# The Hybrid Chronicles

## Book one

# The Awakening

## Robert Stasny

ISBN: 979-8-9889107-0-1

Published by: Robert Stasny

Printed in the United States of America.

# Author's notes

Hello readers, thank you so much for deciding to pick up this book and embark on this journey.

Ever since I was in eighth grade, I have had the idea and concept for these characters in my head. After years and years of telling myself and others "I should put all these ideas down on paper and write a book." I finally got around to actually doing it.

I poured my heart and soul into this book and its characters over the last three years. "Maybe a little too much." I can't wait for you to enjoy getting to know my characters and fall in love with them the way I have, so grab a blanket, get comfortable, and enjoy the story.

Content warnings: Violence, death, mentions of abuse

Dedicated in Memory of
Alan Lynn Stasny

Dad, you always believed in me.
You always told me my imagination
was something special, that the
stories I could come up with in my
head were incredible. I wish you
could be here to read this. This
book is for you.

Robert Stasny

# Table of Contents

## Aiden

## Siri

## Mina

# THE HYBRID CHRONICLES
## Book One

I had the dream again. War, bloodshed. Thousands of people dying. I saw the battlefield, thousands of people from all races fighting. He stood there, sword in hand, as I knew he would be. He stood alone, surrounded by fallen warriors. Blood dripping from his armor. So much blood. He casts his gaze around him, at the carnage he was responsible for. He looks at me, eyes a bright glowing red within a sea of swirling black. He speaks.

"REMEMBER."

# Chapter 1

Aiden woke up screaming, drenched in sweat.

Taking a minute to remember where he was. Aiden looked around at the large, spacious room that doubled as his bedroom and sanctuary. He had been plagued with nightmares for months now. Every night. But always the same dream.

Taking a few deep breaths to calm himself, Aiden lifted himself off the large bed that he sat upon. Walking over to the window next to his bed, he pulled open the curtains.

Early morning sunlight bathed the room in its warm rays as he looked down at the mansion grounds below. Closing his eyes and feeling the sun on his skin, Aiden let out a sigh.

*"Why do I keep having these dreams?"*

Lifting his head, he ran a hand through his jet-black hair before turning and making his way to the adjoining washroom.

*"Might as well get ready for the day."*

Inside the washroom lay a large basin inset into the polished stone floor, used for bathing. This basin was large enough to seat fifteen people inside it and still left plenty of room. On one side of the basin, inserted into the wall was a hand dial that, when turned, would rapidly fill the basin with water for bathing.

Stepping up to the basin, Aiden reached out and turned the dial to fill the large basin. Next to the basin was a pouch full of brightly colored stones. Reaching inside, he picked an orange one up and tossed it into the middle of the basin. On contact, the water instantly began to steam and bubble. Turning back to his room, Aiden walked away as he waited for the rest of the water to heat up. As he reentered his bedroom, a light knock at the door caught his attention.

As the door opened slightly, a slim, young lady silently slipped through. She was short, with bright red hair down to the middle of her back, and bright green eyes that seemed to sparkle as if by magic. She had light skin and graceful movements. But what stood out most was when you looked at her face, your eyes were drawn, not to her eyes, but to the side of her head. Partially covered by her hair, were a set of ears that narrowed and ended in pointed tips.

"Siri, what are you doing in my room?"

The young elf nearly jumped out of her skin.

"Master!" she screeched, falling to the floor. "I didn't see you there, master, you startled me. It's not very nice to sneak up on girls."

Aiden reached out a hand to help the girl up.

"Technically this is my room, you're the one who sneaked up on me. Just because you're not very observant doesn't make it my fault... and I've asked you to stop calling me that."

"Apologies... Aiden, a force of habit." Siri replied.

Breathing out a sigh of relief, she took his hand as he helped her up.

Siri was always surprised by Aiden. Even though she was just a common servant in his father's house, Aiden has always been kind to her. While his father was a very strict and harsh man, Aiden was gentle. When she was sold to his family, she was terrified of his father, and upon learning that she was a gift for his eldest son, she became even more so. Perhaps he would take pleasure in tormenting her? She was so surprised when she met him for the first time. At first, he flat out rejected his father's offer, saying he didn't want to own a slave. But the tone in his father's voice told him he would accept her as his slave, end of discussion. That was nearly three years ago.

"Do you realize what time it is? You're in here earlier than usual today." Aiden asked, pulling her to her feet.

"I was told to come make sure you were awake. After all, you are to be tested today, and your father wants to make sure you don't sleep in again."

Looking up, Siri noticed the fact that Aiden was clothed only from the waist down. Her cheeks blushed crimson. Quickly yanking her hand out of his, she rushed to the side of his bed in order to appear busy.

As she began to make the bed, Siri watched him out of the corner of her eye as she spoke.

"You're up early, another nightmare?"

"Yes." he answered, sinking into a nearby chair. "The same one... over and over, every night. I don't know what it means."

Aiden always felt relaxed around Siri. While he hated the circumstances that forced him into being her master, he was still glad she was his. At least with him as a master she won't be mistreated.

The elven race had been conquered eighty five years ago. Since then, the elves have been integrated into human and immortal society as servants and laborers. Without any rights of their own, the elves were seen as little more than property. Their owners could beat them in the middle of the street, and no one would even bat an eye.

"*Immortals.*" Aiden thought, as he began to eat some bread that was left on his table from last night's dinner. If it weren't for the fact that most humans were blessed with magic, the four nations of immortals would have conquered them as well. Instead, humans were allowed to integrate into immortal society without being conquered.

"*The immortals still ran things though.*" he thought to himself.

Lifting himself from the chair and heading back to the washroom, Aiden called back over his shoulder to Siri.

"Please inform my father I will be down shortly."

As he entered the washroom and looked at the basin of steaming water, he muttered.

"Damn test."

~ ~ ~ ~ ~

*"What am I going to do?"* Aiden asked himself as he soaked in the water.

*"My father expects me to be a strong magic user and impress the Vampyre Council today. But how? Sure, strong magic runs through my family's blood, my younger brother passed his test last year. But he was a natural magic user, using magic came easy to him. But me? I can barely cast the simplest of spells."*

*"All father has ever cared about is power, and his status as one of the Noble families."*

*"After all, Our magical strength is the only reason we became a Noble family."* his father always said.

The vampyres value and respect strength. Physical, magical, it doesn't matter. That's why they granted nobility to the strongest magic users and their families after the war.

Aiden dried himself off and walked back to his room. He noticed that Siri had laid out a set of nice clothing on the end of his bed for the day.

He would have to remember to thank her later.

Now fully clothed and getting ready to head downstairs, a knock on the door, followed by the door opening, and the voice of his brother could be heard.

"Hey Aiden, what happened, you sleep late again? If you're not careful, you'll be late for your own funeral." the man said with a smirk.

"Oh, shut up Thomas." Aiden grabbed a pillow from the bed, throwing it at the younger man.

Catching the pillow, Thomas tossed it back at Aiden.
"Anyway, dad expects to see you in his study before you head out to the test."
"Of course he does."
Aiden had hoped that with today's test and everything, maybe his father would just leave him be for a day.
*"So much for that."*
As they left Aiden's room, they parted ways.
"Good luck today with the test!" Thomas called out as he rounded the corner.

~ ~ ~ ~ ~

Aiden walked along the empty hallways of his family mansion. Looking up, he could see generations of his family ancestors, recorded in portraits lining the walls.
Eight hundred years of "Legacy" his father called them.
Eventually, Aiden came to the door of his father's study. A large door, with a carved figure of a phoenix in the middle. The symbol of their house. The eyes of the phoenix were rubies, while other precious gems were embedded throughout the door.
Taking a deep breath, Aiden knocked twice and opened the door to his father's study.

At the other end of the room, sitting behind a tall, expertly carved desk, sat his father. Across from him on the other side of his desk, sat three people.
*"No, these were not people."* Aiden thought. *"These three were Immortals."*

"Ah, son. Come in please. I was hoping to see you before you set off today." Aiden's father placed his hands together as he leaned back in his chair.

"So, this is the young Aiden we've heard so much about." the first man spoke as he and his companions turned to face Aiden.

The man who spoke up wore a dark grey suit that did little to hide his true nature. The man's skin was pale, and his eyes glowed a soft greenish blue.

"*Vampyre.*"

The two figures accompanying him, set Aiden's nerves on edge.

Aiden instantly recognized them when he looked at them. Their features gave it away. Pale grey, almost translucent skin pulled tight over high cheekbones. Long, bony fingers that ended in inch long, razor sharp claws. Aside from the few strands of scraggily white hair on their head, there was no hair anywhere on their body. Faces that had sharp angles to them that gave an animalistic appearance. Large bat-like ears on the sides of their heads and fangs that stuck out from upper lips as they grinned did little to help. But the worst thing about them was the eyes. The cold, empty, steely-blue eyes that sent a shiver down your spine, eyes of a monster that enjoyed killing.

"*Vampuric*" Aiden thought. "*The watchdogs and intimidators of the vampyre's.*"

The man, having not been introduced, nor introducing himself, stood and walked up to Aiden.

"Good luck today boy. We'll be watching you very closely."

The vampyre's raspy voice caused Aiden's hair to stand on end.

The man placed his hand on Aiden's shoulder. "We hope to see great things from you in the future."

With that, he and his two vampurics left the study.

"Father, what's going on? Why was there a vampyre and two vampurics from the council here?" Aiden asked once the two were alone.

"Son, while your brothers have shown themselves to be quite skilled at magic, you have yet to show signs of much, if any, skill." his father responded.

"The council is concerned about the strength of our house if the oldest and current heir to the family shows no real magical talent. Magic is what has allowed this family to survive and become the noble house it is today."

"I know father, but what does that have to do with the vampyre that came by?"

"The vampyres are beginning to lose patience with our family. We are a very powerful family, but also very popular among the other great houses. The ones in charge want to make sure they keep us in line."

Several seconds passed in silence before either of them spoke.

"Listen son, even if you are not a great magic wielder, you are still my son and I love you. You are the heir to my house. That being said, you need to do your absolute best today, son."

"Why father?" Aiden did his best to hide the worry creeping into his voice.

"They are looking for any excuse they can find to limit our influence. Do well and they will have no cause to make a move against us. However, if you do poorly, they may decide to lower our house status. We will no longer be one of the greater houses, but instead become a lesser house. With less influence and power."

"I understand Father, I will do my best."

"That's all I ask of you son. Now go show them what our family is capable of."

# Chapter 2

The city of Esenor was a rather large, very wealthy city. The human capital of the vampyre nation. Beautiful houses, expensive shops, with a beautiful view of the sea from the harbor. All centered around an exceptionally large, ornate temple made of the purest white marble, standing taller than all the other buildings in the entire city. The city was primarily made up of humans, with a few nonhuman races and immortals scattered here and there. All citizens of the city were required to pay a blood tithe to the vampyres. The greater houses were the only ones not required to pay the blood tithe. Supposedly, the tithe was meant to keep the citizens of the city safe from the vampyre's thirst for blood, to provide for their need for blood without resorting to feeding off random citizens. Still, that didn't prevent some from feeding off the people as they desired. Many stories have been told of the bodies of the peasants being found dead in an alley, drained of blood. Because of this, hardly anyone wanders alone at night, especially in the slums, or near the vampyre district.

~ ~ ~ ~ ~

Siri decided to accompany Aiden to the temple in which he would be tested today. That meant they would have to go through the market square on their way. Siri loved the market. Aiden always let her pick one thing from any of the vendors for herself when they went. Today was no exception.

Aiden handed her a pouch full of coins and told her to have fun, telling her he would be back for her after the test was over. The young elf squealed with delight as she hugged Aiden.

"Thank you, Master!"

Aiden stood there watching her as she happily skipped away between the stalls, with all of the grace her elven heritage had given her.

Turning, Aiden made his way towards the towering structure in the distance.

~ ~ ~ ~ ~

As he ascended the steps of the temple, Aiden could not help but feel incredibly small, and insignificant. At the top of the steps, Aiden passed between two solid granite pillars, transitioning into broad archways leading into the temple itself.

Stepping through the temple doors, he was greeted by high, vaulted ceilings, several stories high. The brightly lit, stained glass hallways were packed full of fancy artwork, and statues of different immortal races all over the place.

As he walked along the white marble floor towards the large audience chamber used for the test, Aiden noticed, among the various artifacts on display, a sword. He had seen it many times at the temple, but this was the first time he actually "looked" at it.

His face froze.

It was an ornate broadsword; its blade was as black as night. Within the blackness of the blade was what looked like a spiderweb of cracks that seemed to glow intermittently with the brightness of a full moon, almost like a heartbeat. And yet, the sword was solid, without any flaw to this strange metal. Along the blade, near the handle, was a set of runes that seemed familiar to him. The handle looked like it was wrapped in braided rope, but this was an illusion. The braided rope pattern had been carved out of solid silver, with the bulk of the handle beneath the silver being made of a pure black stone that was either obsidian, or onyx, Aiden was not sure which. Inside this stone on either side of the centerline, were two immortals, locked in combat. A vampyre on the left, and a hellhound on the right. The cross guard was also made from pure silver, with etchings of the moon phases going from one side to the other, each side ending in a talon. The pommel was a large Moonstone, wrapped in veins of silver to hold it in place.

*"It's the same sword! The same one from my dream!"* Aiden realized.

Aiden instantly wanted to reach out for it but was stopped by someone's voice.

"We have been expecting you. Please, come in."

Aiden snapped back to reality, apologized, and followed the man into the audience chamber.

~ ~ ~ ~ ~

The audience chamber was a large circular room with a high, domed ceiling made of glass, allowing the sunlight to illuminate the chamber. A pedestal sat in the center of the large room. Around it were several hooded figures. Upon reaching the pedestal, Aiden saw there was a clear crystal slightly larger than his palm sitting on it. The man on the opposite side of the pedestal from Aiden spoke up.

"I am Raizel." the man said, removing his hood.

"I will be measuring, and determining your current and innate, or dormant magical potential."

The man was tall, with long, deep brown hair that fell to his shoulders. His canine teeth were slightly longer than normal, and his eyes glowed a greenish blue.

"Please, place your hand over this crystal and we shall begin."

Aiden followed the vampyre's instructions and listened as the man began to speak.

"Magic is all around us, it's in the air we breathe, the ground we walk on, even in the individual cells of your body. Not all people are capable of feeling, or manipulating that magic though, and before you can safely practice magic, you must first understand yourself."

Aiden nodded.

"Magic requires energy to cast. If you don't have enough energy, the spell will fail. But, if you try to do too much, too soon, the energy requirements can drain you of your very life energy and you can die. Do you understand?"

"Yes."

"Good. Remember, the stronger the person, the stronger the spell. Now, I want you to focus on casting the best spell you know. Imagine it being pushed into the crystal from your hands."

Aiden did as he was told, focusing on the fireball spell that his family was known for using, since the phoenix was the symbol of their house. The crystal began to softly glow, then getting brighter. All of a sudden, it stopped, and began to faintly glow and dim repeatedly.

"Interesting." Raizel noted, rubbing his chin.

"You have much potential in you, but your own body seems to be fighting you when you try to use it."

"What does that mean?" Aiden looked at the crystal in front of him as it brightened and dimmed repeatedly.

"Think of it like this. Magic flows like a river... from the world, through you, and then out again. But there seems to be some sort of seal on that flow of power. Like a dam has been built to prevent the power from flowing."

"How do I remove the dam?" Aiden asked, looking up at the vampyre.

"Let me try." Raizel placed his hands over Aiden's. "Let's see if I can find the source of the seal. Now close your eyes."

Aiden did as he was asked, hoping Raizel could remove the seal, so he could actually be good at magic, like the rest of his family.

"Clear your mind. Now look deep inside yourself, find the source of your power, and let it out."

The crystal stopped flashing, and a swirling black cloud began to form inside the crystal.

*"That Sword."*

Wind began to pick up and blow inside the room, even though no doors or windows were open.

*"That Man."*

The entire room began to shake.

*"Those Eyes."*

The hooded men were being pushed to the ground as if gravity had just been increased by tenfold.

"Aiden, Stop!" yelled Raizel, struggling to remain standing. "You must stop, now!"

*"My Eyes."*

Everything froze for a brief moment. And then...

The crystal and pedestal exploded, sending everyone but Aiden flying back twenty meters into the wall. Where the pedestal once stood, was now just a ten foot crater, with Aiden standing in the middle. Eyes a bright glowing red, within a sea of swirling black.

# Chapter 3

Aiden blinked. Glancing around at the devastation that had happened in the room.

*"What happened here?"*

The last thing he remembered was being asked to touch the crystal to measure his magical potential. After that, nothing.

*"Why was the audience chamber in shambles? Where are the hooded men? Raizel, the test administrator, what happened to him?"*

A cough sounded from across the room. Hearing this, Aiden climbed out of the crater in the floor, making his way towards the sound.

Slumped against the cracked wall of the audience chamber, was Raizel, seriously injured and coughing up blood, looking like an explosion had gone off in his face.

"What happened to you? What happened here?" Aiden reached out to help Raizel to his feet.

"Y...you... "cough" ... you did."

"What? There's no way I did all this." he gestured around to the destroyed room.

Raizel started to stand, his body beginning to heal itself. He looked into Aiden's eyes. Normal blue eyes, but now, with the slightest hint of red mixed in.

"The power inside of you, its awake." Raizel told him.

"What kind of power?" Aiden asked.

"I can't say, but whatever it is. It's a power like I've never seen before."

Now that his body was healed, Raizel looked around at the room.

"You should go, people will start asking questions soon. Tell them you passed your test. You were not here when this explosion happened. I'll take care of the rest."

"But..." Aiden tried to argue, but Raizel cut him off.

"Go Home."

As Aiden left the temple, people had begun to gather outside.

~ ~ ~ ~ ~

Avoiding the people, Aiden slipped into the adjoining alleyway. Making his way around the block, he headed back towards the market to pick up Siri and head home.

The moment he stepped into the market; Aiden knew something wasn't right. He began looking around the different shops to find Siri when he heard it. A soft voice cried out in the distance, along with a great commotion. It was Siri's voice, no doubt about it. Aiden sprinted off in the direction of the commotion.

A crowd had already gathered as he pushed his way past them. At the center of the crowd he found Siri, the sky blue dress she had been wearing was ripped, and torn in places, with her hands chained. Tears were streaking down her face, and she was covered in dirt, as if she had been thrown down and dragged through the street. Next to her stood two city guards, talking with a very arrogant looking man pointing at Siri.

Aiden stepped forward to find out what was going on.

When Siri laid eyes on her master, she tried to get up and run to him, but a guard forced her back to her knees as he yelled in an angry tone. "Where do you think you're going, little thief?"

Her red hair now in a mess, Siri looked at her master, and Aiden could see the fear in her emerald eyes.

Aiden rushed forward and demanded to know what was going on.

"Sir, this unsupervised elf here snatched this man's coin purse and tried to get away." one of the guards answered, holding up the pouch of coins Aiden had given Siri earlier. "We are taking her to the dungeon to await execution."

Upon hearing this, Siri broke down, curling up into a ball on the filthy street, sobbing.

Seeing his precious Siri like this broke Aiden's heart. She was just a girl who enjoyed shopping and spending time with her master, she didn't deserve this.

"I'm afraid there has been a misunderstanding here gentlemen." Aiden stepped even closer towards Siri.

"This elf belongs to me, and that coin purse is mine. I gave it to her to buy some things while I was at the temple."

"No way!" the man next to the guards called out.

"She cut that coin purse from my waist. When I demanded it back, she tried to run away." A smug grin crossed his face as he spoke.

Now Aiden understood what was happening. Seeing Siri unsupervised, with such a large coin pouch, this man tried to make her give him her money. But when she refused, he had her arrested.

After seeing the smug look on the man's face, something snapped inside of Aiden. His eyes flashed red for a second, then he was moving. Moving so fast the human eye had trouble following, Aiden closed the twenty foot gap between him and this arrogant man in a fraction of a second, dust kicking up in a trail behind him.

With one hand, Aiden grabbed the man's throat, lifting him off the ground effortlessly, cutting off his airway as the man started to panic.

"Release him now, sir!" one of the guards yelled, placing his hand on his sword.

Ignoring him, Aiden replied casually.

"Gentlemen, if you look inside the coin pouch, you will find a golden phoenix embroidered on the inside."

Lifting his free hand. Aiden revealed a ring on his left hand, bearing the symbol of his house.

"You will find it matches the family ring that I am wearing."

Looking back at the man who was still struggling in his grip, Aiden loosened his grip on the man's throat, allowing him to breath, but still not setting him back on the ground.

"This man has lied to you and has tried to take advantage of my servant simply because she was alone." Aiden's cold glare instilled fear in the man as he struggled against Aiden's grip.

The guards quickly confirmed the matching house crest and handed the coin purse over to Aiden. Lowering the man and pulling him inches from his face. Aiden now addressed the man in front of him.

"I expect an apology, and compensation for damages. Both to my servant, and her belongings."

Aiden tossed the trembling man backwards and into a large water puddle. Shaking with fear, the man got to his knees. Looking at Aiden, he began to apologize.

"I'm not the one you should be apologizing to." Aiden replied coldly, crossing his arms.

Realizing his mistake, the trembling man turned to Siri, bowed his head, and began to apologize profusely to her. "Apologies my lady, I was wrong. I should never have attempted to take advantage of you."

"Now get the hell out of my sight!"

The man wasted no time running down the nearest street as if his life depended on it, shoving people out of the way in his desperation to put as much distance between himself and Aiden as possible.

Aiden turned, seeing one of the guards moving to unshackle Siri.

"Don't touch her!" Aiden commanded angrily, a low growl in his throat causing the guards to jump slightly. "You've done enough damage today."

Aiden pushed past the other guards.

Taking the key from the guard's hand, Aiden knelt down and unlocked the chains around Siri's wrists.

Tossing the chains aside, Aiden picked her trembling body up in his arms.

"I'm here now, you're safe." he whispered, cradling her against him.

As they left the market, Siri buried her face in Aiden chest and spoke softly.

"Thank you, master."

Closing her eyes and gripping Aiden's shirt tightly, she continued crying.

~ ~ ~ ~ ~

It was midday by the time Aiden and Siri arrived at the large, bronze gates that served as the entrance to his family's property.

Entering the house with Siri still in his arms, Aiden began making his way through the mansion toward his room. Along the way, he stopped by the kitchen and requested that some food be brought to his room shortly. The young man and woman who ran the kitchen bowed respectfully, then began preparing the food.

Leaving the kitchen, Aiden continued on his way to his room.

As he ascended the stairs, he came across his younger sister, only fifteen. She was tall for her age, with lightly tanned skin, wearing an elegant blue and white dress that complimented her blue eyes and blonde hair. Upon seeing her brother, she asked how his test went, but stopped when she realized he was carrying Siri.

"What happened?" she asked with concern.

She always liked Siri.

"Hey Maddison, Siri ran into some trouble in the market while I was taking the test. She'll be ok, she just needs some rest. Don't worry, I'll take care of her." Aiden told her.

"Make sure you do." Maddison replied, before continuing on her way.

At the top of the stairs, Aiden turned left to head down the corridor that led to his room. As he turned, he heard the voice of his father call out to him on his right.

"Hey son, I heard good news about your test. I'm proud of you. I'm glad you finished your test before the accident at the temple happened. Come, we need to celebrate."

"Not now father." Aiden ignored him and kept walking.

"But son, we need to..." Aiden's father gripped his shoulder, attempting to stop him.

"I said not now!"

Aiden spun to face his father. The red in his eyes glowing brighter as he spoke, a low growl escaping his throat.

Taken aback, his father lowered his hand.

"Sure son, another time."

His father turned and walked back into his study, closing the door as Aiden continued down the hall to his bedroom.

Entering his room, Aiden immediately brought Siri into the washroom, setting her down next to the washbasin.

As he refilled the basin with water, Aiden retrieved the pouch of stones, tossing an orange one in to heat up the water, and a light green one as well. The water began to glow softly when the green stone was added.

*"That should help to heal her injuries."* Aiden thought to himself as he knelt down next to Siri.

Aiden began to help Siri remove her outer garments, as it seemed to hurt her to move a whole lot. He could now clearly see the toll today's ordeal had taken on her. Bruises and scrapes covered her body almost from head to toe. Apparently, the guards had dragged her through the street by her hair.

Since her outer clothes were in tatters, he stood up and went into his bedroom to fetch one of his large shirts for her to wear, until some of her own clothes could be gotten.

Next to his bed, Aiden opened the dresser and pulled out a bright green tunic.

*"This will work for now."*

Walking back to the washroom, he noticed Siri had already discarded her undergarments and stepped into the bath, facing away from him. As she sank down into the water, she gave out a sigh of relief as the healing waters began to take effect.

"I brought you a shirt to wear once you are done." Aiden placed the shirt down next to the bath, then turned to leave, figuring she'd want to be alone.

"Master?"

Siri spoke softly. Barely above a whisper, yet Aiden found himself hearing her very clearly.

"What is it, Siri?"

"Why are you so kind to me, master?" Siri stared at her feet as she crossed her arms in front of her beneath the water.

Turning back to face her, Aiden walked over to the basin and sat beside it, so that their backs were facing each other.

"Because... I care about you. No one should be allowed to hurt you or lay hands on you the way they did today. I'm so sorry Siri, I should have been there to protect you."

"Why? Why do you care so much about me?" Siri tightened her grip on her arms as she waited for Aiden's answer.

Aiden knew what she wanted to hear, knew she needed to hear it.

Turning so that he was facing her, Aiden reached out his hand, taking her by the chin and gently turning her head to face him. Once they were looking into each other's eyes, he said it.

"Because... You're Mine."

A brief moment of silence occurred. Then they kissed.

After the kiss, Siri rested her forehead against her master's.

"Thank you, Aiden." she whispered.

# Chapter 4

The sun was just starting to rise the next day as Aiden awoke. Attempting to move, Aiden found himself weighed down by something. Looking down, Aiden could see a head of red hair resting on his chest, causing him to smile.

Doing his best to disentangle himself from Siri without waking her, Aiden slid out from under her and got out of bed. Taking a moment to look over at the still sleeping girl next to him, he thought back on the events that led up to this.

Leaning over, he gently placed a kiss on her exposed shoulder and whispered.

"You're mine."

"Promise?" Siri murmured, not fully awake.

"I Promise."

After washing up, Aiden walked back out of the washroom to find Siri standing at his window. The early morning sun streaming through her red hair gave the illusion of her hair being made of fire. She was still wearing the tunic he had given her the day before.

Walking up behind her, Aiden wrapped his arms around her waist and buried his head in her hair.

"How do you feel this morning?"

"I feel like your father will be angry with me for not being up doing the household chores." Siri answered, looking down, a hint of fear showing in her eyes as she held Aiden's forearm against her stomach.

"I'll handle my father. I'm your master, not him."

Siri nodded slightly, her body relaxing.

"You hungry?" he asked.

"No, I'm good, thank you."

Siri's stomach growled.

Grinning, Aiden told her to sit down and eat something. Walking hand in hand together over to his table, they sat down for breakfast.

"Your eyes are different." Siri said, taking a bite of bacon from her plate.

"What do you mean?" Aiden asked, taking a bite of his own food.

"Your eyes, they glow occasionally... and your irises now have a little bit of red around the inside edge."

"Really?"

Siri nodded.

"Also, at the market, how did you move that fast? Or even have the strength to lift that man up the way you did?"

"Adrenalin?"

"I don't think so. It seemed more than that. What happened at the temple?"

"I'm not sure." Aiden replied honestly. "The test administrator said we have accidentally awakened some sort of power hidden deep inside me."

"What kind of power?" Siri asked, taking a drink to wash down her meal before turning to face Aiden.

"I'm not sure. I can't remember what happened."

Aiden began to explain what happened at the temple as best he could.

"Do you think that's how I saved you?"

"No." Siri took another drink of orange juice. "I believe you would have resolved the problem on your own. But I did enjoy watching that man run away in terror."

She leaned over and kissed Aiden on the cheek.

"You were very heroic."

*"I wonder if I can use that power on command."* Aiden thought, looking at his hand.

"Do you feel any different?" Siri asked.

"I haven't really thought about it. But now that you mention it, I feel good. Like, "really good." I feel stronger somehow."

"How so?" The young elf stood up.

Walking behind Aiden, she draped her arms around him, resting her chin on his shoulder.

"It's like... it's like electricity is flowing through my vein.. and I can hear the servants outside the room cleaning the hall."

"But your door is soundproof!" Siri exclaimed, lifting her head to stare at him in shock.

"Apparently not completely." Aiden replied, picking up his own juice and drinking it.

After they had finished breakfast, Aiden figured he should probably go confront a more than likely furious father.

~ ~ ~ ~ ~

As Aiden approached the door to his father's study, he noticed both Thomas and Maddison leaving the study. As he passed them, they both seemed to act strangely. Each seeming to give him a look of both respect, but also of fear, while also giving him a wide berth.

"We need to talk." Aiden said, as he entered his father's study.

"I agree." his father answered.

"First, I want to apologize for what I said yesterday when I returned home."

"No need. I have already been informed of the events that transpired in the market yesterday... which is why I excused her absence from duties this morning." Aiden's father folded his hands across the desk.

"Since you are here, and not currently with her, she has recovered, I take it?"

"She has."

"I sense a "But" coming."

"But... Siri will no longer be serving you, or the rest of the household."

"Is that so?" His father raised an eyebrow as he looked at his son.

"She will never be used again."

Aiden stared at his father for several seconds in silence.

"Very well.. from here on, she is solely your responsibility." His father stood, walking around the desk, approaching Aiden.

"Wait, really?" Aiden asked, confused.

"I'm not stupid son. I've seen the way she looks at you... and you at her. I'm just surprised it took you this long."

Aiden was speechless.

"I hope you know what you're doing, son. Give me your hand."

Aiden placed his hand into the waiting hand of his father.

Closing his son's hand between both of his own, Aiden's father recited a few words. Their hands began to glow for a few seconds, then faded. Removing his hand from his fathers, Aiden inspected his hand. Now, Aiden could see a magical seal glowing on the back of his hand that faded after a few seconds.

"The seal that binds her to this family, is now yours, and yours alone."

"Thank you, father."

"Good luck son, I have a feeling you're going to need it. Now if you will excuse me, I have some business to attend to."

~ ~ ~ ~ ~

Aiden sat beneath a large tree next to a small clearing that was used as his families training ground. Inspecting his hand, he thought back to the previous day.

*"One hand... how did I pick that man up with only one hand?"*

*"More importantly, can I do it again?"*

Leaning his head back, he began to think about how to use this new power he had acquired on command.

*"Up until now I have only used it by reflex."*

Sitting up, Aiden crossed his legs and closed his eyes, bringing himself into a meditative state used to refine combat discipline. Aiden began to listen to the world around him. He could hear the wind rustling through the trees, as well as various kinds of small animals moving around. Way up in the tree, he could hear two birds fighting over a nest.

Feeling the cool breeze blowing against his skin, Aiden pushed a little further.

Outside the training grounds, he could make out the sounds of horses. The family stables were at least a hundred fifty meters away, yet he could hear the horses moving around the pen.

*"This is incredible! If I just focus, I can enhance my hearing even further."*

"You hungry?"

Opening his eyes, Aiden looked up to see Siri standing in front of him, smiling while holding a tray of food.

"What are you doing here?" Aiden was surprised to see her out here.

"Your father told me where you were, and I thought you might be hungry, so I decided to come bring you some food." she told him.

"Yes, I am hungry. Thank you, Siri."

Aiden now realized that he had been out here for several hours. Siri sat down beside him, and they began to eat.

"So, if I focus on just what I want to hear, I'm able to enhance my hearing even more than it already is."

Siri sat there listening to Aiden as he explained what he had come to understand about his power.

"My body knows what it can do, but I still can't manifest my power at will. It's like the power is fighting me."

"So stop fighting it." Siri stated.

"What?"

Picking up a stick beside them, Siri began to draw in the dirt to illustrate her point.

"You said magic flows like a river, right?"

"Yeah."

"So... You're looking at your power as if it is the same as magic."

Aiden looked confused, so Siri continued.

"What if it flows in a different direction than the flow of magic? What if your power isn't magical in origin at all?"

"What are you saying?"

"What if you are trying to use your abilities as if they are magic, but instead, they are something else entirely?"

"So? What if they are?" Aiden asked, still a bit confused as to where this conversation was heading.

"So.. what if you trying to force your powers like you would cast a spell is like trying to swim upstream in a river? Yes, you're swimming, but you're not getting anywhere. You've been trying to force your power to the surface this whole time. Maybe try letting the power flow inwards instead of out."

"I guess it's worth a try." Aiden stood up, walking over to a smaller tree.

Aiden decided to just go for it. To not try to force it this time and to just trust his body to know what to do. Gathering his strength, he punched at the trunk of the tree as fast as he could, trying to see if he could throw a punch at the same speed he had used the day before.

Nothing happened.

Again, he punched at the tree, still nothing. Getting angry, Aiden punched again. This time, he actually punched the tree. A shower of bark and splinters erupted from the point of impact, followed by pain.

Clutching his now broken hand, Aiden dropped to his knees as Siri rushed over to him.

"I guess super strength doesn't mean super durability." Aiden said through clenched teeth.

Siri gasped as she was looking at his hand. Every bone in his hand seemed to be shattered. Tears began to form in her eyes as she looked at his mangled hand.

Just as she was about to reach out to try and help, something happened. Aiden felt it as well and they both looked at his hand in shock. The bones in his hand began to reform themselves and pop themselves back into place.

His hand was healing itself.

"Well.. that's handy." Aiden said, flexing his fingers and clenching his fist, testing to see if it really was healed.

"I think that's enough training for today." Siri said, taking Aiden's hand in hers.

Together, they walked back to the house.

# Chapter 5

Aiden and Siri were just entering his family courtyard when Aiden's father walked out of the house.

Upon seeing his son, the man walked up to Aiden and Siri.

"Son, there is something I need to talk to you about." He then looked at Siri. "Both of you."

"What is it, father?"

"There are things you should know. About this family, and about yourself. Things that have been kept secret. Please, follow me."

The man turned and began walking across the yard toward the family crypt, with both Aiden and Siri in tow.

At the door to the crypt, the man pulled out a ring. This ring did not match the family ring. Instead, this was an ornate signet ring made of pure silver. On one side of the ring was a detailed carving of a vampyre, on the other, a hellhound, with a large black onyx stone carved into the shape of a wolf head on the top. The eyes of the wolf were made from two rubies.

Turning to Aiden, the man offered the ring to his son.

"This ring is your inheritance. It is the symbol of your house. Only it will open the way."

"What are you talking about father?" Aiden asked.

"Inside, you will find the answers you seek." He once again offered the ring to his son.

Looking down at the ring that his father was offering to him, Aiden was hesitant to take it.

"Take it, son. The ring will only work for you."

"What do you mean it will only work for me?"

"Your blood, son." his father replied. "The ring will only work for you, because of your blood. Trust me, just put the ring on."

Although still somewhat skeptical, Aiden took the ring from his father.

Taking a closer look at the ring, Aiden noticed an inscription on the inside of the ring written in an unfamiliar language. Placing the ring onto the middle finger of his right hand, Aiden felt a brief stab of pain, and a small drop of blood oozed out from under the ring. The ring began to glow softly, and then returned to normal.

Somehow, Aiden knew what he had to do.

Lifting the ring to the door of the crypt, Aiden placed the ring into a matching indentation in the smooth stone. A slight popping sound could be heard, then the stone door began to slide into the floor. Before them, a set of steps led down into a dark hallway below.

"Come." Aiden's father said, lighting a torch and handing one to Aiden. "There is much we need to discuss."

Aiden's father stepped into the crypt, followed by Aiden and Siri. The three of them making their way down the dark steps with Aiden's father leading the way while Siri clung to Aiden's arm.

As they walked down the silent corridor, Aiden's father began to speak.

"For the last eight hundred years, my family has held this crypt, and its secrets, in trust."

"What is this place?" Aiden asked.

"A library of sorts. Created to aid you in unlocking your power."

"Eight hundred years ago, during the great war, my family was one of the ones who fought beside a great warrior. He alone was the reason that humanity stood a chance against the four Immortal nations. Even though he himself was also an immortal."

"Why would an immortal fight for the humans?" Siri asked, still holding Aiden's arm in this dark, unfamiliar place.

"Because even among all four immortal races, the Vampyres, the Werewolves, the Hellhounds, and even Vampurics, he was unique."

"How so?"

They exited the corridor and into a large room. Upon entering the room, several torches along the wall of the room ignited themselves, as if to welcome them and acknowledging their presence.

Now lit up, they could see the room clearly. Each wall was not just a wall, but a giant mural that spanned the entire room. Walking over to the wall, Aiden's father motioned for them to look at the mural as he continued.

"Because, he was born to human parents. No immortal blood ran through his veins, nor was he ever turned by another immortal."

Pulling himself from Siri's grasp, Aiden began to inspect the mural. It was a depiction of the story his father was telling him now.

"Father?"

"What is it, son?" His father turned to Aiden, who was staring at the mural.

"Here on the wall, I recognize the symbol for vampyre, werewolf, hellhound, and vampuric, but what does this symbol mean?" Aiden pointed at an unfamiliar symbol surrounded by the symbols for the four immortal races.

"That is his symbol, son... remember when I said he was unique? Well, it wasn't just that he was born to humans. He was born a hybrid."

"Wait.. you mean..."

"Yes son. He was a hybrid of all four races. A perfect hybrid, with all of their strengths, and none of their weaknesses, yet born to human parents. He was an oddity of nature, the first of his kind. Both his blood and his bite were fatal to other immortals. But because of his lineage, he cared for humans."

Aiden then remembered the dream he had been having the last few months. One man, alone on the battlefield, covered in blood, surrounded by fallen warriors.

"After the great war eight hundred years ago, he disappeared. When that happened, the immortals tried to erase every trace and knowledge of his existence from history. In their eyes, he was an abomination, and a traitor to all immortals, no matter how strong he was."

"Now, the legend of the hybrid has been all but eradicated. But before he disappeared, he gave my family a task. To protect his secret and to wait for his return. He told my ancestors that one day he would return, and that it would be my family's job to protect him until he was ready."

"Ready for what?" Siri asked.

"To take up his mantle once again."

Suddenly, Aiden felt very weak. As he dropped to his knees, a flood of visions began to play through his mind.

*Two men stood together, one a normal man. The other, despite being hidden beneath a hood, was clearly the hybrid.*

*"Take some of my blood." the hybrid commanded.*

*"With it, your family will have great natural magical talent... but will also give my power an anchor point to return to."*

*"What do you mean, my Lord?" the man asked.*

*"With my blood now in your veins, one of your descendants will inherit my power, and my memories. I will be reborn through him. Keep my secret, and watch for my return."*

**"Remember."**

Siri knelt to see what was wrong with Aiden when she noticed his eyes, a bright, glowing red in a sea of swirling black.

Suddenly, the room around them began to shake, the air felt heavy and hard to breath. The flames from the torches began to burn brighter and larger.

A series of sharp cracks began to rack Aiden's body, each and every bone in his body breaking, shifting position, healing, and then rebreaking, over and over again.

Aiden began to shift.

Realizing what was happening, Aiden's father grabbed Siri by the arm, dragging her away from his son as Aiden screamed in pain.

Slowly, Aiden's bones began to change shape, elongating in certain places, while shortening in others. His skin began to darken to an almost slate grey color. As his body began to change, his fingernails began to lengthen into claws, his face changing from that of a human, to that of a large werewolf.

After a short while, where once stood a nobleman's son, stood a large, muscular, bipedal werewolf with unusually large fangs, jet black fur covered his body from head to toe, and from his back, sprouted two rather large, bat-like wings.

Watching this unfold, Aiden's father was suddenly gripped with a terrible fear for his own life. He had stood in the presence of immortals before. But never before had he felt such raw power, rage, and animalistic aggression in all his life. All radiating from this thing that had once been his son.

He began to back away towards the wall.

Alerted by the movement out of the corner of his eye, Aiden lunged at his father. Holding his father by the throat, up against the wall, Aiden stared down at his father with those red eyes of his.

Siri had fallen to the floor as a result of watching Aiden go through so much unbearable pain, while not knowing what was happening to him. Looking at him with tears in her eyes, all she could do was whisper one word.

"Aiden."

# Chapter 6

*"Aiden."*

The word echoed through Aiden's mind... bringing him back to reality.

Turning his head, Aiden looked at Siri.
*"Why is she crying? Why does she seem unusually small right now?"*

Turning his head back forward, Aiden finally noticed his father, pinned against the wall, his hand around his throat. No, not his hand, this hand was much larger and stronger than his own hand. And yet, he knew it was his.

Aiden released his grip on his father. Backing away, he began inspecting his own body. His hands were tipped with large claws, his body covered in dark black fur.

*"So, it wasn't a hallucination."* he realized.

Taking a few steps back, Aiden bumped into something.

Turning around, Aiden was now staring at a reflection of himself in a small basin of water surrounding an altar in the center of the room. Dark swirling eyes with bright red irises stared back at him.

*"This can't be real."*

But he knew it was. Knew that he had just tried to kill his father. Had it not been for Siri...

*"Siri!"*

Aiden realized that she must be terribly afraid of him at this moment. Turning away from Siri and his father, Aiden let out a long howl of pain, not physical, but emotional, knowing that he must be a monster in her eyes. How could he face her now?

Aiden bowed his head in defeat, allowing the emptiness to consume him. Until...

Aiden felt a small hand take his own clawed hand. Turning his head, Aiden looked into the bright green eyes of the one he adores most. Looking back at him from her eyes, was not fear, or hatred, but love and kindness. With her other hand, Siri reached up, unafraid, and held Aiden's face in her palm. Looking into his eyes, she spoke softly.

"You're still you... and I still love you."

Guiding his large head down toward her, Siri reached up on her toes, placing a kiss on Aiden's forehead before whispering. "Come back to me."

Pulling away from him, Siri looked back into his eyes. The glowing red was gone. In their place was the eyes of the man she loved.

Aiden pulled away abruptly as his body began changing back to human, being no less painful than when he changed from human.

Seeing that Aiden had ripped out of his clothing when he changed, Siri looked around for something to cover him with. On the altar in the center of the room, Siri found a blanket. Retrieving it, she threw the blanket over Aiden's body as he was in the final stages of shifting back.

Aiden lay on the stone floor, drenched in sweat, he looked up at the woman kneeling beside him.

Looking into her eyes, he asked.

"Did you mean it?"

Not giving him a reply, Siri leaned over and kissed Aiden.

For a few moments, nothing else existed, just the two of them, in this moment.

"What do you think?" Siri asked, once they stopped kissing in order to regain their breath.

Taking his eyes off Siri and looking at his father, Aiden spoke. "I know who I am."

Aiden lowered his eyes, unable to look at his father any longer. "I'm sorry for attacking you."

"It's ok." his father said, still shaking a bit. "I think if you really wanted to kill me, I would already be dead."

"Please don't be afraid of me." Aiden said to them both, but mainly to Siri.

"Never." Siri replied.

As he stood, Aiden noticed both his brother and his sister had joined them in the crypt at some point. They both walked up to him, staying back a few paces, and knelt to one knee.

"My Lord" they both said in unison.

Their father joined them in kneeling a moment later.

"So, you remember?" Maddison asked, after a few moments of silence, looking up at Aiden.

"Yes. I know who I am now."

"And my brother?" she asked, worried that her brother was now gone.

"I'm still me, Maddison, don't worry."

Maddison got up and hugged Aiden, thankful that he was still her brother.

~ ~ ~ ~ ~

Aiden spent the next two nights in the crypt, learning all he could from the multitude of different murals, artifacts and documents that were left in the crypt for him to be able to read. He was finally beginning to understand what he was, but also the man he used to be. But there was still so much that Aiden didn't know; so much he still couldn't remember.

Despite Aiden's constant fear of hurting her if he lost control, Siri refused to leave his side.

With everything that has happened in the last few days, Siri felt equally fascinated by the crypt and its contents, but was also worried about the impact all this would have on Aiden.

Seeing Aiden busy looking over a scroll he was holding, Siri decided to go explore a bit. As she walked along the wall, admiring the artwork painted on them, Siri felt drawn towards the altar at the center of the room.

Walking over to the altar, she began inspecting it.

It was cut from a solid piece of black marble stone. A few feet off the ground, the altar transitioned into a small pool of water surrounding a statue in the middle that served as a fountain. The statue resembled the immortal that Aiden had transformed into two days ago, but with one major difference. This statue did not have the wings Aiden had. Veins of silver worked their way from the base of the statue up to the middle of the statues' torso.

As Siri inspected the statue more closely, she noticed a small, hidden panel that was overlooked earlier. Reaching inside, Siri retrieved what looked to be a book of some sort, bound in leather, wrapped in a red silk cloth.

Glancing over toward Aiden, Siri saw he was still busy reading his scroll.

Siri walked over and sat down in a corner of the room to examine the book she had found. Gently opening the book, Siri began to read what was written inside.

As she read, Siri realized this was not just another book or document left here. This was a journal written by the hybrid. Based on what she and Aiden had learned over the last two days, she realized that this journal had to be over a thousand years old.

The more she read, the more she felt sorry for the man who had written the journal.

Now finished with the scroll he was reading, Aiden finally noticed Siri's absence. Looking around the room, he found her sitting in a corner reading a book of some sort. Standing up, Aiden walked over to where she was sitting.

"Find anything interesting?" Aiden asked, sitting down beside her.

Looking over at Aiden, Siri seemed like she were about to cry.

"What is it?" Aiden asked concerned, brushing a strand of her hair back into place.

"I think it's a journal, your journal." she replied.

"What does it say?"

Showing the journal to Aiden, Siri began to explain.

"This part of the journal talks about his family... apparently, before he became the hybrid, his family were the ones that protected his village from immortals. They were known as the hunters."

"Really?" Aiden asked, his interest peaked.

"That's not all." Siri turned the page.

"Apparently, when he turned for the first time, his family disowned him. His father even tried to kill him just for being what he was."

"Seriously?"

"Yeah... his family then hunted him for years. They saw him as nothing more than a monster. A stain on their family's honor. A stain only his death could expunge."

Turning a few pages, Siri then pointed out another few entries in the journal.

"When he turned for the first time, it was in response to his fiancé being killed by a werewolf right in front of his eyes."

Aiden read the firsthand account of the event, feeling an immense sense of loss, even though he could not remember the event. Turning a few more pages, Siri continued showing Aiden different entries in the journal.

"His entire family was slaughtered by a group of vampurics a few years later. There was nothing he was able to do to prevent it. After that, he stopped letting anyone get close to him. Everyone he ever cared for had suffered a gruesome death, so he decided to fight alone. He decided that in order to do what he does, he couldn't form any attachment with anyone ever again. He said it was the only way, that if he didn't care for anyone, then they couldn't be used against him. They were a weakness he could no longer afford."

Aiden was at a loss for words as he read that entry in the journal.

"Sounds lonely." Siri looked at Aiden, worry in her eyes.

Aiden knew what she was thinking, because he was thinking the same thing.

*"Will that happen to me?"*

*"Is that who I will become when I get all my memories back?"*

"No." Aiden said to himself. *"I don't have to do things the same way he did."*

"Don't worry." Aiden placed an arm around Siri, pulling her close.

"I refuse to end up like him" Aiden kissed the top of Siri's head as he stroked her hair.

"We... will be different".

Siri snuggled a little closer to Aiden, knowing he meant what he said.

# Chapter 7

After a while, Aiden decided that they had spent enough time in this crypt.

Standing up, Aiden reached his hands out to Siri to help her up off the floor.

"Time to go rejoin the world." Aiden smiled. "We can't stay down here forever, can we?"

Smiling back at Aiden, Siri took his hands.

"I guess not." Siri replied as Aiden pulled her to her feet.

As the two of them walked out of the tomb, Aiden placed the journal into a pocket to read later.

It was a little past noon, and having finally brought both himself and Siri out of the crypt, Aiden felt like going for a walk.

They both could use some fresh air.

Leaving the family estate, Aiden and Siri made their way through town. After walking for a bit, they finally came to their destination. A small beach by the edge of a lake on the outskirts of the city.

Looking out across the crystal blue water, Aiden took a deep breath. Turning to his right, he led Siri over to a large tree growing near the edge of the water. Together, they sat down and just enjoyed the afternoon sun.

"So, what happens now?" Siri asked, as they sat beneath the tree.

"I'm not sure. The world the hybrid lived in, the war he fought in, and the things he fought for, no longer exist. I'm not sure what I would do, even if I had all of my memories... our world is just so different from his."

Sitting there, listening to the sound of the insects and the animals, Aiden and Siri dozed off by the lake.

~ ~ ~ ~ ~

Waking up, Aiden realized it was getting close to dark, and that they should probably be getting back to the house. Reaching over, he gently nudged Siri to wake her before helping her to her feet.

"Let's go home."

Making their way home, Aiden and Siri took a shortcut through the market's back alley. As they entered the alley, Aiden heard a small disturbance.

Deciding to investigate, Aiden snuck quietly over to the back window of one of the shops in the market. Looking in, Aiden recognized who's shop this was.

This was the dress shop that Siri always loved going to. The shop owner was always kind to Siri, even if Aiden was not with her. The man and his wife always kept a few nice items back just for her when she came around.

But instead of the nice, orderly interior Aiden was used to seeing, the inside of the shop looked like it had been torn apart. Tied to chairs, with cloth tied around their mouths to gag them, were the shopkeeper's wife and young daughter. The shopkeeper was kneeling on the ground a few meters away, cuts and bruises covered the man's body. Both his wife and daughter were crying.

In the room with them, stood six men.

One of the men who stood over the shopkeeper's body began to walk towards the shopkeeper's wife. The man ran a finger down the woman's face, tracing her jaw, then turned and did the same to his daughter.

"So, which one will be first?" the man asked, looking over to the shopkeeper.

"I asked for some simple information, and you have been very hesitant with your answers... perhaps we need a different form of persuasion." An evil grin crept across the man's face.

"This is what we are going to do." The man turned back to the shopkeeper's wife and daughter. "I'm going to ask a question, and if I don't like your answer... I'm going to drain the blood from those you love."

*"Damn vampyres."* Aiden thought, peering through the window.

"Who is he?" the vampyre asked.

"I don't know what you are talking about." the shopkeeper cried.

"Wrong answer." The man stepped behind the shopkeeper's wife.

Pulling her head to the side, the vampyre sank his fangs into the neck of the terrified woman. Two small streams of blood began to trace their way down the woman's neck, staining her dress.

The shopkeeper tried getting up, but was shoved back down and held there by two other vampyres.

Forced to watch as his wife screamed into the gag and struggled against her bonds while the vampyre drank her blood, the man could only beg.

"Please, I don't know who you are talking about! Please stop!"

Pulling away from the woman's throat, the vampire licked his lips, looking directly at the shopkeeper. "Your wife is quite delicious."

Glancing over at the shopkeeper's young daughter, the vampyre continued.

"I wonder if your daughter is just as tasty." The vampyre smiled, blood still covering his mouth and teeth.

"Please, don't hurt my little girl! I'll tell you anything you want. Please!"

"Now we're getting somewhere." the vampyre said.

Moving behind the man's terrified daughter, the vampire began to rub his hand up and down the girl's arm.

"Don't worry little one." the vampyre whispered into the girl's ear. "This will all be over soon."

Pulling the young girl's hair out of the way, he leaned down, fangs just inches from the girl's throat.

"There was an incident outside your shop a few days ago, a man was attacked by a person who showed signs of not being human. All over a slave girl. We just want to know the identity of this person. Apparently, this slave of his is a frequent customer of yours. Who is he?"

The shopkeeper hesitated.

"Suit yourself."

The vampyre opened his mouth to bite the young girl.

"Aiden! His name is Aiden!" the shopkeeper yelled. "That's what you wanted to know right? Please just leave my daughter alone!"

Smiling, but not pulling away from the man's daughter, the vampyre responded. "Thank you... and where does this man live?"

"He lives in a large mansion on the east corner of town. His family crest is the phoenix, please that's all I know! Just let my wife and daughter go!"

Looking at the other vampyres, the one in charge spoke. "Go to the mansion. Kill everyone, no survivors."

The other vampyres nodded, dropping the shopkeeper, and left the shop, heading towards Aiden's home.

"I told you what you wanted to know. You'll let us go now, right?" the shopkeeper asked.

"Yes, you have been very helpful." the vampyre replied, walking over to the shopkeeper.

The shopkeeper breathed a sigh of relief.

"But..." the vampyre continued.

"We can't have you running off and telling everyone about our little chat, now can we?"

"I won't tell a soul, I promise." the shopkeeper begged.

"Unfortunately, the word of a human means very little to me. Besides, it's not a risk I'm willing to take."

The vampyre walked behind the shopkeeper. "Not when there are much easier... and fun, solutions."

With that, the vampyre quickly snapped the shopkeeper's neck as his wife and daughter screamed through their gags.

As the vampyre snapped the man's neck, Siri, who had also been looking through the window with Aiden, let out a small gasp.

Alerted to their presence, the vampyre walked over to the window.

Before the vampyre could notice them, Aiden grabbed Siri and threw her to the ground under the window and joined her a moment later. Holding a hand over Siri's mouth, Aiden put a finger to his lips, indicating for her to stay quiet.

As the vampyre looked out the window at the empty back alley, he shrugged, pulling the curtains across the window as he turned back to the wife and daughter.

"Now... where were we?" the vampyre asked with a bloody grin as he walked toward the two terrified women.

~ ~ ~ ~ ~

Aiden and Siri were running down the street as fast as they could.

"We have to get home first!" Aiden cried. "We must warn them!"

Turning down the last street before reaching his house, Aiden was suddenly shoved up against the nearest building.

"Get off me!" Aiden yelled, trying to fight back against this unknown assailant.

"Aiden, look at me."

The man's voice was familiar.

Looking into his assailant's face, Aiden recognized the man. Raizel.

"Aiden, you need to listen to me very carefully." Raizel began to speak, his forearm holding Aiden against the wall.

"You need to get out of the city. The vampyres are looking for you."

"I know, I need to warn my family." Aiden pulled at Raizel's arm, trying to free himself.

"It's too late, there is nothing you can do." Raizel responded coldly.

"This is all your fault!" Aiden shouted, continuing to struggle against the vampyre.

"No Aiden, I tried to protect you, but the others picked up your trail faster than anticipated."

"Let me go!" Aiden demanded.

"I can't do that, you're too important to let you get yourself killed."

"Let me go... now." Aiden repeated, no longer raising his voice, but still furious at this vampyre that is preventing him from helping his family.

"Let me go now... or I will Kill you."

Siri, standing off to the side, knew she couldn't just stand there. She had to help. Running up behind Raizel. She put all of her weight into a punch directed just underneath Raizel's ribcage.

Raizel didn't even flinch.

She went to punch him again, but Raizel grabbed her hand with his own free hand.

A blinding pain shot through Raizel's wrist.

Raizel looked down to see Aiden's hand had grabbed the hand that he had used to take hold of Siri with. All the bones in his wrist where Aiden was gripping him were broken. Looking back at Aiden, Raizel saw that Aiden's eyes looked the same as they had that day at the temple.

"*Hybrid Eyes*" Raizel thought.

With the bones in his wrist now crushed, Raizel could no longer keep Siri in his grasp.

As soon as Siri was free, Aiden shoved Raizel, tossing him ten meters away. Grabbing Siri's hand, Aiden looked back at Raizel before speaking.

"Don't even think about following us."

With that said, he and Siri took off towards their house.

~ ~ ~ ~ ~

Bursting through the front door of his house, Aiden yelled for his father.

Hearing a commotion upstairs, Aiden began to run for the stairs, but before he could reach the stairs, he was met by his father, two brothers, mother and little sister.

"Father, vampyres are on their way to kill all of you."

"I know, son. The five that came here earlier have already been dealt with, but I have a feeling more are on their way." his father replied.

"Then we need to get out of here quickly." Aiden said.

"No, son. "You" need to get out of here." Aiden's father said calmly.

"What?"

Aiden stared at his father in shock.

"If we all tried to escape, then we would easily be able to be tracked. You need to survive more than any of us."

"But why?" Aiden demanded.

"Because son... You are the Hybrid. Only your power is strong enough to not just threaten, but potentially overthrow not just the vampyres, but all immortal races. The Hybrid knew that when he disappeared, that the immortal races would begin to establish themselves as the ruling class of society. You need to survive, you will become a symbol of hope, not just for humans, but for all the other races. That is your destiny, son."

Four vampyres burst through the front door, followed by a dozen vampurics.

Stepping forward, Aiden summoned all the strength in his body.

"I can't let you die for me."

Aiden ran toward the vampyres. As he ran, Aiden tried to shift his body into his hybrid form, only to realize he didn't know how to. Slamming into the first vampyre with all his might, Aiden swung his fist at the vampyre's face. A loud crack could be heard, followed by the vampyre's head sailing across the room toward the other immortals.

Aiden charged at the next vampyre, only to be tackled by five vampurics, each one ripping and tearing into his flesh with their claws.

Just as Aiden thought it was the end for him, each one of the vampurics holding him burst into flame, screaming and rolling around the floor in agony. Aiden found himself being picked up off the floor by his brother and Siri.

Making their way back across the room to his father, Aiden's brother then joined in the fight against the vampyres. Fire magic blazed through the air, barely keeping the immortals at bay.

"You're not strong enough Aiden... not yet." his father said. "Go... you and Siri get out of here. We will hold them off as long as we can."

The pain in Aiden's body began to subside as it began healing.

"Father, I can't just leave you all here."

"Yes you can, son. It is not just this family's duty to protect the Hybrid, but also my duty, as a father, to protect my son. You... are the future of this family... and I couldn't be more proud to call you my son."

Aiden's father launched another fireball at the vampurics before turning to face Aiden.

"You need to head south, into the Whitetooth Mountains. Follow your instincts, they will know where you need to go. Trust them. I love you, son. Now Go!"

"Aiden, Listen to your father." Siri said, pulling on his arm.

With tears in his eyes, Aiden took one last look at his family, knowing he most likely would never see them again. As Aiden turned to leave, his mother walked up to him, hugging him as she spoke.

"Be careful, son."

Robert Stasny

Aiden and Siri headed towards the back of the house where his family kept a secret escape tunnel when Aiden's arm was suddenly grabbed by his mother.

"Please Aiden." his mother begged. "Please take your sister with you, she's too young to fight. Please don't let my daughter die with the rest of us."

Aiden looked past his mother, at his father. His father nodded, before going back to fighting.

"Ok mother... I'll take her with me." Aiden replied.

Letting go of his hand, his mother stepped aside to allow Maddison to step forward.

"Take this with you, you will need these." Their mother handed Maddison a small pack full of items.

Accepting the pack and quickly hugging her mother, Maddison grabbed Aiden's hand and the three of them fled into the tunnel.

"Seal the tunnel once they leave!" Aiden heard his father shout to his mother as they drew further and further down the tunnel.

*"There's no going back now."* Aiden realized, as they made their escape.

As the three made their way out of the tunnel, Aiden noticed they were now in the forest outside their property. Taking a glance back at their former home, Aiden wished he hadn't.

Where once, his family mansion stood, was now a giant pillar of fire large enough to consume two city blocks.

# Chapter 8

"Where are we going to go?" asked Maddison, sitting next to the campfire, arms wrapped around her knees.

It had been three days since the three of them had fled their home. Three days of nearly constant running, trying to get as much distance between themselves and the pursuing vampyres.

"I'm not sure." Siri replied. "So much has changed for us in the last few days."

Looking over at the younger girl, who had just lost everything she had ever known, Siri was not really sure how to comfort her.

"I'm going to go check on Aiden." Siri said.

Getting up from the fire, Siri looked around at the cave that they had taken shelter in for the night. It was a good sized cave that narrowed considerably as you got closer to the entrance. Siri walked along the narrow walls of the cave until it widened out to a small opening in the rocks.

Moving a set of vines that had been draped to conceal the entrance to the cave, Siri stepped out into the cool night air. Looking around, she saw no trace of Aiden.

"Aiden?" she whispered, getting no response.

"Aiden? Where are you?"

Panic began to seep into Siri's mind.

Taking a deep breath to calm her nerves, Siri began looking around the area outside the cave for any clue to Aiden's whereabouts. Glancing up at the night sky, slightly obscured by the trees and a few clouds, Siri took note of the moon.

*"Just a few more days until the full moon."*

From the little knowledge she had of immortals, Siri knew that most werewolves could shift at will. At least the older ones who have learned could. But they were still forced to shift against their will on a full moon, losing control for a few hours.

*"What did that mean for Aiden?"* she though.

*"Being a hybrid, how will the full moon affect him?"*

She hated the thought of seeing Aiden go through the pain of his transformation again. She had heard that it was painful to shift, but after watching Aiden shift for the first time five days ago, she now understood truly how painful the process was. It wasn't just a few brief moments of pain, and then it's over. It was an agonizingly slow process. Aiden's screams of pain lasted for what felt like an eternity to Siri. Both his brother and sister had heard his screams from the house and came to investigate. By the time they arrived, he wasn't even halfway through his transformation. The thought of seeing Aiden go through that every month brought tears to her eyes.

"Don't worry about me." Aiden said, walking up.

He had been out gathering firewood.

Seeing Siri looking up at the moon, with tears in her eyes when he returned, Aiden knew what she must be thinking. Dropping the pile of sticks and limbs that he had gathered; Aiden opened his arms invitingly for her.

Walking over to him, Siri wrapped her arms around him and buried her head in his chest, thankful to be in his arms once again.

"Where did you go?" she asked.

"To gather firewood. And...I needed some time to think." Aiden kissed her head, looking down at her.

"What about?" Siri looked up into his eyes.

"About what we do next. We are getting low on supplies, we need to restock."

Letting go of Siri, Aiden pulled out a map. "There is a fishing village called Nurki'l not too far from here, we can resupply there, and maybe, if we are lucky, get some directions."

"Are you sure?" Siri asked, a little worried.

"We'll have to be quick, not stick around long enough to draw attention to ourselves, but we should be fine." Aiden put the map away and picked up the stack of wood he had gathered earlier.

"Come on. Maddison is waiting on us."

Once back in the cave, Aiden explained the plan to Maddison.

~ ~ ~ ~ ~

"How about something to eat?" Aiden asked, pulling a large pouch from his waist.

"Eat what?" Maddison asked, slightly confused.

"We don't have any more food. We ran out yesterday." Siri explained.

"I found some wild strawberries in the woods while I was gathering firewood." he replied.

Pouring out the large pouch of strawberries, Aiden divided them up between the two girls.

"Eat up, then get some sleep. We leave at dawn."

Aiden stood up and began to head back towards the entrance to take watch.

Seeing Aiden had given all of the strawberries to the two of them, and not taking any for himself, Siri spoke up.

"Aiden, what about you? You need to eat something as well."

"No, you two go ahead, you need it more than I do." Aiden replied, not bothering to turn back.

~ ~ ~ ~ ~

Sitting outside the entrance to the cave. Aiden heard Siri coming up behind him.

"Why aren't you sleeping?" Aiden whispered, turning to look at Siri. "You need to get some rest."

"So do you." Siri replied. "You have been standing watch every night since we left Esenor. How much sleep have you actually had?"

"Don't worry about me, I'll be fine." Aiden brushed her comment off, staring back out into the dark night.

"All I can do is worry about you!" Siri snapped.

"You want to protect your sister and me." she continued, more lovingly. "And I love that about you. But you can't protect either of us if you aren't eating or sleeping yourself. Now come to bed."

Siri took Aiden by the hand, trying to pull him into the cave.

"But..." Aiden began to argue.

"The entrance to the cave is hidden, and you can't see or hear anything from the outside. We will be fine for one night, now come to bed." she said again, pulling harder this time. "That's an order."

Walking back into the cave together, they laid down next to the fire, drifting off to sleep in each other's arms.

~ ~ ~ ~ ~

Aiden woke just before the sun began to rise.

Feeling the now familiar weight of Siri pressed against him, Aiden knew he would disturb her if he moved.

Deciding to let her sleep a little while longer, Aiden began to make plans for today's journey in his head, making a mental note of everything they would need to buy at the village. As Siri shifted positions on top of him, pushing him down harder into the rough floor of the cave, Aiden made a mental note to himself to buy some comfortable sleeping mats.

Just after the sun rose over the horizon, Siri began to wake up.

"Morning." Aiden said, smiling at the girl.

"Good morning yourself." Siri teased, shoving her hand into his face so she wouldn't have to look at the stupid grin he was giving her.

Rolling off of him and sitting next to Aiden, Siri began to wipe the sleep from her eyes.

Sitting up behind her, Aiden wrapped his arms around her. Leaning over her, he placed a kiss on the nape of her neck as he inhaled the scent of her body. She was absolutely intoxicating to him.

Aiden felt a peculiar sensation. As he continued to place kisses along her neck, he felt this peculiar sensation continue to build and build. Pulling back temporarily from the onslaught of kisses he was placing on her neck, Aiden ran his tongue across his lips.

That's when he felt it. Fangs.

Realizing what he had almost done, Aiden jumped up and ran out of the cave as fast as he could, leaving behind a still groggy, but very confused Siri.

~ ~ ~ ~ ~

Outside the cave, Aiden ran to a small pond about a hundred meters away, this feeling inside him still raging.

Looking into the pond at his reflection, Aiden could see clearly that his teeth were now showing fangs, as well as his eyes had once again changed to the black and red from his dreams.

Closing his eyes, Aiden took a few deep breaths, and pushed this feeling, this "thirst" as far down as he could, trying to bury it.

After a few moments, Aiden opened his eyes to see that his eyes had returned to normal in his reflection.

Feeling very confused, Siri got up and went looking for Aiden. Blinking into the bright sunlight, Siri found Aiden at the edge of the pond. He seemed to be struggling with something, but she didn't know what.

"Are you ok?" she asked. "Why did you run off like that earlier?"

Aiden didn't respond, but just kept staring into the water.

"Aiden, what's wrong? Talk to me, what happened?" Concern filled her voice.

"I almost hurt you." Aiden finally answered, nearly in tears.

"What are you talking about?" Siri asked.

"In the cave. When I was kissing your neck."

"What about it?"

"Last night we were so worried about what would happen to me during the full moon, that we forgot to remember I'm not just part werewolf." Aiden almost choked on his own words. "I'm also part vampyre."

Now understanding what happened, Siri got down on her knees beside him.

"I'm so sorry." Aiden said, now sobbing.

Siri reached over and gently touched Aiden's shoulder.

Jerking away, Aiden continued.

"Don't touch me! I'm a monster."

"No, you're not." Siri said, reaching up and turning his face to look at her.

"I almost fed off you! I was inches away from sinking my fangs into you and draining you dry." Aiden's fists clenched, thinking about what might have happened.

"But you didn't."

"I wanted to." Aiden said, looking Siri in the eye.

"But you didn't." she repeated, soothingly.

"But..." Aiden tried to argue.

"Shhh, its ok." Siri whispered, pulling his head down into her lap, running one hand through his hair and the other down his arm.

"It's going to be ok. "We" will be ok." Siri said, holding him. "We'll get through this... together."

Siri leaned down, kissing the top of Aiden's head. They sat there for a while as the sun continued to rise.

# Chapter 9

After getting his thirst under control, Aiden and Siri headed back into the cave to pack up and head to the village. Maddison was now awake and getting ready for the day as well.

"Where were you guys?" Maddison asked. "I woke up and both of you were gone."

"Nothing to worry about." Siri said, picking up the pack Aiden's mother had given them.

"You ready to head out?"

"I guess so." Maddison replied.

The three of them stepped out of the cave and began their journey toward the nearest village.

~ ~ ~ ~ ~

After an hour of travelling Aiden and his companions came across a river with a road running alongside it.

"This must be the road to Nurki'l." Aiden said.

As they looked down the road, they could see the outskirts of the village. A small little village, with only a dozen or so buildings, along with various huts that the villagers lived in. Connected to the shoreline of the river, was an old wooden dock that looked like it had seen better days. From this dock, several men and children were fishing using either poles or nets.

As the three of them entered town, several villagers took notice.

"Welcome travelers." An elderly man walked up, greeting them as they entered.

The man was of average height, with a withered face and calloused hands that spoke of a lifetime working with his hands. He had a short grey beard and just a small horseshoe of grey hair left on a mostly bald head.

"We don't get many visitors to our village; my name is Gregory. I'm the leader of this village. Tell me, what brings you here?" The man offered out his hand to Aiden.

"My companions and I are travelling south, and ran out of supplies yesterday morning." Aiden explained, taking the man's hand and shaking it. "Tell me, would your village happen to have a general store that we could resupply at?"

"Oh yes." the elderly man said, turning and pointing down the street. "Third building on your left, you can't miss it. Now if you'll excuse me, I was on my way over to the dock to spend some time with my grandchildren."

"Thank you for your help." Siri said, as the man walked away.

"My pleasure young lady... and please, do enjoy your time in our little village."

Heading down the street to the general store, Aiden pulled a list of items they would need out of his pocket. Entering the store, Aiden took a moment to look around. Behind the counter stood a middle-aged woman with brown hair.

"Welcome, welcome! How may we assist you today?" the woman asked in a cheery voice and a smile.

Walking up to the counter, Aiden handed over his list to the lady.

"We need to restock our supplies. Does your store carry all of these items?" Aiden asked.

Taking a minute to look over the list Aiden had handed her, she smiled back at Aiden.

"We should have everything you need. If you give us a few moments, I will have them brought over."

Calling over her shoulder, the woman yelled.

"Jeffery! We have customers!"

A young man about seventeen walked out of the backroom.

"Yes mother?"

Handing the list over to her son, she continued. "Here is a list of supplies these fine folk need, would you be so kind as to fetch them for us?"

"Ok." the boy said, taking the list and heading back into the back of the store.

"Please have a seat, my son will bring everything you need out of the back shortly."

"Thank you ma'am." Aiden said. "There is one more thing."

"What is it?" the lady asked.

Leaning over the counter Aiden whispered something into her ear.

Blushing slightly, the woman looked over at Siri, smiled, and pulled out a piece of parchment and began writing on it.

After writing on the parchment, she handed it over to Aiden.

"Just down the road, three houses down, two houses to the left." the woman said. "Ask for Anthony. Tell him Margaret sent you, he'll have what you need."

Thanking the woman, Aiden handed a pouch of coins to her. "This should cover everything. Keep the rest as a thank you for your help with my other item."

"But sir, this is at least three times what you owe me for the supplies." Margaret began, her eyes wide.

Aiden held out his hand, silencing her. "I insist. If Anthony has the item I'm looking for, it will be more than worth it to me."

"Thank you sir! Please, don't hesitate to ask us if you need anything else. Girls, if there is anything you two want please, let me or my son know."

"Stay here." Aiden said, turning toward the door. "I will be back shortly, there is something I need to take care of on my own. Is that alright with you ma'am?"

"Oh yes." Margaret answered. "They are more than welcome to stay here while they wait for you."

With that, Aiden left the store and headed to the house that Margaret had directed him to.

~ ~ ~ ~ ~

Stepping up to the house, Aiden knocked on the door of the small log cabin.

A young woman answered the door, opening the door only a crack.

"What do you want?" she asked.

"Sorry to disturb you, but I'm looking for Anthony." Aiden said. "Margaret sent me."

A tall man opened the door from behind the young woman.

"I'm Anthony, what can I do for you?" he asked.

Aiden handed over the small piece of parchment. Reading it, Anthony smiled and moved out of the doorway.

"Please, come in." Anthony said.

Aiden accepted the man's invitation and entered the small cabin. Inside, covering most of the walls and furniture, were stacks and stacks of animal fur. Leading Aiden to a separate room, Anthony began to talk. "So what "exactly" are you looking for?"

~ ~ ~ ~ ~

Aiden returned to the store an hour later to find all the items they had bought had already been packed away. Siri was sitting down at a nearby table with their map spread out across it, talking to Margaret, who was pointing out a few different locations. At another table was Maddison, sitting next to and chatting with

Jefferey. Every now and then, she would giggle at something he said.

Aiden walked up to Siri and Margaret.

"What's going on?" Aiden asked, leaning over to give Siri a kiss.

"I was just telling Siri here about the easiest way to get to the Whitetooth Mountains." Margaret said, pointing at a path on the map.

"We really don't want to be using the roads." Aiden replied, indicating that no other information would be given.

Nodding slightly, Margaret then pointed to a forest to the east.

"You could try crossing through the Lockwood Forest, but I would be careful out there. I have heard reports from travelers that a few trading caravans and whatnot have gone missing in those woods."

"Thanks for the warning." Aiden said. "We will keep an eye out for trouble."

Pointing to an area just past the forest, Margaret continued.

"Once you leave the forest, you will then be heading through the Plains of Aerindor."

She moved her hand a little farther south.

"After that is the base of the Whitetooth Mountains. Where exactly in the Whitetooth Mountains are you heading? she asked.

"We're not sure yet, but thank you for all the help you have given us." Aiden folded up the map, tucking it away.

"Were you able to get that item you were looking for?" Margaret asked.

"Yes, I did. Thank you very much for pointing me in the right direction."

Margaret smiled warmly as she nodded. "My pleasure."

Looking back at Maddison, Aiden had an idea.

"Maddison?"

"Yes?" She paused, looking up from the conversation she was having.

"What do you think of this place?"

Puzzled, Maddison gave her brother a strange look. "What do you mean?"

Walking over, Aiden sat down across from his sister. Reaching across the table, Aiden took her hands in his own. Aiden looked over at Jefferey and then Margaret.

"May I have a moment alone with my sister and Siri?"

"Of course dear. Come Jefferey, let's give them some privacy."

Jefferey begrudgingly got up, following his mother out of the room.

Now alone with Siri and his sister, Aiden began to talk.

"I would like you to stay here, Maddison." Aiden said.

"What? Why?" Maddison asked, shock and confusion written all over her face.

"At the moment, the vampyres are still hunting me." Aiden continued. "They knew about me, and also about Siri... but not you. As far as they know, you perished in the fire along with the rest of our family in order to give me time to escape."

Tears were beginning to form in Maddison's eyes.

Siri sat down next to Maddison and put her arm around her.

"From what I have gathered, this place is a quiet, out of the way village that rarely receives visitors, let alone any immortals. It is a quiet life, but a safe one." Aiden tightened his grip on her hands slightly. "No one knows what you look like, or who you are...you could start a new life here.

"But what about you? You promised to take me with you!" she nearly screamed, squeezing Aiden's hands.

"I promised mother that I wouldn't let her daughter die." Aiden spoke softly.

"Where I'm going... whatever it is that I am supposed to do, it is going to be dangerous. I would feel better about my journey knowing that my little sister is safe. This isn't the end, I'll come back to visit you. Or, maybe once I figure out a way out of this mess, you can come visit me."

"You promise?" Maddison asked, still not completely sure.

"Have I ever lied to you?" Aiden asked.

Maddison shook her head. "Ok, I'll stay."

"So... that boy, Jefferey." Aiden leaned back after letting his sister's hands go. "You like him?"

Looking down at her hands, cheeks blushing, Maddison replied.

"I don't know. He's sweet, and funny... but we only just met!"

"Ok, ok, I'll stop teasing you." Aiden said, getting up from the table. "Just don't forget to actually live your life while you are here. This place isn't a prison, it's your new home."

"I'll try."

Walking back over to the doorway, Aiden asked Margaret and her son to come back into the room.

"Please, sit."

Both mother and son took a seat at the table.

"The road is no place for a young girl like my sister, and where I'm going, it is going to be dangerous. So we have decided to let her stay here in this village."

Jefferey perked up when he hears Aiden say this.

"I would like to ask you to take care of her, Margaret. If that is ok with you... I would also be happy to leave some more money with you to offset the cost of her living here if necessary."

"No, no, that won't be necessary." Margaret answered.

"It would be my honor to take her in. I've always wanted a daughter. My husband and I both did, before he fell ill and died last winter. She will be safe with us, I promise you that. She will be treated as my own flesh and blood from this moment on."

"Thank you." Aiden said, standing up. "I think it's about time we set off."

Walking around to his sister, Aiden wrapped her in a big hug.

"Father was wrong." Aiden whispered into her ear. "I'm not the future of this family... you are."

As he pulled away, Aiden pressed something into her hand.

"Keep it safe." Aiden said, then turned and walked out of the store with Siri following right behind.

Maddison looked down at the object her brother had pressed into her hand.

The family ring with the phoenix family crest engraved on top.

Aiden took one last look back at the village.

"Stay safe." he whispered.

Turning back to the road, Aiden and Siri began their long journey to the Whitetooth Mountains.

"You made the right decision." Siri said, reassuring Aiden.

# Chapter 10

After a hard day of travelling, Aiden and Siri finally came to the edge of the Lockwood Forest. Tall, dense trees who's canopies prevent anything but a few rays of sunlight through.

"I wonder what awaits us inside?" Siri asked as she looked at the intimidating forest before them.

As the two entered the forest, both Aiden and Siri felt a chill run up their spine. The forest seemed quiet, too quiet for comfort. The forest itself seemed to soak up all sound, leaving the surrounding area in an eerie silence.

Aiden and Siri made their way into the forest. An hour later, they came to a small clearing in the forest. Deciding this was as good a place as any, Aiden pulled the pack off his shoulders and got to work setting up camp. Siri headed further into the forest to collect firewood while Aiden set up the tent.

As Siri walked through the forest, she began to really take note of her surroundings. The forest was truly beautiful. Bright green grass and little white flowers covered the ground. The leaves of the trees around her sparked and reflected the sunlight as if they were made of crystals. Despite the eerie quite, the forest gave off a sense of serenity.

As she gathered wood for the campfire, Siri began to get the feeling she was being watched.

Catching a hint of movement out of the corner of her eye, she turned to see what had caught her attention. By the time she turned, there was nothing there. Whatever it was, had fled before she could see it.

Now feeling like she was alone again, Siri figured it must have just been an animal of some sort. Resuming her work gathering firewood, Siri quickly forgot about it.

Reentering the clearing they had chosen to make camp at, Siri could see that the tent that had been set up was not the same one that they had bought at the village store.

Instead of the small, three person tent she had expected, Siri was now looking at a tent large enough to hold at least ten people, tall enough to stand in, with room to spare.

*"Where did Aiden get such a large tent?"*

"So, how'd I do?" Aiden asked, walking up to her, clearly amused at her shocked expression.

"Aiden, where did you get this tent?" she asked.

"I wanted it to be a surprise." Aiden took the firewood from her, placing it on the ground.

"Well I am definitely surprised."

"Not yet you're not." Aiden took her by the hand and led her over to the large tent.

The sun was just beginning to get low in the sky, and darkness would soon be upon them. Reaching the entrance to the tent, Aiden placed his hand over Siri's eyes.

"No peeking."

"Why not?" Siri complained, pouting.

"Do you trust me?"

"With my life." Siri answered, closing her eyes.

Taking each step carefully, Aiden led Siri into the tent.

Once inside, Aiden sealed the entrance to the tent. Turning back to Siri, who still had her eyes closed, Aiden wrapped his arms around her waist and whispered into her ear.

"Remember when I left to go buy my other item at the village?"

"It's all I could think about while we were travelling today... since you refused to tell me what it was." Siri answered.

"Then open your eyes and see for yourself." Aiden whispered, stepping away from her.

Siri opened her eyes, and her jaw dropped.

Inside the tent, covering the floor was a large, luxurious bed made of snow-white rabbit fur. The bed had silk sheets, large fluffy blankets, and several large pillows. Above the head of the bed, was a large orb that glowed faintly with light. Hanging from the ceiling of the tent every few feet, were small crystal orbs that each gave off a soft yellow light to illuminate the tent. Hundreds of smaller gems were attached to the roof of the tent, reflecting the light from the larger crystals, making them sparkle as if they were stars. Off to one side of the tent was even a large tub for bathing, already filled with steaming water. A small table sat in the center of the tent with four chairs next to it. On the table was a plate full of different fruits, bread, and even several varieties of dried meat.

Siri stood in awe of the sheer beauty of her surroundings. Holding a hand over her mouth in shock, she turned to Aiden.

"Was it worth the wait?" Aiden asked, smiling.

Siri could only nod.

~ ~ ~ ~ ~

Aiden stepped outside to start the campfire as Siri removed her clothes and stepped into the warm bath.

Sinking into the warm water, Siri sighed.

*"Oh, I missed this."*

Reveling in the feel of the warm water against her skin, Siri began to scrub the last four days' worth of dirt and grime from her body.

After a few minutes of scrubbing, Siri finally felt clean. Leaning back and resting her head against the rim of the tub, Siri closed her eyes and began to let her body relax and just soak up the warmth from the water.

Having finished getting the fire started for the evening cooking, Aiden returned to the tent.

Seeing Siri in the bath, Aiden walked over and grabbed a bucket of water near the tub. Pulling a small stool from nearby over, he sat behind Siri. Taking his pouch of bathing stones they had bought in the village, Aiden pulled a small one from the pouch and dropped it into the bucket of water at his feet, letting the water heat up. Grabbing a cup from a nearby table, Aiden took Siri's hair in his hands and began to wash her hair as she lay in the tub.

"Hey Aiden."
Siri's eyes remained closed as he continued washing her hair.
"Yeah?"
"Thank you for this... all of it." Siri said.
"I'd do anything for you." Leaning forward, Aiden placed a kiss on her upturned forehead.

Siri opened her eyes as he went back to work on her hair.
"What's going to happen tomorrow, Aiden?"
"What do you mean?" Aiden asked, grabbing a brush from the nearby table and beginning to brush her hair.
"The full moon is tomorrow." Siri continued. "Aren't you afraid?"
"I am, but not as much as I was a few days ago."
"Why not?"

"I've been reading more of that journal you found. Inside, there were a few entries that went into the details of the shift. The journal said that although the shift was always painful, the majority of the pain could be ignored if you have something to keep you focused, and if you don't try to fight back against the shift." Aiden explained.

Siri leaned forward, turning her upper body to face Aiden.

"Fight back against the shift?"

"It means your body's natural reaction to pain." Aiden began to explain further. "If you touch something hot, what happens?"

"You pull your hand away." she answered.

Siri began to understand.

"Exactly." Aiden replied. "Your body's natural reaction is to pull away and fight back against pain. The journal says that if instead of fighting it, you embrace it, and actually lean into that pain, the shift will happen much, much quicker."

"How much quicker?" Siri asked, resting her own arm against his.

"The journal said that he was able to shift back and forth within just a few seconds if needed. Now move over." Aiden ordered, as he began to undress. "You're hogging all the hot water."

Stepping into the tub next to Siri, Aiden began to wash himself as well.

Moving behind him, Siri began to wash Aiden's back as they continued to talk.

"How do you feel?" Siri asked, scrubbing the dirt from Aiden's body. "I've heard that immortals can feel the effect of the moon as it gets closer to being full."

"Yeah... I can feel my senses getting even more sensitive... and I feel even stronger as the full moon gets closer." Aiden replied.

"And what about your thirst, or losing control?"

"The thirst has nothing to do with the moon, and as far as the journal has said... since I am a hybrid, I will still feel a desire to shift, but I won't be forced to. I shouldn't lose control either, I guess we can thank my vampyre side for that."

"That's nice to hear." Siri said, wrapping her arms around him, hugging his back.

"It still won't be easy though." Aiden took one of her hands in his. "The desire to shift will still be very hard to resist, even if I won't lose control. Also... both my emotions, as well as my aggression and temper will be on edge until the full moon is over."

"Couple that with my increased strength, it will still be dangerous. I could still hurt you, or someone else without meaning to." Aiden said.

"You can handle it, I'm sure." Siri said, still holding Aiden.

"How do you know?" Aiden asked, looking back over his shoulder.

"Because... I know you." Siri said.

Taking her hand from around him, Aiden kissed her hand before stepping out of the bath. Wrapping a towel around himself, he tossed one to Siri as she got out.

"I'll go start dinner."

Aiden began making his way towards the entrance, but before he could make it out of the tent, Siri grabbed his hand, pulling him back.

Looking back to see what she wanted, Aiden was ambushed by a set of lips meeting his own.

"Dinner can wait." Siri whispered, pulling him down onto the bed.

# Chapter 11

Lying next to Aiden, Siri could not remember a time she felt happier than she did at this moment. Snuggled beneath the warm blankets, her head rested on Aiden's shoulder, looking up at the twinkling roof of the tent.

"How did you get all this stuff in here?" Siri asked, glancing around the room. "I think I would have noticed you carrying around that bathtub."

"The man I went to go see in the village." Aiden answered, running his fingers through her hair as they talked.

"He worked as the hunter of the village. I originally only planned on getting a nice sleeping mat, but he was also an accomplished sorcerer. After telling the man of our journey, he told me he had something far better than just a comfortable sleeping mat."

"A sorcerer?"

"Apparently, he prefers the quiet village over the noisy city life. He told me that he specialized in temporal magic."

"Temporal magic? What's that?" Siri lifted herself up to look at Aiden.

"Teleporting, transportation, and pocket dimensions." Aiden answered. "Anyway, he said if I was interested... he could create a pocket dimension that existed outside of our current location, anchored by an object. For us, it would be this tent. The entrance of the tent basically would serve as a gateway between our location and the pocket dimension. He said that anything we want could be stored in the tent and would remain there, even when the tent is packed away. So, I took the liberty to get a few extra things added to the tent for our journey."

"Like the bathtub?"

"I figured you would like having access to one while we are on the road." Aiden replied, grinning.

"What time is it?" she asked.

"A few hours till dawn."

"I guess we missed dinner." Siri said, blushing slightly.

Looking down at Aiden, she leaned in and whispered into his ear. "Any chance I could convince you to make an early breakfast?"

Aiden felt the familiar feeling of his thirst start to build.

Pushing it back down, and getting himself under control, Aiden looked up at Siri.

"You do realize... if I go make breakfast, we have to get out of bed, right?" Aiden asked, running a hand through her hair.

Taking a moment, Siri considered her choices.

"Times up!"

Grabbing her with one hand around her waist and the other around her shoulders, Aiden flipped the two of them over, pinning her beneath him.

Looking down into Siri's emerald eyes, Aiden placed a loving kiss on her lips. When they broke their kiss, Siri looked up into Aiden's eyes, noticing that they were glowing softly.

After breaking their kiss, Aiden picked himself up off the bed and began to get dressed, pulling on a pair of trousers. Not bothering with a shirt, he walked out of the tent to make breakfast while Siri remained in bed, staring after him.

~ ~ ~ ~ ~

After breakfast, Aiden and Siri began to pack up camp. After learning about how the tent worked, Siri opted to put everything but a few items in the tent, so that it would be easier and lighter to travel with.

It was still an hour before dawn, so Aiden decided to perform a few tests.

Closing his eyes and concentrating, Aiden followed the instructions he had found inside the journal. Focusing on his hands, Aiden felt a little bit of pain in his fingers. Instead of stopping, Aiden let it happen. Looking down and inspected his hands, his fingernails had now lengthened and hardened into sharp claws.

He had done it!

Even if it was only a partial transformation, Aiden had successfully shifted at will.

Aiden flexed his fingers to test their strength, getting used to the feeling of the claws. Calling Siri over, Aiden explained what he had done, showing her the claws on his hand.

"It's just a small step." he said.

"But its progress." Siri replied, finishing Aiden's statement for him. "You're learning control."

As the sun rose over the horizon, Aiden shouldered their pack and the two of them set off further into the woods.

Making their way deeper into the woods, they came across a dirt path.

"Where did this come from?" Siri asked.

"This must be the route that trading caravans use to get through the forest." Aiden said, inspecting the path.

It was a well-traveled dirt path that was just wide enough to accommodate a wagon, and perhaps a few horses. Recent tracks revealed that someone had come through recently, within the last two days as best that Aiden could guess.

Aiden decided it would be easier to follow the path for a while since it went in the same direction they were headed.

Shortly after midday, Aiden and Siri stopped to eat. Pulling off the pack and setting it on the ground, Aiden pulled a few pieces of bread, as well as a few strips of dried meat out of the pack and handed some over to Siri. After taking some time to eat and regain their strength, the two continued down the road.

A few hours later, Aiden and Siri came across a broken down cart.

"Stay here, I'll go check it out." Aiden stepped towards the cart.

As he got closer, Aiden could see that there were multiple arrows dotting the outside of the cart. Walking behind the cart, Aiden came across the bodies of three men, each of them with an arrow through the chest.

*"This wasn't just some broken-down cart they had found."* Aiden realized. *"Someone ambushed these traders on their way through the forest."*

Aiden remembered the warning that Margaret had given them back at the village.

*"Several caravans and travelers have gone missing in those woods."* she had told them.

As he was examining the corpses, Aiden suddenly heard Siri cry out in terror.

Jumping to his feet as he turned around, Aiden saw five hooded men had grabbed hold of Siri, while another three stood between him and Siri. Lengthening his fangs and growing his claws, Aiden charged at the group of men.

Aiden suddenly felt a sharp, intense pain go through his chest. Falling to his knees, Aiden found it difficult to breathe. Looking down, he saw that he had been shot in the chest by an arrow. Struggling to get back to his feet, Aiden was hit from behind. The last thing he saw before he blacked out was Siri being carried off into the woods.

# Chapter 12

Siri fought back against her captors as best she could... but she was both outmatched, and outnumbered. Seeing Aiden get shot with an arrow and getting hit from behind, Siri knew there was nothing she could do to help him. She also knew that it wouldn't keep him down for long, and that he would come for her.

Still, Siri didn't want to make it easy for them. Screaming and kicking as one of the men carried her away, Siri soon felt a cloth being put over her mouth, smelling strongly of some sort of drug. Siri fell unconscious a few moments later.

~ ~ ~ ~ ~

Opening her eyes groggily, Siri began to take in her surroundings. She found herself in some sort of large, rectangular tent of some kind. Several of the men who abducted her were standing around the room talking.

Noticing her moving around, one of the men gestured to another of the men.
"She's waking up."
Now able to see clearly, Siri looked at the man who was approaching her. As the man got closer, Siri tried to scoot away from the man.
"It's ok, we're not going to hurt you." the man said. "I'm sorry if we frightened you."

Kneeling down in front of Siri, the man pulled back the hood he was wearing, revealing a set of ears just like hers.

"Who are you?" Siri spat angrily. "Why did you attack us and kidnap me?"

"We didn't kidnap you." the elf began.

"We rescued you." he said, reaching a hand towards her face.

Slapping his hand away, Siri screamed at the man.

"Don't touch me!"

"My apologies lady." The man pulled his hand away from her. "I can only imagine what you have been through... being forced to serve that man's every desire. But that's all over now."

"Aiden will come for me." Siri sat up straight, anger and defiance filled her eyes. "And when he does, he's going to kill all of you."

"We know all about your former master." the elf replied, putting special emphasis on the word former.

"We are aware that he is an immortal, and that he is a werewolf. That's why we took special precautions against him. That arrow I shot him with was coated in wolfsbane... he won't last long, even if it is a full moon."

The elf seemed quite proud of himself as he told these things to Siri.

"Right now, he is either dead, or soon to be dead. So you see, there is nothing to worry about." the man said, smiling down at her.

"You have no idea what's coming." Siri warned. "Now let me go."

"I'm afraid I can't do that." the man said. "The seal that binds you to that man must be removed. You clearly still feel obligated to that man, but that is just the binding seal talking. Trust me.. once we remove it, you will feel much better."

Turning away from her, the man called to his comrades as he exited the tent. "Prepare her."

The other four men began approaching Siri.

~ ~ ~ ~ ~

Aiden woke up with a searing pain in his chest. Glancing down, he could see the arrow that he had been shot with was still buried in his chest. Still feeling short of breath, Aiden realized that he must have a punctured lung. Taking his time getting to his feet, Aiden looked up at the night sky.

"*How long was I out?*" he asked himself.

"*I've got to find Siri. But first... I've got to get this arrow out.*"

Walking over to a nearby tree, Aiden prepared himself for what he was about to do.

Taking hold of the shaft of the arrow, Aiden began to pull the arrow out, while simultaneously using the trunk of the tree to snap off the arrowhead sticking out his back. Fighting through the pain, Aiden finally managed to pull the arrow out of his chest. Dropping the arrow, Aiden leaned against the tree as his body healed itself.

Now healed, Aiden focused on Siri's binding seal his father had given him. Not only did this seal act as proof of ownership, but it also had a tracking function to it. Focusing on Siri, Aiden felt a strong tug in the corner of his mind.

"*That way.*" Aiden looked in the direction that the men had taken Siri.

Feeling the strength of the full moon, Aiden kicked his speed into high gear as he dashed into the forest as fast as he could, straight towards Siri.

"*Don't worry Siri... I'm coming.*"

~ ~ ~ ~ ~

Half an hour later, Aiden found himself outside of an encampment of some kind. Around the perimeter of the camp were wooden walls with two guards posted on top, every fifty feet.

Climbing a tree to get a better vantage point, Aiden took a few minutes to familiarize himself with the layout of the camp. Seeing several large structures near the center, as well as many smaller tents surrounding them. Taking note of the patrols roaming throughout the camp, Aiden focused his hearing and listened for the familiar sound of Siri's voice.

It didn't take long for Aiden to isolate the area that Siri was in, as she wasn't exactly being a compliant captive. She was being held in one of three large tents near the center of the camp with several men going in and out of them. With two guards posted outside the door of one.

Dropping back down out of the tree, Aiden had come up with a plan. Closing his eyes, Aiden planted his foot against the tree.

"*This is it.*" Aiden told himself.

Pushing himself off the base of the tree as hard as he could, Aiden went flying towards the two guards nearest him, catching them both by the throat and launching both himself, and them off the top of the wall and into a nearby bush. Looking down at the two guards, with both of their throats crushed, Aiden noticed that they were elves.

In his current state, with the help of the full moon, time seemed to slow down around Aiden. It seemed as if everything around him was moving in slow motion, while he could move freely. Aiden could hear everything around him, he could smell even the faintest of scents. Without even looking, Aiden was completely aware of his surroundings, he knew where each guard was and what they were doing just by scent and sound. Peering out of the bush he was in, Aiden looked around, then quickly moved to the base of the outer wall.

Staying in the shadows, Aiden made his way directly underneath the next guard station. From here, Aiden could hear the guards talking.

"She's cute." one of the guards said.

"Don't get any ideas, Johrra is the one who found her, and he has already laid claim to her." the other guard replied.

"I know, I know. As cute as she is, she's not worth being killed over. I saw the way he looked at her. He wants her, and he is willing to kill whoever tries to challenge him for her."

"Still, it's too bad, there aren't a lot of single elven women left in our camp."

"I heard that when Johrra found her, she was with an immortal." the first man said.

"Seriously?"

"Yeah, apparently Johrra saw him partially transform at his camp. From what he saw, he was either a werewolf, or a hellhound."

"Was?" the second man asked.

"Yeah, Johrra dipped the arrows he had in wolfsbane, just to play it safe."

"You sure it killed him? wolfsbane is not quite as effective on hellhounds as it is on werewolves. If the man was a hellhound, he might have survived."

"No chance, that amount of concentrated wolfsbane could easily kill a werewolf or a hellhound, even on a full moon."

"I hope you're right."

"For the girl's sake, I hope she accepts Johrra, he doesn't take rejection well... and I doubt he will give her a choice in the matter. If she knows what's good for her, she'll not refuse him."

"I feel sorry for her. I'd feel sorry for any woman that catches Johrra's eye."

"Agreed." the other man replied.

Having heard enough to piece together the events that had happened since the ambush at the broken down cart, Aiden slowly climbed the wall until he was standing behind the two guards. As they turned around to see Aiden standing there, Aiden grabbed them both by the throat, giving them just enough air to breath but not enough to be able to yell any louder than a whisper.

"Where is she?" Aiden demanded, baring his fangs at the two of them.

"Middle of the camp, third tent on the right." the first man barely got out, struggling for breath.

"What have you done to her?" Aiden asked threateningly.

"No one has touched her, not yet anyway." the second man said, gasping for air.

"They are attempting to remove her binding seal so that she will no longer feel obligated to you."

"Her binding seal doesn't control her." Aiden growled.

Aiden quickly knocked the two guards heads together to render them unconscious. Staying low, Aiden then began to methodically pick off each and every guard on the wall.

The last guard position Aiden would not be able to take without raising the alarm. Knowing what would happen once he took them out, Aiden looked up at the full moon.

"Ok, *let's do this.*" Aiden said to himself, as he let the red in his eyes take over, glowing brightly within a sea of swirling black. Crouching down, Aiden felt the strength and speed in every fiber of his being, coiled around his muscles, flowing through his veins.

*"Time to make an entrance."*

Launching himself into the air, Aiden grabbed hold of both of the guards, knocking them off their post. Aiden landed in the middle of the camp entrance with the bodies of both guards still in each hand, crouched down into a kneeling position on one knee as the alarm was sounded.

The guard patrol quickly began surrounding him.

Aiden slowly stood to his feet, as he did, he let his body go, allowing himself to shift from his human form to his hybrid form. Not fighting the transformation, Aiden pushed himself into it... embracing it, while keeping his mind focused on Siri. By the time Aiden had stood up, the transformation was complete.

Looking around at the now terrified soldiers surrounding him, several of the elves had fled when they saw him shift. As the remaining men rushed him, Aiden allowed all of his aggression to come out, knocking aside soldier after soldier, tearing through their armor as if it were paper.

Stepping up to the tent that Siri was being held in, Aiden saw that the two guards were no longer outside the tent. Slashing a large gash in the tent, Aiden stepped through to find Siri. The elf she had been arguing with held a knife to her throat, while the two guards stood between them and Aiden. One of the guards rushed forward, thrusting the spear he held at Aiden.

Pushing the spear aside, Aiden eviscerated the man with his claws.

Seeing his chance, the second guard ran up and plunged a short sword into Aiden's oversized torso.

Barely even registering the pain, Aiden grabbed the man by his throat and picked him up off the floor. Looking down at the weapon still lodged in his lower chest, Aiden pulled the weapon out with his free hand, looked at the blade, then slowly pushed the sword back into the struggling elf's own chest.

Dropping the man, Aiden turned to look at the elf who was holding a knife to Siri's throat.

"Come any closer and she dies!" the elf yelled at Aiden.

"Enough!" a woman's voice called out from the entrance to the tent.

Turning to see who it was who had spoken, Aiden saw an elegant elven woman in a bright blue dress. Behind her, stood at least two dozen guards, all shaking in their boots.

"My name is Linorra." The woman stepped forward as she spoke.

"We seem to have had a misunderstanding between you and my people." The woman remained calm, keeping her movements slow.

"The girl, I presume, is yours?" the woman looked past Aiden, at Siri.

"Johrra, release her." Linorra ordered.

"But your majesty..." the man holding the knife to Siri's neck began to protest.

"I said release her!" the woman snapped.

Slowly pulling the knife away from Siri's throat, the elf let go of Siri. Now free of Johrra's grasp, Siri walked forward and held onto Aiden's side.

"I knew you'd come." Siri said, hugging him tightly.

Now feeling like he had no bargaining chip, Johrra made his way around the tent, trying to keep as much distance from Aiden as possible.

Finally making it to the elven woman, Johrra fell into line with the other guards behind her.

Not taking his eyes off of Linorra, Aiden nudged Siri to get behind him, while placing himself in front of her.

"Please, there is no need for any more violence. I am well aware that you could easily kill all of us without even breaking a sweat, and I do not desire to see any more of my people die tonight." The elven woman then knelt down on one knee before Aiden.

"On behalf of my people, I humbly ask for your forgiveness." she said.

"Most elves we meet on the road have had terrible masters... especially those with immortal masters, and all we wanted was to free her."

"Free?"
Siri stepped out from behind Aiden, anger in her eyes.

"I am with him by choice. He does not, nor has he ever treated me like a servant. I have received more kindness from this immortal, than I have from you. If this is the way free elves act, I'm glad to be this man's slave." Venom dripped from Siri's voice as she spoke.

"You have shamed us, young lady." Linorra said as she stood. "Our hatred for what has happened to our race has blinded us to anything else... I'm sorry."

Gesturing with her hand, another young female elf stepped forward holding a set of elven robes, one in black, and the other in green.

"Please, take these as a token of our apologies. If you would like, I wish to invite you to stay with us for a few days... there are some things I would like to discuss with both of you. You can find me in the building at the center of the camp."

Looking back, she spoke, more to her own men than to Aiden and Siri.

"No one will try to stop you, or bring any harm to you from this point on. You are free to leave, if you wish."

Linorra turned and took the garments from the other girl, laying them on a table near Aiden.

"I do hope to see you again." Linorra said as she left the tent, followed closely by the guards.

Aiden turned to look at Siri.

Taking his large hands in hers, Siri smiled up at him.

"You can change back now." Siri squeezed his hands. "I think they've had enough for one night."

# Chapter 13

"Did they hurt you?" Aiden asked, wrapping the black elven robe around himself.

"No." Siri replied, looking at Aiden.

"Let's get out of here."

Taking Siri's hand, Aiden walked out of the tent to see dozens of elves gathered in the courtyard surrounding the tent.

Squeezing her hand a little tighter, they began to walk forward towards the entrance to the camp. As they walked, with Aiden leading the way, the crowd of elves parted, allowing them passage. Looking around at the elves, Aiden was still on alert, keeping an eye out for any signs of danger.

Siri, on the other hand, was paying more attention to the elves who had gathered. Most of them were not soldiers, but rather, ordinary elves who had gathered to see what all the commotion had been about. Siri saw the look of awe on some faces, on others, fear. Still, not one of them dared to get in their way as they exited the camp.

~ ~ ~ ~ ~

Once back at the ambushed caravan, Aiden retrieved the pack he had left when he went after Siri. Shouldering the pack, the two of them headed off the road a few hundred feet to set up camp for the night.

With the tent set up and a fire started, Aiden and Siri sat down to eat.

Placing some strips of rabbit meat over the fire, Aiden sat back and offered Siri a small plate full of nuts and berries. Reaching back into the pack, Aiden pulled out a waterskin. Taking a few drinks, he then handed it over to Siri. The two of them sat in silence for a few moments while they waited for their food to cook.

"I'm sorry." Siri said, after a while.

"For what?" Aiden asked, looking over at her.

"It's because of me you got shot with that arrow." Siri stared down at the ground, unable to bring herself to look at Aiden.

"It's not your fault."

Aiden moved closer to Siri, reaching a hand out to her.

"Yes it is." Siri cried, tears streaming down her face as she pushed his hand away.

"It's my fault you got shot, it's my fault you were forced to have to go through the pain of shifting in order to rescue me, it's my fault you had to kill!" Siri's voice shook as she continued.

"It's my fault we're being chased by the vampires now. If I hadn't been in trouble in the market, you would never have had to use your power and brought attention to you and your family, and your family would still be alive. It's my fault that all this is happening."

No longer able to hold back her guilt, Siri began to sob.

"I'm sorry, Aiden, I'm so sorry." Siri barely managed to say between sobs.

Aiden wrapped his arms around Siri, pulling her close to him as she continued to cry.

"This is not your fault."

Aiden gently stroked his hand along her back.

"And even if it was..." Aiden leaned in, whispering into her ear. "It wouldn't matter to me."

Placing his free hand under her chin, Aiden turned her head to face him.

"You are the most important thing in my life." Aiden said, wiping the tears from her face. "I love you."

Aiden leaned his forehead against hers.

"If it came between you or having my family back, I'd do it all over again. Because you're worth the price.. I can't imagine my life without you."

Tilting her head, Siri kissed Aiden.

"Thank you." she said before leaning into his chest as she finished crying.

~ ~ ~ ~ ~

Waking up the next morning, Siri noticed that Aiden was not in bed with her anymore. Looking around the room, Siri saw him soaking in the bath tub.

Getting up, she started walking over to him.

"What are you thinking about?" she asked.

"That elven woman who spoke to us last night." Aiden answered, looking up at the ceiling as Siri placed her arms around his neck, rubbing his chest.

"While everyone else was terrified, or prepared for battle, she seemed a little too at ease... almost like she knew something that the other elves didn't."

"She did seem rather calm despite you having just killed so many of her men. She seemed to not be afraid of you. While there was fear, she seemed more in awe and had a sense of reverence towards you that seemed a little out of place." Siri noted.

"There's that, and she even invited us to stay with them for a while... said she had things that she would like to discuss with us. What is she hiding? I'm not sure what to think about all this." Aiden said.

"I think we might as well hear her out." Siri said, handing him a towel as he got out of the bath.

"Why do you say that?" Aiden asked as he dried himself off.

"Well... she is obviously smart enough to know not to challenge you, not after last night. She also gave us those elven robes."

"What does that have to do with anything?" Aiden asked.

"It is an elven custom to present gifts when trying to make peace." Siri explained. "If she gave us those robes as a peace offering... for her to go back on her word would be the ultimate dishonor, not just for her, but for her entire clan."

"Interesting."

"That, and she did say she had things that she wanted to discuss with us." Siri handed him a set of trousers to put on.

"Are you sure?" he asked.

"Yes, we could use some more allies... if not allies, then at least we won't make a new enemy." Siri replied.


After getting dressed, Aiden and Siri exited the tent.

As they left the tent, Aiden noticed that the tent was surrounded by two dozen elven warriors, each about a hundred yards away. Two of the elves in armor began approaching them.

Aiden immediately went on the defensive, growing his claws and baring his fangs. He dropped into a defensive stance in front of Siri, ready for a fight.

"Whoa, whoa, no need for that, we come in peace." one of the two guards said, raising his hands in a non-threatening gesture.

"Then why are we surrounded by soldiers?" Aiden asked with venom in his voice, not moving from his defensive stance.

"My men and I were given orders to ensure no one would attack you during the night in retaliation for members of their families being killed." the elf replied. "Queen Linorra tasked us with seeing that her promise to you was upheld."

"I think he is telling the truth." Siri said, taking his hand softly.

As the two elves walked up to them, they knelt onto one knee and bowed to Aiden and Siri. Getting up, the one in charge spoke again.

"My lord, my name is Andarii, the queen has commanded us to escort you back to the camp."

Aiden tensed slightly as the elf continued.

"Or... if you do not wish to return... our queen understands, and she would have us safely escort the two of you out of the forest. The choice is yours."

Aiden relaxed after hearing the second half of his statement.

"When you are ready to leave, just tell us where you wish to go." Andarii said before he and his companion walked away to the edge of trees with the rest of the elves.

"Well, what do you think... shall we go meet with the queen?" Siri asked.

~ ~ ~ ~ ~

After packing everything away, Aiden and Siri began walking towards Andarii.

Seeing them approach, Andarii pulled himself upright from the tree he was leaning against.

"So, my lord, where to?" he asked.

"Why do you call me my lord?" Aiden asked, out of curiosity.

"Two reasons." Andarii replied. "One, our queen has informed us that you are of a noble status... and two, we have been given orders to serve you, and only, you until you have made it out of the forest safely."

"What does that mean?"

"It means that until you leave the forest... me and my warriors are yours to command."

"Why would the queen tell you to serve me?"

"Only the queen can answer that question. Have you decided on where we should take you?"

Aiden looked at Siri.

"Yes, let's head to the camp, it seems the queen and I have a few things that we should discuss."

Aiden nodded to the elf as the company of soldiers began to gather around them.

"As you command."

Andarii turned to address his men, raising his voice so he could be heard. "Move out! We make way back to the camp!"

~ ~ ~ ~ ~

As they neared the elven camp, Aiden could see Siri getting a little nervous. Taking her hand, Aiden looked at her.

"What's wrong?"

"I'm worried about seeing that elf who kidnapped me again." Siri answered.

Looking at the men around them, Aiden motioned Andarii over.

"What is it my lord?" Andarii asked as he walked over.

"When we get to the camp, please keep an extra close eye out for the man who kidnapped Siri yesterday." Aiden said.

"You mean Johrra?"

"Yes. I want you and your men to make sure that he does not come within fifty feet of myself, and especially Siri. Whatever it takes, I don't want him anywhere near Siri ever again."

"Of course, that can easily be arranged." Andarii turned to his lieutenant, having him pass down the order to all of his soldiers.

Turning back, Andarii looked at Siri.

"Don't worry my lady, he won't come near you. Me and my men will make sure of that."

As he spoke to Siri, a group of five soldiers walked up to them. Seeing their arrival, Andarii motioned to them as he spoke to Siri.

"These are my five best men; they will look after you personally my lady. If you need something, or feel uncomfortable at any time just let them know."

Andarii turned to the five soldiers.

"Men, you are to be this lady's personal guard while inside the camp, understood?"

"Yes sir!" they said in unison, falling in line behind Siri.

Andarii turned back to Aiden.

"The rest of my men will keep an eye out for any trouble as well as keep Johrra away."

"Thank you." Aiden said.

"You ready?" Aiden asked Siri, taking her hand.

Squeezing his hand tightly Siri smiled at Aiden.

"let's go."

~ ~ ~ ~ ~

As they entered the camp, Aiden and Siri took note of their surroundings.

After last night, they expected an increase in guards patrolling the camp, but they noticed that instead, the streets were filled with elves of varying ages and occupations going about their day as normal. Acting almost as if the events of last night never happened, only the occasional glance, or nod in their direction gave any indication of them even being noticed.

As they entered the courtyard near the center of the encampment, Aiden and Siri were met by a small group of elves.

"Who are these people?" Aiden asked.

"It has been a long time since an outsider has been allowed inside our camp." Andarii replied. "Many are curious about you."

Looking up at the building in the center of the camp, Aiden squeezed Siri's hand and headed inside. As they approached the door, Aiden heard a voice yell out.

"How dare you touch me! Get your hands off me!"

Glancing over at the commotion, Aiden and Siri could see that Andarii's men had blocked Johrra from approaching them and were dragging him away from the building. With a slight smile of amusement, they entered the building as two of Andarii's men stood guard at the door.

Inside the building, Aiden and Siri were met by a young elf woman.

"Greetings, we have been expecting you. My name is Irina, please follow me."

Nodding to the woman, Aiden and Siri followed her down the hall to a set of doors.

"Queen Linorra awaits inside."

Irina opened the doors, bowed to Aiden, and then left.

Entering the room, Aiden saw Linorra sitting at a large table.

"Please, come in, I'm so glad you decided to return." Linorra said.

Standing from the table, Linorra crossed the room to greet them.

"I hope the two of you had a pleasant journey?"

"We were a little surprised to wake up this morning surrounded by your soldiers." Aiden told her.

"My deepest apologies, but given the circumstances, I didn't want them bothering you so soon after last night. So I told Andarii to simply watch over you until morning and to keep their distance. Please sit, we have much to talk about."

Linorra gestured to two chairs at the table opposite her own. Once Aiden and Siri took a seat, Linorra walked back around the table and sat down in her own chair.

"So, I'm sure you have some questions for me." Linorra said, folding her hands together and placing them on the table in front of her.

"Why are you being so polite to us?" Aiden asked. "I killed many of your people, and instead of attacking me and seeking vengeance, you let us go, give us gifts, and tell your men to guard us and follow my commands... why?"

"Because... you're the hybrid." Linorra said.

Aiden tensed up when Linorra called him the hybrid.

"Don't worry." Linorra said calmly. "You have nothing to fear from me."

"How do you know who I am?"

"That... is a long story."

# Chapter 14

"As you already know, my name is Linorra, but what you don't know is that, while I may look young, I am actually over 600 years old. My mother was queen Reanna, and during her life she had the honor and privilege of not just fighting alongside, but also becoming friends with the original hybrid. And yes, I know you are not the original, he disappeared eight hundred years ago. Based on what I have seen of you, your personality is very different from his. But you are still unmistakably the hybrid."

"How did you know?" Aiden asked.

"When you came for your woman." Linorra answered, looking over at Siri.

"When you made your entrance, several of the guards that saw you transform, ran to me to inform me of the situation. They described a werewolf that stood upright, and who also had wings. They had never seen anything like you before, but I grew up listening to the stories of the hybrid from my mother. So when they described an immortal of matching description, I knew there could be no mistake, the hybrid had returned. Having grown up hearing the stories, I knew that my men didn't stand a chance against you, especially on a full moon... not that they would have stood any better chance had it not been the full moon."

"I see." Aiden nodded his head as the queen told her story.

"But I was confused as to why the hybrid was attacking my people... we had done nothing to earn his wrath. But then I remembered the men telling me about you." Linorra looked at Siri.

"They told me they had found a young elven girl traveling with an immortal. They said that they had shot the immortal with a wolfsbane arrow and had rescued the elf and were currently working on removing the magical seal placed on her."

"When they told me that you had arrived, and that you were making your way towards the tent she was being kept in, as well as your description, I put the pieces together and realized that it must have been you that the men had attacked... and that you had come for her. So I decided to go to you in person and try to apologize, and to attempt to fix things between my people and you before it was too late."

Finally having the full picture of what had happened the day before, Siri and Aiden both began to relax slightly.

"So you knew who I was based on my description alone?"

"Yes, the hybrid transformation is very unique." Linorra answered. "My mother told me of the transformation. How your body took different aspects of all four races, the vampyre, the werewolf, the vampuric and the hellhound, combining them all into one single transformation, with each one manifesting in a different way. Having grown up hearing about it, it was still quite a shock to see it in person."

"You seem to know a great deal about me and my transformation. Is there anything you know that could help me to understand my power?" Aiden asked, leaning forward.

Linorra stared at Aiden in shock for a moment.

"What do you mean?" Linorra asked, regaining her composure. "Do you mean to tell me that you don't have control of your power?"

"If I am being honest..." Aiden leaned back in his chair. "Last night was the first time I ever transformed."

Again Linorra was shocked.

"How could last night have been your first transformation?" she asked.

"Well, up until a few days ago, I was just a normal human without any knowledge of who I was. But something happened that unlocked that part of me, unleashing the power of the hybrid that was dormant inside of me. Since then, Siri and I have been on the run. Last night was my first full moon as the hybrid."

"I see... as far as your powers are concerned, I'm afraid I don't know much about how it works, or the extent of them. I always assumed that when the hybrid returned, he would come back knowing who he was. But from the moment I met you, I could tell you were not him."

"How?" Aiden asked.

"Because, you do not act like him. The original hybrid never allowed himself to get close with anyone... clearly you have." Queen Linorra looked between Aiden and Siri.

"Also, a lot more of my people would have died last night if you had been more like the original hybrid, he was not known for showing mercy very often. In that regard, I am thankful that you are different. You have much more compassion and mercy than your predecessor, but you are also similar in many other ways. You are bold, unquestionably strong, you also think like him."

"What do you mean I think like him?"

"When you got to the camp looking for Siri, you looked at the situation logically, you figured out her location, and then began to take out the guards one by one. From what I've been told about last night, you only revealed yourself once there was no other choice, and when you did, you made sure to put as much fear into the soldiers as possible."

"It just seemed like the smartest thing to do." Aiden replied.

"Agreed, if you can make an enemy fear you, then you've already won half the battle." Linorra responded. "The original hybrid, as well as yourself, are quite perceptive and can keep a calm head even in a time of crisis. Now, what else would you like to know?"

~ ~ ~ ~ ~

A few hours later Aiden and Siri left the office, accompanied by Linorra.

"Thank you for trusting me enough to come and speak with me today. I would also like to offer an invitation for you to stay with us for a day or two before continuing on your journey. It would be an honor for us to host the two of you."

"Thank you." Siri said, looking at Aiden. "I think we could use a day or two of rest."

Aiden nodded his head in agreement.

"It's settled then." Linorra clapped her hands together, summoning two elves from the side.

"A room has already been prepared for you. These two will show you to your room, please let them know if you require anything."

As she spoke, the two elves stepped forward and bowed slightly.

"Please, follow us."

~ ~ ~ ~ ~

Aiden lay asleep in the bed as Siri sat at a nearby table. Looking over at Aiden, Siri was thankful that he was finally able to get some rest.

"*He has been hyper vigilant ever since we left our home.*" she thought.

"*He hasn't had a good night's sleep in days, and even when he does sleep, he tosses and turns, like he is wrestling with someone in his sleep. It's only when I lay next to him, that he seems to relax.*"

"*What's going on inside that head of yours, Aiden?*" Siri asked herself.

Picking up a book from the table, Siri began reading. As she was reading, Siri noticed Aiden starting to mumble in his sleep. Placing the book down, Siri stood and walked over to the side of the bed. Listening closely, Siri was able to make out some of the words that he was saying... but what she heard didn't make sense to her. A few words she could understand, but there were many that she could not. The words seemed both familiar, and yet foreign to her at the same time.

Suddenly, Siri gasped and covered her mouth with her hand, realizing what it was that Aiden was speaking.

He was speaking elvish, but not the same elvish that she could speak.

"*He can speak ancient elvish.*" Siri realized.

Most of the ancient elvish language has been extinct for almost twelve hundred years... and yet here Aiden was, speaking it fluently in his sleep. Siri could hardly believe it.

Siri thought back to the stories that her mother used to tell her as a child.

"*Our people used to speak a different kind of elvish.*" her mother told her. "*But it wasn't just a language, the words themselves were not just words... they were pure, undiluted magic. To speak a word was to command the very thing you were speaking of. Both magic, and language in its purest form. Only the most powerful of our people were ever able to learn and master the language. Those who did, found they no longer had to channel and shape magic into spells, incantations, or hand signs, but could cast and manipulate magic simply by speaking. But it took immense concentration, as well as both physical and mental strength to wield such raw power... since the power itself could destroy the wielder just as easily.*"

*"These must be the memories of the hybrid."* Siri realized. *"Just how powerful was the hybrid?"*

Looking down at Aiden, she couldn't help but wonder to herself.

*"How much are these memories going to affect him? When he does remember, what will happen to the Aiden I know? How much of Aiden will be left?"*

~ ~ ~ ~ ~

Aiden tossed and turned in his sleep, memories of a life that wasn't his flooding through his mind.

Aiden saw himself sitting across from several others gathered together.

*"Why should we help you?"* one man said. *"You are not one of us... and to enter ourselves into this conflict would bring war and death to our own people."*

*"War and death are already coming to our people."* a woman said, *entering the room and taking her place at the table.*

*"Every day, the kingdoms of the immortals conquer more and more land. Do you really believe they will be content to simply leave us alone?"*

*No one in the room could speak.*

*After a few moments, an old man at the table stood up.*

*"Very well, what is it you suggest?"*

~ ~ ~ ~ ~

Aiden woke up to the early morning light shining through the window. Looking across the room, he could see Siri sitting at a table eating breakfast while she read a book.

"Did you sleep well?" Siri asked, noticing that Aiden was now awake.

"I'm not sure how to answer that." Aiden swung his legs off the bed and stood up.

"Another dream?"

Siri already knew the answer.

Aiden simply nodded as he stood up and walked over to the window. Setting her book back down, Siri stood up and walked over to where Aiden was standing.

"What's wrong?" Siri asked, wrapping her small arms around Aiden's torso, hugging him close.

"Who am I?" Aiden whispered as he looked out of the second story room they were staying in.

"What?" Siri looked up at him.

"No, I'm serious, just who am I?" Aiden said angrily.

"Ever since this thing happened to me." Aiden lifted his hand, inspecting it. "Nothing has felt the same, I don't seem to feel anything anymore. The man in the square who tried to have you arrested, yelling at my father when he tried to congratulate me on so called "Passing" my test. Confronting my father about you the next day, discovering what I am. Even when the vampyres attacked our home and my father, mother and two brothers gave up their lives so that I could live. Seeing that pillar of fire consume our house, throughout all of that, I felt almost nothing. I haven't even shed a single tear for my family, how is that normal?"

Tightening his hand into a fist, Aiden began to shake. "Even the killing of the elven guards that kidnapped you. When did I become such a cold, heartless killer?"

"You're not a cold, heartless killer Aiden." Siri said, tightening her grip on him.

Reaching down, Aiden pulled Siri's hands off him as he spoke.

"Everything that I touch has fallen apart, everywhere I go, destruction follows me. I am a walking calamity, a monster."

"You're not a monster Aiden, you're..." Siri began.

"You really think so?" Aiden half yelled as he turned to look at her.

"Every time I look at you... every time you are near me, all I want to do is sink my fangs into you, to drink your blood. Even now, your scent is intoxicating to me. What is that, if not a monster?"

Aiden didn't wait for her reply as he turned to the open window and leapt out.

"Aiden wait!" Siri cried out as Aiden landed two stories below her in a dead sprint.

Siri ran downstairs, not caring that she was till in her nightclothes.

As she burst through the front door of the house she saw a group of elves nearby. Upon seeing Siri, the group of elves pointed in the direction Aiden had run off.

Siri thanked them as she rushed past, desperate to catch up to Aiden.

# Chapter 15

Siri began to search the woods surrounding the camp looking for Aiden in the direction he had run off, calling his name over and over again.

"Aiden... Aiden!" she yelled.

The only answer she got back was the sound of the wind through the trees, and the cold echo of her own voice.

"Aiden, where did you go?" Siri asked as she stopped to catch her breath.

"Away from you." came a voice from behind her.

Siri jumped at the sudden intrusion of an unfamiliar voice in the quiet woods she had chased Aiden through. Turning to look in the direction of the voice, Siri noticed a man sitting on the branch of a nearby tree, leaning against the trunk.

"Who are you?" Siri asked, taking a cautious step back.

As Siri spoke, the man jumped down from the tree, stepping into the light so Siri could see him.

Siri took a moment to look at the man. He was a tall man who wore a style of armor that she did not recognize, dark black leather armor, clearly meant for mobility, with accents of metal plate as well as some dark red accent color. He wore a dark black cloak with a hood that he used to conceal his face from the girl. Along the edge of the cloak's hood, as well as along the bottom edge of the cloak were magic runes and symbols that emitted a soft white glow. On his waist, the man carried a set of daggers on one side, on the other, a sword. Across his back, the man had a bow strung, as well as a quiver of arrows. Beneath the bow and quiver, was what looked like another sword, only this one was wrapped in cloth as if to protect it, or hide something about it. The gloves on his hands were of the same color as the armor, and each finger ended in nails tipped with silver.

"Who are you?" Siri asked again, preparing to flee from the man if necessary, as well as looking around for something she could use to defend herself.

"Who I am doesn't matter for the time being." the man replied, taking a step toward her.

"What do you want?"

Siri caught sight of a tree branch she could use as a makeshift weapon laying a few feet away from her.

"To help." the man answered, taking another step towards her. "You see, Aiden is having a bit of a difficult time right now."

Siri lunged for the branch.

Picking it up, Siri looked back where the man was standing, but saw only empty air.

"Where did he..." Siri looked around, trying to find the stranger.

"Not very wise." the man said.

It sounded as if he had just whispered into her ear.

Siri spun around, swinging the branch as hard as she could, only to have it caught by the man who was standing directly behind her. Now standing face to face with the man, she could see his facial features. Long brown hair down to his shoulders, sharp features, fangs, and eyes that glowed a soft bluish green.

"If you're going to kill me, then just do it." Siri said, letting go of the branch as she slumped to her knees, knowing she didn't stand a chance against this man.

Tossing the branch aside, the man took a step back.

"Why would I do that?" the man said as he looked down at her. "I already told you... I want to help."

As Siri looked up, the man pulled back his hood.

"Besides, the last time I laid my hand on you, Aiden broke it."

Suddenly, Siri recognized the man.

"It's you."

~ ~ ~ ~ ~

Aiden stood at the base of a very large tree, smashing his fists against the trunk, finally letting some of the pent up emotions he had been suppressing come to the surface. In his anger, his claws had come out on their own, each one burying themselves into his palms, drawing blood with each blow he made against the tree. After several minutes, Aiden collapsed to his knees, closed his eyes, and for the first time since he left home, cried for his family.

After a few minutes of crying, Aiden regained his composure.

Wiping his tears, Aiden turned his attention back to the problem at hand.

"It's getting harder and harder to stop myself from drinking blood." Aiden thought to himself.

"It's not just an urge anymore... it's like an itch, a dryness in the back of my throat that won't go away no matter how much water I drink. On top of that, my heightened sense of smell doesn't help the situation either. I can smell peoples blood through their skin, and it pushes my thirst into overdrive."

Aiden continued to sit there, eyes closed in contemplation.

"And it's even worse around Siri. I don't know why, but her scent... and the scent of her blood is so much sweeter and potent than any other... It's nearly impossible to resist. I tried to keep it under control by drinking some animal blood, but my body rejects the blood immediately, my body spasms, and I clutch my stomach from the pain before throwing it up within seconds of drinking it. It has to be fresh blood, and animal blood won't work. What am I going to do"?

Aiden felt two small hands holding his own hands.

Opening his eyes, Aiden found Siri kneeling in front of him, gently inspecting his hands, as they were covered in blood.

"Siri..."

"I know." Siri whispered, looking up from his hands and into his eyes.

"I'm sorry I ran off, I just needed to..." Aiden started to apologize, before getting cut off by Siri.

"Why didn't you tell me?" Siri asked, near tears.

"Tell you what?"

"Why didn't you tell me how bad the thirst was? What it was doing to you, or how hard it was to resist?"

"I..." Aiden tried to say.

"We were supposed to be in this together, so why keep this from me?" Siri asked, tears freely flowing down her face now.

"I'm sorry." Aiden replied.

"Aiden, you need to feed." Siri said, looking into his eyes.

"I've tried to. I really have... I've tried drinking blood from animals, but it doesn't work." Aiden tried to explain.

"No." Siri said, cutting him off. "You need to "Feed" and you need to do it now."

Siri tilted her head to the side, offering him her neck.

"No!... I can't feed off you, I can't hurt you. I could never forgive myself if I hurt you."

Aiden tried to pull away, only for Siri to tighten her grip on his hands and once again look him directly in the eyes.

"You need blood, and not animal blood. You may be a hybrid, but you are still part vampyre, and that means you need to feed. The longer you go without it, the weaker you will become, and the more likely you will be to attack someone innocent. You don't want that on your conscience."

Siri softened her grip on his hands.

"When a vampyre turns for the first time, the need and desire to feed will be the strongest it can be. Feeding for the first time allows their abilities to settle. Without it, they will die. Unless that need is satiated, it will drive them insane... do you hear me? I refuse to lose you simply because you are afraid of hurting me."

Siri let go of Aiden's hands, drew a dagger and held it to her throat.

"Either take what you need, right here, right now... or kill me, because I refuse to watch you suffer needlessly anymore."

After hearing and seeing this, Aiden was completely defeated.

"Okay." Aiden said, his shaking hand reaching up, pulling the knife away from her neck.

"You win... I'll do it... promise me you will stop me if I start hurting you." he pleaded.

"Take what you need, I trust you." Siri said, once again offering her neck to Aiden.

Leaning forward, Aiden inhaled, her scent pushing his thirst into a frenzy. Aiden took Siri into his arms, leaned in, and gently placed a kiss onto her collarbone before finally giving in to his urges as he closed his eyes and sank his fangs into Siri's neck.

Aiden hugged Siri close as he sank his fangs into her neck. Feeling her tense up slightly as he bit her, Aiden thought about releasing her and not going through with it... only to be stopped by Siri placing her hand on his head, preventing him from pulling away as the rest of her body relaxed. A moment later, the first drop of blood entered Aiden's mouth.

The moment the first drop of blood touched his tongue, it was as if a switch had been flipped inside of Aiden. Everything around him disappeared, it felt like liquid fire was spreading throughout his body, and yet at the same time, he felt like a man dying in the desert given water for the first time in days.

Aiden thought the blood flowing into him would be repulsive, but instead was refreshing, revitalizing even. Every fiber of his being felt alive, euphoric, her blood the most delicious thing he had ever tasted, with a hint of sweetness to it that couldn't possibly be real... and with it, an urge, like a voice in the back of his mind, urging him on.

*"More... more... more!"*

Aiden opened his eyes, no longer the blue they used to be, but red, bright red, glowing in a sea of swirling black.

Losing himself to this new feeling, Aiden became more aggressive, pinning Siri down against the ground as he began to bite down harder. All the while, Siri never fought back, nor even made a sound, simply letting him take what he so desperately needed after denying himself for so long.

Aiden's vision went dark.

~ ~ ~ ~ ~

Looking around, Aiden found himself in a vast, empty nothingness. Everything around him was dark. Nothing but blackness in all directions as far as the eye could see. After floating in this sea of nothingness for what felt like hours... eventually, Aiden felt his bare feet touch the ground.

Aiden found himself standing in a few inches of water that rippled out away from him when he landed. The scene around him seemed to shift and change as the ripples dissipated. Ahead of him where once was empty nothingness, was now a large wooden archway.

Not knowing what else to do, Aiden made his way to the archway, water rippling behind him as he walked. As he passed through the archway, the scene around Aiden changed once again.

This time, he was standing in the middle of an open field of grass as far as the eye could see. A small pond of water directly in front of him reflected a bright full moon that hung in the sky along with thousands of twinkling stars.

"*What is this place?*" Aiden thought to himself.

"Welcome." A voice from behind him startled Aiden.

Turning around, Aiden saw a man standing twenty or so paces behind him, wearing a black robe.

"Come, sit." The man gestured with his arm. As he did, two small floor mats appeared beside him.

"We have much to discuss."

The man sat down on one of the mats.

"I've been looking forward to meeting you." he said with a smile.

"Who are you?" Aiden asked, taking a seat on the mat, facing the stranger.

"I am you. Or, specifically, you... are me." the stranger replied, glowing his own eyes at Aiden, a bright red within a sea of swirling black.

# Chapter 16

"You're him." Aiden looked at the man across from him.

"You're the Hybrid, aren't you?" he asked, already knowing the answer.

"Indeed." the man replied, bringing his hands up, a cup of tea materialized in his hands. "Here, drink this, it's quite good."

He held out the cup, offering it to Aiden.

"Go ahead, it's perfectly safe." he said reassuringly.

Taking the cup from the man, Aiden took a sip of the tea.

"What is this place?" Aiden asked, motioning to the ever-changing scenery around them.

"A genetic memory, although... to be overly simplistic about it, you can just call it the dreamscape. Now down to business." the man replied.

"My name is Sebastien Arlet. I am, or was, the hybrid many centuries ago. You are here because you have finally awoken my power deep inside of you. Originally, you were simply supposed to be a vessel for my own consciousness." Sebastien said looking across at Aiden.

"What do you mean?"

"You see, when I decided to disappear and be reborn, I fully intended to come back as myself."

"Wait, are you saying you were planning on taking over my body?" Aiden screamed, standing up and backing away a few steps.

"Originally, yes. But you inadvertently unlocked my power before you were supposed to. Since that moment, I have been watching you."

As he spoke Sebastien waved his hand and different scenes from Aiden's life were brought to life right in front of them.

"You seem to possess many of the same character traits that I myself possess. You are brave, intelligent, able to make quick split second decisions when necessary, yet also are able to form complex tactics to ensure you have the best probability of success in battle. While watching you, I have noticed that you are quite similar to myself, although, with one major difference."

Sebastien waved his hand once more. The figures of Aiden disappeared, but were quickly replaced by a figure of Siri.

"Siri!" Aiden exclaimed as he reached for her, only for her to disappear into smoke just as he touched her.

"While I pushed people away, you have grown quite attached to this one particular elf." Sebastien said with a smirk.

"You leave her alo..." Aiden began to say, only to realize he could no longer speak.

"I wasn't finished." Sebastien said, his voice darkening as he walked over to Aiden.

"I thought others to be a weakness, and while I have seen that in you, I have also seen that they are also a source of great strength for you."

"I never wanted to be the warrior I became, never wanted to lead legions of people to their deaths. I actually tried to stay out of the war, seeing as it didn't concern me. I just wanted to be left alone. But, I had a certain friend at the time, he knew what I was, but never judged me. He had a terrible knack for always trying to do the right thing. One day, some werewolves came through town and began terrorizing the people, he asked me to use my strength to help the townspeople fight back. I told him that it wasn't my problem. I didn't owe these villagers anything. I told him to just let it go, don't cause a scene and to stay out of it, that he was no match for them."

"He didn't listen, and started rounding up villagers to try and make a stand against the werewolves... and what did he get for his efforts? The werewolves killed them all and made a public spectacle of him by ripping his stomach out right in the middle of the town square and left him to bleed out, laughing as they walked away."

As he recalled the memory, the scene around him showed the events to Aiden as if he were there.

"As he lay dying, I came up to him, asking why he did it, why he insisted on challenging them. What he told me changed me forever. The words he spoke to me that day started me down the path I would follow for the rest of my life."

Looking at Aiden, Sebastien continued.

"Do you know what he said to me?"

"He said he did it because I wouldn't, even as he lay there coughing up blood and was about to die, he grabbed me by the arm and said..."

*"You have power, you can do things that nobody else is capable of. That means you don't have a choice anymore, that makes you responsible, that you don't have the luxury of sitting on the sidelines. You were given these powers for a reason, and it wasn't to just hide away the rest of your life while the rest of the world burns."*

"Those were the last words my friend ever spoke to me, and from that day on, I stopped sitting on the sidelines, no one else would die because of my inaction. But I also believed that my power put anyone I cared about at risk, so I stopped letting anyone get close. My time away from others made me cold, and I see now that may have been a mistake... I see a lot of my friend in you, you have a strong moral compass, and will stand up for what you believe. You are willing to fight for the ones you care about, despite the risk to yourself. Perhaps, if I had someone who cared for me the way you do, I would never have disappeared." Sebastien said with what appeared to be a sorrowful expression on his face.

"I have come to a decision." Sebastien waved his hand toward Aiden.

Aiden felt his voice return to him.

"Oh yeah, and what decision is that exactly?" Aiden spat as he held his hand to his throat.

"I had my time. I'm tired of waging this war by myself, and I know I've made my share of mistakes. Even if I were to take over your body, I'm old... and set in my ways. Maybe it's time I entrust the future of this world to the next generation."

Sebastien looked at Aiden. "I've decided to entrust my power to you, to do with as you wish and, hopefully, to do better than I did."

Sebastien took a step back and bowed slightly to Aiden.

"But I already have your power, don't I?" Aiden asked, confused.

"Yes and no." Sebastien turned around, motioning for Aiden to follow as he began walking.

As they walked, Sebastien continued.

"While your body has become a hybrid, it is not at full power. Up until now I'd say you have only been able to use my power at about three or four percent of its full strength. Your body has not had enough time to adjust to the sudden intake of power that it received when you first unlocked my power, your body just isn't strong enough yet. Over time you will gain more and more of my power, along with my memories."

Aiden was speechless.

"Although there was one time where you were able to use my full power, even though it was done unconsciously." Sebastien said.

"Really? When?" Aiden asked.

"When you defended Siri in the market right after awakening my power. Tell me, have you been able to move that fast ever since?"

"No, I haven't." Aiden answered, knowing what Sebastien was talking about.

"Under moments of intense emotion, stress, or when in desperate need of it, your body is capable of using my full power, but only for a very brief moment."

Aiden nodded in understanding.

"With everything that has happened since awakening my powers, you should be able to use at least fifteen percent of my power now that your body has grown stronger. Drinking her blood has allowed your body to become even stronger." Sebastien commented as they came to a stop.

Waving his hand once more, Aiden now saw a figure of himself drinking the blood from Siri's neck.

"From now on, you need to drink blood regularly. Blood strengthens you, and also amplifies your own healing abilities."

Looking at himself drinking Siri's blood, Aiden became concerned.

"Have I been drinking her blood this entire time?" Panic began to rise in Aiden's voice.

"Yes, but time moves a bit differently here. You feel you have been here for hours, but in reality, it has only been a few seconds." Sebastien answered.

Aiden's body began to relax upon hearing that.

"Don't relax just yet." Sebastien's voice turned cold once more. "A vampyre can drain the life from someone in under two minutes... and by my calculations, you have been feeding off her very aggressively for twenty to thirty seconds."

Aiden's panic set in once again.

"Why isn't she telling me to stop?" Aiden asked.

"Because she loves you, and she knows you need it." replied Sebastien as he turned to Aiden.

"The longer you go without feeding, the more you need to feed... and the more you will have to take."

Sebastien grabbed hold of Aiden's hands. "Listen closely, if you feed regularly, feeding won't be a problem. Once every two or three days should be enough to sate your thirst. Up to a week at the longest, otherwise you will start to feel the thirst increase in severity. Now... it's time to send you back. You need to stop yourself from draining any more from her, if you don't, she will die. It is going to be the hardest thing you have ever done, nearly impossible. Your body is in a feeding frenzy since you have refrained from feeding for so long. It will take everything you have to stop yourself. Your entire body will keep fighting to drain her dry, but you must overcome it, now go." Sebastien pushed Aiden down.

"I wish you luck... Hybrid."

~ ~ ~ ~ ~

"More... more... more!" Aiden felt the voice in the back of his mind repeating, over and over again.

"No, enough... you've had enough." he told himself.

"More... More...More!!!" it screamed.

"I said you've had enough!" Aiden screamed at himself, feeling the voice grow quieter and quieter, finally falling silent as Aiden pulled his fangs from Siri's neck.

Aiden picked his head up from Siri's neck and looked down at her. She looked even paler than she usually did, and her usual pink lips had turned blue from blood loss. Tears began to flow from Aiden's eyes as he looked at what he had done.

Looking up at Aiden, Siri smiled.

"I'm alright." Siri said, lifting her hand to cup the side of Aiden's face, looking into his eyes.

Siri noticed, for the second time in her life, Aiden's eyes had changed. Now, instead of blue eyes with a tinge of red in them, Aiden's eyes were now dominated by bright red irises with only the smallest hint of blue left around the inside of the irises.

*"Different... but still his."* she thought as she dropped her hand from lack of strength, passing out.

Seeing Siri pass out caused Aiden to start panicking, until he listened closely and could hear her heart was still beating and that she was still breathing.

Taking a breath and calming himself down, Aiden decided to bandage Siri's neck before she lost any more blood. Ripping off a piece of his clothes, Aiden turned Siri's head to the side, afraid of what he might see... only to find that the wound on her neck, despite how aggressively he had been feeding off her, was nonexistent. Where he had bitten her, the flesh had somehow healed itself.

Deciding to figure it out later, Aiden picked up Siri and began to head back to the village. Looking down at her in his arms, Aiden thought to himself.

*"Thank you Siri, now rest."*

# Chapter 17

Siri woke to the sound of shuffling feet nearby, as well as feeling a hand being placed on her forehead.

"Aiden?" Siri called as she groggily opened up her eyes.

"Oh you are awake." Siri heard an elven woman say as she withdrew her hand from Siri's head.

"Who are you?" Siri asked, trying to sit up in the bed she was in, only to find she had very little strength.

"Easy, you've been unconscious for three days... you lost a lot of blood, and you are going to be a bit weak. My name is Narii, one of the healers in the village." the elf replied, stopping Siri from sitting up, while giving her a reassuring smile.

Hearing this, Siri remembered what happened in the forest. Lifting her hand to her neck, Siri was surprised to not find a bite wound.

"Where's Aiden?" Siri asked as she looked around with concern.

"Relax." Narii placed her hand on Siri's shoulder. "He's right here."

Narii moved out of the way, revealing Aiden, asleep in a chair directly behind her.

"He has refused to leave your side since he brought you back from the forest. He hasn't eaten or slept since he brought you in, but after three days of waiting by your side, exhaustion finally overcame him a few hours ago." Narii spoke in a hushed tone so as not to wake him up.

Seeing Siri relax a bit upon seeing Aiden, Narii leaned in and whispered into her ear.

"You're a lucky girl, I wish my husband paid half as much attention to me as this man does to you. Although I would like to know just what happened that would lower your blood levels this much." Narii had a mischievous grin on her face.

A panicked, and very embarrassed look crossed Siri's face as Narii giggled.

"Relax, he hasn't said anything, but between you and me, he IS part vampyre, and you are a very pretty girl. So I put two and two together on my own."

Siri could only stare at her own hands, her face red, and her ears burning from embarrassment.

"Although..." Narii said, looking over towards Aiden.

"He is very handsome. I'd let him drink my blood too."

"It's not like that!" Siri stammered, embarrassment written all over her face.

"Oh?" Narii cocked her head to the side, looking at Siri.

"It's just..." Siri began.

"He just..."

"He needed it." Siri finally managed to say, her voice lowering as she reached her hand back up to her neck.

"I just didn't realize how much he needed."

"Wait, so you've never let him...?" Narii asked.

"He has never needed to drink blood up until now."

"I see." Narii gave Siri a knowing smile.

"Don't worry, it'll be our little secret." Narii put her finger up to her lips and patted Siri on the leg before exiting the room.

Looking over at Aiden, Siri noticed him shifting uncomfortably in his chair before waking up from sleep himself.

As his vision began to clear, Aiden rubbed the sleep from his eyes, only to suddenly stop when he noticed Siri was awake, sitting up, and smiling at him.

"You're awake." Aiden nearly yelled as he jumped up and ran over to Siri.

Leaning over her, Aiden placed his palms on either side of her face before leaning in and kissing her.

"I'm so sorry." Aiden said, pulling away from the kiss momentarily, only for Siri to grab the back of his head as she forced their lips back together.

After finally separating to catch their breath, Siri looked at Aiden.

"You have nothing to be sorry for. You are what you are. I have accepted that from the beginning."

Siri could see tears running down his face.

"I thought I lost you." Aiden said as he began sobbing. "I thought I had killed you."

"Shhh, it's ok now." Siri said, pulling Aiden's head down into her chest, running her fingers through his hair soothingly.

"Just promise me you won't fight your urges like that ever again, promise me you'll talk to me." Siri spoke in a soothing voice, laying her cheek against the top of Aiden's head.

Placing her arms around his shoulders, they just sat and held each other.

After a few minutes of holding each other, Aiden picked his head up and looked into Siri's eyes, getting lost in the sea of green.

Looking into Aiden's eyes, Siri noticed something. Along with all the love and kindness she was used to seeing, Siri could now see something else as well, something less human and more animal. There was now a primal look to his eyes.

Suddenly, Aiden leaned forward and kissed Siri, in a way they had never kissed before. This kiss was powerful, strong, and needing, without restraint. Siri was caught off guard by the abrupt aggressiveness that Aiden was displaying, but quickly surrendered herself to the kiss as Aiden climbed onto the bed, pressing her further into the mattress as their mouths began fighting for dominance. Aiden released Siri's lips, only to begin drawing a line of kisses along her jaw, up to her ear. Siri felt the hot breath on her ear, and it sent her into overdrive as she pulled at his shirt, wanting more. Aiden pulled back from her only long enough for Siri to pull the shirt over his head before he was once again tracing kisses from her ear, and down her neck, stopping occasionally to suck or to nip at the tender flesh on her neck.

At this time, an older elven man walked through the door to check up on Siri.

Upon hearing the intruder, Aiden's desire for Siri, as well as his newfound animalistic need to protect what was his triggered, causing Aiden to instinctively cover Siri with his own body, before turning to the man and letting out an animalistic roar at the intruder that seemed to shake the entire room as well as causing his eyes to glow bright red as he did so.

Dropping the piece of parchment he was carrying, the old man fled from the room, looking like he was about to have a heart attack, leaving Siri and Aiden once again to themselves. Looking back at Siri, she simply giggled as she pulled him back down into another kiss.

~ ~ ~ ~ ~

Siri woke the next morning and blushed when she saw the state of disarray the room was in.

Looking around, she saw that the blankets, as well as many of the clothes they had been wearing the night before had been torn to shreds all round them. Looking down at Aiden's bare chest underneath her, Siri snuggled back up to him and absently ran her fingers through his chest hair as she thought about last night.

From the moment Aiden first transformed down in his family crypt, Siri knew that there was an animalistic side of him. She also knew that it eventually would come out. Despite everything, Siri found she was never afraid of Aiden, even when he was in that state. She didn't know why, but she knew somehow that that side of him was just as much a part of him as his human side. before, that side of him only came out when he transformed. But seeing him now, since he drank her blood, Siri could no longer separate the two personalities.

"I guess this is the real you, isn't it?" she asked, looking at his sleeping face.
After a few more minutes of watching him sleep, Siri felt Aiden's fingers gently stroking her naked hip. Smiling, Siri laid her head down, running her hand across his chest, enjoying the attention his fingers were giving her.

*"What's that?"*
Noticing a new sound, Siri Picked her head up.

Hearing it Again, Siri focused on it, a sound starting so faintly she could hardly hear it. As she lay there and listened, it got louder, turning into a deep rumbling. Siri was confused until she realized that the sound was coming from Aiden. A deep, rumbling growl was coming from Aiden, resonating in his chest.
Siri simply smiled as she laid back down against Aiden, letting the sound wash over her.

"Hey Aiden." Siri said, placing a kiss on his chest.

"What is it?" Aiden asked, looking down at a pair of emerald eyes, hidden behind a tangle of red hair.

"I think your purring."

Siri giggled as she sat up.

"I don't purr." Aiden sat up, wrapping his arms around her.

"Maybe not purr, but it's definitely something similar." she said, looking at Aiden.

"What happened here?" Aiden asked, looking around at the destroyed room.

"I think "We" happened." Siri answered, blushing slightly and giving Aiden a quick kiss before getting up and searching for any clothing that was still usable.

Finding only the shirt Aiden had been wearing and taken off before things got out of hand, Siri picks it up and turns to Aiden.

"Finders Keepers."

Siri stuck her tongue out at him and pulled his shirt over her head.

Once on, the shirt came down to mid-thigh on Siri, doing a decent job of covering her up, being just a little loose around the shoulders.

Looking around himself, Aiden grabbed a portion of shredded bedding large enough to make a makeshift towel out of. Just as Aiden wrapped the towel around himself, there came a knock at the door.

After a few seconds, Siri realized that after last night, no one wanted to enter the room without permission. Chuckling to herself, Siri looked over at Aiden to make sure he was covered before calling out.

"You may enter."

The door to the room cracked open for a few seconds before being fully opened.

The older elf from last night cautiously stepped into the room, followed by Narii, and two other elves, his eyes going wide and blood draining from his face as he saw the state the room was in.

A combination of last night's encounter, as well as the current state of the room made the old man so nervous that he forgot to speak to Aiden in his own language.

"Ahnvae Ent Nesh, Tel' Leha Sal, Et Lor Nae." The man stumbled over his words in fear.

Since he had spoken in elvish, Siri decided to translate the words for Aiden, but before she could, Aiden responded.

"Arta Tel' Etriel, Ausa Va."

Everyone in the room just stared at Aiden for a few seconds.

"What's everybody staring at me for?" he asked.

The old elf spoke up.

"I'm sorry, I didn't realize you spoke elvish."

"I don't." Aiden answered, causing even more confusion.

After a few moments of silence, Siri spoke up.

"Aiden, he spoke in elvish when he walked in... and you answered him in elvish before I could translate."

# Chapter 18

Aiden and Siri returned to the room they were given after Narii did a small checkup on Siri to make sure she was alright, since the old doctor fled the room in panic when Aiden growled at him for telling Siri she would have to remove her shirt for him to do a full examination.

Once properly dressed, they made their way back into the village. As they walked amongst the different shops, Siri was admiring some elven jewelry when queen Linorra walked up behind them.

"I heard you two caused quite a stir in the infirmary last night." the Queen said, with an unmistakable smirk on her face.

Siri could only blush, and bury her face into Aiden's arm as Aiden began to apologize to the queen.

"It's quite alright." Linorra held up her hand to stop Aiden from apologizing.

"I remember what it is like to be young and eager, although I don't recall ever destroying an entire room before." she said with a smile.

Standing a ways away, having listened to the conversation, was Johrra. Still seething with anger after already being humiliated by Aiden, who, in his mind, was an obstacle keeping him from what should rightfully be his, that being Siri. Having already seen them walk back to their room from the infirmary with him wearing nothing but a towel, while she wore only his shirt, Johrra couldn't stand it anymore as he ran up to the three. Johrra pointed at Aiden and yelled.

"Amtoll! I invoke Amtoll Riis!"

"Johrra, stand down." Queen Linorra began to say.

"No!" Johrra yelled, stamping his foot. "This outsider... he keeps one of our own people as his slave, kills many of our own, and you treat him with respect? Even worse is that you allow this... this "Animal" to defile this elf in our own village! She should be mine, not his! I declare Amtoll Riis, it's my right!"

"Johrra, don't do this." Linorra begged.

"My decision is made." Johrra turned to Aiden. "Today, you die."

Turning to Siri, Johrra grinned. "By tonight, you will belong to me."

Johrra turned, storming off.


"What just happened?" Siri asked, holding onto Aiden's arm, who was trembling with rage.

"It's his way of dealing with being humiliated by you the other night." Linorra said, shaking her head.

"He invoked Amtoll Riis, a trial by combat used in ancient times to settle disputes. It is a fight to the death. Winner inherits everything that belonged to the loser."


Siri gasped, now understanding what Johrra said.

"Yes, unfortunately, that means you as well, since you are his."

"All this because he wants another man's woman." Aiden spoke under his breath.

"Can't you order him to back down?" Siri asked, continuing to try calming Aiden down as his claws had already extended into his own fists, causing them to bleed.

"I'm afraid not. Even as queen, I cannot break this tradition... I'm sorry."

~ ~ ~ ~ ~

As evening approached, Aiden and Siri were led to a large circular arena. The arena was roughly one hundred and fifty feet across, with a wall separating the crowd that had gathered from the participants of the arena. The wall was about four feet tall. On the other side of the arena, stood Johrra, dressed in his elven plate armor, a silver sword at his waist and a bow, with arrows dipped in wolfsbane.

As they neared the arena, Linorra came around the corner.

"As per our customs, to ensure a fair fight, since you are an immortal, you must fight without armor." Linorra said.

"How is that fair?" Siri yelled, as two royal guards came forward and held her so she couldn't interfere.

"You may also not transform, although you may use weapons, and magic, if you know any." Linorra said, looking at Aiden.

"You're sending him to his death!" Siri screamed, struggling against the guards holding her.

"Hey! Don't damage the merchandise, I plan on collecting it after I kill this dog." Johrra yelled at the guards holding Siri.

Aiden stepped into the ring, having removed his shirt and taking nothing but a small dagger with him.

"Have any last words to tell your precious dog, girl?" Johrra yelled over to Siri.

"Begin!" Linorra shouted.

Johrra fired off several arrows at Aiden. While Aiden managed to dodge or deflect most of them, one caught him in the left shoulder, momentarily staggering to the ground in pain from the arrow. Dropping the bow, Johrra charged at Aiden, drawing his

136

sword and slashing at Aiden's neck, intending to decapitate him and end this battle right then and there. Aiden, however, had other plans.

Rolling to his left underneath the sword swing, Aiden then retaliated by bringing his dagger up into Johrra's wrist guard, hitting with precision between the folds of armor plate, drawing blood from Johrra, as well as causing him to drop his sword.

Stepping back, into a defensive posture taught to him by his father, Aiden waited for his opponent to make the next move.

Backing away while holding his arm, Johrra yelled at Aiden.

"How dare you cut me, you filthy dog!"

Aiden remained silent, remembering back to the lessons taught to him by his father.

*"Never give in to taunts."* he would always say.

*"Focus on the battle."*

Johrra tried to feint a rush only for Aiden to not fall for it, nor move.

*"Watch your opponent's movements... every step, every muscle movement can give away what they are planning to do next."*

Johrra took two steps to his left.

Aiden mirrored his movements as the two circled each other.

*"Anticipate your opponent's next move."*

Johrra pulled a dagger out from behind him and threw it at Aiden. Aiden rolled forward, dodging the dagger by only a few inches, then counterattacked with a precision slice to the bottom of Johrra's wrist, cleanly cutting through the tendons, effectively disabling his hand as Johrra screamed.

*"Get inside your opponent's head, and you've already won."*

Johrra jumped back and began weaving his other hand through the air, shaping and channeling magic into an offensive attack.

*"We are the house of the phoenix, our power is fire, everything else is just a cheap imitation."*

Aiden dropped his dagger as Johrra threw a large fireball at him, hitting him in the chest and causing a large amount of dust and smoke to appear.

"No!" Siri screamed from the sidelines.

"You see?" Johrra held his arms up in victory.
"Nothing but a pathetic, filthy dog! I'll be taking my prize now." Johrra began walking towards Siri, a menacing gleam in his eyes.

"Is that it?"

Aiden's voice stopped him in his tracks.

Johrra's sadistic grin was instantly replaced by one of dread as he turned back to face the cloud of smoke.
Walking out of the smoke was Aiden, the fireball that should have killed him had wrapped itself around him like a cloak of fire, surrounding him in the shape of a phoenix.

"That's impossible!"
Aiden's eyes had changed.
"There's no way you could have survived that!" Johrra yelled, taking a step back.

Recognizing his family battle cloak, Siri realized that whatever it was that kept Aiden from using magic growing up, no longer affected him. No longer afraid, Siri stepped to the side of the ring as she yelled to Aiden.
"You can do it Aiden! I believe in you!"

"My family is the house of the phoenix." Aiden began to say, taking a step towards Johrra.
"Stay back!" Johrra yelled, taking another step back.

"Our power is fire."

"What the hell are you?" Johrra began stepping back even further.

"Everything else is just a cheap imitation."

The flaming phoenix cloak surrounding him dissipated.

Johrra lunged at Siri, drawing another dagger, deciding if he couldn't have her, then no one else could either.

"Nar Talas."

Johrra's hand was mere inches from grabbing Siri when his entire body froze, unable to move, no matter how much he struggled.

"*What the hell just happened?*" Johrra thought to himself. "*Did he just cast magic with a single word?*"

Fear began to overwhelm Johrra.

"Meir't." Aiden said, as Johrra's body flew across the arena towards him.

Just as Johrra reached Aiden, he found himself once again able to move, but it was too late.

"Nohkra."

Aiden punched Johrra in his stomach, caving in a part of his plate armor, as well as sending him across the arena at incredible speed.

Johrra's back slammed into the wall of the arena, blood bursting from his mouth as the air was driven from his lungs from the impact. Every witness in the audience was completely stunned and in perfect silence.

Johrra struggled to catch his breath as Aiden slowly walked towards him.

"W... wa...wait!" Johrra coughed as he held out his right arm out in front of him while holding his stomach with his left.

"Nihckt."

Johrra's right arm twisted outwards, the bones in his forearm shattering, while the elbow dislocated with a sickly pop.

Johrra grabbed his arm, screaming in pain.

Stepping up to him, Aiden grabbed Johrra's shattered arm. Twisting and pulling, Aiden hauled the elf over his shoulder, tossing him back into the center of the ring.

"Meir't."

Johrra once again flew towards Aiden, this time, Aiden brought his knee up and rammed it into Johrra's chest.

"Sal Theur."

The entire breastplate Johrra was wearing instantly shattered into tiny pieces upon impact with Aiden's knee.

Struggling to his knees, Johrra looked up at Aiden as he stood over him. A powerful right hook from Aiden threw him face down on the ground yet again.

The broken bones in Aiden's hand popped back into place as Johrra spat out several of his teeth, along with a mouthful of blood.

"I yield!" Johrra coughed, looking up at Aiden, expecting mercy. Johrra lifted his remaining good arm up in front of him.

Aiden grabbed the elf's arm at the wrist, looking directly into his eyes.

"Amtoll Riis."

A quick twist of his hand, and Johrra's wrist dislocated with a pop, bones cracking, as the tendons snapped.

"There is no yielding... It's to the death."

Aiden drove his free hand down into Johrra's elbow, shattering it as he forced the arm to bend backwards.

Dropping the elf's now useless arm, Aiden spun on his heel, delivering a powerful kick to the side of Johrra's head, sending him tumbling several feet away.

Opening his eyes, Johrra watched as Aiden stepped towards him again.

*"I don't get it. I planned this entire fight out perfectly. I was supposed to humiliate him and then take his woman as my own. I even dipped my arrows in wolfsbane to weaken him further, even though it was against the rules. So why? Why is he winning? How is he so strong? I have to live, I have to get away, honor and tradition be damned... I want to live!"*

Despite the injuries to his body, and his blurry vision, Johrra struggled to his feet and began limping away from Aiden.

"Nihckt."

Johrra's left leg snapped, his lower leg shattering, as his knee joint dislocated.

Johrra fell to the ground, screaming in pain.

The majority of onlookers were sickened at what they were witnessing. Though they had no love for Johrra, this was just too much. To them, Aiden looked like a predator toying with its prey, dragging out the kill for its own amusement. Siri could only watch as she covered her mouth with her hand.

"First, you shoot me with arrows in the forest." Aiden began, taking a step towards him, taking his time.

"Then you abduct Siri, thinking you could have her to yourself."

"No." Johrra whimpered, attempting to crawl his way away from Aiden, desperate to put as much space between himself and this monster as possible.

"When I came for her, you tried to use her as a shield."

"I swear, I wouldn't have hurt her."

Johrra tried to reason with Aiden, willing to say whatever he had to in order to survive.

"And when that didn't work, you decided to rig a fight so that you could kill me, just so you could have what doesn't belong to you." Aiden said, as his eyes began to glow even brighter.

Aiden stood over Johrra as he was trying to crawl away, with two shattered arms and a shattered leg. Aiden kicked him in the ribs, breaking three ribs while turning him over onto his back. Reaching down, he grabbed Johrra by the throat and lifted the man into the air.

"Please, you don't have to do this." Johrra squeaked around his constricting airway. "Please, have mercy."

"Seek mercy from your gods, for you'll find none with me." Aiden replied.

Reaching down to Johrra's waist, Aiden drew Johrra's last remaining dagger from its sheath, twirling it in his fingers for a moment.

"Your life ends here."

Aiden slowly and carefully slid the blade of the knife into the side of Johrra's neck, intentionally avoiding any major arteries, sliding the blade between the bones of his neck and his airway.

"Any last words?"

Johrra attempted to speak, but Aiden never gave him a chance.

Aiden twisted the blade sideways, severing his airway then shoved the hilt backwards towards the base of the skull, the pivot point ripping the blade out the front of Johrra's neck, spraying blood everywhere.

Aiden tossed Johrra's body to the ground as he bled out, gasping for air that would never come.

Pulling the arrow from his left shoulder, Aiden began walking towards Siri, his eyes returning to normal.

Siri, in tears, jumped over the wall and ran to Aiden, just in time for him to collapse from exhaustion, falling into her arms.

"You did it Aiden, you did it." she sobbed, holding him.

"Thank you." she whispered, so no one else could hear.

# Chapter 19

"The fight is over." Queen Linorra declared. "The victor is Aiden."

Linorra stepped into the arena and began walking over towards Aiden and Siri, followed by eight of her royal guard.

As they approached, Aiden noticed that the guards following the queen had their weapons half drawn, trembling in fear. Realizing the danger, Aiden told Siri to get behind him, getting to one knee, about to rise. Out of panic, the guards rushed forward, surrounding the two of them, fully drawing their weapons.

Realizing what was happening, Linorra quickly ordered her men to stand down.

The men did not obey at first, as they were too focused on Aiden.

"I said stand down!" Linorra screamed, finally getting the attention of the guards.

"My queen, you saw what he did." one of the men said, still frightened.

"Yes, I did, and it was done during combat. Now stand down."

The men still didn't want to fully drop their weapons.

"Now!"

The guards finally dropped their weapons and returned to the queen's side.

"Leave us." the queen told her men.

"Your majesty, I don't think that is a very wise decision after what just happened."

"What just happened." Linorra said angrily, turning to face the men.

"Is that an honored guest has just been insulted, challenged to a trial by combat, and came out the victor. Only to have the royal guard, who are supposed to honor the old ways, surround him and draw their weapons on him for no other reason than that the man has frightened them." Venom dripped from her words as the queen berated her men.

All of the royal guards, knowing she was right, could only bow their heads in shame as the queen yelled at them.

"Now get out of my sight!" Linorra commanded.

As the guards left, Linorra turned back to Aiden and Siri.

Aiden was doing his best to stand up, despite being so weak and exhausted, leaning against Siri as she struggled to keep him upright.

Linorra knelt down in front of Aiden and Siri.

"I apologize for my guard; they should have known better. That battle was... hard to watch."

"He deserved it." Siri said with anger in her voice, looking over at Johrra's dead body.

"Yes, he did." Linorra agreed. "Even though deserved, it was still difficult to watch."

Linorra stood, extending her hand.

"Here... let me help you, you need rest after what you did out there." she said, offering her support to Aiden and Siri.

"No thank you." Siri replied a bit coldly as she looked at Aiden.

"Besides, it's not rest he needs, it's..." Siri eased Aiden back to the ground.

"May I borrow your dagger?" Siri asked.

"Of course." Pulling her dagger from her waist, Linorra handed it to Siri.

Taking the dagger from the queen, Siri ran the blade lightly across her wrist to draw blood before offering it to Aiden.

"No." Aiden said, shaking his head. "I'll be alright."

"Shut up and take it already, it'll help you heal faster... or do I need to force feed you?" Siri said, slightly aggravated.

"Fine." Aiden conceded.

Taking Siri's wrist, Aiden closed his mouth over the wound. Upon tasting her blood, Aiden's thirst kicked up, but to Aiden's surprise, it was only a tiny fraction of what he felt the other day. Feeling more confident that he wouldn't hurt her again, Aiden bit into Siri's wrist to take in more blood, as he felt his strength returning.

Siri felt a sting in her wrist as Aiden bit down, followed by a pleasant tingling that ran through her arm as he drank. After a few seconds, Aiden felt that he had enough and released Siri's hand and looked at it, only to watch the wound seal itself and heal on its own.

"*Interesting.*" Aiden noted.

"Now if you will excuse us your majesty, it's been a long day." Standing up, Aiden took Siri's hand in his.

"Of course, we can speak tomorrow." Linorra said, stepping out of their way as they headed back to their room for the night.

~ ~ ~ ~ ~

Aiden sat on the edge of his and Siri's bed in their tent. After what just happened, Aiden didn't feel comfortable staying in the elven village. Instead, choosing to set up the tent just outside the village. He felt more comfortable here with just the two of them.

"*At least here the walls don't have ears.*" Aiden thought, wanting some privacy.

Looking down at his own body, Aiden noticed something that he hadn't noticed before.

The years of training he had gone through growing up in his family left him in excellent physical condition. Despite this, looking at himself now, Aiden looked as if he had put on twenty pounds of pure muscle.

*"When did this happen?"*

Aiden was so focused on himself that he hadn't noticed Siri move across the bed to him until she placed her arms around his chest, pressing herself into his back as she rested her head on his shoulder.

"It happened when you drank my blood." Siri said, as if she knew what he was thinking.

"What?" Aiden turned his head to look at her.

"Your body changed after drinking my blood."

"I didn't even realize." Aiden looked back at his body.

"I thought not." Siri pulled herself off him, laying down on the bed.

Turning to face her, Aiden noticed that Siri had changed back into the shirt that she had salvaged from the destroyed infirmary room that morning.

"That's mine." Aiden growled.

"Nuh-uh, mine." Siri shot back, smiling as she scooted up the bed away from him.

"Since when?" Aiden asked, making his way after her.

"Since you shredded mine last night."

Siri rolled to the side, just as Aiden pounced at her, getting up and fleeing to the other side of the tent.

"Give it back." Aiden followed her like an animal stalking its prey.

"You want it back? You're gonna have to take it." Siri smiled mischievously.

"That can be arranged."

Aiden lunged for her.

Siri squealed as she tried to run from Aiden, only to be caught in his strong arms, kicking her arms and legs as he dragged her back to the bed.

"No fair! You're faster and stronger." she said as she was partially pinned beneath him, face down on the bed.

"All is fair in love and war." Aiden replied, his body pressing into hers.

"So we're at war?" Siri asked playfully, turning her head to the side to look back at Aiden.

"Guess again." Aiden leaned down, nibbling on her ear, causing her to squirm beneath him.

Aiden released her, rolling off of her onto his back. Siri snuggled up against him, letting him run his fingers through her hair.

"I feel different." Aiden said after a few minutes just enjoying each other's company.

"Not surprising." Siri lifted her head, looking down at Aiden as her hair fell across his chest.

"Your blood?"

"Exactly." Siri laid her head against his chest, listening to his heartbeat.

"Drinking my blood allowed your powers to properly settle into your body, but there's more to it than that."

Aiden kissed the top of her head, pulling his arms up around her shoulders.

"When you drank my blood, I believe that was the first time you actually accepted what you are... at least in part." Siri looked up into Aiden's eyes as he sat up in the bed, bringing her with him.

"You've been pretending to be something you're not ever since you found out what you are." she said, turning to straddle his waist, facing him.

"You're a hybrid... not a human. Now that you have accepted it, really accepted it, your dormant animal side has finally come to the surface. And with it, you have become even stronger as a result." Siri pushed Aiden back down onto the bed before leaning forward and kissing him.

Sitting back up, Siri looks into Aiden's eyes as they begin to glow softly.

"I think I like the new you." she said, running her hands across the muscles of his chest.

~ ~ ~ ~ ~

Siri laid on top of Aiden for several minutes, trying to find a way to ask him about what happened with Johrra. The way Aiden used ancient elvish to cast magic worried her. Siri wasn't afraid of him knowing the language. She knew sometimes Aiden would go into some sort of trance, like he was there, but only as an observer to what he was doing. Each time, he came back with more memories of the hybrid, and occasionally new power. But still...

As the anxiety started to build inside her, Aiden began to purr, the deep resonating vibration from his chest washing over her. Siri felt all the tension and anxiety simply melt away as she instinctively pulled herself closer to Aiden.

"What's wrong?" Aiden asked, wrapping his arms around her. "What's bothering you? Please tell me."

Aiden rolled them over onto their side, propping himself up on one arm while looking into her eyes.

Taking a deep breath, Siri answered.

"What do you remember about your battle today?"

Knowing there was more to it than just the question itself, Aiden closed his eyes for a few moments before answering her.

"I remember that I used magic... and that for the first time in my life, casting spells was actually easy for me."

"That wasn't just magic." Siri sat up on the bed, crossing her feet underneath her.

"What do you mean?" Aiden took her hand as she continued.

"Aiden... you didn't cast any spells."

~ ~ ~ ~ ~

Siri woke to find Aiden missing from their bed. Getting up and pulling on a robe, Siri opened the front of the tent as she finished fastening her robe.

"Aiden?" Siri called quietly, not wanting to be too loud, seeing it was still dark outside.

A few yards away, Siri recognized one of the elven guards that were meant to protect her and Aiden. She suddenly felt a bit embarrassed, knowing all she had on was the robe.

*The guard either doesn't notice, or rather... doesn't care."* Siri thought after he silently nodded to her before pointing off in the distance.

Looking where he pointed, Siri could just barely make out Aiden in the distance. Feeling a little better now that she knew where Aiden was, Siri disappeared back into the tent to put on a few more clothes before going back outside.

Aiden stood in a small clearing about ten meters across, and about forty meters from the village and the tent he was in earlier. Wearing nothing but a loose fitting pair of shorts, sweat poured from his body as he continued his combat training.

Waking up earlier, Aiden had realized that he had not kept up with his father's combat discipline since they fled Esenor, and after his fight the day before, Aiden felt it was time to get back into it, as it was good for him as well as it helped him to clear his mind.

Finishing up his workout routine, Aiden walked over and sat down on a large rock. Pulling his feet into a cross-legged position, Aiden lowered his hands into his lap, bringing his fingers together to form a circle in his lap. Straightening his back, Aiden closed his eyes and began to take slow, controlled breaths... in through his nose, hold for two seconds, then back out through his mouth. Something that his mother had taught him to help him focus. Right now, he needed to focus.

Siri stepped back out of the tent, having made herself decent, and went to go find Aiden. Looking up at the moon in the sky, Siri estimated it was about two hours after midnight.

*"What is he doing out here this late?"* Siri thought to herself, making her way over to where Aiden was sitting. Siri was about to call out to him when she noticed the stance that Aiden was sitting in.

Deciding not to disturb him while meditating, Siri opted to just sit down across from Aiden and wait a while.

As she approached him, Siri noticed a few other guards gathered together around twenty feet or so from Aiden.

"What's he doing?" one of the guards asked her as she made her way past them.

"He hasn't moved a muscle in fifteen minutes." another said as she stopped momentarily to look at them.

"He's meditating." Siri told them, keeping her voice down to not disturb Aiden.

"It helps him focus." she explained, then continued on her way toward Aiden.

After reaching Aiden, Siri sat down facing him, and simply watched him as she waited for him to finish.

*"It must be something important if he is out here at this time of night."* Siri thought to herself.

As she wondered what he must be thinking about, Siri couldn't help but be a bit distracted as she looked at Aiden. A few strands of Aiden's unkempt hair had fallen down in front of his face. Siri fought the urge to reach out and move his hair back into place as she continued looking at him, her eyes traveling further down. Seeing his lips, Siri wanted nothing more than to lean forward and press her own lips to his.

Shaking her head, Siri pushed the thought out of her mind as her eyes kept travelling further down his body, despite herself.

Siri's eyes wandered over Aiden's broad shoulders and chest, reminding her of that strange purr that he does when they are together, admiring each and every muscle from his well-defined chest, to his six pack abs.

Unable to contain herself anymore, Siri stood up and launched herself into him, pushing him down onto the ground as she ran her hands across his abs and chest, looking into his eyes before smashing her lips against his.

"That's very distracting."

Siri snapped out of her daydream to find she was still sitting across from Aiden, fidgeting with her hands in her lap as she looked at Aiden. Aiden was still sitting in front of her with his eyes closed, a slight smirk on his face.

Realizing she had been caught, Siri turned bright red as she quickly glanced down before looking back at Aiden.

Opening his eyes, Siri saw them glowing red within that sea of swirling black, only for the swirling black to disappear, before his eyes finally stopped glowing and returned to normal.

As Aiden stood, Siri stood up as well, brushing grass and dirt off her pants before looking up where Aiden had been, only for him to be gone. Looking around for him, Siri was suddenly picked up from behind as Aiden scooped her up in his arms and started walking back towards the tent.

"I was trying to figure some things out." Aiden said, looking down at Siri in his arms as she held onto his neck, pushing open the tent and heading back towards the bed.

"But since you are so distracting..." Aiden tossed her onto the bed before climbing on himself.

"You now have my undivided attention." Aiden eyes glowed and a low growl escaped from his lips.

Siri's mouth suddenly went dry as Aiden made his way towards her.

# Chapter 20

Aiden sat in the large bath, enjoying the warm water as he cleaned off the dirt and sweat from last night's training session. Across the room, Siri sat at a mirror brushing her hair.

"We can't stay here much longer, Siri." Aiden said, looking over at her.

"I know." Siri said, lowering the brush and looking at her lap.

"I know they are your people, and you would like to know more about them, but the vampyres won't give up looking for me. You know that."

"It's not that."

Siri stood up and walked over to Aiden, dropping her robe as she climbed into the tub with Aiden.

"Then what is it?" Aiden asked, picking up a cloth and starting to wash Siri's back for her.

"I just wish we knew where we were headed. All your father told us was to go to the whitetooth mountains. But what do we do when we get there?" Siri asked. "I don't want us to be on the run our entire lives."

She motioned for him to turn around so she could wash his back as well.

"We won't." Aiden promised.

Once clean, Aiden got out of the bath, grabbing a nearby towel to dry off, leaving Siri with the bath to herself as he got dressed for the day.

Siri, now finished with her bath as well, began to stand up and step out of the bath. As she reached for a towel, Aiden and Siri noticed the entrance to the tent move slightly as it began to be opened from the outside.

"You open that flap, you die."

Aiden's warning caused whoever was on the other side of the tent flap to stop.

"My Lord, there is something out here you should see." Andarii said from the other side of the entryway.

Tossing a set of clothes to Siri, Aiden made his way out of the tent, making sure Siri was covered first.

Stepping outside, Aiden noticed it was already mid-morning. Next to the entrance stood Andarii, captain of the men assigned to Aiden's command while he remained in the forest.

"My apologies for disturbing you, but..." Andarii gestured to a spot nearby.

Over the last few hours, piles of clothing, elven armor, as well as an assortment of weapons and miscellaneous goods had been brought over and placed next to Aiden's tent.

"What is all this?" Aiden asked, looking back at Andarii.

"They are the personal belongings of Johrra. Won through the right of Amtoll Riis, what was once his, now rightfully belongs to you. They are still collecting the remaining possessions Johrra had, but this is the majority of them, awaiting your inspection."

"All of this now belongs to me?" Aiden asked in shock, as Siri stepped out of the tent.

"Yes, my Lord, including..."

"MOVE!" someone yelled, catching Aiden's attention.

Rounding the entrance to the village, an elven man was pulling on a length of rope. Attached to the rope, was a person.

"I SAID MOVE!" the man yelled, pulling against the rope harder while the person struggled against him.

Aiden looked closely at the person struggling against the man, his eyes going wide as he stared.

It was a female prisoner; she wore nothing but a tattered sackcloth tunic. Her hands were tied at the wrist as she was being dragged, clearly against her will, the rope cutting into her skin as she struggled. She had hair as black as a raven's feather. Atop her head, she had a pair of cat ears. Her tail frantically swished back and forth behind her as she struggled desperately against her bonds. Her fingers were tipped with long, sharp fingernails. She was barely able to put up a fight as the elf dragged her over to where Aiden and Siri were.

"What is she?" Aiden asked, unable to take his eyes off the girl.

"She is a Nekomata." Andarii answered.

"A catgirl." the elf holding the rope added.

"I thought the Nekomata were hunted to extinction years ago." Aiden said.

"A few survived and went into hiding." Andarii answered. "This one was caught sneaking into Johrra's place attempting to steal food. Instead of killing her, Johrra decided to make her his slave."

The elf holding the rope roughly pushed the Nekomata forward a few feet towards Aiden.

"And now she belongs to you, as per our law." the elf said, as the young catgirl stared at her own feet.

Siri wanted to speak up and say something, but stopped when Aiden held his hand out at his side, motioning for her to keep quiet.

Stepping forward, Aiden approached the girl.

Now able to get a better look at the girl, Aiden saw that she was covered in dirt from head to toe. She wore no shoes, and was clearly malnourished. She had bruises all over her body, with quite a few scars along her bare arms and legs, as well as those that were hidden beneath the sackcloth tunic. Scars caused by repeated beatings and whippings. A crude collar had been placed around her neck.

Looking at the scars, an immense rage began to build within Aiden for reasons he couldn't explain.

"*What had Johrra put this girl through?*" he thought to himself. "*And all for trying to steal some food she clearly needed.*"

Any guilt over what he had done to Johrra yesterday vanished as he looked at this girl.

"What is your name?" Aiden asked the girl as she shivered, out of both fear, and the cold morning air.

"M.. Mi.. Mina." the girl stammered.

Without realizing it, Aiden subconsciously reached a hand toward her, only for her to hiss at it and try to bite his hand.

"How dare you attack your master, slave!" the elf holding the rope yelled, reaching to his side where he kept a small whip. Raising the whip to hit the girl, she hunched her shoulders and tensed up, expecting pain.

When none came, she cautiously looked up.

In the blink of an eye, Aiden had grabbed the hand that was holding the whip, preventing it from hitting the girl.

The man began to cry out in pain as Aiden began tightening his grip, increasing the pressure. The man howled as Aiden slowly broke every bone in the man's hand, one by one.

"You think this is Pain?" Aiden asked, glaring down at the man who had fallen to his knees as Aiden continued applying pressure on his broken hand.

Andarii and his men took a few steps back.

"You like causing pain to others?"
Aiden's eyes began to glow.
"You like leaving scars on other people?"

Aiden's own bones began to crack as he began to shift while still holding onto the man's hand.

All guards present ignored the man's cries as Aiden passed judgment... acting as if they hadn't seen or heard a thing.

Now standing at his full height of seven feet in hybrid form, Aiden lifted the terrified man up by his broken hand. Holding the man into the air, Aiden raise his other hand, claws glinting in the sunlight.

Aiden brought them down across the man's face, down his neck, and across his chest, being careful to not cut so deep as to kill the man, but to permanently scar him with a reminder of the consequences of his own actions.

Releasing the man, Aiden dropped to the ground on all fours, howling in pain as his own bones once again began to crack, reverting back to his human form.

Siri looked to Andarii as Aiden began shifting back. Nodding his head to her, he pulled his cloak from around his shoulders, handing it to her before she ran over to Aiden to cover him as he turned back. As Aiden was in the final stages of shifting, he glanced back to the girl he had just saved.

The girl had slumped to the ground as she stared at Aiden, her bright, vibrant blue eyes locked with his.

"*Did he really just save me?*" she thought to herself, as they continued staring at one another.

~ ~ ~ ~ ~

Aiden remained on the ground for a few moments, his body shaking from the pain of the shift. Although he could now shift on command, it still hasn't gotten any easier, or any less painful for him.

After a minute, Aiden broke eye contact with the girl as he stood up, wrapping the cloak around himself.

After throwing the cloak over him earlier, Siri had ran back into the tent and fetched a pair of trousers for him.

Returning just as Aiden stood, Siri handed him the trousers.

Pulling on the trousers, ignoring the cries of pain from the man he just mutilated... Aiden then turned back around to the girl collapsed in the dirt.

Aiden saw Siri bend down to try to talk to the girl.

"Are you ok?" Siri asked, but got no response from the girl, who just kept staring at Aiden.

Getting no response, Siri reached out her hand and touched the young girl's shoulder. Feeling Siri touch her, broke the girl out of the daze she was in.

"No!" she screamed, flinching away, falling over onto her side.

"It's ok." Siri said, holding out a hand to help the girl back up, only for her to crawl away as fast as she could with her hands bound.

"Wait."

Siri started to follow the girl.

"Siri." Aiden's voice caught her attention.

Aiden silently waved Siri away from the girl as she curled herself into a ball against a nearby tree. Realizing she wasn't helping the situation, Siri stood up and took a few steps back.

"Leave us." Aiden said to the guard, never once taking his eyes off the girl.

Without a word, each guard there nodded and began heading back into the camp, picking up the man writhing in pain and taking him to the infirmary. Soon it was just Siri and Aiden left.

Siri made her way over to Aiden.

"You too Siri."

Siri stared at him in disbelief.

Keeping his eyes on the girl, Aiden takes Siri's hand before speaking.

"She's terrified." he says softly.

"Of course she is." Siri began. "After what just happened..."

"Not of me." Aiden cut her off. "I don't know how I know this... but I need to be alone with her, just for a few moments."

"Do you trust me?" Aiden asked, squeezing Siri's hand.

"Of course." she replied.

"Go."

Aiden released her hand as she walked away, following in the direction the guards went.

Aiden glanced around him. Seeing a small dagger on top of a pile of boxes that had been brought over, Aiden walked over and picked it up before making his way over to the girl laying against the tree. The girl had curled up leaning against the tree, pulling her knees up to her chest and hiding her face.

Reaching out, Aiden carefully took the girl's bound wrists in his hand, feeling her tense up under his touch, but otherwise not moving.

"Please, Mina will be good... please don't hurt Mina. Mina's sorry, Mina won't do it again. No more... please." the girl pleaded, barely above a whisper.

Aiden carefully cut the bindings on her wrists, freeing her arms as she slowly lifted her face to look at him.

"No one's gonna hurt you." Aiden said softly, tossing the knife away as he sat down next to the girl.

The two of them just sat there in silence staring at each other for a few minutes before she finally spoke.

"Mina's sorry, Mina shouldn't have tried to bite you... master." The catgirl lowered her eyes as she spoke.

Aiden inwardly winced as she called him master, but said nothing. This girl has just been through hell, and Aiden didn't want to push the girl over the edge, seeing just how close she was to being broken.

"What did Johrra do to you?" Aiden whispered under his breath, not realizing she could hear him.

Hearing Johrra's name, the young girl suddenly grabbed ahold of Aiden tightly.

"Please... Mina is sorry master! Mina will do better! Mina will be a good girl, just don't send Mina back to him!"

Aiden wrapped his arms around the girl, taking notice of the way she winced when he touched her back.

"Shhh, it's ok. He can't hurt you anymore."

"Y...you won't send Mina back to him?" she asked, her forehead leaning against Aiden's chest.

"No, I won't. Besides, he's dead."

Mina picked her head up to look into his eyes.

"Johrra is... dead?"

"Yes, he is. I killed him." Aiden said softly. "He can't hurt you anymore... no one will."

Hearing this, she collapsed into his lap, crying.

"Thank you." she managed to get out between sobs, barely loud enough for Aiden to hear.

Aiden slowly rocked back and forth as Mina cried against him, doing the best he could to comfort the girl. After several minutes the sobbing turned to crying, then to hiccups, and eventually, just the occasional sniffle. Looking at the goosebumps on the girl's skin, as well as the way she was shivering, Aiden knew he needed to get her out of the cold morning air, and fast.

Looking over the girl again, Aiden noticed the bottoms of her feet were bruised and cut, with blisters in places. He was surprised she was even able to walk at all.

Being as gentle as he could, Aiden slid his arm underneath her legs and picked the girl up. Turning back towards the village, Aiden saw Siri watching from the entrance. Nodding to her, Siri followed Aiden as he walked back towards their tent, carrying a now unconscious Mina in his arms.

# Chapter 21

Aiden threw open the doors as he burst into the throne room of the queen, nearly breaking them off the hinges, his eyes glowing a bright crimson in a sea of swirling black. Standing near the fireplace, queen Linorra let out a sigh. She knew this moment was coming, although she was not looking forward to it.

One of the queen's guards stepped in Aiden's way only to get knocked clear across the room with a single swing from Aiden.

"How long?" Aiden demanded, slamming his fists into the queen's desk, splitting it in two and sending pieces of wood everywhere.

"Excuse me?"

Linorra was slightly shaken, but not entirely surprised with Aiden's outburst.

"How long did you let that monster torture that poor girl and not lift a finger to help her!"

"I'm afraid it is a bit more complicated than that."

"How long?" A growl escaped his throat as Aiden fought the urge to shift.

Linorra sighed. "Seven months." she replied, knowing he wouldn't listen until he had his answer.

Aiden's eyes stopped glowing out of pure shock, returning to their normal color as the reality of the situation hit him.

Johrra had tortured and abused that girl for seven whole months.

"There is a law in our village." Linorra turned to face Aiden.

"Thievery is not permitted. Those that steal from another would typically be put to death. It is hard enough to live out here without people stealing from one another. Although death is usually the judgement, the victim may choose to spare they guilty parties life in exchange for servitude. Unfortunately, that young Nekomata stole from Johrra."

"But you could have made him stop. Instead you chose not to." Aiden accused her.

"She was his slave, his property, there was nothing we could do. That's why he wanted Siri, all the women in the village knew how he treated the girl and refused to marry him." Linorra stated.

"You could have told him to stop. You could have..."

"And just how do your own people treat elves?" the queen spat back.

Aiden stopped, realizing that Linorra was right. No one had the right to tell someone what they could or couldn't do to their slaves.

"That's also why no one batted an eye when you mutilated that man earlier." Linorra continued.

"By our law, she was your property. Even if he was bringing her to you, he did not have the right, or the authority to lay a hand on her, and he will forever bear the scars to remind him."

Aiden took a few calming breaths.

"I want to trust you, if not for my own sake then for Siri's... as you are her people. But lately, I'm finding fewer and fewer reasons to trust your people." Aiden said.

"I see." Linorra lowered her head, knowing where this conversation was headed.

"We are leaving."

"I understand... when?"

"Two days." Aiden answered flatly.

"I'm sorry that we have disappointed you." Linorra turned away from Aiden as she continued.

"At one time, the elves were the greatest allies the hybrid had. I had hoped to rekindle that alliance... but it appears we have fallen much farther than we thought we had." Linorra looked up at a portrait of her mother.

"Don't be sorry." Aiden said as Linorra turned back to look at him.

"Be better."

Linorra nodded, setting her jaw and straightening up, knowing he was right and that all was not lost.

"We will be. Should you ever need our assistance, all you need do is call on us and we will rally to your side on swift wings." Determination filled the queen's voice.

~ ~ ~ ~ ~

Leaving the building, Aiden decided to once again walk through the elven market, anxious to return to Siri and Mina. He had laid Mina down on the bedding in the tent before going to confront the queen. He didn't know why... but he was worried about the girl, and what would happen if she woke up and he wasn't there. Aiden knew he needed to be quick.

Walking through the market, Aiden kept his eyes peeled for what he was looking for. Glancing around, Aiden finally found what he was looking for as he turned and walked up to the stall. It was a small shop that had a variety of different herbs, medicines and potions.

"Excuse me." Aiden said to the owner of the stall, who was turned away from him, placing some potions on the shelf.

"Oh good heavens, you startled me." The woman jumped as she turned to look at Aiden, one hand covering her chest.

She wore an apron around her waist that had a few dirt smudges on it, revealing to Aiden that many of the herbs she sold were probably picked by hand herself. She had light brown hair pulled back into a tight ponytail to keep it out of the way when mixing potions. Soft hazel eyes reflected a kind soul.

After seeing who it was that came up to her shop, her eyes widened in recognition as she became slightly nervous.

"C.. can I help you?" the woman asked, trying to keep a smile on her face.

Seeing the woman's nervousness, Aiden took a half step back before speaking.

"I was wondering if you had any herbs or salves that can be used for healing?"

"Certainly." The woman relaxed slightly. "What kind of injuries are you dealing with?"

"I'm not entirely sure." Aiden responded.

Aiden thought back to Mina wincing in pain when he touched her, as well as the cuts and bruises on her feet.

"Cuts, bruises, perhaps even some lacerations and blisters." Aiden wanted to get everything he would need to help the girl before returning.

Realization dawned on the woman as Aiden said this.

"This is for the catgirl isn't it?" The woman lowered her voice, sounding concerned.

Aiden nodded.

"Everyone knew Johrra abused the girl, my husband and I lived next door to him. We would constantly hear her wailing as Johrra beat her." she said, a tear rolling down her cheek.

"We wanted to help, but Johrra kept her on a short leash. She didn't deserve what happened."

Looking at Aiden, the woman reached across the stall, grabbing Aiden's hands.

"Please don't treat her the way he did... I know who you are, and I know you are quick to temper, it comes with being what you are, and I'm scared for her. Please... allow me to buy her from you. Just name your price. I don't want her to suffer anymore, please." the woman begged, with tears in her eyes.

"No." Aiden said quietly, but firmly.

Letting his hands go, the woman placed her hands on the counter as she looked at Aiden.

"But..." she began before Aiden cut her off by holding up his hand.

"You are a kind person, and I can tell you wouldn't abuse her, but no. I feel it will be better if she came with me. I plan on taking her away from this place, away from where she endured so much trauma, and hopefully, help her to heal."

Reaching down, Aiden picked up the woman's hands from the counter.

"She is safe with me, I promise. Despite the things you may have seen or heard about me, I am not like Johrra. I do not enjoy causing unnecessary pain." Aiden released her hands.

"But the man this morning..."

"Tried to strike her with a whip."

Aiden's eyes began to glow softly.

"And I repaid his kindness tenfold. A lesson he will not soon forget."

The woman wiped the tears from her eyes, relieved by Aiden's words.

"Thank you, sir."

Grabbing a crate, she began filling it with supplies.

After filling the crate, she turned back around to Aiden. She explained each of the herbs, potions and salves she had placed in the crate, as well as how to apply them, and how often to change out the dressings.

"Thank you for your help." Aiden said, looking at the crate full of supplies. "How much do I owe you?"

The woman shook her head at him.

"Simply knowing she will be taken care of is payment enough, especially after what she has endured." The woman handed the crate of supplies over to Aiden.

Aiden thanked the woman once again before leaving her shop and heading straight back to his tent.

Arriving at the tent, Aiden heard an ear shattering scream come from within.

Dropping the crate, Aiden rushed into the tent to find Siri standing next to the bed trembling, while Mina writhed on the bed clutching at the collar around her neck, screaming in pain.

# Chapter 22

Climbing onto the bed, Aiden gathered the young catgirl into his arms as she writhed in agony.

"What happened?" Aiden asked, looking over at Siri.

"I'm sorry." Siri said, tears in her eyes. "She was sleeping... I felt bad about what Johrra did to her... I'm sorry."

"It hurts! It hurts!" the catgirl screamed, as she struggled in Aiden's arms.

"What happened Siri?" Aiden asked again, gritting his teeth as the catgirl struggled against him, her claws raking across his arms, chest, and shoulders as he held her, leaving deep gashes in his skin.

"I just wanted to remove the collar." Siri said, collapsing onto her knees at the side of the bed.

"It's a master's collar." Aiden replied, placing his hand against the catgirl's neck, directly over the collar. "It causes extreme pain if attempted to be removed by anyone other than the girl's master."

Siri began crying even harder, realizing that by trying to take the collar off her, she had almost killed the girl.

Closing his eyes, Aiden began to recite an incantation before opening his eyes as he spoke.

"Release!"

The girl in his arms collapsed as the pain subsided, curling into a ball in Aiden's lap as she continued to cry.

"I'm sorry, I'm so sorry." Siri cried, looking at the girl, as well as Aiden's arms and chest, which had been torn to shreds by the girl's claws.

Siri wanted to get up and help Aiden with the cuts in his flesh, but could only sit motionless after what just happened. A part of her wanted to be angry with the catgirl for clawing, and hurting Aiden, but she also knew that she was the reason it happened.

Siri got up from the floor, knowing that, for the time being, her presence was only making the situation worse for the poor girl. Leaning over to Aiden, she spoke quietly.

"Are you gonna be ok?"

Looking down at himself, Aiden could already feel his body trying to heal.

"I'll be fine, don't worry about me."

Looking down at the girl crying in Aiden's arms, Siri felt guilty.

'I'm sorry.'

The girl in Aiden's lap didn't respond.

"Let me know if there is something I can do to help." she told Aiden.

He nodded, knowing what she was thinking as she left the tent.

Aiden laid his hand gently on the girl's head as she cried, causing her to flinch slightly before relaxing as she realized he wasn't going to hurt her as he rubbed his hand against her head and ears.

They sat like that for the better part of an hour, until the girl turned her head slightly to look up at Aiden. He had closed his eyes at some point as he stroked her hair.

Looking up at Aiden, the girl noticed the jagged marks all across his arms, shoulders, and torso that her claws had inflicted.

*"Had Mina done that to her previous master, she would have been whipped until she passed out, only to be woken up and whipped again."*

Fear welled up inside her at the thought of that, but something inside her told her he wasn't mad.

Looking at Aiden's face, Mina felt a strange, new sensation inside herself. This man had saved her twice today, and while she didn't know what he was... or if he would hurt her, she felt safe with him. This feeling inside her confusing her, yet comforting her at the same time. She felt connected to him, and she had hurt him.

"Mina is sorry." the girl said, finally gathering the courage to speak.

Opening his eyes, Aiden looked down into her own bright blue eyes, which were brimming with tears.

"For what?" Aiden asked, giving her a slight smile.

*"Is he serious?"*

"Mina hurt you." Mina tentatively reached up and touched the claw marks she had left on his chest.

"Mina is sorry." she said, hiding her face once more.

Reaching down, Aiden gently turned her head so she would look into his eyes before speaking.

"You have nothing to be sorry for. I knew the risks when I grabbed you. It was my choice, and I'd do it again." Aiden said, looking into her eyes.

Mina knew he meant it, he really wasn't mad at her.

Relief flooded through her as he spoke those words.

"Does it hurt?" Mina asked, trying to sit up a bit, only to lose her balance, falling back into his chest.

"Not really, they are already healing, so don't worry." Aiden replied trying to reassure her.

Aiden couldn't understand what was happening. Since the moment he first laid eyes on this girl, he felt inexplicably drawn to her. He had only just met this girl, yet Aiden knew he was already willing to lay down his life for her. Her scent washed over him, being this close to her, and it was the sweetest smell Aiden had ever experienced. Her skin, cool to the touch, a stark contrast to his own as she leaned against him. Looking down at her, Aiden couldn't help but wonder.

*"Who is this girl? And why does she make me feel this way? Why do I feel so protective of her?"*

"What are you, master?" Mina tried to sit up again, this time succeeding.

"That's... complicated." Aiden replied.

Mina lowered her head and stayed quiet, but Aiden could tell she wanted to say something.

"What is it?"

Mina shook her head.

"Mina."

"Apologies master! Slaves should only speak when spoken to. Slaves should not ask questions." Mina scrambled off the bed, getting down on her knees before him, lowering her head and not looking at him.

"Mina, look at me."

Aiden placed a hand on her trembling shoulder. Her chest was heaving as she began to hyperventilate.

Finally looking up into Aiden's eyes, Mina expected to see anger, but instead, saw only concern.

"I am not him." Aiden said gently, looking into her eyes. "And I will not hurt you."

Aiden could see her body start to relax as her breathing slowly returned to normal.

"Better?" Aiden asked, once she had calmed down a bit.

"Better... thank you, master."

"What happened?" Aiden asked, kneeling down beside her.

"Mina forgot her place, Mina asked questions. Slaves aren't supposed to ask questions." Mina answered.

Aiden reached over, touching near the collar on her neck.

"Please..."

Mina closed her eyes, expecting to be punished.

"Mina, look at me."

Mina slowly opened her eyes to look at Aiden.

"What did I say earlier?"

"Master?" she asked, confused.

"Do you remember what I said?" Aiden asked, running his hand along her neck, but not touching the collar yet.

"Master said that he would not hurt Mina?" she asked, not knowing if it was the right answer.

"Have I hurt you yet?" Aiden ran his free hand along her shoulder and upper arm.

Mina shivered slightly at his touch.

"No... master."

Taking his hand off her arm, Aiden brought it up to her face, wiping away a tear with his thumb.

"Do you trust me?"

Mina subconsciously nuzzled into his palm.

"Mina trusts you, Master." she said, closing her eyes, enjoying the feel of Aiden's palm against her cheek.

"Look."

Mina opened her eyes, blinking a few times, not believing what she saw as Aiden held up the collar that used to be around her neck in his fingers.

Slowly, Mina reached her hand up and felt her own neck, tears welling up in her eyes as she realized it wasn't a trick.

*"Master has really removed Mina's collar!"* she thought to herself.

Tears of joy rolled down her face as Mina tackled Aiden in a tight hug, knocking them both over.

"Thank you so much, Master!" Mina cried.

# Chapter 23

Mina felt that peculiar sensation again. Mina knew that she should be frightened of this man, yet couldn't bring herself to pull away. The warmth of his skin felt like heaven against her own. Taking a deep breath, Mina inhaled his scent. Her mouth watered, and her muscles relaxed as she familiarized herself with his scent. Why did she feel this way?

Hugging him right now, Mina never wanted this moment to end. What are these feelings she is experiencing?

These feelings confused her, but also made more sense, and felt more right than anything she had ever experienced in her life. Mina thought about her mother, about the things her mother told her about Nekomata... but also about immortals.

*"Can it? Is it possible? Could Master be Mina's..."* she wondered.

Mina wasn't sure, but she hoped.

~ ~ ~ ~ ~

"How do you feel?" Aiden asked, after a few minutes of Mina hugging him.

"Mina is happy, Master." Mina said, finally letting go of Aiden.

"How about we get you cleaned up?"

"Yes, Master." Mina nodded as Aiden got up from the floor.

Walking over to the bath, Aiden was thankful for the enchanted water never having to be replaced or cleaned. Dropping a fire stone from the table next to the bath into the water, Aiden turned to Mina as the water heated up.

Aiden's jaw dropped when he looked at Mina. Mina had pulled up and licked the corner of her tunic before rubbing it on her hands and arms, trying to clean herself the best she could.

Walking over to her, Aiden reached out a hand as he called out to her.

"Mina." he called gently.

Looking up from what she was doing, Mina saw Aiden holding out his hand to her.

Mina did not know what her master had planned, but she trusted him as she took his hand.

Helping her to her feet, Mina winced as the pain in her tired and abused body returned. Aiden picked her up as her legs began to give out on her.

"Easy there." Aiden said as he caught her.

"Thank you, Master." Mina said, blushing ever so slightly.

As Aiden began to walk towards the bath, Mina finally saw it. Her eyes went wide, and her jaw dropped.

"Is that for Mina?" she looked at Aiden in shock.

"Yes, it's for you, who else would it be for?" Aiden asked, not really wanting her to answer.

"Mina can have a real bath... with hot water?"

"Only if you want one... do you?"

Mina couldn't answer, only nod her head as they got closer to the tub.

Sitting her down on the edge of the tub, Aiden turned to leave.

"Master?" Mina called after him.

"What is it?" Aiden asked, turning back to look at her.

"Will Master help Mina?" Mina looked down at the dirt covering her body.

"I'll go get Siri; she can help you." Aiden said quickly, turning to get Siri.

"No!" Mina screamed, reaching for Aiden.

As she lost her balance on the edge of the tub, Aiden caught her.

"What is it? What's wrong?" Worry filled his voice as he looked at Mina.

Feeling embarrassed, Mina lowered her head as she answered him.

"Master... only Master." she whispered, lifting her head to look into his eyes pleadingly.

"It's ok Aiden, go ahead." Siri called from the slightly open entrance of the tent where she had been listening the whole time.

"Are you sure?" Aiden asked, looking over at the entrance of the tent at Siri.

Siri gives a reassuring nod to Aiden as she answered. "She needs it."

Siri turned, closing the tent fully, giving them privacy.

Aiden looked back at Mina as he lifted her back onto the edge of the tub.

"Ok, Master will help."

Aiden let go of her, grabbing a bench and placing it next to the tub.

Mina smiled slightly, but Aiden failed to notice.

"You sure about this?" Aiden asked, looking at Mina.

Mina nodded, lifting her arms so that he could untie the knot in her tunic below her arm and at her hip, before shrugging the uncomfortable material off.

Looking at the sackcloth tunic in his hands, Aiden growled as he tossed the piece of cloth she had been forced to wear to the side, making Mina jump slightly as she sank down into the water.

Turning back to Mina, Aiden's breath caught in his throat when he saw what Johrra had done to her. He had already seen the few scars on her arms and legs, but nothing prepared Aiden for what he saw next.

Mina's back was covered in scars, crisscrossed all up and down her back. Some short and thin, others longer and thicker. Older ones now barely visible, while newer ones stood out more. Some scars were placed on top of older ones, making them look worse than they actually were.

Looking at her back, Aiden saw around twenty welts across her back that were very recent... enough to still be visible after a few days, but not enough to scar. Along with the welts, were three fresh marks that had been done with a whip, running from her right shoulder to her left hip. The cuts were deep.

Aiden now understood why she winced when she moved, or was touched.

Out of shame, Mina tried to slide further into the tub to hide her scars, but Aiden stopped her.

"Don't... don't hide from me." Aiden spoke as gently, and soothingly as possible.

"Mina is sorry." she said, as she began to cry.

"Sorry for what?" he asked, picking up a cloth as he began carefully cleaning her back.

Mina had originally been excited when Aiden agreed to help bathe her. In her excitement, she had forgotten about the scars covering her body until now. Now, she only felt shame.

"Mina is broken." Mina lowered her head as she spoke. "Mina's skin is marred. Can't be appreciated by Master...ugly...broken."

"That's not what I see."

Aiden lifted one of her arms as he washed. Starting from her neck, running down her shoulder, and along her arm.

"It's not?"

Mina turned to look at Aiden, wincing from the pain in her back.

"No, it's not." Aiden said, turning her back around so he could continue. After a few minutes of careful, gentle cleaning, Mina spoke up.

"What does Master see when he looks at Mina?" She spoke barely above a whisper, as if she was afraid of hearing the answer.

"I see a strong, beautiful woman... who the world tried to break, but couldn't." Aiden answered truthfully.

"But Mina did break." Mina replied, lowering her head.

"Did she? Because as I remember, when I met her, she hissed at me and tried to bite me." Aiden replied, smiling.

Remembering this, Mina held her hands together in front of her as she chewed on her thumbnail.

"Mina was scared, thought Master would hurt Mina, just like Johrra... didn't know Master was kind." Mina said after a few seconds.

"That means they didn't break you. If they had broken you, you wouldn't have tried to protect yourself."

A slight smile crossed Mina's lips as she continued chewing on her nail.

Aiden handed her the washcloth, which she reluctantly takes.

"Can you lean back so I can get your hair?" Aiden asked.

Mina nodded, leaning back in the tub with Aiden's help. Wincing slightly as her back touched the side of the tub, she let her hair hang outside the tub as she finished washing herself.

Aiden went to work pulling pieces of dirt, twigs and other things out of her hair before reaching over to the table and grabbing a brush.

As Aiden began brushing her hair gently, Mina spoke up.

"Does Master like Mina's hair?" she asked, turning her head slightly, trying to look at Aiden.

Mina really hoped that Aiden would like her hair, it was the only thing that was still the same after Johrra would beat her.

"I do.. I think it's beautiful, just like you." Aiden even surprised himself with his answer.

"Master thinks Mina is beautiful?" she asks, looking up at Aiden longingly.

"Head back."

Mina complies, letting her neck rest against the edge of the tub as she looks up at Aiden.

Mina really hoped Aiden felt the same things she was feeling. Hoping it wasn't just because he wanted to be nice to her, or felt sorry for her.

"Yes... I think you're beautiful." Aiden begins to wash her hair.

"Scars and all?" she asks, looking at him with hope.

"Scars and all."

Mina closed her eyes as she began crying happy tears.

*"Scars and all."* Aiden thought, looking down at all the freshly healed scars she had inflicted on him.

~ ~ ~ ~ ~

After Mina had been cleaned. Aiden pulled a green healing stone from the pouch of bath stones next to the tub. Dropping it into the tub, Aiden told her to stay in the bath a little while longer, as it will help heal the smaller injuries on her body.

Walking over to the entrance to the tent, Aiden stepped outside to find Siri talking to Andarii. Seeing Aiden, Siri walked over, stepping up to him, as he wrapped his arms around her.

"How is she?"

"Not as broken as we feared... she'll be ok... given time." Aiden rested his chin on her head.

"Good... she's important to you." Siri said.

"What do you mean?"

Taking his hand, Siri led him over to a set of boxes for them to sit on.

"I never told you this, mainly because I thought I imagined it. On the day your father brought me home as a gift for you. After fighting with your father over not wanting me, you took me up to your room. Afterwards, when you first looked into my eyes, your eyes changed color."

"My eyes turned red when we first met?"

"No not red... green." she corrected.

"You mean..."

"Yes Aiden, just like mine. But only for a second, so I thought I imagined it. Ever since that moment, I have been slowly falling in love with you."

"You thought you imagined it? So what changed your mind?" Aiden asked.

"She did..." Siri nodded towards the tent. "When you shifted back after saving her, I saw you look back at her. You locked eyes with her, and I saw something."

"What did you see?"

"You already know." Siri cupped his face in her hand.

"They turned the same color as her eyes, didn't they?"

"Yes, and I think it has something to do with you being a hybrid." Siri replied.

Aiden looked at her puzzled.

"Aiden, have you heard of a mate bond?" Siri asked.

"I've heard of a mate, but not a mate bond, why?

"It's very rare, but when an immortal meets the one they are destined for... their eyes change color, and a bond is formed between them that constantly draws them together. My mother told me about it before she died."

"What else?" Aiden asked.

"Not much else is known about the mate bond, at least, not shared publicly." Siri told him.

"You think that's what happened to us back then?" Aiden took Siri's hands in his own.

Siri nodded her head.

"It would explain why I was not afraid of you when you first shifted."

"And why your voice brought me back when I lost control." Aiden added.

"That means... we are mates?"

"I believe so." Siri leaned forward, kissing him.

When they broke the kiss Siri looked him in the eye as she spoke.

"I think she is also your mate."

"How can that be possible if you are my mate?" Aiden asked, clearly confused.

"I think it's..."

"Because I'm a hybrid." Aiden finished for her, sighing as he placed his forehead against hers.

"I think you're right... even now, I feel drawn to go back into the tent." Aiden said, looking over at the tent Mina was in.

"Then go to her... the first few hours are crucial." Siri said.

"But I don't want to betray you."

Aiden kissed Siri on the forehead, holding her close.

"You're not... besides, I'm a big girl... I can share." Siri said as she kissed him.

"Go... right now, she needs you more than I do. I'll still be here in the morning." she said, pushing Aiden towards the tent.

# Chapter 24

Entering the tent, Aiden saw that Mina was just stepping out of the bath.
He quickly closed the tent to hide her from prying eyes.

*"Yep, definitely mates."* Aiden thought, laughing at himself over his possessiveness over both Siri and Mina.
Looking across the room at Mina, Aiden couldn't help but stare. Even malnourished as she was, to him, she was stunningly beautiful.
"Master?" Mina called, knocking him out of his daze.

Mina just stood there, shuffling from one foot to the other, staring at her feet, not knowing if she should cover herself or not.
Walking over to her, Aiden grabbed the bench he was sitting on earlier, placing it on the ground in front of him.
"Sit." Aiden said, patting the bench in front of him.
"Yes Master." Mina said, sitting down.
"How are you feeling after the bath?"
"Wonderful, Master. Mina is grateful you allowed her to bathe with hot water."
Aiden secretly wished he could resurrect Johrra, just so he could kill him again. This time even more slowly and painfully.

Holding back a growl, Aiden walked behind her to inspect the three whip marks.

"And what about your injuries? Does anything still hurt?" Aiden gently traced the lacerations with his fingers.

"Mina feels much better, although Mina's back still hurts a bit, Master." she answered shyly, knowing Aiden was looking at her scars again.

Taking out a container of healing salve, Aiden thought about using it on the lacerations when he had an idea. Setting the healing salve down, Aiden placed his hands on Mina's shoulders, causing her to tense up.

"Relax, it's just me."

Aiden leaned forward, brushing his face against her cat ear.

"What's the first thing I told you?" he asked, whispering gently into her ear.

"Master will not hurt Mina." she replied, her body relaxing under his hands.

"Good girl."

A shiver ran down Mina's spine when he said that.

Aiden ran his hands off her shoulders, and down her arms, sending sparks through Mina's skin wherever his hands touched, repeating the process several times as she purred. Mina whimpered when he pulled his hands away, but gasped when Aiden kissed her on her shoulder.

Mina closed her eyes, enjoying his attention.

After placing a series of kisses along her shoulder, Aiden began to move down her back, taking extra care to kiss each and every scar he came across.

"Master!.. those are Mina's... those are..." Mina tried to speak, but couldn't find the words as his lips left a trail of fire across her skin.

"Beautiful, just like the rest of you." Aiden kissed another scar.

"Beautiful."

And another.

"Beautiful."

Mina kept gasping and mewling as she clenched and unclenched her fists at her sides, his attentions driving her wild.

Aiden finally came to the lacerations that still weren't healed. Deciding to test his theory now, Aiden kissed the sensitive tissue before lightly licking it. Looking at the wound, Aiden saw that the part he had licked was sealed, and rapidly healing.

Aiden stopped what he was doing and stood up, earning him a whimper from Mina.

"Master..." she begged.

Aiden smiled.

Leaning into her ear, Aiden nibbled on it, causing a small moan to escape Mina's mouth... her reaction causing him to growl in response.

"Would you like the pain in your back to go away?" Aiden continued nibbling on her ear, making her squirm in her seat.

"Please Master, make it go away. Make Mina feel better." she pleaded.

Dropping back down to her back, Aiden began kissing and licking his way along all three lacerations on her back. Where he had licked, the lacerations left no scar. Happy with the job he had done, Aiden stood and walked back around in front of Mina.

Mina's eyes were dilated as she stared at Aiden's chest... craving for his touch, but also to touch him.

*"But Master hasn't given Mina permission to touch him."* she reminded herself.

As if reading her thoughts, Aiden leaned forward and whispered in her ear.

"You may touch... if you want."

Slowly, Mina reached out and touched Aiden's chest, palms flat, enjoying the warm heat from his skin. Slowly, she began to explore, feeling every curve of muscle, every scar that she caused.

A single tear rolled down her cheek as she whispered.

"Mina scarred Master. Mina is sorry."

"I'm not." Aiden took her face in his hands, wiping the tear from her face.

"Why?" Mina asked. "Why is Master not upset with the scars Mina gave him?"

Mina looked into his eyes, trying to figure out why he didn't hate her. Hoping that he didn't hate her... hoping for more.

"Because... you gave them to me." Aiden leaned forward, stopping just millimeters from her lips.

Mina whimpered when he stopped, squirming in her seat as her tail swished behind her in both anxiety, and excitement.

"If you want something, ask for it." Aiden whispered, his breath hot against her lips.

"M.. Mina wants Master to kiss her." she said shakily, just before Aiden finally captured her mouth with his own.

Mina moaned into his mouth as Aiden growled through the kiss.

Without breaking their kiss, Aiden picked Mina up as she wrapped her legs around his waist, placing her arms around his neck.

Aiden carried her to the bed, laying her down gently. Finally breaking the kiss, Aiden looked down into her bright blue eyes, getting lost in the ocean within.

Looking up into Aiden's glowing eyes, Mina felt safe. Mina felt happy.

"Thank you... Master." Mina whispered.

"Not Master..." Aiden finally corrected her.

"Mate." Aiden said, as he kissed her again.

Mina smiled through the kiss as she cried tears of joy.

~ ~ ~ ~ ~

"So... Mina is confused." Mina said, laying on top of Aiden. "Master is a Werewolf?"

"Yes." Aiden answered.

"But, Master is also Vampyre?" she asked.

Aiden nodded.

"Also Hellhound and Vampuric?"

"Yes, Mina, I am a hybrid." Aiden said, trailing his fingers up and down Mina's bare back as she lay on top of him, eliciting a shiver from the catgirl.

"How? Mina doesn't understand. Did Master get bit?"

"No, I wasn't bit, I was born this way." Aiden explained.

"Can Mina see Master's fangs?" the catgirl asked.

Aiden allowed his fangs to slip out as he grinned up at Mina.

Mina smiled after a few moments.

"Mina likes Master's fangs."

"Just my fangs?" Aiden asked, raising an eyebrow as Mina began to draw patterns on his chest with her nails.

Mina blushed as she shook her head.

"No, Mina likes all of Master."

Mina began rubbing her face against Aiden's chest, relishing in his scent.

"Master is perfect." she purred.

After a few minutes, Mina yawned, before shaking her head, trying to stay awake.

"What's wrong?" Aiden asked.

"Mina is tired." the catgirl answered.

"And this is a bad thing?"

Mina nodded.

"You don't want to go to sleep?" he asked.

Mina shook her head vigorously.

"Why not?"

"Mina is scared." she replied.

"Of what?" Aiden sat up, holding Mina in his arms.

"Mina is scared that if Mina goes to sleep, Mina will wake up and Master will have been just a dream." she says quietly, holding onto Aiden tightly.

"It's ok." Aiden whispered into her ear. "I'm not going anywhere. I promise."

"Master will still be here when Mina wakes up?" Mina looks up at him, a silent question lingering in her eyes.

"Yes, I will. Get some rest, I'll be here when you wake."

Shifting in his arms, Mina began to let herself fall asleep.

"Master will stay with Mina?" Mina mumbled.

"Always." Aiden whispered.

Mina didn't hear him answer, as she had already fallen asleep in his arms, feeling safe for the first time in seven months.

Aiden sighed as he laid back down, bringing the sleeping catgirl with him. Being careful not to wake her, realizing this was probably the first time in months she hasn't fallen asleep afraid. Aiden lay there listening to the sound of Mina breathing against him, feeling the coolness of her skin pressed up against his, and the soft swish of her tail as it brushed his leg, finally falling asleep himself.

~ ~ ~ ~ ~

Aiden woke up feeling a sharp pain in his side. looking down, he saw that Mina had accidentally scratched him in her sleep. Aiden smiled, deciding a little discomfort on his part was worth Mina getting a good night's sleep. No longer tired, but refusing to risk disturbing the sleeping girl laying across him, Aiden just lay there watching her sleep, her ears twitching every now and then.

Aiden heard someone quietly open the flap of the tent.

Looking over, Aiden saw Siri silently slip into the tent, shutting it behind her.

Aiden held his finger to his lips, letting her know Mina was still asleep.

Making her way across the room, Siri smiled at Aiden, not bothered by the naked girl draped over his chest. Siri held up a small bundle in her arms, showing it to Aiden before pointing at Mina. Aiden nodded to her before Siri placed it on the table and exited the tent as silently as she entered.

Thirty minutes later, Mina began to stir, showing signs of life.

Mina had draped herself across Aiden during the night, resting her head against his opposite shoulder.

Keeping her eyes closed, a still groggy Mina went to stretch, only to realize she wasn't alone. The sudden realization caused her to stiffen.

Mina sniffed a few times, recognizing Aiden's scent, before hugging herself closer to him as she relaxed and opened her eyes.

"Master kept his promise." Mina said sleepily, with a slight smile.

As she lifted her head out of Aiden's shoulder, Mina looked down at Aiden. After a few seconds, Aiden reached up, guiding her down for a kiss.

Breaking the kiss, Aiden looked into her bright, sapphire eyes.

"Still think I'm just a dream?" he asked.

Mina shook her head as she slowly climbed off Aiden, allowing him to sit up.

"I'd like you to meet somebody today, if that's okay with you."

"Does Master mean the elf girl?" Mina asked nervously.

"You know about her?"

Mina nodded her head before speaking.
"Mina can smell her on Master's bed." she answered quietly.

Aiden wanted to say something, but his mind just kept drawing a blank. Aiden didn't know what to say.
After a few moments Aiden turned to look at Mina. Mina sat on the bed, looking at Aiden, her bottom lip quivering, not knowing what Aiden's silence meant.
"Come here." Aiden opened up his arms for her.
Mina climbed into his lap as she melted into his arms, face buried in his chest.
"You don't have to worry about me liking her more than you." Aiden said soothingly, running his fingers through her hair.
"Mina doesn't?" she asked, looking up into his eyes.
"Mina, do you know what a mate bond is?" Aiden asked.
"Mina knows." A smile formed on her face, happy she was right about him.
Several seconds later, Mina's eyes widened in realization.

Pulling herself slightly away from Aiden, Mina looked him in the eyes.
"Master has multiple mates?"
"Does that bother you?" Aiden asked, worried.
Mina thought for a moment before answering.
"No."
Aiden was shocked by her response.
"It doesn't?"
"It is normal for Nekomata males to take multiple females." Mina paused, taking a moment to think.

"Mina will share Master with the elf... but no more."
Mina looked down at her lap before continuing. "Mina doesn't want to compete for Master's attention."

She whispered so quietly, Aiden barely managed to hear her.

"No more... I promise." Aiden reached up, cupping her face in his hand.

"The two of you are more than enough for me."

Mina nuzzled his hand happily.

"Mina would like to meet her sister mate." Mina said after a few moments.

"But Mina is still worried sister mate will not like Mina... will think Mina is trying to steal Master for herself." Mina said sadly.

"I wouldn't worry about that." Aiden took Mina's hands in his as he stood up from the bed.

"She is the one who told me to go to you yesterday."

"Elf girl is ok sharing Master with Mina?" Mina was surprised as she followed Aiden over to the table.

"She even left this for you." Picking up the bundle that Siri had dropped off earlier, he handed it to Mina.

Opening the package, Mina's eyes widened as tears began forming in her eyes.

Inside, was a beautifully made, loose fitting black dress, with thin straps at the shoulders. The inner lining of the dress made of satin, with outer layers of thin, transparent black silk that flowed from the waist, all the way to the ground. It even had a hole for her tail to fit through!

Mina could only stare at it for a few moments until Aiden stepped behind her, wrapping his arms around her waist as he whispered in her ear.

"It's beautiful."

Mina nodded.

"Want to try it on?"

"Mina wants to..."

"What is it?" he asked.

Mina turned to look at Aiden.

"Mina wants to wear it. Mina wants to have Master admire Mina in it. But not villagers... villagers don't deserve to see Mina like that. Only Master." she told Aiden.

Chuckling with relief, Aiden bent down and kissed Mina's nose. "Very well, what do you want to wear instead?

Mina looked around momentarily before looking back at Aiden, a shy smile on her face.

# Chapter 25

Stepping out of the tent, Aiden glanced around looking for Siri, finding her twenty yards away, sitting on a wooden crate looking through some of the supplies.

Noticing him, Siri stood up and walked over to Aiden, pulling him down for a kiss before talking.

"So how's our girl this morning?" Siri asked, despite it already being past noon.

"What? I didn't want to wake her up. I figured she needed the sleep. Besides, I was kind of trapped if you hadn't noticed." Aiden said with a wide grin on his face.

"Oh, I noticed." Siri teased.

"And I'm sure the "view" had nothing to do with you not wanting to wake her." she added with a smirk and a raised eyebrow.

"I don't know... the view's pretty nice from out here too." Aiden replied, admiring the bright green dress she was wearing.

Rolling her eyes as she laughed, Siri looked past Aiden at the tent.

"She wants to meet you." Aiden stepped behind Siri, grabbing her waist.

"Really?" Siri looked back at him, surprised.

"She also loved the dress."

"Is she going to wear it?" Siri's voice filled with excitement.

"No."

"Why not?" she asked, frowning.

"She loved the dress and wants to wear it, but thinks the villagers don't deserve to see her like that, and frankly, I agree with her." Aiden answered.

"I agree as well." Siri added after a few seconds.

"Hey Siri?"

"What is it?" Siri asked, looking up at Aiden as he held her.

"I know you and Mina are both my mates, but why didn't I experience the same thing when you and I first met?" Aiden asked. "How did we not realize we were mates earlier?"

"Well... our mate bond would have formed when you were still a human, and gradually grew stronger over time. That's why we didn't notice it. Humans and elves have a harder time noticing the effects of the mate bond at first, for them it is more gradual. But immortals are more sensitive to the mate bond... when they make the bond, it hits them in full force, all of it, all at once. That's what happened when you saw her for the first time, isn't it? That's why you reacted so strangely around her yesterday. Afterword, your body automatically picked up on her emotions and distress. That's why you act differently with her than you do with me. Your body instinctively knows what each of your mates need, and adapts to each one's individual needs." Siri squeezed Aiden's hand as he held her around the waist.

Aiden listened as Siri continued talking.

"You're an immortal now, it's part of who you are. Drinking my blood changed you... and the bond between us also grew stronger after you fed on me. I noticed it that night in the infirmary, I just never put the pieces together until yesterday."

Aiden lifted his hand, motioning to Andarii, who had been standing near the village entrance.

Andarii clasped his fist over his heart as he came up to Aiden.

"My Lord, you need something?"

"Mina is still terrified of this village, and I don't want to overwhelm her. Please make sure no one attempts to come near her. Even if they have good intentions, it's still a bit much for her to handle right now." Aiden told him.

"Not to worry sir, the three of you will not be bothered."

Andarii rushed off, giving orders to his men.

As Andarii's men established a perimeter around them, Aiden looked down at Siri.

"Ready to meet her?"

Siri nodded.

Letting go of Siri's waist, Aiden walked back over to the tent, opening the flap slightly.

Reaching his hand out, Siri watched a small hand reach out and take his. Slowly, Mina emerged from the tent, clutching Aiden's hand in a death grip, eyes scanning the environment for danger. Siri noticed that Mina was wearing one of Aiden's shirts, her tail swishing behind her nervously.

Mina locked eyes with Siri and neither girl moved for a minute or so. Mina, out of fear, and nervousness, and Siri, because she didn't want to spook the girl.

After a while, Aiden leaned in, whispering something into Mina's ear. Mina turned to him, and Aiden gave her a peck on the lips before nodding in Siri's direction. Siri watched as Mina started walking towards her, slowly, and with trembling legs, never letting go of Aiden's hand as he led her over to Siri.

Now standing just a few feet apart, Siri slowly held her hands out in front of her.

Mina, not being sure what to do, looked up at Aiden. He nodded, letting go of Mina's hand as he slid himself behind her, wrapping his arms around her waist for encouragement.

Slowly, Mina reached out her trembling hands and placed them in Siri's.

Siri gently squeezed Mina's hands as she gave her a warm smile.

"I'm Siri." Siri said gently.

"M.. Mina." the catgirl stuttered. Pulling her hands out of Siri's, she began fidgeting with the hem of the shirt she was wearing.

"That shirt looks nice on you."

"It smells like Master." Mina said quietly as she looked at the ground. "Mina is sorry for not wearing the dress you gave her."

Mina shifted her weight uncomfortably from one foot to the other, Aiden's thumb gently caressing her abdomen, calming her.

"It's ok." Siri said, already knowing why she didn't want to wear it. "Besides, I think a dress that pretty should only be worn for the man you love. Am I right?"

Mina quickly nodded her head in agreement.

"Let's sit down." Aiden said, leading Mina and Siri over to a nice patch of grass. Aiden sat down first, pulling Mina into his lap as Siri sat next to them.

For the next few minutes, Siri tried to make small talk, but only got the occasional nod or shake of the head from Mina. Aiden held Mina against his chest, occasionally kissing her shoulder and collarbone.

Mina finally built up the courage to ask Siri what she had been wanting to ask, but couldn't look Siri in the eye as she asked.

"Are you mad at Mina?" Mina asked quietly.

"Why would I be mad at you?" Siri asked, puzzled by Mina's question.

"Mina stole your mate, Mina is sorry."

Mina looked up at Siri with a guilty expression.

Siri smiled warmly back at Mina. Reaching over, Siri placed her hand gently onto Mina's thigh.

"Like I told Aiden when we found out you were also his mate, I'm a big girl.. I can share." Siri said in a reassuring tone.

Hearing the word share triggered something in Mina, her eyes going wide as she tried to scramble out of Aiden's lap.

"Mina is sorry... Mina is hogging Master all to herself.. Mina is supposed to share Master with sister mate. Mina is sorry!"

The catgirl began to panic, her body trembling.

Aiden held on tightly, pulling Mina back into his lap as he nuzzled his face into Mina's neck, kissing her as he began purring. The sound washed over her, causing her to relax, melting against him, calming her.

Siri sat patiently waiting for Aiden to calm her before speaking again.

"You're not hogging him at all Mina. You have just as much right to be close to him as I do... I've had Aiden all to myself for the last three years... you still have a lot of catching up to do." Siri brushed a strand of Mina's hair that had fallen out of place during the struggle back into place.

Mina stared at Siri in shock.

"Sister mate is not mad at Mina? Not jealous of Mina?" Mina looked back and forth from Siri to Aiden.

"How can I be mad? I know what it feels like to have a mate bond with Aiden too. I can't be jealous of you feeling the same things as me, and denying you, would also hurt Aiden, and that's something I refuse to do."

Mina began to cry as she looked up at Aiden, feeling the safety of his strong arms around her. His scent felt like home... this was where she belonged, and she never wanted to leave, having found what she had been missing all this time.

"Mina loves Master, Mina never wants to leave Master's side." the catgirl said.

"I can work with that... as long as I get his other side." Siri said with a grin.

Mina nodded her head before turning and curling up in Aiden's lap, falling asleep.

# Chapter 26

"Mina, wake up... Mina."

"Tired Master... Mina want to sleep, Master promised." Mina tried to ignore Aiden's fingers tracing her jaw, before pawing at his hand to leave her alone.

"Mina, I have food." Aiden whispered into her ear.
"Food?" Mina asked, her ears perking up.
Mina's eyes shot open as she sat upright in bed, her tail swishing back and forth in excitement.

It had been three days since Johrra had given Mina something to eat, and Mina was starving.
Looking over, Mina saw Aiden sitting on the edge of the bed. After meeting Siri, Mina was exhausted, so Aiden had carried her back to the bed so she could rest.

Mina looked at Aiden, sniffed the air, and then pouted.
"Master lied to Mina." Mina said, lowering her head, worried that Aiden might not give her food, just like Johrra.
She was so hungry and didn't want to miss another meal.
"Mina, I didn't lie." Aiden said, as Mina looked up at him excitedly.
"But first, I have a question. After you answer, we can eat, ok?" Reaching his hand towards her, Mina began to nuzzle it.

Mina quickly nodded, as her stomach growled.

"Did Johrra deny you food?" Aiden asked.

"Yes Master, he said food was expensive, told Mina to be grateful for what he did give her. Mina sometimes, didn't get food for days, and only getting scraps when Mina was allowed to eat."

"How long since your last meal?" Aiden asked, afraid of the answer.

"Three days." Mina answered, tears in her eyes.

"Mina is very hungry, Master."

Aiden gently cupped Mina's chin, making her look at him.

"I will never deny you food Mina. From now on, if you are hungry, tell me and we will get some food, I don't care what time it is, or if we have already eaten. Ok?

"Thank you Master... Mina is hungry now." Mina looked at him, hopeful.

'Let's eat." Aiden said, holding out his hand. Mina took it, following him out of the tent into the early night air.

As they stepped outside, the smell of cooked meat, as well as all kinds of food found its way to Mina's nose.

Just outside the tent, a series of tables had been set up and prepared. Originally, Queen Linorra wanted to hold a banquet to honor Aiden before they left, but Aiden refused, saying it might be too much excitement for Mina. Instead, the whole village came together to cook the best dishes they had to offer, wanting to provide a good meal for the group of them, then giving them their privacy.

Many of the villagers took special care to make things they thought Mina would enjoy, knowing Aiden wouldn't treat her the way Johrra had.

Mina's mouth watered at the sight of so much food.

"Is all this for Mina?" she asked, looking at Aiden.

"All for Mina."

Aiden watched as Mina took a few steps towards the table, unsure of what to eat first. Suddenly, Mina's tail started swishing around erratically as she noticed something on the table. Walking up behind her, Aiden whispered in her ear.

"Find something interesting?"

Mina pointed to a spot at the end of the table, where a large plate of grilled fish had been placed.

"Go ahead, eat as much as you want." Aiden said as Mina rushed over to the plate of fish, taking the whole plate before sitting down at a nearby table.

A set of four long tables had also been set up with nothing on them.

Aiden picked himself out some food as well, before joining Mina. Siri joined them a few moments later with her own plate of food.

Looking at Mina, Aiden was grateful to the villagers for making Mina so happy right now.

"Are you going to eat all of those, or can I have one?" Aiden asked Mina, seeing as she had already eaten half of the plate of fish and showed no signs of stopping, or slowing down.

Mina shyly picks one up and hands it to Aiden before going back to work on the plate of fish.

Aiden laughed, then he and Siri started to eat as well. After several minutes, Mina looked up from the table. Not a single fish had been spared.

As she looked around at all the food remaining, Mina leaned over and whispered into Aiden's ear. Aiden looked at her for a few seconds before nodding.

Mina stood up from the table, followed by Aiden. Her legs were shaking as she made her way away from the table towards the entrance to the village, holding Aiden's hand for courage.

"I can do it; you don't have to." Aiden offered, only for Mina to shake her head at him.

"Mina wants to do it." she replied.

Andarii spotted them moving towards him at the entrance to the village and was about to walk up to see what Aiden needed when Aiden motioned for him to stay where he was.

Reaching Andarii, Mina stood in front of him, holding onto Aiden with one hand, and fidgeting with the hem of her shirt with the other while staring at the ground.

"S.. sir?" Mina finally said.

"What can I do for you my lady?" Andarii asked.

"M.. Master says y.. you and your men p.. protect Master, Siri and M.. Mina while we sleep?" Mina asked, still looking at the ground.

"That's right my lady." Andarii looked at Aiden questioningly.

Aiden just shrugged his shoulders, nodding towards Mina.

"M...Mina w...wanted to in... invite you and y... your men to e... eat with us." Mina finally managed to say as she looked up.

Andarii smiled warmly as he answered.

"We would be honored to join you, my lady."

# Chapter 27

As the night went on, Aiden stood off to the side of the banquet table, leaning against a tree as he watched Siri, Andarii, and the rest of his men having a good time at the feast. Even Mina was having a good time. Although she rarely spoke or lifted her head, her happily swishing tail told Aiden she was enjoying herself for once.

Deciding to let the girls have their fun, Aiden turned around and walked into the forest.

Aiden didn't get very far into the wood line before he heard someone following him.

"Master?"

Aiden turned to see Mina standing at the edge of the trees, staring at him.

"Where is Master going?" Mina asked.

"I was just going for a quick walk... you want to come with me?"

Mina perked up as Aiden asked that question.

"Mina would like to go with Master, but if Master would rather be alone... Mina understands."

Mina fidgeted with the satchel around her waist, hoping Aiden would take her with him.

Aiden held out his arms, letting Mina step forward as he wrapped his arms around her.

"Company would be nice."

Together, they turned and walked into the woods.

~ ~ ~ ~ ~

Aiden and Mina had been walking for some time, just enjoying the sounds of the forest as well as each other's company when the pair came across an opening in the trees.

"Master look!" Mina said excitedly as they stepped out of the trees.

In front of them was a small, beautiful lake. This lake really stood out compared to others that Aiden had seen.

As the terrain transitioned from forest to beach, the sand was neither white, tan, brown, or any other color Aiden was used to seeing on a beach. Instead the sand was a very dark black, with hints of white and green mixed in, making the sand seem to shimmer in the moonlight overhead. The sand was not coarse like regular sand, almost like a finely ground powder, extremely soft to the touch. There were large outcroppings of rock scattered around the beach made of a similarly colored black stone, with white veins running through them that glowed softly, as if absorbing the moonlight, that could easily be used to sit on. The water was a deep, crystal blue, and a soft glow seemed to come from beneath the surface, making the whole lake give off a dim glow. In the center of the lake was a small island. With the bright moon overhead, the whole place had an ethereal look to it.

Both Mina and Aiden just stared at the lake for a few moments.

"Master, it's so pretty." Mina said, marveling at the place they had found. "Come on Master!"

Mina grabbed Aiden's arm and began pulling him towards the lake excitedly.

Mina pulled Aiden over to one of the strange black stones.

"What is this place, Master?"

Aiden sat down on one of the black stones. Mina sat down in his lap as he held her.

"I've never seen anything like it." Aiden told her. "It's beautiful."

Aiden looked out across the water, watching small lights flick back and forth just above the water's surface.

"Thank you for letting Mina come with Master." Mina said.

Mina leaned back against Aiden, getting comfortable. A few minutes felt like hours as they sat there just admiring the scenery.

"Mina has a present for Master." Mina stood up, turning to look at Aiden.

"Really?"

Aiden tried to stand up, only for Mina to place her hand on his chest.

"Master stay here, wait for Mina." the catgirl said, rushing off behind a larger rock nearby, clutching the satchel in her hands.

"Are you gonna tell me what this present is?" Aiden asked, as Mina hid herself behind the rock.

"Uh-uh, it's a secret." Mina said from behind the rock.

His curiosity getting the better of him, Aiden started to stand up to follow her, only for Mina to poke her head out and catch him.

"No peeking Master!" Mina yelled at him, making him sit back down.

"Mina doesn't want Master spoiling Mina's surprise." she added, a bit quieter.

"Ok fine, I'll wait."

Mina nodded before pulling her head back behind the stone.

A few minutes later, Aiden heard Mina's soft voice call to him.

"Master?"

"What is it?"

"Master needs to close his eyes." Mina said shyly.

Aiden laughed but did as he was told.

"Are Master's eyes closed?"

"Master's eyes are closed." he answered.

"Master wont peek until Mina tells him to?" Mina asked, concerned.

Aiden could tell whatever this was meant a lot to Mina, and Aiden didn't want to spoil this for her.

"No peeking." Aiden said.

"Promise?"

"I promise Mina, I won't open my eyes until you tell me to." Aiden answered honestly.

Aiden heard her come out from behind the rock, but kept his eyes closed, listening as she walked closer to him.

"Master can open his eyes now." Mina said quietly.

As Aiden opened his eyes, his mouth fell open, and he was at a complete loss for words. Standing ten feet in front of him was the most beautiful sight he had ever seen.

Mina stood there wearing the black dress that Siri had bought her. The loose black dress accentuating her curves, contrasting with her pale skin. Her long, silky, raven hair hanging down, blowing slightly in the wind. The long transparent black lace flowed from her waist, down past her bare feet, trailing a few inches behind her. Her tail swayed nervously behind her. On her neck, she wore a thin black choker necklace that matched the dress. Her light pink lips pulled slightly apart, and bright, blue eyes stared back at him.

"Does Master like it?" Mina asked, shifting weight from one foot to the other, fidgeting with her hands, not knowing how to interpret Aiden's silence.

Finally managing to swallow the lump in his throat, Aiden stood up. Walking over to Mina, he placed his hands on her bare shoulders, causing her to shiver in response.

Slowly and tenderly, Aiden pulled Mina in for a kiss.

"I love it." Aiden whispered once they stopped kissing, making Mina smile.

Aiden reached down, taking Mina's hands as he led her down to the water's edge.

"What about Mina's dress?" Mina asked worriedly, not wanting to ruin the pretty dress.

Aiden smiled as he pulled his shirt off, tossing it to the side before pulling Mina close, whispering in her ear.

"I guess you'll just have to take it off." Aiden growled, slipping the straps of the dress off her shoulders, the dress pooling at her feet as she stepped out of it.

Aiden picked her up as she wrapped her legs around his waist. Her lips captured his in a deep longing kiss as he began to walk backwards into the water. Aiden made his way deeper into the lake, with Mina wrapped around his waist.

Mina broke their kiss when she felt the water touch her legs.

As they moved through the water, the water that was disturbed by their movement seemed to glow a bit brighter, leaving a trail of light from the shore where they had started. Once the water reached Aiden's chest, Mina looked at him with worry in her eyes.

"Master?" she squeaked, holding him a bit tighter.

What is it, love?" he asked, running his hands along her bare back.

"Mina can't swim Master."

Mina felt embarrassed, fearing she had ruined the moment.

"It's okay, just hold onto me, everything will be alright." Aiden replied, calmly and soothingly.

"Trust me?" Aiden asked, looking into her eyes.

Nodding her head and tightening her grip, Mina answered.
"Mina trusts you."
Aiden leaned back in the water, letting go of Mina's back so
that he could start swimming.

# Chapter 28

Siri noticed that both Mina and Aiden had disappeared from the banquet. Looking around and not finding them, Siri went back to the tent.

*"Not here either."* Siri said to herself.

Thinking of Aiden, Siri felt pulled towards the forest.

Siri followed that feeling for fifteen minutes, coming to the same lake Aiden and Mina had discovered.

Siri stopped to admire the lakeshore for a moment, then she noticed movement out in the water. Looking out into the water, Siri recognized the silhouette of Aiden and Mina in the water. Siri made her way down to the shore before spotting the dress she had given Mina in a heap near the water.

Siri smiled as she called out across the water.

"So this is where the two of you ran off to."

Aiden and Mina looked towards the shore and saw Siri standing there, waving at them.

"Sorry if we worried you." Aiden called out. "I decided to go for a walk and Mina asked to come with me. We ended up finding this place and decided to go for a swim."

"I can see that."

"Well? You gonna just stand there, or are you gonna join us?" Aiden asked sarcastically.

Siri quicky discarded her own garments, adding them to the already existing pile of clothes before jumping into the water and swimming out to Mina and Aiden.

As Siri got closer, Aiden saw the mischievous look in her eyes.

"Before you try anything."

Aiden swam out of reach of Siri, knowing what she was planning.

"Mina can't swim." Aiden said, causing Siri to give up on trying to dunk Aiden, realizing it would cause Mina to panic.

Siri swam up, giving Aiden a kiss before looking at Mina, who was using Aiden as her own personal boat.

"What are you doing out this deep if she can't swim?" Siri asked, treading water beside them.

"Master said he could swim for both of us." Mina said, blushing. "Mina is also having fun."

As the three continued to talk and swim, the flickering lights that Mina and Aiden saw earlier began to get closer. Tiny specks of light darting to and fro began surrounding them.

"What are they?" Aiden asked.

"They're beautiful." Siri said.

"They are water spirits." Mina answered.

"Water spirits?" Aiden looked up at the catgirl sitting on his chest.

Mina nodded before continuing.

"Yes, they come out at night here in the forest, dance on the water."

Mina reached her hand out as one zipped by.

"Are they dangerous?" Siri asked.

Mina shook her head.

"Mina's mother said water spirits are very pure, not capable of harm, but skittish, will rarely come near people." she said.

The three of them watched in awe as the lights flitted back and forth, dancing around them for a few minutes before wandering off to a different part of the lake to continue their dance.

Aiden now realized that they had swam almost all the way to the island.
"Want to explore the island?" he asked.
Mina and Siri both nodded their heads.
Siri got to the island first, since Aiden was carrying Mina.
As he got near shore, Aiden let Mina down.

As the three walked up a small path, shielded from the outside by a group of trees, was a small cabin. At first, Aiden was worried someone might see them, but quicky realized this place hasn't had visitors in years.
As they neared the cabin, Aiden noticed a small forge in the yard, as well as some of the stone from the shore. A pile of wood was stacked beside the cabin, and the cabin itself seemed to be in very good condition. He stared at the cabin for a few moments, feeling like he had been here before.
"I know this place." Aiden said, getting Siri and Mina's attention.
"You've been here before?" Siri asked.
"Not me, the Hybrid." Aiden shook his head as he stepped up to the door.
Opening the cabin, Aiden found there was surprisingly little dust inside, despite it being abandoned for so long. The cabin was practically empty other than a small table, a single chair, and a small bedroll. A desk sat against the wall next to the bedroll.

Aiden, Siri and Mina began looking around the interior of the cabin.
"Did the Hybrid live here?" Siri asked.

"No, I think this was a getaway, and based on the tools and forge outside... I think this place was also used for crafting." Aiden answered, going through the desk.

Inside the bottom drawer of the desk, Aiden found a false bottom.

"I think I found something." he said, pulling a stack of papers, and a few scrolls from the drawer.

After confirming there was nothing left inside the small cabin, Aiden decided it was about time to return to the village for the night.

Leaving the cabin, the group made their way back down to the water.

"Master, how will we keep these dry?" Mina held up the papers they had found.

"I have an idea." Aiden said, turning to the two girls.

"Are you sure?" Siri asked, realizing what Aiden was planning.

"Yes, take Mina back to the cabin until I'm done."

"What is Master doing?" Mina asked, as Siri tried to lead her away.

"Come on Mina, let's go."

"No, Mina will stay." Mina said, pulling free of Siri.

Aiden stepped up to the girls, placing his hands on Mina's shoulders and looking her in the eye.

"Mina, if I let you stay... I need you to not interfere. Can you do that?"

"What is Master going to do?"

"I'm going to shift... It's extremely important that you do not interrupt me during the shift."

"Mina understands, but why does Master not want Mina to see Master shift?"

"Because, I don't want to frighten you." Aiden answered. "The shift is also extremely painful for me, and I don't always have full control while shifting, and I don't want to hurt you." Aiden answered, taking Mina's hands.

"Mina understands... Master doesn't want Mina to see Master in pain." Mina squeezed Aiden's hands.

"Mina can handle it. Mina is also not afraid to see Master shift. Mina is not afraid of Master. Mina trusts Master, and will not leave Master alone when Master is in pain." Mina told Aiden.

"Are you sure?"

"Master did not leave Mina when Mina was in pain." she whispered, remembering how Aiden stopped the master's collar, putting himself at risk to save her, and staying by her side as she cried.

"It's going to be difficult to watch."

Mina shook her head, determined. "Mina wants to watch."

"Ok, you can stay." Aiden let go of Mina as he took a few steps back.

Aiden began taking off the trousers he was still wearing.

"Why is Master getting undressed?" Mina asked Siri, who stood beside her, taking her hand.

"Because if I don't, I will rip out of them as I shift." Aiden answered, tossing them over to Siri.

Aiden closed his eyes, preparing for what came next.

*"This won't be like the other times I've shifted"* he told himself.

*"Each time I have shifted, it has been with the help of anger, or an outside force causing me to shift. But this time, I won't have anger to help me through it, nor a desperate need for power to give me focus. This time, the shift will have to be voluntary."*

Aiden clenched his teeth as the bones in his body began to break one by one.

Mina held Siri's hand tightly as she watched Aiden fall to his knees, as the bones beneath the skin began to break and reshape themselves. She wanted to step forward and hold him, but Siri's tight grip on her hand held her in place.

Mina had watched Aiden shift the first time they met, but she had been so frightened of everything going on that day, that she hadn't noticed the effect shifting had on Aiden. Now, Mina understood why Aiden didn't want her to see him shift. It was the worst pain imaginable... and it was not quick.

Aiden felt the pain each time a bone ripped itself apart as they changed shape. The ligaments and tendons attached to those bones snapped like rubber bands, only to reattach themselves, before snapping again, the muscles literally tearing themselves apart as they changed size and shape.

Slowly, Aiden's body began to change shape as he forced himself to continue shifting, his skin darkening, as thick black fur began to cover his body. Aiden hunched over... hands tipped with claws digging into the soil as two giant wings forcibly ripped themselves out from beneath the skin.

After several grueling minutes of shifting, the pain in Aiden's body stopped as the transformation was completed.

Seeing that the shift was complete, Siri let go of Mina's hand as Mina rushed forward, hugging him tightly.

"Does it always hurt Master this much?" Mina asked, crying.

Feeling Aiden's hot breath on her ears, Mina looked up just in time to feel Aiden rub his face against hers. His way of telling her he was alright as he wrapped her in his large arms.

Aiden felt his wings stretch out behind him as he let go of Mina and stood up.

Flapping his wings a few times to test their strength, Aiden was confident that this would work. Looking over at Siri, he motioned her over.

As she approached, Aiden got on one knee.

Realizing what he wanted, Siri climbed onto Aiden's back, nestled between his wings as she held onto his neck. Aiden picked Mina up in his arms as he stood back up, facing the water.

Siri held on tighter as she felt the muscles in Aiden's back flex as his wings moved, preparing for what came next. Aiden looked down at Mina in his arms to make sure she was ready.

Mina gave Aiden a small nod.

Aiden crouched down as low as he could go, looking up at the sky, he tightened his grip on Mina, being careful with his enhanced strength so as not to hurt her. Pushing off as hard as he could, the three of them were propelled a good ten meters into the air as Aiden's wings opened, catching the air.

Although difficult, Aiden found he was able to carry them across the lake. His body instinctively knowing what to do and how to fly. What he didn't know, however, was how to land.

As Aiden's feet hit the ground, his legs buckled, and his forward momentum caused him to pitch forward, losing his balance.

Letting go of Mina's legs, Aiden braced his arm in front of himself while still holding onto Mina. All the weight of the crash was absorbed by Aiden's arm, preventing him from falling on top of Mina as Siri was thrown off his back, bouncing over his head as she landed in the soft black sands of the lakeshore.

Aiden began shifting back to his human form.

While still painful, shifting back was always easier and quicker for Aiden. Once started, his body would continue the shift on its own without being forced.

Looking down beneath him, Aiden checked to make sure Mina was alright.

"You ok?" Aiden asked as Mina began to giggle.

"That was fun Master." Mina smiled up at Aiden.

"Speak for yourself." Siri said, brushing sand off herself as she stood up.

"You're not the one who got thrown off."

Siri threw Aiden's trousers at him, hitting him in the face.
Mina just stuck her tongue out at Siri as she walked up.
Both girls began laughing.

"Ok, let's get dressed and head back." Aiden said, standing up.

# Chapter 29

Aiden woke to the now common sensation of being pinned down. Looking over to his right, Siri was curled up beside him, one leg draped across his legs, with one of her arms across his chest, her head resting against his shoulder. On top of him, lay Mina, the full weight of her body pressing down on his torso, with her face buried in his neck opposite Siri.

Aiden found it strange that this all felt completely normal to him. looking down at the two sleeping girls, Aiden smiled.

Aiden looked at Siri.
Siri was his anchor... always understanding, ever inquisitive. She kept Aiden calm when his emotions ran wild. Not afraid to call him out if needed, even though it infuriated him. Siri was intelligent, always looking for the bigger picture. She was his link to his humanity.

Aiden then looked at Mina.
While Siri was his anchor, Mina.. was his treasure, driving his need to protect. So full of insecurity and fear, Mina brought out the softer side of Aiden, a side Aiden didn't know he had till he met her, but also a strength he didn't know he possessed. Mina understood the animal side of Aiden better than Siri, coaxing it to the surface much more frequently. She connected him to his animal side.

Aiden stared up at the ceiling, finally feeling whole, wondering how he ever survived before they came into his life.

Aiden closed his eyes for a few moments before feeling a sharp pain in his neck.

Aiden winced, followed by Mina giggling.

"Morning Master." Mina said, sitting up as Aiden saw a drop of blood on Mina's lip.

"Did you just bite me?" Aiden asked, staring at her.

"Now why would Mina do that?" the catgirl said, wearing a wicked grin on her face.

"Ok, you asked for it... come here!" Aiden reached for her as Mina squealed, trying to get away from him as she crawled across the bed.

"Not fast enough." Aiden said, grabbing her by the ankle, dragging her back across the bed.

"Sister mate help!" Mina screamed as Aiden pinned her beneath him.

"Don't look at me, you brought this on yourself." Siri mumbled, rubbing the sleep from her eyes after being woken up.

"You look good enough to eat." Aiden whispered into Mina's ear before looking into her eyes, his fangs showing through his smile.

Mina's eyes widened before baring her neck to Aiden in submission.

"Go ahead, Master." Mina whispered.

No longer worried about his thirst, or having any fear of hurting Mina or Siri, Aiden bent down and kissed Mina's collarbone before sinking his fangs into her. As Mina relaxed beneath him, Aiden released his grip on her.

Taking the opportunity, Mina leaned her head forward and sank her own teeth into the space between Aiden's collarbone and neck.

Aiden groaned, but kept drinking for a few more seconds before pulling away once Mina stopped biting him.

"What was that for?" Aiden asked as he kissed Mina, licking his blood from her lips.

"Master is Mina's mate. Mina marked Master... now everyone will know Master belongs to Mina."

The catgirl smiled as she touched the newly formed scar on Aiden's neck.

Looking over at Siri, Mina smiled.

"Sister mate should mark Master as well." Mina enthusiastically tried waving Siri over.

"I'm not biting him." Siri said, coming over and giving Aiden a quick kiss before heading off to get dressed.

"But how will people know Master is yours if you do not mark him?" Mina asked, concern in her voice.

"What are you talking about?" Siri asked, coming back over to the bed and sitting next to Mina.

"When one finds their mate, they mark each other, to show others you are taken... and that your mate is also taken. It is a symbol of their love." Mina touched her own neck where Aiden had just bit her.

"It is important... not just a mark. It connects them, makes mate bond stronger."

Aiden looked at Mina's neck to see that there was now a small scar on Mina's neck as well.

"Why didn't it heal like it usually does?" Aiden asked, gently fingering the scar on Mina's neck.

"Because Master marked Mina." she replied, smiling as she touched the mark Aiden gave her.

"Mina saw it in Master's eyes before Master bit Mina... Master wanted to claim Mina as mate, to mark Mina as his."

Sitting up, Mina looked at Siri as tears began to form in her eyes.

"Does sister mate not want Master's mark?" the catgirl asked, as tears began to flow.

"Does she reject mate bond with Master? Does she not love Master?" she cried as Siri pulled her into a tight hug.

"I'm sorry Mina, I didn't know... I didn't realize how important it was. Please don't cry, I'm not going to reject the mate bond." Siri looked over Mina's shoulder at Aiden, nodding her head.

"Then will sister mate mark Master now?" Mina asked, wiping tears from her eyes.

"Yes, I will." Siri replied, as Mina moved out of the way.

Scooting closer to Aiden, Siri looked into Aiden's eyes. She too, now saw what Mina was talking about, the animal just beneath the surface. Siri instinctively bared her neck in submission, just as Mina had done.

Pulling her close, Aiden kissed Siri on the collarbone as well, before sinking his fangs into her, marking her as his. As Aiden pulled away, Siri reached up and sank her own teeth into Aiden's neck, marking him as hers.

~ ~ ~ ~ ~

Aiden sat on the bed as the two girls were getting dressed. Reaching up and touching the mark Mina had put on the left side of his neck, before moving his hand to the other side where Siri had left hers, Aiden couldn't help but smile.

Standing up, Aiden began getting ready for the day, changing into his traveling clothes, knowing they would be leaving the village this afternoon to continue on their journey. While he wanted to stay for Siri's sake, Aiden also knew he had to get Mina as far from this place as possible.

Stepping outside, Aiden was greeted by Queen Linorra, as well as Andarii.

"Knowing that the road ahead is going to be difficult…" Linorra said, walking up. "I have asked our master smith to commission some travelling armor for you and the girls."

She turned aside, allowing three of her servants to step forward. Each carried a set of light, elven plate armor.

"That's really not necessary." Aiden said.

"I know, but it's what my mother would have done. Besides, I'll sleep better knowing that you and the girls have some decent protection." Linorra answered.

"Thank you, I appreciate it."

"Speaking of protection." Andarii said, turning to the queen.

"My queen, I ask that when they leave the forest, that I may be allowed to remain with them." Andarii knelt on one knee.

"You want to go with us?" Aiden asked.

"If my Lord would have me, I would pledge my life and sword to his service."

"I think that's a great idea." Siri said, exiting the tent, followed by Mina.

"Agreed." Queen Linorra said, turning to Andarii. "I Linorra, Queen of this tribe, hereby relieve you of your oath to me, and to this people." the queen proclaimed.

Andarii stood before going over to where Aiden was with Siri and Mina.

Kneeling before them, Andarii drew his sword. Holding the blade in front of him, Andarii gripped the blade with his off hand, running it along the edge, drawing blood.

"I, Andarii of the elves, hereby swear fealty to Lord Aiden, Lady Siri, and Lady Mina. To serve them in all things. To be their hand and their blade, to fight on their behalf... willing to lay down my life for theirs if necessary. From this moment on, until the day I die... or Lord Aiden releases me from my oath." Andarii spoke with a loud voice before sheathing his sword while remaining kneeled.

Taking a step forward, Aiden held out his hand for Andarii. Aiden spoke as he pulled Andarii to his feet.

"I Aiden, hereby accept the oath of fealty from Andarii of the elves. Likewise vowing to never abuse his loyalty... and to treat him with both the honor and dignity he is owed. Now rise."

Suddenly a horn sounded from the forest as a group of twenty hulking figures burst from the forest, weapons raised.

# Chapter 30

"Orcs!" one of the guards around the queen yelled, dragging her back into the camp, as the rest rushed forward.

"Take the girls inside, and watch over them!" Aiden told Andarii as he turned to face the group of orcs.

"My Lord, I can help." Andarii said.

"Protect them!" Aiden said, as one of the nearby guards tossed him a sword.

Aiden caught the sword just in time for him to quickly duck as the first orc swung a crude heavy piece of sharpened metal at Aiden.

Ducking below the barbaric weapon, Aiden brought his own sword up, cleanly cutting the orc's forearm off before rolling behind him, thrusting his blade back through the orc's spine and out his chest.

Chaos erupted all around the camp as Andarii pulled Siri and Mina into the camp just before they closed the gate.

~ ~ ~ ~ ~

Trees and buildings were burning as the sounds of battle raged all around the camp.

Aiden and the gate guard had dispatched the twenty orcs who had initially attacked, losing three guards in the process. Another wave of orcs came shortly after, this one with twice as many orcs.

Aiden realized that the elves would quickly get outmatched by the sheer brute strength of these hulking figures.

Dropping the sword, Aiden quickly began shifting. Doing so caught the orcs off guard, as many of them stopped fighting for a few moments as Aiden shifted.

As Aiden began to shift, Aiden felt a sense of control wash over him he had never felt before. Suddenly, he could consciously feel each and every muscle in his body, having perfect control over each one.

Aiden felt no pain as he shifted, letting out a deafening roar that caused several of the orcs to run in fear before Aiden tore into a group of the remaining orcs.

Siri and Mina stood atop the wall watching the fight take place, fearing for Aiden's life. Both girls gasped as Aiden dropped his sword and began shifting. Neither Siri nor Mina could believe what they were seeing. Aiden effortlessly shifted in the span of a few seconds. But that is not what shocked them. They expected Aiden to come out of his shift in his seven foot tall hybrid form, but instead, Aiden was on all fours, as a very large, black werewolf, without any wings. Siri could only stare while Mina gripped her arm.

*"This feels different."* Aiden thought, looking down at his hands, only to see paws instead of fingers.

In this form, Aiden was much sleeker, built for mobility and speed as he charged into the group of orcs. Grabbing one by the ankle with his mouth, Aiden disappeared into the woods dragging the orc behind him... only to reappear a few moments later, landing on the back of another orc, tearing into him with his claws before taking the orc's head into his jaws and twisting.

Dropping the orc's severed head, Aiden sped off into the brush.

A series of growls, screams, and the sound of tearing flesh could be heard all over the place as Aiden moved with inhuman speed, tearing into one enemy after another. The cheers of the elves echoed throughout the camp as they thought they had all but won the battle.

~ ~ ~ ~ ~

Only one orc remained, having been surrounded by several elves.

Though surrounded, no elf attempted to attack, as this orc easily killed any who got within range of him.

The elves parted as Aiden walked up to the group, blood dripping from his jaws, and splattered all over his fur. Once again, Aiden began shifting. Leaning back, Aiden's legs began to straighten, as his front legs cracked and rearranged themselves as he stood upright. Paws became clawed hands as a portion of the fur on his forearms, thighs, and stomach receded, leaving a dark grey skin.

The orc's eyes went wide as Aiden shifted into a hellhound. Aiden stared at the orc, eyes a bright red in a sea of swirling black.

The orc raised his heavy, crude, and rusted piece of metal that served as his sword above his head, bringing it down with all of his might, only for Aiden to catch it with two fingers.

The elves could not believe their eyes. Aiden had caught the sword with two fingers. The sheer strength it would take to do such a thing astounded them.

The orc let go of the sword, falling to his knees, resigned to his fate.

Tossing the sword aside, Aiden stepped up to orc, placing one clawed hand on his shoulder as he brought his other hand into the orc's stomach, claws piercing through his flesh as if it were nothing. Aiden curled his claws upwards as he lifted the orc's body, the orc's own weight causing Aiden's claws to push further up his abdomen, eviscerating him from the inside.

Aiden pulled his hand, coated in the orc's blood, from his abdomen, ripping his heart out before dropping it.

As the elves cheered, a distant sound came from the forest as a huge ogre burst through the trees.

"They brought an ogre!" one of the elves yelled as they fled.

Aiden looked up just in time for the ogre to slam his giant fist down on him.

Aiden attempted to block the blow just as he had the orc's sword, only to underestimate his own strength as his left arm shattered under the weight of the ogre's attack, just as a second ogre appeared.

Aiden was repeatedly slammed into the ground by the ogre's fists as he could barely fight back against such brute strength. The ogre picked up Aiden in its powerful oversized hands and began to crush him. Wanting the last thing he sees to be the ones he loved, Aiden looked over at Siri and Mina as his ribs began to break.

"Master!" Mina's voice rang out as vines burst from the ground around the ogre.

The vines snaked their way up the ogre's body, as other vines wrapped themselves around the ogre's wrists, prying its hands apart, forcing him to drop Aiden.

Minas eyes glowed, her hands stretched forth, commanding the vines. Mina screamed as the ground began to shake, splitting open beneath the ogre, the vines dragging the beast into the depths before closing.

Aiden's broken body lay on the ground as Siri and Mina jumped from the wall, racing to his side.

Mina grabbed Aiden as she cried, clutching him to her chest as Siri joined her.

"Master, you can't die, Mina just got you. Please don't leave Mina alone!" the catgirl cried, oblivious to everything around her.

Siri used a sword she saw on the ground to cut her wrist as she placed it to Aiden's lips.

"Drink Aiden, please drink." Siri whispered, tears in her eyes as Aiden didn't respond.

The second ogre turned and began charging at the three of them.

Aiden was barely conscious as he saw the ogre bearing down on them. The ogre's throat suddenly split open as it fell only a few feet from them, dead.

As Aiden's vision faded, he saw a hooded man walking towards them, sword in hand, eyes glowing a bright greenish blue.

"Looks like I arrived just in time." Raizel said as Aiden passed out.

# Chapter 31

"Two days! He's been asleep for two days!"

Aiden could hear Siri arguing with someone.
"You said he would be fine, so why hasn't he woken up yet?"
Siri screamed.

Aiden opened his eyes to find himself in the infirmary of the elven village. He shifted positions, only to find Mina was laying on the bed next to him.
"Master?"
Mina turned to look at Aiden as tears began streaming down her face.
"There's my girl." Aiden lifted his hand, gently rubbing her ear.
"Master!" Mina screamed, tackling him in a tight hug, her head knocking the wind out of him as she collided with his chest.
"Aiden... thank the gods you're alright!" Siri said, rushing over, joining the group hug.
"Never better." Aiden wheezed, trying to catch his breath as both girls were on top of him.
"Mina was so scared Master, please don't scare Mina like that anymore!" Mina wailed, hugging him as she nuzzled her face into his chest.

"Do I get to join the group hug?" Raizel asked from the doorway.
Aiden growled as Raizel interrupted the reunion.

"Another time perhaps." Raizel commented, stepping out and closing the door.

"Did you say I've been here for two days?" Aiden looked at Siri.

"Yes." Siri answered, taking Aiden's hand in hers.

"After the battle, you were badly injured. They brought you here for treatment. You were given blood, and Raizel said you would be fine after a few hours... but it's been two days." Siri told him as she kissed his hand.

"Raizel?" Aiden asked, not recognizing the name.

"He's the vampyre I was arguing with when you woke up."

"Wait, a vampyre is here?" Aiden asked, trying to sit up.

"Don't worry, he's not after us. I think he's been covering our tracks since we left Esenor, although I'm not sure why." Siri answered as Aiden relaxed a bit.

Aiden looked down at Mina.

"Mina, do you remember what happened out there?" He began rubbing her ears as she looked at him.

"Mina was so scared, saw Master getting hurt. Mina wanted it to stop. And then... vines answered Mina. Came to help... saved Master." Mina said.

"Have you ever done anything like that before?"

Aiden moved his hand from her ear to her cheek as she nuzzled into his palm.

"Never. Mina was too young to learn. Mother and father never taught Mina."

"Mina, you used magic." Aiden said.

"Mina knows. Nekomata are good at magic, but Mina doesn't know how Mina did it... never used magic before."

"Listen, magic has rules. What you did took extreme amounts of energy, it should have killed you." Aiden said, looking into her eyes.

"But Mina is fine." Mina looked at her own body, confused.

"Mina, I put the remainder of my own energy into your spell, letting it draw on my strength instead of yours."

"That's why you were asleep for two days, isn't it?" Siri asked, looking at them.

"Yes, my body was healed, but I hadn't recovered."

"Mina keeps hurting Master."

Aiden leaned down, hugging Mina to his chest, placing his chin on her head as he began to purr.

As Mina began to calm down, Aiden spoke.

"Feel better now?"

"Yes Master, thank you." Mina said.

"You didn't hurt me, ok? I wasn't hurt, just tired." Aiden said. "So, do either of you have anything to eat?"

"Mina will go get Master some food!"

Mina hopped off Aiden and left the room.

~ ~ ~ ~ ~

Leaving the room, Mina made her way down the hall. Rounding the corner, she bumped into Raizel.

"Watch where you're going girl." Raizel said, turning to face Mina.

"Apologies m.. mister. Mina was on her way to get Master some food, d.. didn't see you there." Mina tried to step around Raizel.

Raizel stepped in front of Mina, blocking her way.

"Fascinating... I thought all the Nekomata had been hunted to extinction... although I really shouldn't be surprised a few survived." Raizel said, grinning.

"Mina doesn't want trouble." Mina said, taking a step back, not liking the look he was giving her.

"What great luck to find a living, breathing Nekomata here in this forest."

The vampyre took a step towards her.

"Please let Mina past." Mina said quietly, trying to squeeze past him.

Raizel placed his arm against the wall, blocking her. Mina backed up against the wall as Raizel inched closer.

"It's been a few days, and I'm a bit thirsty. Care to help me out?" he asked, fangs glinting.

"No." Mina said, her body beginning to shake.

"It wasn't a question, girl." Raizel growled, leaning closer.

Mina hissed as she swiped at him with her claws.

Grabbing her wrist, Raizel roughly pinned it above her head against the wall.

"Stay quiet." Raizel ordered, forcing Mina to stop talking.

"A slave should know better than to try to strike their betters, now quit struggling." Raizel commanded, his eyes glowing.

Mina's body was frozen as she began to cry.

"Don't worry, I won't kill you, I just want a taste." Raizel said, leaning in towards Mina's neck.

"Master... help." Mina managed to whisper.

Raizel was caught off guard as Aiden tackled him, sending both himself and Raizel out the third story window.

~ ~ ~ ~ ~

Aiden landed on top of Raizel as they hit the ground, baring his fangs and slashing at him with his claws as Raizel kicked Aiden off himself.

The vampyre quickly dodged as Aiden got up and charged at him once again.

"What the hell is wrong with you Aiden?" Raizel yelled, flipping over Aiden, then landing a kick to Aiden's back, knocking him to the ground.

"You touched her! You tried to hurt her! I'll kill you!" Aiden screamed as he got up, charging again.

"Aiden, wait. It's not what you think."

Raizel sidestepped, grabbing Aiden's wrist as he tripped him, pinning his arm behind his back as Raizel held him against the ground.

"She's not yours! How dare you touch her!" Aiden yelled, struggling to free himself from the vampyre's grip.

Raizel knew that Siri was Aiden's mate. He had seen his mark on her as she spoke to him over the last few days. Therefore, Raizel never gave much thought to the Nekomata slave that always referred to Aiden as Master, while always shying away from people.

Looking down at Aiden struggling beneath him, Raizel noticed two distinct marks on either side of Aiden's neck. One was a crescent moon shape, clearly done by someone without fangs. Raizel knew that it was Siri's mark. On the other side, was a more jagged mark, done by something with fangs. A werewolf... or...

"*Crap.*" Raizel thought to himself, realizing Mina wasn't just a servant, and why Aiden was trying to kill him.

"Aiden, I'm sorry... I didn't realize she was your mate. I will never lay a finger on her again." Raizel said. "I'm letting go now."

Aiden's muscles relaxed slightly as Raizel released him and stood up.

Aiden stood, turning to face Raizel, fangs and claws still extended. Raizel held his hands to the side, palms out as Aiden stepped up to him.

"We good?" Raizel asked.

Aiden punched him in the face.

Raizel fell to one knee, not bothering to defend himself as Aiden continued to punch him over and over.

Raizel didn't resist, knowing he deserved what was happening. To touch another's mate without their consent was a strict taboo for immortals. But to feed from another's mate was an unforgivable offense, a crime punishable by death, and he had nearly done just that.

Raizel's face was bloody and bruised when Aiden finally stopped. Aiden's hand was broken from the force of the punches he had been throwing, fingers popping back into place as he stood over Raizel.

"If you ever so much as look at Mina or Siri the wrong way again, I will kill you." Aiden growled, kicking Raizel in the stomach before storming away, heading back into the infirmary to find Mina.

Aiden found Mina crumpled in a heap on the floor where Aiden had tackled Raizel, Siri doing her best to calm the girl as they held each other.

Seeing Aiden, Mina ran to him, jumping into his arms as she cried. Aiden picked her up as she wrapped her legs around his waist before taking Siri's hand and leaving the Infirmary.

As they exited the infirmary, several guards, as well as Andarii and Queen Linorra were running up.

"My Lord, your awake." Andarii said.

They looked at the crying Mina in Aiden's arms, as well as the bloodied Raizel who hadn't moved from where Aiden had beat him to a pulp.

"What happened here?" Linorra asked, only for Aiden to ignore them and continue walking, still fighting the urge to shift.

~ ~ ~ ~ ~

Once back inside the safety of their tent, Aiden laid Mina down on the bed. She had fallen asleep in his arms as he purred to her the entire way back.

Aiden and Siri walked over to the table and sat down. Aiden began to eat some food from the table as Siri seemed lost in her own thoughts.

Several minutes went by as they sat in silence.

"Your purr seems to have really calmed Mina down on the walk over here." Siri said, looking over at the sleeping catgirl.

"I think that is its purpose." Aiden said.

"Its purpose?"

Aiden sighed, leaning back in his chair. Closing his eyes, Aiden ran his fingers through his hair.

"I've been giving it quite a bit of thought lately." Aiden started to explain, as Siri got up and began rubbing his shoulders to ease his tension.

"While I can do it on command, my body does it on instinct whenever you or Mina are stressed."

Siri moved from his shoulders, to his chest, continuing her massage as Aiden's body began to relax beneath her fingers.

"It's not just a sound. It causes a physical reaction in both you and Mina, your bodies relax, any anxiety, fear, or stress just seems to melt away. It also causes you to instinctively want to draw closer to me."

"So it responds to stress?" Siri asked, walking around and sitting on Aiden's lap, facing him.

"Specifically, yours and Mina's."

"Because we are your mates?"

Aiden nodded.

"I believe its entire purpose is to help calm and control the emotions of our mates... as well as to gently lure them back into their mate's arms." Aiden said.

"That would make sense."

"Master is right."

Mina rubbed her eyes as she sat up in bed.

"You knew about it?" Aiden asked, as Mina joined them at the table.

Mina nodded her head as Siri got off Aiden's lap, sitting closer to Mina.

"It is known as the Calling. It is a common thing amongst both immortals, as well as beastkin... including Nekomata." Mina picked up some food and began to eat as well.

"What else do you know about it?" Aiden asked, wanting to learn all he could.

"Only males can use the calling." Mina said.

"They can use it to control and subdue their mate, through gentle coaxing of the mate bond. But can only be used through love. Love is what allows the calling to subdue their mate. That is why Master uses it when Mina or sister mate is upset. It will calm us and make us want to come back to Master's arms, to feel safe and loved. Even works from a distance."

Aiden sat quietly for a few moments, letting this new information sink in. Hearing that Aiden could use the calling to control Mina and Siri worried him.

"Master."

"What is it Mina?" Aiden asked.

"The calling is not malicious, Master. Mates still have free will, just helps bring mates together, to be united. Mina hopes Master will not quit using it, Mina enjoys it. The calling is greatest expression of love a female can feel from their mate." Mina said, knowing what was bothering Aiden.

Aiden got up and walked over to the bed. Turning to look at both girls, he allowed the calling to slip out. Mina and Siri looked at each other before smiling, then followed Aiden onto the bed.

# Chapter 32

Aiden and the girls had begun packing away supplies... Andarii also insisted on helping. There could be no more delays, too many things had happened here, and Aiden was anxious to leave this place behind them.

Aiden started a fire and began to prepare lunch for the group. Mina and Siri sat nearby, chatting. Aiden looked up from the fire just as Raizel rounded the entrance to the village, walking towards them.

Aiden kept a careful watch on Raizel as he approached. Seeing Mina and Siri, Raizel turned and headed towards them as Aiden quickly stood and followed. Just as Raizel was about to reach the girls, Aiden stepped in front of him, blocking his way.

"Not one step closer." Aiden warned, a deep growl escaping his throat as Mina hid behind him.

"I would like to apologize, Lady Mina, for attempting to feed off you." Raizel said, looking at the catgirl hiding behind Aiden.

Mina hissed at the vampyre, holding Aiden tightly.

"You have every right to be angry with me. I did not realize that you were Aiden's mate, nor about your past. I am sorry."

"Vampyre tried to hurt Mina, tried to take Mina's blood against her will. Mina will not forgive vampyre so easily." Mina hissed, her claws slightly digging into Aiden's arm as she peeked around him.

"You are right, even if you weren't his mate, what I tried to do was wrong. My curiosity got the better of me, it will never happen again, I swear." Raizel said, getting down on his knees, bowing his face to the ground..

"Just what curiosity did you have?" Aiden asked, his eyes glowing briefly, before feeling Siri take his hand in hers, helping to block Mina from Raizel.

"Mina's blood." Mina whispered.

"Aiden, do you know why the Nekomata were hunted down?" Raizel asked, before standing.

"Because they would not submit to the immortals." Siri answered.

"That's just the story the public was told." Raizel walked over and sat down by the campfire.

Aiden turned, pulling Mina into his arms as he let the calling wash over her.

"Ok without me for a few minutes?" Aiden asked, resting his chin on Mina's head.

Mina nodded, pulling away as Aiden walked over to Raizel.

"I see you have already discovered and learned to use the calling." Raizel stated.

Ignoring him, Aiden sat down.

"Why were the Nekomata hunted down?" he asked.

"For their blood." Raizel answered, looking at Aiden.

"It is said that the Nekomata are special, that their blood is unique. It has the ability to temporarily increase the strength of any immortal who feeds off it. During a time of war, as well as for just a lust for power, the Nekomata were hunted down, just for a taste of their blood."

"And you wanted that power for yourself?" Aiden's fists clenched at his sides.

"No, although a part of me is intrigued by the temptation of more power."

"Why else would you try to drink her blood?" Aiden demanded.

"I was curious if the legends were true. I simply wanted a small taste to satisfy my own curiosity... but she resisted."

"Of course she did!" Aiden yelled.

"You've felt it too, haven't you?" Raizel said, picking up a stick and tossing it into the fire.

"What?"

"All immortals feel it, that desire for domination, the instinct to chase when your prey runs... to relish in the hunt. The primal drive of an apex predator." Raizel continued. "The older you are, the easier it is to control... but it's still there."

Aiden knew all too well what Raizel was talking about.

"I had no intention of hurting her, I swear."

"After what you just said, how can I trust you won't just try again?" Aiden asked, giving Raizel a cold stare.

"You only just became an immortal, and are not familiar with our customs." Raizel began.

"The mate bond is sacred to immortals. Although still common, It is a rare occurrence. Only one in twenty-five immortals are lucky enough to find their mate. The link between mates is the most powerful driving force an immortal will ever experience. It allows them to literally feel each other, even over great distances. It also allows you to feel each other's emotions. With that bond, comes an overwhelming desire to guard, and protect... more powerful than a vampyre's thirst, or even a werewolf's blood lust and need to shift on a full moon. Wars have been started because of it."

Taking his eyes off the fire, Raizel looked at Aiden.

"Because of this, when an immortal discovers his mate, no matter who it is or where they come from, the two are allowed to be together. It is an extreme taboo amongst immortals to attempt to keep an immortal and his mate apart. Immortals cannot lay a hand on another's mate without their approval, and for an immortal to feed from another's mate is even worse, it is a crime that is punishable by death." Raizel finished.

"That's why you didn't fight back when I started hitting you earlier."

"Correct, I laid my hand on your mate without permission, and I nearly fed off her. For that, I would have had to give up my life had you not stopped me. For that, I am grateful... I swear to you, from this moment on, no harm will come to either of your mates by my hand."

Aiden nodded his head.

"I understand, but it's not me you will have to convince." Aiden glanced over at Mina and Siri.

"I'm aware." Raizel said, seeing where Aiden was looking.

"Why are you here?" Aiden asked after a few minutes of silence.

"I was once a close friend with Sebastien Arlet." Raizel answered.

"The original hybrid." Aiden stated.

"So you know the name... anyway, for centuries, I looked forward to my friend's return. He had told me his plan in great detail. I know awakening your powers has prevented him from fully returning in your body. That is why I am here."

"It won't work." Aiden said. "I've been to the dreamscape. I've met Sebastien. He already told me he has chosen not to possess my body."

"Let me finish." Raizel said.

"I am here, because Sebastien told me he was tired, and that when his successor showed up... if he was unworthy of inheriting the Hybrid's power, he would take over the host's body. But if he was found worthy, then the full power of the Hybrid would be transferred to the successor... In truth, I have known you were

Sebastien's successor for three years now. During that time, I have been evaluating you on Sebastien's behalf. You passed every moral test placed in front of you, proving that you were a good person. But there was still one more test that you needed to pass."

Raizel stood.

"And what test is that?" Aiden asked, standing up as well.

"Has the term "absolute power corrupts absolutely" ever been explained to you?" Raizel asked as he began walking, followed closely by Aiden.

"No, I've never heard of it.."

"It means those that have power, ultimately are not satisfied with the power they have, and will constantly seek more power, and with more power, they begin to abuse that power. Even the kindest of people eventually become the very opposite of who they used to be." Raizel explained.

"I get it." Aiden said as they continued walking.

"The final test was to unlock your powers. Before that, you did not have much in the way of power because of the seal keeping the Hybrid's power dormant. The test was to give you a taste of that power, and to see what you would do with it. I've been following you since Esenor, I have watched you struggle to maintain the man you used to be. You never actually gave in to the power. Sure, you were tempted by it, and sometimes indulged in the power, which was to be expected. Even Sebastien flaunted his power at times. But you never let it change who you are as a person. That was the test. I am standing before you now, because you passed, and it is now my honor to perform my friends last wish."

"What was his last wish?" Aiden asked.

Raizel smiled at Aiden before responding.
"To train his successor."

# Chapter 33

Two weeks had passed since the group left the elven village. Over the last two weeks, Raizel had been teaching Aiden as much as he could about immortal customs, as well as the history of Aiden's predecessor, Sebastien Arlet.

"Ready?" Raizel asked, looking at Aiden.
Aiden stood a few feet away from Raizel.

"I already know how to fight." Aiden said, looking at Raizel. "My father trained me."
"Did he now?" Raizel laughed.
"Yes, he did." Aiden replied in irritation.
"Ok, let's see have a look at this so called training."
Raizel tossed his sword to Aiden.
"What about you?" Aiden asked, looking at Raizel.
"Oh... right." Raizel replied, looking at his empty hands.

Raizel looked around himself, before picking up a stick.
"You're kidding right?" Aiden laughed.
Raizel took his position.
"You realize this won't be a fair fight?" Aiden asked, readying himself.

Aiden rushed at Raizel, swinging his sword. Raizel quickly parried the sword before spinning behind Aiden and striking him in the back with the branch.

"Your right, not a fair fight." Raizel said, grinning.

Shaking the pain off, Aiden faced Raizel once more. Dropping into the fighting stance his father taught him, the two opponents circled one another.

"Are you going to fight or just keep circling me?" Raizel asked.

"Not every fight is won by attacking first."

"True, but being passive is just as dangerous.. as I'm about to show you." Raizel thrust the branch at Aiden's stomach.

While bringing the sword down in order to deflect the branch, Aiden received a right hook from Raizel.

Seeing stars momentarily, Aiden recovered. Raizel placed two more lashes on Aiden's body, one on his left shoulder and the second across the back of his legs, causing Aiden to fall to his knees.

"I can see the effect of your training."

~ ~ ~ ~ ~

Siri was preparing dinner, while Mina explored the area where they had set up camp. Andarii accompanied Mina as she explored.

Two days ago, they had crossed over out of the forest, entering the Plains of Aerindor. Miles and miles of open grassland stretched before them. Several hills, rivers and lakes dotted the landscape, along with several wooded areas and a few cliffs. Herds of animals could be seen from the hill that Mina was sitting on, moving and grazing across the land.

"Is that the mountain Master was talking about?" Mina asked Andarii, pointing off in the distance.

"Yes, those are the Whitetooth Mountains. That is where we are headed." Andarii answered, looking back to keep an eye on Siri and the campsite, before sitting down next to Mina.

"What do you think Master will find there?"

"I'm not entirely sure he even knows the answer to that question." Andarii replied.

Together, they sat and watched a herd of buffalo in the distance.

"Guys, Aiden's Back!" Siri yelled up to them, before turning back to finish dinner preparations.

"Ok. Let's get back to camp." Andarii stood, offering Mina his hand.

Mina hesitated for a moment before taking his hand, allowing him to help her to her feet. Once she was on her feet, Mina quickly pulled her hand away from Andarii, wiping her hand on her trousers before heading back down the hill to the camp. Andarii watched her for a few seconds before following.

It had been almost three weeks since Aiden rescued the catgirl from the abusive elf who owned her before him. When Aiden found her, she was a wreck, beaten and broken. At the time, Andarii didn't think there was much hope for the poor girl.

Andarii was glad that Johrra had challenged Aiden to a fight to the death. In doing so, Aiden gained possession of Mina. As it turned out, Mina was one of Aiden's mates, the other being Siri. Since then, Mina has made much progress, although she still flinches when anyone other than Aiden touches her. Even though she liked Andarii, Mina still hated it when anyone other than her mate touched her.

"You still fight like a human." Raizel said as he and Aiden entered the camp.

"Immortals are faster and stronger than any human. The training your father gave you was thorough, but it is ultimately ineffective. You still fight, and react like a human."

"I get it." Aiden replied.

Aiden and Raizel had been gone for three hours. During that time, Aiden never landed a single blow on Raizel. He, however, had no problem landing blows on Aiden, leaving him sore from head to toe.

"You could have gone a little easier on me." Aiden said in frustration.

"An enemy won't go easy on you in battle. They won't have mercy just because you are weaker than them." Raizel responded.

Aiden knew he was right, asking Raizel to go easy on him would only hinder his training.

"Tomorrow, you learn to fight like an immortal."

Aiden nodded.


"How was training?" Siri asked, handing Aiden a bowl of stew.

"Informative." Aiden answered, rubbing his shoulder.

Taking the bowl of stew from Siri, Aiden thanked her before walking over to Mina, who was already eating her own bowl.

"So, is it any good?" Aiden asked, sitting next to Mina.

"Even better with Master here to share." Mina said, leaning against Aiden, rubbing her face on his arm.

"Mind if I sit?" Raizel asked, only for Mina to hiss at him.

"I guess not."

Raizel walked away, taking a seat on the other side of the campfire.


Mina was still angry with Raizel for trying to drink her blood without permission, and didn't want him anywhere near her. Just because he was teaching Aiden to control his power, doesn't mean she had to like him.

"Why do you do that?" Aiden asked.

"Do what, Master?" Mina asked, looking up.

"Why do you still hiss at Raizel?"

"Mina doesn't like vampyre."

"I get that, but he is trying to make amends."

"Mina knows." the catgirl said as she lowered her head.

Aiden placed his bowl down, wrapping his arms around Mina.

"Vampyre scared Mina, made Mina feel powerless... Mina told him no, but vampyre didn't listen. Took away Mina's choice, just like Johrra." she whispered.

Aiden now realized why Mina always hissed at Raizel, knowing full well how far the scars Johrra had left on Mina went. Leaning down, Aiden kissed her shoulder, causing Mina to press herself further into him.

"May I?" Aiden asked as he nibbled on her shoulder.

"Master doesn't have to ask... Mina belongs to Master." She tilted her neck to give Aiden better access.

"I know, but I also want you to always have a choice." Aiden whispered, before gently biting down.

"No fair! What about me?" Siri asked, sitting down beside Aiden and Mina.

Aiden released his hold on Mina, withdrawing his fangs before licking the wound in order to heal it.

"What? You were busy serving everyone else." Aiden teased, as Mina sat up.

Siri pouted as she batted her eyelashes at Aiden.

"Although... I could go for some seconds." Aiden smiled, showing his fangs.

Siri beamed, holding out her wrist.

Aiden shook his head, pulling Siri close as she leaned into the kiss. Aiden allowed his fangs to lightly rake along Siri's bottom lip, drawing blood as they kissed. Pulling away, Aiden licked Siri's lip before trailing kisses down her jaw, finally sinking his fangs into her shoulder, causing her to gasp.

After a few seconds, Aiden pulled his fangs free.

"Happy now?" Aiden asked, leaning down to pick up his bowl of stew.

Siri nodded.

Aiden finished eating his bowl of stew before standing up and walking over to Andarii.

"So, you miss the forest yet?" Aiden asked, sitting down.

"Very funny." Andarii said. "How did your first training session go?"

"You remember how I fought against Johrra?"

"It's something I'll never forget. Magic use aside, you're fighting technique alone was extremely impressive."

"I couldn't even land a single blow on him." Aiden said honestly.

"Seriously? Not a single blow?" Andarii asked in disbelief.

"Apparently, I need to learn to use both my enhanced strength and speed while I fight. Until I can do that, I'm at a severe disadvantage when fighting."

"Don't you already do that?

"Not when I fight." Aiden shook his head. "Years of training has conditioned my body to react a certain way during a fight. It has become muscle memory. I have to break that conditioning in order to fight effectively with my new abilities."

"Don't worry, I'm sure you will get the hang of it in no time." Andarii said, encouraging Aiden.

"I have to. Especially if I'm going to keep them safe." Aiden replied, looking over at Siri and Mina, who had fallen asleep leaning against each other.

"I don't know what it's like having a mate bond my lord, but I can see the way the three of you look at each other. They are the center of your entire world, aren't they?" Andarii said.

"I can't live without them. Not now... not anymore." Aiden replied.

"I am your sword and your shield, I will stand by your side to defend them from the world, until the day the world kneels at your feet." Andarii said.

"Thank you, Andarii. Let's hope it never comes to that." Aiden said. "Now, if you will excuse me, I've got two tired ladies over there waiting for me to come to bed."

# Chapter 34

Waking up a few hours before dawn, Aiden spent several minutes trying to escape the tangle of arms and legs that seemed positively determined to keep him prisoner.

Having successfully extracted himself from the bed, being careful to not wake Mina or Siri, Aiden began getting ready for another day of training with Raizel.

Aiden hated getting up so early and leaving the girls alone. Especially since Mina tended to get nightmares from her past whenever he left. But he also knew that the training with Raizel was important. After pulling on a set of trousers, Aiden heard a small whimper from the bed.

Looking over at the bed, Mina had curled herself up into a ball, pushing the blankets off, whimpering as she began to have another nightmare.

"Please... Mina is sorry. Mina was just hungry, please let Mina go." she cried softly.

"*Let Raizel be angry if he wants.*" Aiden thought to himself, dropping the shirt he was holding.

Walking over, Aiden sat on the edge of the bed, gathering the catgirl into his arms.

"No, Mina doesn't want to... let Mina go. Mina will leave." she cried.

"No! Please, it hurts... no more! Mina is sorry... someone help Mina!" Mina screamed as she held Aiden tightly.

Aiden hissed as Mina tightened her grip, her claws digging into his back. Aiden let the calling slip out as he continued holding the girl.

"Shhh... Master's got you." Aiden whispered into her ear as Mina began to relax.

Mina slowly opened her eyes.

"Master?" she asked, looking up as Aiden stroked her hair gently.

Mina realized that her claws were buried in Aiden's flesh.

"Mina is sorry." she said, carefully removing her claws.

"Don't be." Aiden replied, smiling down at her.

"But Mina keeps causing Master pain." The catgirl felt the wounds begin to heal beneath her fingers.

"It's only pain."

Mina looked at him with a puzzled expression.

"Only pain?"

Aiden nodded his head, pulling her closer.

"Watching you or Siri suffer causes me more pain than any of the scars you give me, and if it can ease your suffering, then I welcome the pain it causes me." Aiden told her as he laid his cheek against hers.

"Besides, since I became a hybrid, pain and I have come to an understanding."

"What does Master mean?" Mina asked, sitting back up as Aiden released her.

"Watch."

Aiden placed his right hand around his left wrist. With a quick twist of his hand, Aiden snapped both bones in his forearm as Mina gasped.

"Master, your arm!" Mina said, grabbing his arm.

"Will heal." Aiden replied as Mina watched, feeling the bones snap back into place beneath her fingers.

"You think this... or anything you've done, comes close to the pain of shifting?"

Mina calmed down, realizing what Aiden was trying to tell her.

Aiden laid back down on the bed, pulling Mina with him.

"Wanna tell me what happened?"

Mina shook her head.

"I know you're scared, but you can tell me."

"Master has already seen Mina's scars. Mina doesn't want to cause Master more pain by telling Master Mina's past." the catgirl whispered.

"Mina." Aiden said, making her look at him.

"Please tell me."

Nodding her head lightly, Mina began to tell Aiden about her nightmare.

"Mina was back at the elf village, when Mina first tried stealing food from Johrra. Johrra pulled Mina outside and tied Mina to a pole before whipping Mina. Was the first time Mina ever got whipped. Elf enjoyed Mina's screams as Mina begged. Kept whipping just to hear Mina cry more."

Mina cried, telling Aiden the story as he held her in his arms.

"Thank you for telling me." he whispered.

Mina fell asleep against his chest, listening to the sound of Aiden's heartbeat.

Aiden slowly slid Mina's sleeping form off him, placing her back down onto the bed.

"She have another Nightmare?" Siri asked.

Aiden rolled over to look at her.

Siri sat up in the bed as Aiden leaned over, placing his head in her lap.

"She finally told me about one." Aiden told Siri, as she ran her fingers through his hair.

"I heard."

"Do you think she'll ever find peace from the demons of her past?" Aiden asked.

Taking one of Siri's hands in his, he started caressing the back of her hand with his thumb before intertwining their fingers and kissing the back of her hand.

"I believe she already is. Her nightmares are becoming less frequent, and she has improved so much from when we first met her." Siri noted. "You should go, you're already late for training with Raizel."

"Raizel can wait... besides, not like he can start without me." Aiden rolled over, bringing Siri with him.

Aiden stood up from the bed, with Siri wrapped around his waist.

"What are you doing?" Siri asked, when Aiden pulled a cloak over her shoulders, carrying her from the tent as she ran her hands through his hair.

"After your pouting last night, I figured you could use a little extra attention this morning." Aiden growled as he nipped at Siri's neck causing her to grab a handful of Aiden's hair.

"Any objections?"

Aiden looked into Siri's sparkling emerald eyes. Her desire for him driving him wild.

"Let's find a quiet spot where we won't be disturbed." she whispered into his ear before kissing him passionately.

~ ~ ~ ~ ~

"You're late." Raizel said, folding his arms in front of his chest.

"Maybe you're just early." Aiden replied, walking up to Raizel.

"Hilarious. I hope you have a good reason for being almost three hours late."

"Mina had another nightmare." Aiden replied flatly.

Raizel's face softened, all irritation disappearing as he heard Aiden's excuse.

"How is your mate?"

Aiden sat down across from him.

"Well, she still hates you." Aiden said jokingly.

"I'm well aware, and I don't blame her. Having heard just a few of the things she has gone through, I now know just how badly I hurt her... ok, let's get started."

~ ~ ~ ~ ~

Mina woke to the smell of food reaching her nostrils.

"You awake Mina?" Siri asked, entering the tent with a plate of breakfast for the catgirl.

"Mina is now." she grumbled, crawling out from beneath the blankets she had covered herself with.

Siri sat on the edge of the bed next to Mina before handing her the plate of food.

"Thank you si..." Mina stopped, giving Siri a strange look.

"What is it?" Siri asked, hoping everything was alright.

Mina put the plate down, leaned towards Siri and sniffed the air a few times.

"What are you doing?" Siri asked, as Mina gave her a knowing smile.

"Sister mate has been with Master." Mina said, picking up the plate and starting to eat, causing Siri to turn bright red.

"Mina is happy for sister mate." the catgirl said between bites.

Siri let out a breath she didn't realize she had been holding. She wasn't sure how Mina would react, since Mina was very possessive of Aiden.

"Thank you, Mina." Siri said.

"Mina doesn't want to hog Master all to herself." Mina said, finishing the plate of food.

Setting the empty plate aside, Mina took Siri's hands in her own, looking into her eyes before speaking.

"Mina needs to explain things to sister mate."

"Ok, what is it?"

"Sister mate knows Mina is Nekomata, but sister mate does not know what that means." the catgirl began.

"Nekomata are very affectionate, especially the females. Physical contact is how they show love. Mina likes touching Master, not because Mina wants Master to herself, but because it is Mina's nature. For Mina, touching Master is important, just as important as breathing. Master's touch makes Mina happy. When Mina is away from Master, Mina feels sad, like piece is missing. Master saved Mina, and Mina adores Master. Mina doesn't like being separated from Master, makes Mina nervous, like world is closing in." Mina told Siri, being honest with her feelings.

Siri now understood Mina's behavior towards Aiden.

"If sister mate wants time with Master, Mina wants sister mate to say so... otherwise, Mina won't know. Mina wants sister mate to be happy too." Mina said as she squeezed Siri's hands.

"Ok, I promise if I start feeling left out, I will tell you." Siri replied with tears in her eyes, before pulling Mina in for a hug.

"Mina gets Master next." the catgirl said with a grin as she pulled away after the hug.

"I was planning on going down to watch Aiden train this afternoon, want to come with me?" Siri asked as Mina was getting dressed.

"Mina would like that." Mina answered.

"Ok then, we'll go and surprise him." she said as they walked out of the tent together.

# Chapter 35

"Not fast enough."

Aiden felt the sting of the branch as Raizel brought it down across his back.

"When you are fighting an immortal, you can't aim for where they are, they are too fast. Instead... aim for where they are going to be."

Aiden swung at Raizel once again. Despite the many failed attempts at landing a strike on Raizel, Aiden had been watching Raizel's movements, learning his patterns. Aiden knew Raizel favored his left side when dodging. Using this knowledge, Aiden adjusted his trajectory, bringing his sword within inches from hitting Raizel.

"Not bad... again."

Despite Raizel's harsh training, Aiden had made remarkable progress since yesterday. While the vampyre still held back when fighting, he never handed victory over to Aiden, not once. Going easy helped no one. While Raizel still landed quite a few blows on Aiden, Aiden had managed to start deflecting many of them.

"Alright, let's take a break." Raizel told Aiden after a few more minutes of training.

Aiden sat down, picking up a waterskin and taking a drink as Raizel sat next to him.

"You're making remarkable progress." Raizel stated.

"Yeah right, tell that to the bruises that are still healing."

"And yet, in less than twenty four hours, you have managed to start deflecting some of my strikes... not an easy feat."

"So why am I not allowed to transform during our training?" Aiden asked. "I'm stronger, and faster in that form, it would make sense to use it."

"True, you are faster and stronger when you transform, but sometimes, you may not have the opportunity to shift before battle. At other times, you may not have the option to shift at all."

"What do you mean?" Aiden asked.

"Ok, say you are in the middle of a town, and you are attacked. You may be able to shift, but what are the consequences of shifting? Let's say the townspeople are human. Will they trust you after that, or will they turn on you? What if your assailant isn't an immortal?" Raizel started explaining.

Aiden nodded as he listened to Raizel.

"Concealing who, and what you are from those around you is a very important skill for an immortal. It allows you to move undetected through areas you would rather not draw attention to yourself. Take me for example; the color of my eyes, as well as my fangs are a dead giveaway that I am a vampyre. But if I wear a hood to conceal my eyes, not looking people in the face, it draws less attention to me, and they more than likely won't even notice my fangs."

"Pick and choose your battles." Aiden said.

"Precisely. Besides, fighting in your hybrid form is substantially different from fighting in human form. When you change, that animal side of you is given just a bit more control, making it harder to focus. While shifted, you will be more likely to act on instinct and reflex. Also your size should be considered, a seven foot tall immortal is an easier target to hit than a human."

"I guess you're right."

"Although... you have demonstrated a strong control over yourself when you shift." Raizel stated.

"Master!"

Aiden turned to see Siri and Mina coming down the hill toward them. Aiden waved to them as he began to stand, only to be tackled back to the ground as Mina pounced on him.

"Mina missed you Master." Mina said, rubbing her face against his chest.

"I can see that." Aiden replied, rubbing her ears.

"Mina, you're interrupting his training. We came to watch, not distract him." Siri said, sitting down.

"Sorry Master, Mina was just excited to see you."

Mina climbed off him and sat down by Siri.

"That's quite alright, we were taking a break anyway." Raizel said, as Mina hissed at him.

Aiden reached over, picking Mina's hand up and kissing it.

"Play nice." Aiden said before he leaned in, giving her a quick kiss.

"Ok, Master." Mina said.

"Good girl." Aiden whispered in her ear.

"Alright, let's get back to it." Raizel said, standing up.

Raizel shook his head as Aiden reached for the sword.

"No sword."

Raizel held his hand out, taking the sword from Aiden.

"Hand to hand combat?" Aiden asked.

Raizel shook his head.

"Something a little more challenging... and a lot more fun." Raizel raised the sword.

"Wait, you want me to fight you with my bare hands while you have a sword?" Aiden nearly shouted.

"No, I want you to shift. Show me the control you have in that form. Your strength and speed will be increased, and you will be a much more dangerous opponent to face, hence, the sword." Raizel said.

"I already regret agreeing to this." Aiden said, taking his place, facing Raizel.

Raizel grinned.

Aiden closed his eyes as he began to shift.

Since the orc attack on the elven village, Aiden discovered shifting no longer caused extreme pain, instead, only mild discomfort. Almost as if his body no longer registered his bones breaking repeatedly as pain, even though he could still feel everything. With this, Aiden also found he had more control over his transformation, deciding that unless they were needed, to not include his wings whenever he shifted.

After a few seconds, Aiden had shifted into his hybrid form, minus the wings. Lowering his body posture and readying his claws, he looked at Raizel.

"Impressive. It took Sebastien years to learn to shift that quickly. Even longer to gain control over the transformation. Maybe you're further along than either of us thought." Raizel said, with a hint of admiration.

"let us begin." Raizel lunged for Aiden.

Aiden quickly sidestepped, raking his claws against the ground to adjust his position before counterattacking. Bringing his other hand forward, Aiden quickly slashed at Raizel with his claws.

Several minutes went by as Siri and Mina watch the two immortals going back and forth. Both girls winced every time Raizel would land a blow on Aiden, drawing blood momentarily before the wound healed. Mina nearly jumped for joy every time Aiden's claws dug into Raizel's flesh.

"Looks like I need to kick your training up a notch." Raizel said, clearly impressed with Aiden's control in this form.

Raizel smiled before moving in a blur. Both Siri and Mina had trouble following his movements.

"Master look out!" Mina yelled as Raizel got behind Aiden, thrusting his sword at Aiden's back.

The whole world seemed to slow down around Aiden as he spun around. The sword in Raizel's hand appeared to only be moving a few inches every second.

"*Woah.*" Aiden thought as he suddenly realized he had all the time in the world to dodge the blade.

Aiden casually stepped out of the way of the incoming sword, moving himself behind Raizel.

"*Two can play that game.*"

Raizel found himself staring at empty air, sword having not met its target. Neither Raizel, Siri, nor Mina had seen Aiden move.

"What in the...?" Raizel began to look around, just as he felt a set of claws begin tapping against his throat.

"Well... this is awkward." Raizel said, lowering his sword.

Aiden released Raizel's throat as the vampyre turned to look at him.

"Perhaps I was mistaken about your skill in combat after all." he said, as Aiden began to shift back.

Siri rummaged through the pack Aiden took to the training session. Pulling a spare set of shorts out, Siri tossed them to Aiden as he and Raizel made their way back over to them.

After pulling on the shorts, Aiden sat down, followed by Raizel. As he sat down Aiden opened his arms for Mina, but was surprised when Mina shook her head slightly before motioning at

Siri. Seeing what Mina was trying to do, Aiden instead pulled Siri into his arms, wrapping his hands around her waist.

"Mina, come here." Aiden said, knowing how important physical contact was to Mina, not wanting her to be left out.

Mina scooted closer to Aiden as he wrapped one arm around the catgirl, pulling her against his side as she nuzzled into his neck.

"That's enough training for today." Raizel said.

"You were incredible Master." Mina said.

"I'm glad we got to see it" Siri added, leaning back against Aiden as he kissed her shoulder.

"It seems you've finally unlocked your heightened awareness." Raizel said, looking over at Aiden.

"Heightened awareness?" Aiden asked, puzzled.

"Heightened awareness allows you to perceive the world in slow motion." Raizel began. "When coupled with your enhanced speed and strength, it allows you to do things like you did today. To you, it felt like everything was moving slowly, but in reality, it is actually you who have sped up."

"Seems useful."

"It is, although it won't happen every time you fight, and it is less effective against other immortals that can move just as fast as you." Raizel told him.

"Let's head back to camp." Aiden told the girls.

"That's a good idea, head back and get some rest. Tomorrow we continue on our journey." Raizel said as he left.

# Chapter 36

Aiden, Mina and Siri bolted upright in bed as they heard a loud disturbance just outside the tent.

"What the hell?"
Aiden quickly threw on a pair of trousers and headed for the entrance.
"Wait here." Aiden said as he opened the tent.

Outside, Aiden saw traces of blood all over the place, the still glowing embers of the fire were scattered, as if someone had been thrown into the fire pit. Just a few yards away, Aiden caught sight of Raizel and Andarii.
Both men were panting hard, Raizel knelt on the ground, pinning the body of an unfamiliar person down. Andarii likewise had another in a chokehold. Several other men lay scattered around the camp. Aiden looked around at the scene before him.
"My lord, vampyres." Andarii said.
"A scouting party by the looks of it." Raizel said as he tied up the struggling vampyre beneath him.

Aiden saw one of the vampyre's on the ground begin to move. Running over, Aiden delivered a blow to the back of the vampyre's head, knocking them unconscious, before tying them up as well.

"Should we be worried about more showing up?" Aiden asked, looking at Raizel.

"No, we should be good for now. Scouting parties are only comprised of ten individuals."

Looking around, Aiden could see seven dead bodies around the camp, aside from the three that had been tied up.

"Bring them." he ordered, walking back to the tent and ducking inside.

What happened?" Siri asked.

Mina and Siri had both gotten dressed and were sitting at the table waiting for Aiden to return.

"Vampyre scouting party found us... it's time for us to leave." Aiden answered, putting on the rest of his clothes.

"Is everyone ok?" Siri asked.

Mina rushed to Aiden, holding him tight.

"A few bumps and bruises, but everyone is ok."

Mina continued holding Aiden in a death grip as Aiden tilted her chin to look her in the eyes.

"I'm alright, don't worry... I need to go address our uninvited guests." Aiden said, pulling Mina's arms off him.

"They are still alive?" Siri asked.

"We managed to capture three of them, the rest are dead." Aiden said. "I think it's time to get some answers."

Aiden exited the tent, followed by Mina and Siri.

~ ~ ~ ~ ~

Two vampyres were bound with their hands behind their backs, on their knees with makeshift gags tied around their mouths. Raizel and Andarii stood behind them, preventing them from trying to escape when Aiden exited the tent. The third, and final one, was still unconscious, bound and gagged off to the side.

Aiden stepped up to one of the two vampyres kneeling in front of him. Siri stood at his side as Mina held his waist, peeking around Aiden at what was happening.

"Who are you?" Aiden asked.

Andarii removed the gag from the vampyre's mouth.

The moment the gag came out, he started cursing in vampiric, only to receive a right hook from Aiden, knocking him over, blood splattering on the ground.

"You will speak to me in my own language, or I will remove your tongue from your mouth." Aiden said coldly, towering over him as Andarii hauled the man back into a kneeling position.

"Filthy Abomination." the vampyre replied, blood dripping from his mouth as he spat at Aiden's feet.

Andarii grabbed the man by his hair, yanking his head back, forcing him to look Aiden in the face.

"We've been looking for you." the vampyre stated.

"Why?"

"Your very existence is an insult. You're an abomination of nature. We won't allow you to interfere again... my master has been waiting a long time to kill you himself."

"Who is your master?" Aiden demanded.

The vampyre began to laugh as he looked at Siri and Mina.

"Doesn't matter, you don't have long, now that we have picked up your trail."

Aiden didn't like the way the vampyre was looking at Siri and Mina.

"After killing you, my master will enjoy getting to break those lovely companions you have there."

Aiden fought the urge to shift and tear the vampyre apart.

"I'm sure the elf will provide plenty of entertainment for my master and his friends."

"Enough!" Aiden yelled.

"Aiden, he's trying to rile you up." Siri told Aiden, as she tried to calm him down.

"As for that little "pet" of yours... well, it's been decades since we heard the delicious screams of a Nekomata."

Aiden surged forward, gripping the vampyre by his throat as he hauled him into the air, his claws digging into the side of his neck.

"You enjoy the sounds of screaming, do you?" Aiden's eyes glowed brightly. Deep red in a sea of swirling black.

"Let me show you what it means to scream." Aiden growled, as he began dragging the vampyre behind him.

"Bring the others!" Aiden ordered. "We're getting our answers, one way or another."

Raizel and Andarii quickly obeyed.

"Aiden wait, you can't..." Siri started to protest, following Aiden.

"Yes, I can. They have information we need. I will force it out of them if I have to."

"It's not right, Aiden."

"Stay here." Aiden began dragging the vampyre away from the camp.

"Aiden, listen..."

"Stay here!" Aiden shouted at Siri, causing her to jump.

"Take Siri back inside."

"Yes Master." A frightened Mina responded, pulling on Siri's arm.

"Aiden, Stop!" Siri yelled after him.

~ ~ ~ ~ ~

About a mile away from the camp was a small cave carved into the cliffside. Andarii worked to place three anchor points into the roof of the cave as Raizel slipped away to retrieve a few things.

Once secured, Aiden and Andarii attached rope to the vampyre's bound hands, running the rope through the anchor point and lifting him off the ground, causing extreme pain in the man's shoulders as he was suspended by his hands behind his back.

"Hang the other two normally." Aiden ordered.

Andarii had just finished suspending the other two vampyres by their wrists when Raizel returned, carrying a bag.

"Andarii... go back and watch over the girls, Aiden and I will make sure our guests get comfortable." Raizel said, dropping the bag and opening it.

Andarii listened, not wanting to leave the girls alone.

All three vampyres now hung from the ceiling of the cave, spaced evenly apart, each in full view of the other two. Raizel walked up to the vampyre still unconscious.

"Wake up!" Raizel shouted, slapping the vampyre in the face.

Aiden looked at the three vampyres. The one he had strung up, strained painfully against his bonds, clearly the oldest and the leader. He had short stubble across his face, medium length blonde hair, and a small scar across the left jaw. The second vampyre was younger, a shaved head, with tattoos running up and down his arms.

Aiden looked towards the third and final vampyre. This vampyre had been unconscious and Aiden hadn't gotten a good look at them until now. Hanging from the ceiling, with their hood pulled back from their face, was a female vampyre, with long, dirty blonde hair. She was clearly the youngest of the group, although it was hard to estimate age for a vampyre. Terror gripped her when she saw the predicament her and her colleagues were in.

"Now that we're all awake... let's all get to know each other a little better." Raizel said with an evil grin that even made Aiden shudder.

Raizel placed a pair of thick leather gloves on his hands before picking up a strange tool, walking over to the vampire with the shaved head.

"Time for a little show and tell." Raizel held the thing up in the torchlight for everyone to see.

"This here is a device of my own invention. It is relatively simple, as the three of you will soon see. I call it the extractor." Raizel said, grabbing the man by the face.

Raizel could see the vampyre's fangs in front of the gag placed in his mouth. The gag prevented him from talking, as well as forced his mouth open slightly.

The device was made of silver, and had an adverse reaction when it came in contact with a vampyre's skin. A small loop just big enough to fit around a vampyre's fang was attached to the tip.

Slipping the loop around the man's fang, Aiden could hear the gums and lip around the fang sizzle before Raizel forcibly "extracted" the man's fang as he struggled and screamed into the gag.

"That's one, still one to go." Raizel laughed, before repeating the process on the other fang.

"Souvenir?" Raizel asked, offering the fangs to Aiden.
Aiden shook his head.

"Suit yourself, hand me that small vial would you?" Raizel asked, pointing to a vial of liquid next to the various tools Raizel had brought.

As Aiden retrieved the vial, Raizel walked over to the vampyre Aiden had attempted to interrogate earlier.

"Now, I know you won't talk, that means I won't have to hold back." Raizel ripped the shirt off the man, causing pain as it put more pressure on his strained shoulders before the fabric finally tore free.

Taking the vial from Aiden, Raizel pulled the gag from his mouth.

"I will kill you!" the vampyre screamed, just before Raizel poured the contents down the man's throat, quickly replacing the gag as the man thrashed back and forth in excruciating pain.

"What was that?" Aiden asked, as the man continued struggling, traces of blood seeping out around the gag.

"A mixture of blackthorn, hawthorn and juniper. For a vampyre, it's the equivalent to drinking acid." Raizel answered.

The bald vampyre was furiously trying to break his bonds as he watched his commander thrash about. The third vampyre was heaving, tears flowed freely from her eyes, she was on the verge of hyperventilating, despite the gag in her mouth.

# Chapter 37

Two hours later, the commander's body hung lifelessly from the ceiling, burns and deep cuts covered his body. There was a hole in his chest where his heart used to be.

"So... anybody have anything they wish to share?" Raizel asked, turning to the two remaining vampyres.

Blood covered the man's clothes as he grinned at them, still holding the commander's heart in his hand.

*"I don't know anything... please, I don't want to die. Oh gods. Please."*

Aiden hear a small female voice in his head. He looked over at the female prisoner.

Now that Aiden's anger had calmed down, Aiden could see much more clearly. The girl hanging from the ceiling was shaking in terror. A sudden realization hit Aiden.

This girl was no soldier.

*"Who are you?"* Aiden thought to himself.

The girls eyes suddenly snapped to his.

*"Did... you just hear me?"*

The girl nodded her head.

Raizel took a step towards the girl, intending to start on her next.

*"Please. I don't know anything. Please don't kill me."* the voice repeated in Aiden's mind.

The girl's eyes were glued to the device Raizel held in his hand as he approached her.

"Stop." Aiden said, catching Raizel's attention.

"Yes?" Raizel turned to look at Aiden.

"Find out what you can from him." Aiden said, pointing to the bald vampyre.

*"Don't worry."* Aiden thought, knowing she could hear him.

"I'll interrogate this one myself."

*"I'm not going to harm you."*

Aiden stepped up to the girl.

Pulling a knife from his waist caused her to flinch.

*"I'm cutting you down."*

"I don't think that's a good idea, she might run." Raizel said when he saw Aiden begin cutting the rope holding her up.

"She's not going to try to run... are you?" Aiden asked, looking at the girl.

Unable to answer because of the gag, the vampyre frantically shook her head.

"Aiden..."

"You have your orders." Aiden snapped at Raizel.

After cutting her loose, the vampyre girl slumped to the floor.

Reaching down, Aiden removed the gag from her mouth, allowing her to breathe easier.

"You're coming with me, and you will not resist." Aiden said in a strict voice.

"Okay." she whispered as she struggled to her feet.

*"Is he going to kill me?"* the girl thought to herself, silently following Aiden out of the cave.

Once outside the cave, Aiden turned to the vampyre.
"No, I'm not going to kill you."
The girls eyes widened in shock.
"So I wasn't imagining it, you really did hear me." the girl said, lowering her head and looking at the ground.
Aiden cut the rope binding her hands together.
"Follow me, I have a few questions, don't try to run. I promise, I am faster than you." Aiden told her as he began walking back to camp.
The girl quickly followed as she heard the screams from the cave start up again.

~ ~ ~ ~ ~

"What's your name?" Aiden asked, halfway to the camp.
"Sylvia, sir."
"How old are you?"
"Twenty one."
"Pretty young for a vampyre."
"Half-Vampyre." Sylvia said, under her breath.
"Half-Vampyre?" Aiden asked, stopping to look at her.
Sylvia nodded.
"My mother was a vampyre." Sylvia said.
"And your father?"
"Father was a hellhound." she answered, her voice dropping.
"I thought different immortal species couldn't mix." Aiden asked.
"They can, but children will either be one or the other, hybrids do not exist."
Aiden chuckled.
"What's so funny?" she asked.
"Oh, nothing... just that you're talking to a hybrid."

Sylvia's eyes went wide in disbelief. After a few moments of silence, she looked at Aiden.

"Though I am technically still a vampyre, I'm not as strong as a pureblood... and half breeds are looked down upon. If you really are an actual hybrid, they would do anything to kill you. That must be why they are after you." the girl said.

"So you didn't know who you were tracking?"

The vampyre girl shook her head.

"I'm surprised you haven't tried to run away yet." Aiden said.

"You told me not to, that you're faster than I am."

"Even so, I still expected you to at least try."

"If I did, you'd catch me and kill me... I don't want to die." she answered honestly. "Besides, if I returned without my squad, I'd be killed for abandoning my mission."

"I wouldn't kill you... besides, you don't look like a soldier to me."

"I was conscripted, forced to serve as a scout because I was good at tracking. Mother didn't even put up a fight when they came for me." Sylvia said.

"I'm sorry about back there... I don't like being cruel. But that man not only insulted me, but he threatened my mates, and even though it made me sick, a part of me enjoyed watching him suffer for it." Aiden said softly.

As they entered the camp, Andarii, who had been standing guard, rushed over, sword drawn.

"Stand down Andarii, she's not a threat."

"As my lord commands." Andarii said, sheathing his weapon.

"How are they?" Aiden asked, looking past Andarii, at the tent.

"Good luck if you plan on going in there... she's right furious." Andarii warned.

"Give me half an hour, then send her in please." Aiden said motioning at the vampyre girl.

Walking over to the tent, Aiden took a deep breath, then stepped inside.

# Chapter 38

"SLAP!"

"How could you!" Siri screamed at Aiden as she slapped him across the face.

"You didn't have to torture them!" she yelled.

The room was completely destroyed, as Siri have been venting her frustration for the last hour. Mina, who had hidden under the blankets during Siri's tantrum, peeked out.

Aiden saw the bookcase he had placed in the tent for Siri had been turned over. Many of the books had been spread across the room.

Aiden walked over, putting the bookshelf back in place before starting to pick up Siri's books and place them back onto the shelf one by one as Siri continued her rant.

"I can't believe you would do something like that! You don't torture people Aiden!"

Aiden continued cleaning up the mess Siri had made.

Mina expected Aiden to calm Siri with the calling, but Aiden hadn't said a word since he entered the tent. Mina knew something was wrong.

"I hate you! I hate you! Why wouldn't you listen to me! You monster, I told you not to torture them!" Siri screamed.

Aiden stopped cleaning, looking at the blood splatter on his clothes and hands.

"*She is right, what I did was unforgivable. I only cared about my own anger and revenge. I could have gotten information another way, but I wanted to torture that man. I wanted him to suffer. In doing so, I betrayed her trust.*" he realized.

Aiden slowly went to his knees.

"*What do I do? I can't take it back. Their blood is on my hands. I can't fix this. She should hate me... I've finally become a monster in her eyes.*" Aiden thought to himself.

"Stop fixing the damn bookcase and look at me!" Siri screamed, picking up a large glass vase from the table before throwing it at Aiden.

Siri expected Aiden to dodge, or at least duck, but instead he just sat there as the vase shattered across the side of his head and shoulder, pieces of glass cutting, and imbedding into his skin.

Siri stopped, her eyes going wide.

"Oh gods, Aiden. I'm sorry." Siri said as she started walking over to Aiden.

"Sister mate." Mina said, crawling out from under the blankets.

Siri glanced at Mina.

"Something is wrong with Master."

Looking back at Aiden, Siri realized he hadn't moved from the kneeling position he was in before she threw the vase, and that he hadn't even flinched when he got struck by the vase. Mina and Siri both slowly crossed the room towards Aiden.

Aiden's hands were trembling.

"Master?" Mina said quietly.

"Aiden?" Siri called.

Siri carefully knelt down in front of Aiden.

"Aiden, can you hear me?" Siri asked.

"I finally became a monster, even in her eyes." Aiden whispered, not even registering Siri or Mina's presence.
"Aiden?" Siri said, lifting his chin to look into his eyes.

Siri expected to see Aiden's red and blue eyes, or his red and black hybrid eyes. But what she saw startled her. Aiden's eyes had changed. No color remained, only a cold, empty darkness.

Aiden stood, bolting out of the tent as Siri chased after him.

"Aiden wait!" Siri called out to him, but he was already gone, shifting into his werewolf form and running off faster than she or Mina could follow.

"We need to follow him." Siri said, looking at Andarii.
"How? There's no way we can keep up with him." he answered.
"I don't know, I don't know, but this is my fault. I need to find him." Siri said, in tears.

"The river." Mina's voice caught their attention.
"What?"
"Master is down at the river."
Mina took Siri's hand, placing it against her own chest.
"Think about Master, mate bond will tell you how to find him."
With her hand against her chest, Siri did as Mina instructed. Thinking about Aiden, Siri could swear she could hear the sound of the river, as well as a tug in the same direction Aiden had run off in.
"Let's go get Master." Mina said, pulling Siri in the direction of the river.

~ ~ ~ ~ ~

Aiden sat, staring at his own reflection in the water for what felt like hours.

*"What kind of man have I become?"*

Closing his eyes, Aiden shut himself off from the world around him, wanting nothing more than to simply fade away.

After what felt like an eternity, Aiden felt two pairs of small hands take his own.

Opening his eyes, both Mina and Siri had knelt down at the edge of the water, each of them taking one of his hands in their own.

"What are you doing here? he asked.

"We love you." Siri answered, lifting his hand.

"I'm a monster, you said it yourself."

Aiden pulled his hand away, standing up and turning his back to them.

Before he could flee, Mina wrapped her arms around his waist, hugging him tightly from behind.

"Master is not a monster. Master is kind, caring, Master protects Mina.

Stepping around him, Siri took his hands in hers again, looking up into his eyes as she spoke.

"I'm so sorry, Aiden. I didn't mean what I said. I was angry, I didn't realize how much my words were hurting you. Please, come back. I need you. I can't live without you."

"Mina needs you too, Master. Please don't leave Mina all alone." Mina whispered.

Aiden collapsed to his knees, his eyes returning to normal.

Aiden was kneeling in front of Siri, his entire body shaking. Siri lifted one of Aiden's trembling hands in hers.

"I'm sorry Aiden, you're not a monster... and I could never hate you. You're the man I love, the man I'd die for. I'm right here."

Siri said, placing his hand against her cheek, which was damp with tears of her own.

"I'm not going anywhere." Siri whispered soothingly.

Aiden collapsed into Siri's lap, sobbing, as Mina leaned over him, hugging him tightly.

~ ~ ~ ~ ~

Aiden sat in a chair next to the table in their tent, with Siri and Mina.

"I'm sorry I lost my temper with you." Siri said, gingerly picking pieces of glass from Aiden's shoulder, as Mina worked to remove the ones in the side of his neck and face.

"You had every right to be angry with me." Aiden said, wincing as Siri pulled a larger piece from his skin.

"Not for this." Siri said, glancing around the room.

"And definitely not for this." she said, kissing the wound as it began to heal.

"I'll heal." Aiden replied, dismissively.

"Not the point." Siri said, shaking her head.

"You've seen me angry, seen me lose control." Aiden said.

"It's different for you." Siri said, pulling another piece out.

"How is it different? How is it ok for me to get angry, but not you?" Aiden turned to look at Siri.

"Master stay still so Mina can work. Argue with sister mate... but no moving." Mina scolded him, pushing his head back into place so she could keep working on the glass shards.

"It's different, because you literally have a wolf inside you, trying to tear its way out. You spend more effort trying to keep it contained, to not shift, than you do actually being angry. I threw a tantrum simply because I felt like it. I should have talked to you, instead of screaming those hurtful things at you. I'm sorry." Siri said, tears forming in her eyes.

"Just because I don't grow fangs and claws when I get angry, doesn't make it ok."

A few minutes went by in relative silence as the girls finished pulling pieces of glass out of Aiden's flesh.

"Mina is done." Mina said, letting go of Aiden's head.

"Me too." Siri said, pulling away.

"I'm sorry for questioning you in front of your subordinates." Siri said, placing her hands in her lap.

"What?" Aiden asked.

"Questioning your decision in front of Raizel and Andarii, as well as the three vampyres. I shouldn't have done that."

"What difference does that make?"

"You are a wolf... and, by extension, we are your pack."

"My pack?"

"Our group... though not an actual pack, the dynamics remain the same."

"Where are you going with this, Siri?"

"Master, be quiet and listen to sister mate." Mina said, covering Aiden's lips with her fingers.

"Packs are typically ruled by an Alpha, that would be you. We, as your mates, would be your Lunas. Andarii and Raizel would fall under the rank of Beta. The Alpha and Luna should have a united front. If we have a disagreement, it should be behind closed doors. In front of your pack, and especially in front of non-pack members, I should stand by your decisions and let you handle things the way you deem fit." Siri said.

"I can't expect you to agree with everything I do." Aiden countered.

"Sister mate and Mina don't have to agree with Master. Sister mate and Mina can voice our opinion, but Master is the Alpha. If Master makes a decision, Mina and sister mate should support Master's decision. Alpha and Luna are supposed to rule together.

Sometimes Luna will make decision. As her mate, the Alpha should also support her, even if he doesn't fully agree." Mina said.

"Challenging your decision in front of those who serve you, undermines your authority and can make you appear weak. If we are to survive, we must support each other. Our enemies must never see us as weak." Siri said, taking Aiden's hand.

"Okay then, let's do better... together. Sound good?" Aiden asked.

Siri and Mina both hugged Aiden.

"Mina?"

"What is it Master." Mina asked.

"I get the comparison, but you do know I'm not actually an alpha werewolf, or alpha hellhound?"

"Master may not have alpha status, but Master is still alpha of his pack."

After a few Minutes, Aiden spoke up.

"There is a girl outside I want the two of you to meet." Aiden told the girls.

"Master promised no more!" Mina said, pouting.

"And I'm keeping that promise. No more." Aiden nuzzled Mina's neck.

"I want the two of you to give me your opinion of her before I decide what to do about her." Aiden said.

"I saw her earlier when you ran off, who is she?" Siri asked.

"One of the scouts from last night." Aiden answered, causing Mina to hiss slightly.

"Although I don't think she was working for the vampyre's voluntarily. I also don't think she knew exactly who it was they were having her track down." Aiden told them.

"How can you be sure?" Siri asked.

"Well for one, she didn't even think that hybrids were possible."

# Chapter 39

"You know, you could help." Siri said, trying to put the room back together.

Looking over at Aiden and Mina, Mina had ahold of Aiden's hand and was leading him across the room.

"Sister mate made mess... sister mate can clean mess." Mina replied, pushing Aiden backwards onto the bed.
"Besides, Mina is busy."
The catgirl climbed on top of Aiden, smothering him in kisses.

"Maybe we should..." Aiden began to say, attempting to sit up.
Mina roughly pushed Aiden's shoulders back down onto the bed.
"Master will stay put." Mina growled, causing Aiden to raise an eyebrow at her.
"Oh really?" Aiden responded, giving the catgirl a look, grabbing Mina's wrists and holding them in place.
"Master please stay put?" Mina asked, softening her voice, her lower lip beginning to tremble.

Aiden simply stared into her eyes for several seconds, letting the tension build.
"Master?" Mina squeaked.
Aiden softly pulled Mina's hands around his neck, running his hands up her arms and across her back, pulling her close.

"Kiss me." he growled.

"Yes Master." Mina said, blushing as she leaned in for the kiss.

Siri spent the next thirty minutes cleaning alone.

~ ~ ~ ~ ~

Aiden sat on the edge of the bed as Siri sat beside him. Mina sat behind him, one arm hanging over his shoulder, draped across his chest. Her head rested on his shoulder, her hair still a mess.

A chair from the table had been brought over and placed in front of Aiden, fifteen feet from the bed, facing them.

"Andarii." Aiden called.

A few moments later, Andarii entered the tent, leading Sylvia by the arm.

Andarii pushed Sylvia forward towards Aiden before taking a position by the door. Sylvia's eyes darted from Aiden to Andarii with unease.

"Leave us." Aiden ordered, waving his hand to Andarii.

Andarii clasped his fist over his heart before stepping out of the tent, shutting it behind him.

"Sit." Aiden said, softening his tone while motioning to the chair.

"Thank you, sir." the vampyre girl replied nervously, quickly sitting down.

Aiden could see the girl was on the verge of having another panic attack.

"Breathe... we're not going to hurt you." Aiden said, giving the girl a few moments to calm down.

Sylvia looked at the three of them. Her eyes darting from Aiden, to Siri, to Mina, then back to Aiden. She knew her future depended on these three, and did not want to anger them.

"Sir.. I do not wish to assume, or to offend by not addressing you correctly. Which of them is your mate?" Sylvia asked, not wanting to insult or offend his mate as her commander had.

"I am." Mina and Siri said in unison.

"I'm sorry, but I don't understand." Sylvia said, looking between the two girls, confusion written on her face.

Aiden chuckled before clarifying.

"They are both my mates. Apparently, I have been blessed to have two different mates." Aiden told her, taking Siri's hand and kissing it. Mina began kissing his neck, making Sylvia blush.

Seeing the girl's embarrassment, Aiden tapped Mina on her arm, getting her to stop kissing his neck and laying her head back down on his shoulder.

"I apologize if my mate made you uncomfortable. Her species tend to be quite "attached" to their mates, as you can see." Aiden turned his head, whispering something in Mina's ear.

"Mina is sorry for making you uncomfortable." Mina said, sliding off Aiden's shoulder to sit beside him on the bed.

"I... It's quite alright." Sylvia stammered, trying to regain her composure.

"Everything ok?" Aiden asked.

"Yes, thank you. it's just... I have heard of a double mate bond, but I have never actually seen one before. It is extremely rare, even amongst immortals." Sylvia stated.

"Anyway, my mates and I have a few questions for you." Aiden said.

"What would you like to know?"

Siri stood up from the bed before speaking.

"Aiden tells me you were able to hear his thoughts. Is that true?"

"Y.. yes Ma'am." the half-vampyre answered, not liking the question.

"Has anything like that ever happened to you before?"

"No, it surprised me when it happened. I thought I imagined it at first, until it happened again a few seconds later." Sylvia answered truthfully, afraid of how Siri might react to her hearing her mate's thoughts.

"Don't worry, I'm not going to get upset with you." Siri said, sitting back down.

"We are just trying to determine if the link came from you, or from me... that's all, no need to be afraid." Aiden told her.

Sylvia relaxed a bit.

"Is there anything special about your bloodline... from either side?" Aiden asked.

"Not that I know of Sir, neither my mother, nor father are particularly powerful in terms of vampyres, or hellhounds."

Aiden nodded his head, before rubbing his chin. Mina leaned over, whispering something in Aiden's ear, causing him to look at her before nodding.

"Mina has a question for vampyre girl." she said.

"Ok." Sylvia responded.

"Master says he heard vampyre girl begging for her life, that she didn't know anything, and didn't want to die." Mina stated, looking for confirmation from Sylvia.

"Yes, I was scared, terrified that I was going to be tortured and killed for information that I didn't even have."

Sylvia began fidgeting with her hands.

"Mina believes you."

"You do?" Sylvia asked, shocked.

"Vampyre girl did not know Master could hear her, had no reason for deceit."

Sylvia breathed a sigh of relief.

"Mina has one more question. Answer honestly." Mina said.

"Alright."

"Just before Master heard vampyre girl beg, what was going through vampyre girl's head?"

Sylvia took a few moments to answer.

"I was thinking that I didn't want to die, that I was going to be killed to protect the secret of the same people who dragged me from my home and forced me to be a tracker for a scouting party. I was willing to do whatever it took to live. Even... even..." Silvia tried to say, tears forming in her eyes.

"Even what?" Siri asked.

"Even if I had to offer myself to you as a slave." she finished, before crying.

Sylvia cried for several minutes as Mina whispered to Aiden and Siri.

Aiden stood up and left the tent.

Outside, Aiden motioned for Raizel to come over.

"Yes?" Raizel asked as he came up to Aiden.

"Do you know if Sebastien was able to read minds?" Aiden asked.

"Sort of." Raizel answered. "When an immortal gets powerful enough, they learn to mind link with those of their pack or coven. Sebastien didn't have a pack or coven, but he was able to mind link with those around him... Why?"

"That girl in there mind linked with me back at the cave." Aiden answered.

"That shouldn't be possible. A mind link doesn't just happen between random people. She would have to be very powerful to force her own thoughts into your head." Raizel replied.

"More like desperate."

"How so?"

"She was gagged, so she couldn't talk, but in her mind she was begging for her life, terrified of being tortured and killed for information she didn't have. She didn't even know I heard her. At least, until I unknowingly responded back."

"What did you say?" Raizel asked.

"After hearing a voice begging in my head, I asked myself "Who are you?" When I did that, her eyes shot to mine, and I knew she had heard me too."

"She may have an affinity for telepathy. The intense stress of the situation could have awakened any dormant ability as a last ditch effort to survive." Raizel told Aiden.

"Should I be worried about her?"

"At her current level, no. With training, her abilities could become quite impressive if she was able to push into your mind out of desperation, having just unlocked them." Raizel said.

"Thank you, that's all I needed to know." Aiden told him, before turning and reentering the tent.

Siri had handed Sylvia a cloth to wipe her tears on as Aiden came back inside. Walking over to Mina, he motioning Siri to follow.

Aiden spoke where only the three of them could hear. Telling them what Raizel had told him.

"What do you want to do Aiden?" Siri asked.

"Mina would prefer vampyre girl not die if possible, Master."

"The two of you will support my decision?" Aiden asked.

Mina and Siri both nodded in agreement.

Turning to the half-vampyre, Aiden walked up, stopping a few feet from her. Mina and Siri sat on the bed, having agreed to let Aiden make the final call.

"I've decided what we should do with you." Aiden said, getting the girl's attention. "The easiest and safest course of action would of course, be to kill you."

Tears once again began to flow from the girls eyes. Sylvia was about to start begging again when Aiden held up his hand, silencing her.

"However... seeing as you are not a threat, I have decided to let you go. Although from what I have gathered, if you return to the vampyre army, you will be killed for abandoning your team and mission. Am I right?"

Sylvia nodded her head.

"And if you run, you will be a deserter. Also punishable by death."

The half-vampyre dropped to her knees.

"Please sir, take me with you. make me one of your slaves. I don't want to die. If you leave me behind, I'm as good as dead. Please... I can cook, clean, or do anything you would ask of me... you may even have my body if you desire, just please, don't leave me to die." the girl begged, gripping the hem of Aiden's shirt, looking up at him as she cried.

"My mates are more than enough to satisfy my desires... but as I was saying..." Aiden looked down at the girl.

"I'm letting you go, but I will also give you a choice. You can leave and be on the run the rest of your life. Or... you can come with us. I will accept you as one of my servants. Should you accept my offer, you will be bound to me, to serve me the rest of your days. If you are loyal, you will be treated well... as well as have my protection. But if you betray me... you will have preferred death. The choice is yours."

Sylvia let go of Aiden's shirt. Bowing her head to the ground, she spoke between sobs.

"My life is yours. For the rest of my days, I will serve you. Thank you." Sylvia said, returning to a kneeling position.

"Stand up. My servants do not wait on their knees." Aiden said, walking over to Siri and Mina.

"Yes sir, I mean master." the girl said, standing to look at Aiden.

"Never call me master, ever again!" Aiden raised his voice, turning back to her, eyes glowing.

Having seen the marks on Mina's arms and shoulders, Sylvia flinched as she closed her eyes, expecting Aiden to lash out.

"I'm sorry." Aiden said, lowering his voice as Sylvia slowly opened her eyes.

"I do not like the name master, and will not have my servants refer to me as such." Aiden said, sitting on the bed.

"I'm sorry... I thought... well... your mate..." the half-vampyre started to say.

"My mate is a special case." Aiden replied. "She knows my name. But because of her past, as well as her own nature, she prefers to call me Master... and I allow it, because she is my mate, and it makes her happy."

"Her past?" Sylvia asked out of reflex. "I'm sorry, I shouldn't have asked."

"It is quite alright. If you are coming with us, you should know about our past." Aiden said.

"I have been with my mate Siri for over three years. She was a servant gifted to me by my father. Since then, I have given her freedom in all but name. Free elves are not tolerated in society, therefore she still bears my master's mark, but that is all it is." Aiden continued.

"Mina, on the other hand, is a different story." Aiden pulled her into his lap before continuing.

"I met Mina two and a half weeks ago in an elven village. Her previous master had a grudge against me. He challenged me to a trial by combat, a fight to the death. As was their custom, the winner inherited all the belongings of the loser. At that time I didn't even know she existed, not until they dragged her across the village, hands bound and barefoot, to my feet."

Aiden continued to tell the story as Mina hugged him tightly, burying her head in his chest as she cried, reliving the memory.

"The marks you see on her were not caused by me. Her previous master enjoyed hearing her scream, and would beat her daily just for the fun of it." Aiden said, tears forming in his own eyes.

"For seven months he tortured her. Had he not challenged me, she would still be getting abused to this day. She was nearly broken when she came to me. She actually hissed at me and tried to bite me when we first met, but then the mate bond formed. That, her past, and the way I treated her when we met is why she chooses to call me Master." Aiden said, stroking Mina's hair.

"Master saved Mina, made Mina feel safe. Mina loves Master." Mina said, looking up from Aiden's chest.

"I'm so sorry you had to go through that."

Sylvia tried to reach for Mina, offering a hug, only for Mina to scoot away, hugging Aiden closer.

"Mina does not like to be touched. After what happened, me and Siri are the only ones who can touch her without her flinching away." Aiden told her, explaining Mina's reaction.

"Sorry." Sylvia said, putting her hands back at her side.
"At least she doesn't hiss at you like she does Raizel." Aiden said, chuckling.
"Mina doesn't like vampyre." Mina hissed.
"She means him, not vampyres in general."

"There is also one more thing you should be aware of. I don't want you being caught off guard in the future, so I will show you this now." Aiden said.
Aiden slid Mina off him as he stood up.
Slowly removing his shirt, Aiden revealed the many scars covering his arms, shoulders and torso.
Sylvia gasped as she looked at the scars.

"Mina's previous master had placed a master's collar on her. I did not realize what it was and tried to remove it, causing Mina extreme pain." Siri told Sylvia.
"I picked her up into my arms as she thrashed about in pain, to keep her from hurting herself, despite the danger to myself." Aiden added.
"Master deactivated the collar, even though Mina hurt him. Master didn't know Mina was his mate yet either." Mina finished, her head down, looking at the floor.

Aiden turned back to Mina.
"And I'd do it again, even if you weren't my mate... that's just a bonus." Aiden lifted her chin and kissed her, causing Mina to smile.

Aiden turned back to Sylvia as he put his shirt back on.

"I showed you this, because I don't want my scars to be a shock to you. I am often shirtless, especially around them." Aiden gestured to the girls. "You will also see them when I shift."

"Sir... you said you are a hybrid... what kind?" Sylvia asked.
Aiden smiled before answering.
"I am a perfect hybrid of all four species of immortals. I'm the only one of my kind."
"What?" Sylvia nearly screamed, eyes bulging.

Aiden walked over to the bedside table, picking up Sebastien Arlet's journal and handing it to Sylvia.
"Read this and it will make a lot more sense.
"I will, thank you sir." Sylvia replied, taking the journal.

"Now, as far as your duties are concerned... occasional cleaning is expected. I also want you to assist Mina and Siri with anything they may have need of. They prefer to do many things themselves, so help where you can. You are to be their personal handmaid, answerable only to them, or myself. Understood?" Aiden asked.
"Yes sir."
"Just call me my lord, calling me sir make me feel old."
"Of course, my lord."
"You will also be responsible for preparing the meals. Siri or I may choose to prepare the meals on occasion. When that happens, just let us do the work ourselves. If Siri, Mina, or myself do not have anything for you, feel free to spend your time doing whatever you want. You may be our servant, but you are not a slave, understand?"
"Yes, my lord. Thank you."

"When it comes to your thirst and needing to feed. Andarii is willing to give you some blood when needed. Mina and Siri are strictly off limits. Feeding off them will not be allowed, under any circumstance. I am the only one that may feed from them. Andarii will give you a bit of blood each morning to sate your thirst. It is your responsibility to tell us if you require more. Also, this should go without saying, but do not attempt to feed from me either. In fact, try to avoid getting anywhere near my blood. As a hybrid, both my blood, as well as my bite, are fatal to other immortals, no matter the species. Any questions?"

"No, my lord."

"None other than Siri, Mina and myself are allowed to enter this tent without direct permission. Special exceptions will be given to you regarding that rule, as you are our personal servant. But it would be wise to announce your presence before entering... lest you see something you shouldn't. The girls and I are mates, after all." Aiden said, looking back at Siri and Mina.

"Understood, My Lord." Sylvia said, a slight blush crossing her cheeks.

"Very well, go prepare lunch, we will be packing up and leaving immediately afterword. Send Raizel and Andarii in as you leave, I shall explain the situation to them.

"Right away, my lord." Sylvia bowed slightly before leaving the tent.

Aiden turned to Mina and Siri. "So how'd I do?" he asked.

Siri and Mina smiled at him.

"I may not understand why you did everything exactly the way you did, but I think you made the right decision." Siri said, getting up and hugging him.

"Mina agrees." Mina said, joining the hug as Raizel and Andarii entered the tent.

# Chapter 40

After an awkward lunch, everyone began packing. Raizel and Andarii were not too thrilled when Aiden told them that Sylvia would be joining them on their journey.

Sylvia was assisting Siri packing up the tent as Aiden walked over.

"Sylvia, take a walk with me, let the others finish packing." Aiden turned and began walking away, the half-vampyre following quickly behind.

After they had been walking for a while, they came across a tree that had fallen over. Sitting down, Aiden patted the tree beside him. Sylvia sat beside him as Aiden began to speak.

"Raizel believes you may have an affinity with telepathy, the ability to read minds and communicate without speaking." he told her.

"Really?" the girl asked.

"We believe the stressful situation you were put in allowed some of your dormant power to awaken. Even though you had no idea what you were doing, you subconsciously linked with me out of desperation."

"I wanted you to understand that I didn't know anything, that I just wanted to live." she responded.

"And that is perfectly understandable. But the fact you were able to link with me, shows that you have much potential. There are not many who can push their own thoughts into my mind. The fact that you did without intending to is very impressive."

"Why tell me all of this, my lord?" the girl asked, turning to look at Aiden.

"I want you to develop your skills. Hone them and make them stronger, learn to use them at will." Aiden answered.

"How do I do that?"

"Each day, you will spend one hour with myself, Raizel, or Andarii, attempting to establish a link between you and the person you are training with. As it gets easier, we will resist you more and more. For now, you will practice on me. Since you have already established a link with my mind, it should be easier for you to reconnect." Aiden explained.

Sylvia nodded in understanding.

"For what purpose am I training, my lord?" the half-vampyre asked.

"A strong telepath would be a great asset. They can be extremely adept at information gathering, as well as detecting lies. If you are as powerful as I believe you may be, you could read a person's entire mind like an open book. Not just what they are thinking, but anything they know would be yours for the taking, whether they want to divulge that information, or not. That is a valuable skill, but I will not force you to use it on someone against your own will." Aiden told her.

"You spared my life, my lord, choosing not to torture me when you could have. You allowed me to stay with you instead of leaving me to die on my own... even though I brought those men to attack you. Even as your servant, you gave me freedom to do what I want. By taking me in, you saved my life. If my powers can be of use to you someday, I will train hard, and when that day comes, my powers will be yours to command." Sylvia said with determination.

"Then let's begin your training." Aiden said. "Close your eyes and try to imagine being inside my head again. Think of me, and nothing else."

Sylvia closed her eyes as she was told.

"Focus on my voice."

Sylvia focused, trying to remember the way she felt when she first felt Aiden's voice in her head. The fear, and confusion of what was happening. The calm, almost caring sound in his voice when he realized she had heard his thoughts.

*"Can you hear me?"*

Aiden's voice was soft inside her head.

*"Yes."* Sylvia answered.

*"Nicely done."*

*"It feels strange being in someone else's head."* Sylvia commented.

*"Take your time... get familiar with how it feels. Right now I'm not resisting your advances. When you're ready, try to look through my memories. Find the memories of the night we met, see the events from my perspective... then tell me what you see."* Aiden said.

Sylvia spent the next twenty minutes getting used to the feeling of Aiden's mind, learning how to sift through his thoughts... his memories... everything. Reliving his memories as if she were there, feeling his emotions as if they were her own. Eventually, she opened her eyes to see Aiden looking back at her.

"Well?" he asked.

A few tears slipped down her cheek. She no longer had any fear of this man, now having a deep understanding of his character and personality.

"You've been through so much." Sylvia whispered. "I only caught a few glimpses, but I saw what you have gone through... I'm sorry."

Aiden knew she had seen parts of his past. He could feel it each time she went through a memory. Allowing her to freely explore his mind, Aiden was glad she hadn't gone through all of his memories. If she had tried to look through memories he did not want her looking at, he would have resisted, and pushed her back.

"And the night we met?" he asked.

"It was like I stepped into your skin. I felt your anger towards the commander, at what he said about your mates. I also know how sick you felt watching Raizel torture him, your compassion when you realized I wasn't a soldier. You really aren't the person I thought you were." Sylvia said.

"I have my moments of anger and ruthlessness. It's part of being immortal, but that doesn't mean I have to enjoy being cruel." Aiden told her.

"I must admit, I'm a little envious of your mates, they're lucky to have you." she said.

"Don't tell them that, Mina's quite possessive. Also, you have it backwards. I'm the lucky one, I don't deserve either of them." Aiden replied, causing them both to laugh.

"I simply meant the relationship you have with them. I felt the strength of your mate bond in your memories. I wonder if I'll ever find someone like that."

"I'm sure you will one day. When that happens, you are free to leave and be with them if that is what you want to do. I will not make you choose me over your mate." Aiden told the girl.

"Thank you, my lord." the girl said.

"Let's head back, it's time to leave, and they are probably waiting on us." Aiden said, standing up.

As they walked back to camp, Sylvia kept staring at Aiden. She knew without a doubt that the man before her was worthy of her devotion. She now saw what Andarii saw in him, kindness beyond measure. Ruthless, yet fair. A man of power and authority, yet will humble himself, treating even his servants as equals. She loved this man, not in the way Mina or Siri loved him, but a deep seated admiration and respect. She knew one day, the world would be at his fingertips. She made a vow right then and there to always remain by his side, and gods help anyone who stood against him. She would burn the entire vampyre kingdom to ashes if he asked. All for him, her Lord, her King, her Alpha.

~ ~ ~ ~ ~

"Go help Mina with her pack." Aiden told Sylvia as the got back to camp.

Aiden watched as Sylvia rushed over to Mina, taking Mina's pack from her and placing it onto her own shoulders.

In the last two weeks, Mina had been eating well. Although she no longer looked malnourished, she still remained rather slim. Aiden also knew she was still physically weak compared to the rest of them, and wouldn't let her carry her own pack, as she still became exhausted easily, even choosing to carry her when she could no longer keep up.

"Ready to go?" Aiden asked, walking up to the group.

"Ready, my lord." Andarii said, shouldering his pack as the rest of the group nodded their heads in agreement.

# Chapter 41

"My lord, stop." Sylvia knelt down, looking at the ground. They had been following the river for several miles before splitting off, following a game trail in the direction of the distant mountains.

Aiden knelt beside her, Mina holding onto his back with her legs around his waist. Mina had grown tired half a mile back, so Aiden shifted his pack onto one shoulder to allow Mina to climb on his back for the rest of the day's journey.
"What do you see?" Aiden asked.
"You see these scratch marks?"

Long scratch marks littered the area. Each set of scratch marks were six to eight inches long, coming in sets of five. Four spaced evenly apart, with the fifth slightly further from the four. These weren't just scratches in the dirt, they were tracks left by something. Something with five fingers and claws.
Aiden nodded his head.
"Werewolf maybe?" Aiden asked.
"Not a chance, look here. These marks are deep and long, Like something was digging into the soil to propel them forward, leaving behind long scratches in the dirt... and these others are much shallower, pressing down into the soil before lifting off." Sylvia said, pointing out the differences.
"Do you know what made them?"
Sylvia nodded her head as she stood up.

"Vampurics, no doubt about it. a large group of them, moving fast." she said.

Aiden shuddered at the revelation.

Of the four immortal races, vampurics were the most hated. The least evolved among the four. Not much more than savage bloodthirsty beasts unless controlled by an elder vampyre.

"How many?" he asked.

"Difficult to tell. My best guess is around seventy or eighty. Could be more, as the tracks overlap each other." Sylvia answered.

"Suggestions?"

"Tracks head off to the southwest, into that valley." she said, pointing.

"I recommend heading southeast, climbing up the cliff and following the ridgeline. Hopefully they won't catch our scent. We still have a few hours of daylight, I suggest we keep moving. Vampurics can't come out in daylight like regular vampyres, the sunlight burns their skin. Most likely they are hiding in a cave, or they have buried themselves beneath the ground until dark. Either way, we should be extra vigilant tonight." Sylvia stated.

"Alright, let's get moving." Aiden said, all of them picking up their pace.

~ ~ ~ ~ ~

After another hour of hiking, they came to the ridge Sylvia had pointed out.

"How do we get up there?" Siri asked, looking at the nearly two hundred fifty foot sheer cliff face.

Aiden had Mina get off his back as he began to go through his pack, pulling out two long coils of rope. Aiden tossed one to Raizel before taking off his shirt, pulling the coil of rope over his shoulder, and under his opposite arm.

"You and me, we're climbing." Aiden said.

"Why me?" Raizel asked.

"Get up the damn wall." Aiden said, as he began to climb.

Aiden and Raizel began slowly making their way up the cliff face. Aiden carefully tested each handhold and footing as he climbed higher. Halfway up the cliff, Aiden lost his footing, sliding down a foot before digging his claws into the side of the rock.

Aiden cursed under his breath as he regained his footing. Continuing their way up the cliff, the two finally reached the top half an hour later.

Looking out at the horizon, Aiden saw the sun was setting and that they needed to work fast.

Lowering the ropes, Aiden and Raizel began to pull Mina and Siri up the cliff, just as a cacophony of howls and screeches rose from the valley below.

"Damn it!" Aiden swore, pulling Mina to safety, as Raizel pulled Siri to safety as well.

Using his enhanced vision, Aiden could see a horde of at least a hundred and fifty vampurics heading their way, and closing fast. Tying his rope off before throwing it back down, Aiden turned to Raizel.

"Go... I've got this. I'll get them up." Raizel said, already knowing what Aiden was planning.

Aiden walked up to Siri, kissing her before turning to Mina.

"I'll be back, I promise, but I've got to go help our friends." Aiden said before kissing her.

As Aiden turned, Mina grabbed his hand.

"I have to go." Aiden said.

"Take some of Mina's blood, Master." Mina said, tilting her head.

Aiden pulled her to him, biting into her shoulder. After a few mouthfuls of blood, Aiden sealed the wound, then turned, jumping off the cliff.

Mina and Siri's breath caught in their throat for a few moments, until Aiden soared back up the cliff in his hybrid form, taking off in the direction of the horde.

Time stopped for Sylvia when she saw him jump off the top of the cliff. Watching as Aiden shifted for the first time in front of her eyes. She gasped when two giant wings burst from his back, catching the air ten feet above her, buffeting her with wind as he soared back into the air.

"Incredible." she whispered.

"Admire later girl, we gotta move!" Andarii yelled, handing her a rope before starting to climb his own.

~ ~ ~ ~ ~

Aiden soared over the heads of the vampurics, just out of reach as they shrieked and hissed. Several of the beasts jumped and slashed at Aiden as he passed by.

*"Time to put my training to the test."* Aiden thought to himself.

Retracting his wings, he crashed into a vampuric, feet first, caving in its chest as he landed. Within seconds, Aiden was surrounded by rabid vampurics, shrieking and clawing over one another to get at Aiden.

Aiden began slashing his way through the vampurics as fast as he could. Slashing the throat of one, only for two more to take its place. Some of the vampurics began feasting on the bodies of the fallen, while others continued attacking Aiden.

The stench of blood filled Aiden's nostrils, causing his thirst to flare up.

Being momentarily distracted, one of the vampurics launched itself at Aiden, latching onto his back, claws tearing into his flesh as it sank it's teeth into his shoulder.

Aiden reached up, grabbing the entire head of the vampuric in one hand, his claws cutting through the scalp, digging into its skull for grip. Ripping the creature's teeth from his shoulder, Aiden hurled the vampuric over his shoulder and into another group of the creatures.

The creature that had bitten him let out a blood curdling scream, causing many of the beasts to look at it as it writhed on the ground.

*"Serves you right for biting me."* Aiden thought as they focused back on Aiden.

*"My Lord, we are safely on top of the cliff, Raizel is on his way. Just hold on a few more minutes."* Sylvia's voice broke through, speaking directly into his mind.

*"Easy for you to say, the damn things are rabid."* Aiden answered.

Aiden continued fighting, slamming the body of one down onto the ground, before turning to catch another by its throat midair as it pounced at him, crushing its throat in his claws. Aiden could feel his body weakening, more and more of the creatures were landing hits on him, tearing his flesh.

*"I'm not sure how much longer I can keep going."*

"Need a hand?"

Aiden turned to see Raizel, hacking his way through the creatures towards him.

"Here, this should help."

Raizel pulled the clothbound sword from his back, tossing it to Aiden. As the sword flew through the air, the cloth it was bound in unraveled and fell to the ground.

Snatching the sword from the air, Aiden felt an electric hum radiate through him as he gripped the hilt with his clawed hand. The sword sang as he pulled it from its scabbard, a black sword, with pulsating veins of light flowing through the blade. Aiden felt a rush of energy as he held the sword.

Aiden grinned, his lips pulling back over his teeth in a wicked snarl.

Aiden and Raizel began fighting in unison, as if they had been fighting together for years. As Raizel turned, Aiden turned to cover his back. Raizel did the same for him as they began making quick work of the remaining vampurics.

Once the battle was over and the last remaining vampuric lay cut in half, Aiden placed the tip of the sword in the ground as he leaned against the hilt, shifting back to human as he caught his breath.

"Not bad, not bad at all." Raizel said, slumping to the ground next to him.

"Not so bad yourself... for an old man." Aiden smacked Raizel with the side of his foot.

"As I recall, this old man just saved your ass." Raizel said.

"Your memory has gotten bad in your old age. I totally had that handled." Aiden said, as they both began laughing.

"That was a brave thing you did... incredibly foolish... but brave." Raizel said, after a moment of rest.

"Bravery had nothing to do with it." Aiden replied, reaching his hand out and helping Raizel to his feet.

~ ~ ~ ~ ~

Mina heard the rocks and rubble at the edge of the cliff being disturbed as Aiden and Raizel hauled themselves over the edge.

"Master, are you..." Mina began to ask, before bursting into a fit of laughter and giggles.

"What's so funny?" Siri said, looking over before joining in the laughter.

"Yeah yeah, laugh it up." Aiden said, walking past them, wearing a small loincloth made from the bit of cloth the sword had been wrapped in.

"We're safe for the moment. I think we should rest for the night." Raizel said.

~ ~ ~ ~ ~

Aiden waited anxiously for the bath water to finish heating. He was covered in sweat and blood, and wanted to get clean.

Sinking into the water, Aiden relaxed.

As Aiden washed the dirt, sweat and blood from his body, Siri sat at the nearby table, reading one of her books while Mina rolled around on the bed.

Aiden chuckled as he watched the catgirl getting comfy.

Dipping his head beneath the water, Aiden quickly washed his hair before leaning back against the side of the tub.

Leaning his head back over the side of the tub as he closed his eyes, Aiden enjoyed the warmth of the water on his skin. He had nearly fallen asleep in the tub when he felt the water move.

"What are you doing?" Aiden asked, his eyes still closed.

"Mina is joining Master." Mina said, stepping into the bath.

"I was enjoying my bath." Aiden said, opening his eyes as Mina sat down in his lap, facing him.

"Master will enjoy it better with Mina." she purred, hugging his chest.

Aiden felt another pair of hands begin to run along his shoulders, massaging his muscles.

"So what's with all the attention?" Aiden asked, looking up into Siri's emerald eyes as she massaged his neck and shoulders.

"The hero deserves a reward after a triumphant battle." Siri answered, a sultry undertone in her voice.

"Does he now?" Aiden asked amusingly.

Mina nodded her head as she picked Aiden's arms up, placing them around herself.

"Master deserves Big reward." Mina said, staring into his eyes seductively.

Aiden could get lost in the deep, blue ocean of Mina's eyes.

"Just how big of a reward are we talking?"

"As big as Master wants." Mina whispered, nipping Aiden's ear, causing him to groan.

Reaching beneath her, Aiden gripped her backside, lifting them both out of the water.

"You sure about that? I can ask for quite a lot." Aiden warned, carrying her toward the bed.

Mina squealed as he dropped her on the bed, devouring her with his eyes before capturing her mouth with his own.

Siri silently slipped to the door of the tent.

"Sylvia." Siri called.

"My lady, you need something?" the girl asked from the other side.

"I have a feeling we will be skipping dinner." Siri stared back at Aiden on the bed. "Possibly even breakfast... let no one disturb us."

Siri turned, walking back towards the bed, disrobing as she went.

"The two of you are absolutely insatiable." Aiden growled as he nibbled on Mina's ear, making the catgirl moan as her nails dug in, leaving long scratches down his shoulder blades.

"Then what does that make you?" Siri asked, climbing onto the bed, pulling his head towards her for a kiss.

"A man who gets very little rest." Aiden answered, once their lips parted, his eyes glowing softly.

# Chapter 42

Siri woke up, hearing the sound of movement in the tent.

"Aiden?" she asked, rubbing the sleep from her eyes.

"Apologies for waking you my lady." Sylvia answered.

"Sylvia?" Siri asked, pulling the sheet up to cover herself.

"Yes my lady. When you and lady Mina are ready, I have prepared a tray of food for each of you." the vampyre girl responded, before going back to her duties.

"Thank you. Have you seen Aiden?" Siri asked, grabbing a robe from beside the bed.

Siri looked at the bed beside her, trying to figure out how Aiden always manages to get out of bed without disturbing her or Mina.

"My Lord said he was going for a run, and that I should lay out some clothes for the two of you, as well as a set of clothes for him when he returns." Sylvia replied, laying several different options of clothing at the foot of the bed.

"If you will excuse me my lady, I have other things to attend to. Does my lady require anything before I leave?" she asked.

"No. Thank you Sylvia, you may go." Siri said, wrapping the robe around her before getting up and sitting at the table.

Sylvia bowed once then left the tent.

~ ~ ~ ~ ~

Aiden had decided to do a little scouting before Siri and Mina woke up.

Finding a small, secluded spot to store his clothes, Aiden shifted into his werewolf form. This form was faster than his hybrid form, and would allow him to cover more ground in less time.

Aiden enjoyed the feel of the wind in his fur as he raced along the ridgeline, before cutting away from the edge to begin a large circle, checking for danger as he made his way back.

~ ~ ~ ~ ~

Siri finished eating her breakfast before waking Mina.

"What does sister mate want?" Mina asked begrudgingly, when Siri pulled the blankets off the sleeping catgirl.

"Breakfast is on the table. Get dressed." Siri said.

Mina ignored her. Rolling over, she grabbed Aiden's pillow, pulling it to her chest and burying her face in the pillow. Mina inhaled Aiden's scent as she tried to go back to sleep.

"Fine, I'll eat your food too then." Siri said.

"Sister mate wouldn't dare!" Mina said, quickly sitting up and looking at Siri. A slight hint of anger and worry in her eyes.

"Get dressed." Siri tossed the clothes Sylvia had laid out over to Mina.

"Your food is on the table." she said as she exited the tent.

Outside, Siri found Sylvia sitting across from Raizel. With Aiden being gone, he had agreed to help her with her powers. Twenty meters away, stood Andarii, looking out over the ridge at the valley below.

Siri walked up beside Andarii and took in the view.

"Always vigilant, don't you ever relax?" Siri asked.

"Good morning my lady, I'm surprised to see you up this early." Andarii said, bowing his head slightly.

"Beautiful view isn't it?"

Siri looked out over the green landscape.

"It is."

A series of howls came from the trees on the other side of camp.

Raizel grabbed his sword as Andarii and Siri ran over.

From the edge of the trees, emerged six large wolves, each one having different colored fur. The wolves approached, stopping at the edge of the camp.

"Now what?" Raizel asked, glaring at the wolves, as his eyes narrowed.

One wolf stepped forward from the group, his fur a deep reddish orange. Lowering its head slightly before its bones began to crack, shifting into a human form.

The man pulled on a set of shorts he had tied around his left leg before standing and facing the group.

"Greetings." the man said.

"Who are you?" Raizel asked.

"What do you want?" Andarii said.

"A pack of feral vampurics have been plaguing our land for several months now. Last night, someone managed to eradicate the entire pack. We've been battling those creatures for weeks, and never managed to kill more than a few each night. We have come looking for the one responsible."

"I am the one responsible." Raizel said, stepping forward.

"Don't insult us, vampyre." he scoffed. "It would not be wise to make an enemy of us... especially this close to a full moon."

The man let his claws slip out as four other werewolves moved forward, surrounding Raizel.

Sniffing the air as the wind shifted directions, his eyes snapped to Siri.

"You."

He began walking toward her.

Andarii stepped in front of the man, only to be knocked aside with a single blow.

Stepping up to Siri, the man took a good look at her, noticing Aiden's mark on Siri's neck.

"No, not you... your mate. it's the same scent." he said, sniffing the air again. "His scent is all over you. Where is your mate?"

Mina stepped out at that moment, the stranger's eyes snapping to her. The stranger looked past Siri, staring at Mina.

"Nekomata." the stranger said with a grin.

"He's not here." Siri said, stepping back, allowing Mina to get behind her.

"Based off your reaction, I assume the Nekomata is yours?" The stranger took another step closer.

"Leave her alone." Siri warned.

"Siri." Raizel said, trying to take a step toward her.

The wolves surrounding him growled and snapped at him, preventing him from moving.

"You don't want this fight, believe me. If he slaughtered those vampurics, what do you think he would do to you and your friends after threatening his mates?" Siri said defiantly, nodding towards the other wolves surrounding Raizel.

"That's enough Jonas."

The last remaining werewolf had shifted and was walking towards them.

"I'm just following orders." the stranger said, eyes still on Mina.

"Your orders were to make contact with their alpha, not pick a fight with his luna." the man replied.

The stranger ignored him, taking another step forward.

"I said stand down Jonas... or I will put you down." the man stepping up to them, claws extended, his eyes a burning yellow.

Jonas growled under his breath, but backed away several paces.

"The rest of you, stand down as well. We are not here to fight." he ordered.

The four remaining wolves backed off from Raizel, lowering their heads as they retreated back to the edge of the camp.

"My deepest apologies, I believe we may have gotten off on the wrong foot. My name is Damien, First Beta of the Silver Moon Pack." he said, bowing before Siri.

Raizel checked on Andarii, before moving to Siri's side.

"Please forgive my associate, he is young and arrogant. Thinks just because his uncle is the alpha he can do whatever he wants." Damien said.

"Our mate may not see it that way." Siri said, motioning behind Damien.

Damien looked over at Jonas. Since Mina had left the tent, he had not taken his eyes off her. Jonas was still staring at Mina, his eyes darkening into black pits.

Damien rushed up to Jonas, slapping him squarely across the face, knocking him down.

"What the hell?" Jonas yelled, looking up and glaring at Damien.

"Keep your damn eyes off another man's mate!" Damien roared, causing Jonas to shrink back a bit.

"Go back to the pack. I won't have you embarrassing our alpha any more than you already have... and you can be sure your uncle is going to hear about you leering at another man's mate. Now get out of my sight before you cause any more damage." Damien yelled, kicking Jonas in the chest, making him fall into the dirt.

Jonas quickly ran off, following Damien's orders.

"Thank you." Siri said as Damien walked back up. "Aiden is very protective of her."

"Aiden... is that the name of your mate?"

"Yes. What is it you came here for?" Siri asked.

"If you don't mind, I would prefer we wait until your mate arrives... to avoid any further misunderstandings." Damien answered.

# Chapter 43

Returning to the spot he had placed his clothes, Aiden felt something was off as he was getting dressed. Returning to the camp, Aiden caught the scent of several unfamiliar individuals.

"Siri! Mina!" Aiden yelled, breaking into a sprint.
"It's alright Aiden, we're fine!" Siri called back, easing his worry.
Rounding the tent, Aiden saw Siri talking with Raizel and Andarii. At the edge of the camp, Aiden noticed four shifted wolves as well as a man leaning against a nearby tree.

Quickly walking to Siri, Aiden took her in his arms.
"What happened? Who are these people, did they hurt you?" Aiden asked, looking her over.
"I'm fine. Mina is inside the tent. She's ok, she just wanted to wait for you inside the tent."

Damien quit leaning against the tree, and was about to walk over to introduce himself when Siri motioned for him to wait. Knowing Aiden's mates would be his first priority, Damien nodded and stayed put.

Stepping into the tent, Aiden found Sylvia sitting at the table. Seeing it was Aiden who entered the tent, Sylvia pointed to a bundle huddled beneath the blankets on the bed.
Aiden nodded, motioning for her to leave.

Once Sylvia had left the tent, Aiden made his way over to the bed, allowing the calling to slip out. Aiden watched Mina begin to stir beneath the blankets. Lifting the edge of the blankets, Aiden peeked inside.

"You alive in there?" Aiden asked.

"Master..." Mina whispered, reaching for him.

"I'm here now, no need to worry." Aiden soothed the girl as he picked her up.

With Mina wrapped in his arms, Aiden walked back outside to deal with their visitors.

Damien watched as Aiden returned from the tent, carrying the catgirl in his arms, the girl hiding her face in his chest.

*"Jonas, you moron."* Damien thought as Siri motioned him over.

Keeping his hands out, Damien approached Aiden slowly, fully aware that he would have to tread lightly. Stopping twenty feet from Aiden, he bowed and opened his mouth to speak.

"Before you say anything, I want to know who is responsible for this." Aiden said, gesturing to the frightened catgirl in his arms.

Damien knew this was coming, no sense denying it, or avoiding it.

"One of the younger wolves from our pack, his name is Jonas. He overstepped his own authority and has been reprimanded and sent back to the pack to await punishment from our alpha." Damien said.

"What are you doing here, and what are your intentions?" Aiden asked, his voice tense.

"We mean you no harm, we only wish to speak to the alpha, that is you, is it not?" Damien answered.

"Harm has already been done." Aiden growled. "And I'm not sure I trust you when you say you only wish to talk. If that was the case, why are there four shifted wolves just outside my camp?"

"Point taken." Damien said, waving to the wolves, instructing them to shift.

After shifting, three men and a woman stood behind Damien.

"Siri, take Mina and go stay by Andarii." Aiden told her, setting Mina back onto her own feet.

Mina refused to let go of Aiden as Siri pulled gently on her arm. Leaning down, Aiden whispered something into mina's ear. After a few seconds, Mina nodded before releasing her grip on Aiden.

Before Siri led Mina away, Aiden removed his shirt, handing it to Mina, who held it close as she followed Siri to the other side of the camp.

Damien and the others watched as Mina followed Siri, clutching Aiden's shirt.

"My scent calms her." Aiden said.

Nodding, Damien bowed before speaking.

"We humbly apologize for upsetting your mate, that was not our intention." Damien replied respectfully.

"Now, who are you and why are you here?"

"My name is Damien, First Beta of the Silver Moon Pack. My alpha sent us to make contact with your pack's alpha." Damien answered.

"I am not an alpha, but I am the leader of this group. Why were you sent to make contact with me?" Aiden crossed his arms across his chest.

"We were sent to inquire about the individual who defeated the vampurics that have been terrorizing our lands. One of our pack members told us he saw a hellhound single handedly facing the horde of creatures. By the time we arrived with a small hunting party, the entire horde lay slain. Is it safe to assume you are the one responsible?"

Aiden nodded.

"You truly faced the horde of creatures alone?" Damien asked.

"They caught wind of our scent and posed a threat to my pack. I chose to take action."

A wave of both fear, and awe passed over the group of werewolves.

"If I may ask sir, where is the rest of your pack?" Damien asked.

"The rest of my pack?" Aiden asked.

"Surely a hellhound of your strength must belong to a much larger pack." Damien looked at Aiden's companions off to the side.

"I do not belong to any pack, nor am I seeking one. We are simply passing through." Aiden said.

"Well then, in the name of our alpha, I would like to invite you and your companions back to our pack to meet with Alpha Logan. At the very least, allow us to show our gratitude by replenishing your supplies."

"I'm not so sure that would be a good idea." Aiden said.

"My lord." Raizel said from the side.

Walking over, Raizel whispered where only Aiden could hear.

"Not all immortals are bad, and not all wish for your death either. Remember that many immortals stood beside Sebastien in combat, myself included. I advise you not throw away a potential ally just yet."

Nodding his head, Aiden looked back at Damien. "Very well... we will accept your invitation on three conditions."

"Name them... if they are within our power, they will be done." Damien answered.

"Condition one... my pack and I will not be escorted within your home. We will be allowed to go where we want, when we want."

"That should not be a problem."

"Condition two... we will not be accepting an offer to join your pack, nor shall it be asked of us."

"Alpha Logan will be disappointed to hear that, but I believe we can accommodate your request." Damien replied. "And the third condition?"

# Chapter 44

Half a day's journey, down into the valley, lay the outskirts of Vanora.

"Welcome... to the Silver Moon Pack." Damien announced, as they walked through the gates of the small town.

Small wooden houses lined the dirt paths that served as streets. Children played openly in the street as people went about their daily lives.

Though not as large or impressive as Esenor, Aiden and Siri were still impressed with the size of it. Mina, who had grown up in the forest, and had never been to a town or city before, held Aiden's hand so tightly he thought she might break it. Her tail swished about in a panic, her body beginning to tremble as her legs became weak. Aiden felt her distress through their bond.

"Master..." Mina barely got out as she began to hyperventilate, not knowing what to do, or what to expect in this strange place.

Aiden pulled Mina close, leaning his head down so their foreheads rested against each other, staring into each other's eyes.

"Just look at me... no one else, only me." Aiden whispered, staring into her bright, sapphire eyes.

Taking her hand, Aiden placed it over his heart.

"Feel my heartbeat."

Mina splayed her fingers out across his bare chest, feeling the steady beat beneath her palm.

"Listen to my voice... drown everything else out." Aiden ran his thumb across her cheek, wiping away her tears.

"You are with me... only me." he whispered soothingly.

"Only Master." Mina repeated quietly.

Aiden allowed the calling to slip out, gently purring to her to calm her, while never breaking eye contact. As her breathing began to slow, Aiden could hear her heartbeat slowly returning to normal as well. Lifting her up, he placed her legs around his waist as she buried her head in his chest, closing her eyes and focusing on his heartbeat, breathing in his scent as she surrendered to the calling's effect on her body.

Looking up, Aiden saw that many of the townsfolk, both men and women, had stopped to watch their interaction.

"That is the sweetest thing I've ever seen." a woman nearby said under her breath to another woman she was talking to.

"Strong and gentle." another said, wiping a tear from her eye.

"She's so lucky." said another.

"What are they doing mama?" a young boy asked, pointing at Mina wrapped in Aiden's arms.

"Don't you worry about them. Come, let's give them some room." his mother said, taking his hand and leading him away.

After witnessing Aiden comfort Mina, the atmosphere in the town seemed to change. Men nodded their heads to Aiden in respect, while women stared at him in awe.

Holding Mina with one arm, Aiden slipped the other around Siri's waist as he continued down the street. Raizel, Andarii and Sylvia followed closely behind.

Damien led them through the streets of the town, pointing out areas of interest.

"Over here is the town blacksmith. If you require weapons or armor, he is the one to see... this shop sells herbs and potions in case your group is in need of any healing supplies. Two buildings down on your left is a general goods shop. It is usually kept well stocked. If you need something, they should have it. The town market is down to your right at the end of the street if you, or any of your group is interested."

Finally, Damien led them through a large, open area with a raised platform connecting to a small stage. Just past it was a building much larger than the others in the town, with a small porch wrapping around the side. Just in front of the house, two young men were engaged in a sparring match, striking, kicking and grappling with each other. They reminded Aiden of how he and his brother Thomas would often get into sparring matches, just to see who the better fighter was.

Standing on the porch was a young woman in a blue dress with brown curly hair falling to her shoulders, with a broom in her hands as she swept the dirt from the porch. Seeing them approaching, the woman scolded the two young men.

"You two, knock it off, we have guests." she said, getting the two men's attention as they stopped fighting.

"Welcome, Beta Damien." the girl beamed, cheeks flushed as they approached.

"Hello Alice, how are you?" Damien replied.

"How was your mission?" she asked excitedly.

"See for yourself." Damien answered, stepping aside. "May I introduce Aiden... the one single handedly responsible for eradicating the vampuric scourge from our land."

Alice dropped the broom as she looked at Aiden. She had heard about the rumor that someone single handedly killed the entire horde of vampurics. She had thought about what such a person would look like, given the strength needed to kill that many vampurics. Seeing Aiden now, she could only stare. Even with the catgirl wrapped around him, Alice could see that he was indeed extremely well built, chiseled abs and a strong chest. Those strange eyes of his, bright red with just a hint of blue in them, his jet black hair making them stand out even more. But it was the scars that had caused her to drop the broom. Never before had she seen that many scars on someone before.

As the broom hit the ground, the sound snapped her out of her shock.

"I...I apologize for staring, it's just... I just..." she stammered, trying her best not to appear rude, or to offend.

"It is quit alright young lady, I am fully aware that my scars can come as a shock to most people, no need to apologize." Aiden told her.

"Were they caused by the horde of vampurics?" Alice asked.

"No, something far worse." Aiden chuckled.

"What could be worse than a horde of feral vampurics?

"That's... personal." Aiden replied, looking down at the catgirl curled up against his chest.

"Of course, I understand. Please, forget I asked... and who are your companions?" Alice asked, looking at Siri standing next to Aiden as well as the girl he was holding.

"This charming redhead beside me is my mate Siri." he answered.

"Nice to meet you." Siri said.

"And this shy thing in my arms is my other mate, Mina." Aiden continued, causing the catgirl to look up at him for a few seconds when she heard her name, before snuggling back into his chest.

"Well welcome Aiden, Siri and Mina, to the Silver Moon Pack. My name is Alice. Alpha Logan is my father. Please come in, your friends are welcome to join us as well." Alice said cheerfully, opening the door and gesturing inside.

Once inside, Alice led them to a large room with several couches as well as a few chairs.

"Please have a seat, I will let father know you are here." the young girl said, disappearing into the next room, followed by Damien.

Aiden and the group took a seat, waiting for Alice to return.

Several minutes later, Alice reappeared.

"Alpha Aiden, If you would follow me please. Your mates, and the rest of your pack must stay out here." she told them.

"Where I go.. my mates go. Period." Aiden replied sternly.

"Of course... as you wish, I meant no disrespect. Please follow me." Alice stammered, caught off guard by Aiden's abruptness.

Aiden stood and followed Alice, still carrying Mina as Siri followed close behind.

Alice led them down the hall to her father's study, knocking twice before opening the door. Once they were inside, Alice left, closing the door behind her.

"I thought I told my daughter to tell you to come alone." Alpha Logan said, narrowing his eyes at Aiden when he saw Siri and Mina.

"She did."

"I do not talk business with females present." Alpha Logan said sternly, attempting to intimidate Aiden.

"And I do not talk business without my lunas... let's go Siri." Aiden replied casually, turning to leave.

"Wait." Logan said.

"I don't believe we have anything left to talk about." Aiden replied, leaving the study.

Two steps outside the door, Aiden suddenly felt a weight pressing down on him from all directions. Mina whimpered as Siri struggled to stand.

"We're not done." came the angry voice of Alpha logan.

Aiden turned to see Alpha Logan stand and walk towards him, the pressure getting worse.

"This is my pack, and I'm the alpha. I will not be disrespected." he told Aiden.

Siri was forced to her knees as the pressure around them increased even further, while Mina continued to whimper loudly in Aiden's arms.

"Only another alpha can resist the aura of an alpha. You've already told my beta you are not an alpha. So even if you are a hellhound, you must still obey the commands of an alpha... now submit." Alpha Logan commanded as he increased the force of his will on them.

Aiden had dropped to one knee as Siri and Mina writhed in pain. Aiden too felt the pain, doing his best to resist.

"You think all that power means you can do whatever you want? I was willing to reward you for dealing with the vampurics, but not now. Now, you will do as I command. Now kneel!" Alpha Logan commanded, forcing his will on them in full force.

Andarii, Raizel and Sylvia came running into the hall when they heard the yelling. Alpha Logan's aura hit them like a wall, forcing them to the ground as well.

Aiden saw his group being affected by the aura Alpha Logan was emitting, but still wouldn't kneel. Something inside him told him to stand tall, to stand for his group of comrades... no, Aiden finally realized... not his comrades... his pack... and they would not kneel to the likes of this pathetic alpha.

Placing Mina on the ground, Aiden closed his eyes and began to rise.

"I said kneel! Alpha Logan yelled, hitting Aiden with another wave of his aura.

Aiden dropped a few inches but continued to stand.

"That's impossible!" Alpha Logan said, watching Aiden resist his aura, continuing to stand.

Aiden felt a new strength flow through his body, and he knew what it meant. Aiden opened his eyes, a bright red in a sea of swirling black. Bright red irises glowing brighter than they ever have before.

"You have to obey me, I'm the alpha!" Logan screamed at Aiden, fear in his eyes.

"No."

Alpha Logan's aura shattered, unable to push against Aiden's own aura as it poured out of him, washing over his own pack members, freeing them from the pressure of Alpha Logan's will, stopping the pain, and allowing them to stand.

Siri helped Mina to her feet, then stood by Aiden's side. Raizel, Andarii and Sylvia fell in line behind Aiden.

"I am not a beta... nor am I a hellhound, or a werewolf." Aiden spoke, glaring at Logan.

Alpha Logan took a step back as Aiden stepped forward.

"What the hell are you?" Logan cried.

"I am Aiden." Aiden continued walking towards Logan, his pack behind him.

"Stay away!" he screamed.

"Heir to the throne of the vampyres, the vampurics, the werewolves, and the hellhounds."

"No."

"I am all of these and none of them. I am the Hybrid. I am the Apex of apex predators... and now... I am an alpha."

The room around them began to shake.

"The Alpha of alpha's... and I kneel to no one."

Alpha Logan stood, backed up against his desk, staring at Aiden, unable to believe his own eyes.

Aiden dropped his aura, having successfully risen to the status of alpha. The room stopped shaking.

Looking across the room at Logan and Damien, Aiden roared at them, forcing them both to their knees with just the power of his own voice.

Logan and Damien knelt in submission as Aiden turned and left, his pack following him.

As they entered the waiting room they were in earlier, Logan's daughter was there.

"Alpha." Alice said, kneeling in submission, lowering her eyes.

Aiden ignored her as he walked out of the house.

~ ~ ~ ~ ~

A crowd had gathered outside the alpha's home after hearing the commotion from inside as well as the shaking that came from the house.

"What's going on here?" Jonas demanded, stepping forward from the crowd.

Mina grabbed Aiden's hand as Jonas marched forward, demanding answers.

Jonas looked at Mina, then looked at Aiden, before looking back at Mina. Aiden noticed his gaze as Mina squeezed his hand. Aiden turned, looking at Mina, silently asking a question. Mina nodded, not needing Aiden to ask the question out loud.

"I asked what's going on here? Where's my uncle... the alpha? Tell me!" Jonas yelled, grabbing Aiden's arm.

Aiden spun, grabbing Jonas by the throat and lifting him up.

"So you are the one who can't keep his eyes off another man's mate." Aiden growled.

Jonas' eyes went wide in fear, suddenly realizing the vast difference in power between them as he struggled in Aiden's grip.

"And not just anyone's mate either, but you dare to ogle at an alpha's luna?" Anger dripped from his voice.

Jonas pissed himself out of fear, the rage in Aiden's eyes instilling a primal sense of terror in him.

"I'm sorry, it won't happen again Alpha. I swear." Jonas choked around Aiden's fingers.

Aiden lowered Jonas to look him in the eyes before responding.

"You're right, it won't happen again. In fact... you will never look at another man's mate ever again."

Aiden extended his claws, growling as he plunged his fingers into Jonas' eye sockets, permanently blinding him.

Aiden dropped the screaming man onto the ground as he turned and picked up Mina. Once she was in his arms, Aiden stepped over Jonas as he lay on the ground screaming, holding his face.

"Were leaving."

# Chapter 45

"Well, that went well." Raizel commented as he and Andarii sat around the campfire.

"More like a waste of time." Andarii replied.

"I wouldn't say a complete waste of time." Raizel corrected, looking into the distance where Aiden and the girls were.

"He is an alpha now."

"So what happens now?" Siri asked, leaning against Aiden's side.

"We wait." Aiden said, staring out into the darkness.

"What is Master waiting for?" Mina asked, leaning against his other side.

"A response."

~ ~ ~ ~ ~

After a few hours, Siri began drifting off to sleep.

"It's getting late, let's get you girls to bed." Aiden said, noticing the girls' exhaustion.

Aiden picked Siri up and carried her back to the tent, doing his best to not wake her. Sylvia opened the tent for him as he stepped inside, Mina following behind him.

Walking over, Aiden gently laid Siri down onto the bed. As Mina got ready for bed, Aiden moved to Siri's feet and began to carefully remove her travelling boots, before continuing up her body. Aiden carefully removed each item of clothing, before pulling the blankets across her. Leaning down, Aiden placed a kiss on Siri's forehead as he whispered.

"Sweet dreams, my love."

Mina climbed into bed beside Siri, and Aiden repeated the process on Mina.

Turning to leave, Aiden heard Mina call to him.

"Master?" Mina whispered, so she wouldn't wake Siri.

Aiden looked back to see Mina reaching for him.

Sitting back down on the bed, Aiden pulled her in for a hug, wrapping his arms around her.

"I'm sorry baby, not tonight. I have something that must be taken care of, and it can't wait till morning." Aiden whispered in her ear as she held him tight.

Mina looked up as Aiden leaned in and kissed her.

"Sleep, my angel. I promise I'll be here when you wake up." Aiden whispered, laying her back down. Aiden reached over, grabbing his pillow and giving it to Mina. Mina hugged it close as Aiden pulled the blanket over her, her eyes fluttering closed.

~ ~ ~ ~ ~

Raizel, as well as Sylvia had already retired for the night as Aiden stepped out of the tent. Andarii sat near the fire, taking first watch of the night.

"My lord, what are you still doing up? Why are you not with your mates?" the elf asked.

Aiden sat down beside him. looking into the fire.

"The day's not over yet. There's still something I must do." Aiden replied.

"What exactly would that be, my lord?"

Aiden tilted his head slightly, as if listening for something.

"She's here." Aiden said, standing up as he looked out into the darkness.

"Come out. There's no point in hiding, I can hear you." Aiden spoke, command in his voice.

Alice slowly came out from behind the tree she was hiding behind. Aiden knew she had been there for the last hour, but decided not to address it until now.

As she got closer to Aiden, she stopped and turned her head slightly, baring her neck in submission.

"Why are you here?" he asked, acknowledging her submission.

Stepping forward, Alice knelt on the ground a few paces from Aiden's feet.

"Alpha Aiden... my father wishes to make peace with you. He acknowledges his mistake and wishes to make amends."

"And he thought by sending a woman, I would be less likely to retaliate and kill the messenger?"

Tears formed in her eyes when he said that.

"Stop crying... tears will not help you here." Aiden told her.

"I'm sorry, Alpha... my father sent me for two reasons. One is as you have said, the other is that I am not as valuable as my brothers. If you were to kill me, he would still have his heirs." she answered, wiping the tears from her face.

"You haven't answered my question." Aiden said, looking down at the girl.

"Sir?" she asked, confused.

"I didn't ask why your father sent you. I asked why you are here."

"Then... you know?" Alice asked.

Aiden nodded.

"I knew the moment you first knelt in submission to me in your father's house. You did not submit out of fear, like your father, or his beta. You submitted because you wanted to." Aiden informed her.

Alice leaned forward, burying her face in the dirt.

"Alpha Aiden, please... take me with you when you leave. There are many others who also wish to leave Alpha Logan's tyrannical rule, but he won't allow it. Please... take us in, let us be a part of your pack. We would serve you faithfully. Not all of us agree with my father's way of ruling, but we cannot stand against him, only another alpha can do that. We cannot just leave his pack on our own. But if we shift loyalty to another alpha, and if he accepts us as pack members, then my father would have no choice but to allow us our freedom. Please, Alpha Aiden, I beg you... save us."

Alice had not lifted her head once while she begged.

"Tell your father I will come to see him tomorrow. As for your other request... those that desire, should make camp just outside my camp tomorrow afternoon after I meet with your father. When ready, I shall evaluate each person before making my decision. But under no circumstance are they to enter my camp. Doing so will automatically disqualify them for pack membership." Aiden told her.

Alice finally looked up at Aiden from her bowed position.

"Thank you, Alpha Aiden." she said through tears.

"Once you have informed your father of my visit, return here immediately, have those you trust spread the word about tomorrow on your behalf." Aiden instructed her.

"You wish for me to return tonight?"

"Yes Alice, you will stay here, with your pack. I, Alpha Aiden, accept you as part of my pack. Now go."

"Yes, my Alpha." Alice said, leaving to give her father Aiden's message.

"You sure that was wise my Lord?" Andarii asked, stepping up beside Aiden.

Aiden nodded his head as he turned to the elf.

"Earlier today, Raizel advised me not to just throw away a potential ally, and we may need them. When she returns, provide her with some bedding and a place to sleep. We have a long day ahead of us tomorrow." Aiden said, then retired to his tent.

# Chapter 46

Mina woke to the sensation of Aiden's fingers dancing along her spine.

"mmm... that feels good Master." Mina cooed, pulling herself closer to him.

"Mina, I need to go back into town today. I'm taking Siri with me. You can either come with us, or stay here. Which would you prefer?" Aiden asked.

"How long will Master be gone?" she asked, rubbing her face on his chest.

"Only a couple of hours, it shouldn't take long." Aiden answered, sliding his hand down and playing with the catgirl's tail, causing her to shiver on top of him.

"Master go... Mina still want to sleep. Master spend time with Mina when he gets back?" she asked, still not fully awake.

"Sure, just the two of us." Aiden assured her, sliding her off his chest.

Aiden pulled the blanket back up over Mina, kissing her shoulder before getting dressed.

~ ~ ~ ~ ~

As Aiden exited the tent, he caught sight of Siri chatting with Sylvia as she prepared breakfast.

Walking up behind her, he wrapped his arms around her waist, kissing her neck.

"She decided to stay and sleep." he said between kisses.

"I thought she would." Siri responded.

Aiden had already discussed the events of last night, as well as his plans for today with her when she woke up earlier this morning.

"Good morning Alpha, Luna." Alice greeted them as she came over.

Aiden nodded to her before continuing his assault on Siri's shoulder and neck.

"When are we leaving?" she asked.

"Right after breakfast gets done cooking." Siri said, lightly pushing Aiden's head away, not really wanting him to stop.

Knowing she didn't want him to actually stop, Aiden ignored her as he kept kissing her.

"I'm not sure I can wait till then." Aiden whispered, gently biting into Siri's neck.

Aiden released her a few seconds later, sealing the wound before kissing where he had just bitten.

Alice stood there, watching them with a confused look on her face.

"I guess we should explain." Aiden whispered into Siri's ear when he saw the look on Alice's face.

Aiden and Siri sat down with Alice and explained to her about Aiden being a hybrid. Having not been in the room yesterday, she still did not know he wasn't just a hellhound.

"Wow, that's... a lot to take in." Alice said.

"Does it make you uncomfortable that I'm part vampyre and vampuric?" Aiden asked.

"No, but it may take a little time to get used to." she answered honestly.

"His powers are still evolving and getting stronger. We're still not sure just how powerful he will become." Siri commented.

"Alright, time to go see your father." Aiden said.

~ ~ ~ ~ ~

"Where have you been all morning young lady?"

Alice's father was upset because she was not there to fix breakfast for himself and his sons this morning.

"We'll deal with this later, now get to work, you have chores to do." Logan commanded his daughter.

Alice did not move from her seat next to Aiden and Siri.

"Are you ignoring me girl?"

Her father tried to not lose his temper in front of Aiden, knowing how well it went the last time he tried pulling rank.

"I'm afraid she no longer falls under your authority." Aiden said, leaning back on the couch across from Alpha Logan.

"What are you talking about? She's my daughter, of course she is under my authority." Logan replied, looking at Aiden.

"Not anymore... as of last night, she is now one of my betas."

"What!?" Alpha Logan yelled, standing up from his chair.

"Sit Down." Aiden commanded. The sternness in his voice and the glow in his eyes causing Logan to shut up and sit back down.

"I will be blunt with you, you are a tyrant. You force others to do your bidding simply because you can, and she has had enough living beneath your thumb. Had you not sent her to me last night, she would have come to me on her own anyway. I am not like you Alpha Logan, my subordinates do not follow me because they have to. They follow me because they want to, and I, in turn, am willing to lay down my life for theirs. You asked me here to make peace, because you know you cannot afford to go to war with me."

Alpha logan knew what Aiden said was true, he truly could not afford to go to war against this man.

"You want to talk peace, so let's talk peace." Aiden said. "You and your pack have offended me three times in the last twenty four hours. I come here to meet you, by your own request, only for you to insult my lunas in front of my face."

"That wasn't my intention." Alpha Logan said.

"Because I chose my mates, over your authority... you tried to force me and my pack to submit." Aiden continued.

"Although I should be thanking you. Your need to dominate gave me the push I needed to become an alpha myself."

Logan remained quiet.

"Then, there is still the matter of your nephew." Aiden leaned forward, crossing his arms.

"What about him?" Logan asked.

"He still hasn't paid for the disrespect he showed me and my luna."

"You already blinded him. He has already paid for his actions." Logan said, raising his voice slightly.

"He is lucky I let him live at all! He paid for his inappropriate behavior towards another man's mate by losing his sight. But he has not paid for the damage he caused to my luna. As alpha, it is your responsibility to see to his punishment." Aiden yelled, causing the other alpha to shrink back in his chair.

"If that is what it takes to have peace between us... so be it. What would you have me do?" Alpha Logan asked, head down in defeat.

"Fifteen lashes with a wolfsbane soaked whip." Aiden answered.

"Fifteen?" Logan nearly yelled.

"One for each hour I spent comforting my mate." Aiden replied flatly.

Lowering his voice, Logan looked across the table at Aiden. "Very well."

"Carried out publicly, before the entire pack." Aiden added. "Anything else?"

"Should any of your pack members wish to leave your pack and seek another, you will allow it." Aiden told him.

Alpha Logan looked across the room to his beta, Damien. "Do it." Alpha Logan said.

~ ~ ~ ~ ~

An hour later, Aiden, Siri, and Alice left Alpha Logan's home. The pack had already been gathered before the platform next to the alpha's house.

Damien was dragging Jonas through the crowd with his hands tied.

"Get up!" he commanded every time Jonas stumbled in his blindness.

Dragging him onto the platform, Damien tied Jonas' hands above him to a wooden post in the middle of the platform, then secured each leg to an anchor point in the floor, preventing the man from moving.

"What's going on? Why are you doing this?" Jonas asked, not knowing what was happening.

"For the crimes of looking at another man's mate with bad intentions, the trouble it caused his mate, and the embarrassment to this pack... you, Jonas, are hereby sentenced to fifteen lashes with a wolfsbane soaked whip. May it serve as a reminder to you, as well as to all others, the consequences of having impure intentions towards another's mate." Damien called out, loud enough for everyone to hear.

Jonas screamed and struggled against his bonds as Damien ripped his shirt, leaving his back exposed.

"No! Please, don't do this, I'm sorry!" he begged, straining with all his might against his bonds.

Reaching down into a bucket, Damien pulled out a whip that had been soaking it's lower half in a wolfsbane solution for the last forty five minutes.

"One!" Damien said as he brought the whip down across Jonas' back, splitting the flesh as the wolfsbane burned the wound, preventing him from healing.

"Two!" he called, as the whip cracked once more.

Damien did not hold back as he swung the whip, not willing to go easy, for fear of what might happen if he did. Jonas screamed until his voice was hoarse... each lash adding more pain. Unable to move, and unable to heal, Jonas had no choice but to take each and every lash.

By lash five, Jonas could no longer support his own weight as he hung limply from his bound wrists. On lash nine, he passed out, only to be woken with a bucket of water to the face before resuming.

Aiden watched the entire thing. He knew the punishment was excessive, but he also knew it was necessary. An example had to be made. Neither Aiden nor Siri felt bad for Jonas.

Wrapping his arm around Siri, they left the area, heading down the street once the people began to dissipate.

~ ~ ~ ~ ~

Making their way down the street, Aiden decided to take a detour before heading back to camp.

"Alice, head back to camp and help organize those that wish to join us." Aiden instructed her.

"Yes, my Alpha." she answered.

"Once the selection is done, I will have another task for you. Also, if any complain about the order, or about the wait, dismiss them from the selection immediately. There is also to be no fighting."

"Of course, it will be done." Alice said, bowing slightly before running off.

Aiden and Siri continued walking. The end of the street opened up into a large market square, similar to the one they had back in Esenor, just slightly smaller. Siri's eyes lit up as she realized where they were and why Aiden had chosen to take the detour.

"One hour, anything you want. Have fun." Aiden told her as he pulled her close, leaning down for a kiss before releasing her.

Soon, Siri was dragging him back and forth between the different shops. Aiden smiled, seeing the happy look on Siri's face as she raced between the shops and stalls with a bounce in her step.

Aiden and Siri stepped into what appeared to be a book shop.

As they entered, an older man greeted them as he was packing away some books into a box behind the counter.

"Please come in, take a look around, but be aware, the shop is closing soon. My wife and I have an appointment this afternoon." the man said, not looking up from what he was doing.

"That's disappointing, I was hoping to get a few books for my mate before leaving town." Aiden replied.

Looking up from the counter, the man saw who it was that had entered his shop.

"Apologies Alpha, Luna... take as much time as you want." the man stammered.

"It's no problem. Please don't rearrange your schedule just for us." Siri insisted.

"Of course, Luna... truth be told, my wife and I were closing early today to come see you and your mate." the old man replied.

"What did you wish to see me about?" Aiden asked.

"We heard you were holding interviews for pack membership to anyone who wished to leave Alpha Logan's pack. Besides, no one in this town seems to care about books or reading anymore. Alpha Logan doesn't care for anyone other than the young and strong. Business has been declining more and more over the years. Soon, we won't be able to afford to stay open, and Alpha Logan doesn't accept useless wolves in his pack."

"I see. While I'm not much of a reader myself, My luna here, is an avid reader. She finds much value in books." Aiden told him.

"Then please, take a look around. If you have any questions, feel free to ask." the man told her as he went back to work.

Siri stood in front of a bookshelf, dozens and dozens of books of different sizes and subjects filled the shelf. Aiden walked up behind her, wrapping his arms around her waist as she scanned the shelf for anything that catches her eye.

"Find anything worth reading, love?" he asked.

Nodding, Siri held up three books she was holding as she continued looking for more.

"Aiden?" Siri whispered, pointing to a book that was placed on a shelf too high for her to reach.

Instead of grabbing the book for her as she expected, Aiden picked her up by the waist, causing her to squeal as she dropped the books she was holding.

"That's not what I meant, and you know it." Siri said, retrieving the book and smacking Aiden with it, her face red with embarrassment.

Setting her down, Aiden kissed her on the forehead before apologizing.

"Ready to go? I promised Mina I'd spend some time with her once we got back." Aiden asked, picking up the books Siri had dropped.

Siri nodded, walking over and placing the book on the counter, followed by Aiden.

"We would like these four books." Siri said as the old man came over.

"Certainly. For the Luna who loves to read, they are free of charge." the man said, smiling at Siri.

"We appreciate it, but I would rather pay for it. This is a shopping spree after all, and I enjoy spoiling her." Aiden replied, the old man nodding in response.

Once the books were paid for, Aiden shook the man's hand before speaking.

"Don't bother coming to the pack evaluation with everyone else. I already know everything I need to know. On behalf of my luna, I invite you and your family into my pack. We will be leaving tomorrow, pack what you need and be at the camp, ready for travel in the morning."

"Thank you Alpha. We appreciate your kindness. My name is Gerald, please let me know if there is anything you need in the future." he said.

"Just keep some books on hand. I'm sure my luna will provide you with plenty of business in the future."

"Certainly, when you are ready for another book, please don't hesitate to seek me out." Gerald replied.

"What was that for? Why invite them to the pack? We are still travelling, and he won't be able to set up shop." Siri asked, after they stepped outside.

"What if I told you I don't care about his shop, but that I did it just for you?" Aiden asked.

Siri reached up, wrapping her arms around Aiden's neck as she gave him a deep kiss.

"I'd believe you." she giggled.

# Chapter 47

Arriving back at the camp, Aiden could see quite the crowd had formed, seeking entry to his pack. He knew they expected him to begin the evaluations now that he was back, but Aiden had other things to do before then. Dropping off the bags of things Siri had bought, Aiden went looking for Mina.

Just as he thought, Aiden found her still asleep in bed.

Grabbing the clothes Sylvia had laid out for her, Aiden made his way across the room to the table. Sitting down at the table, he let the calling slip out, causing Mina to stir beneath the blankets.

Mina turned to look at Aiden, eyes pleading with him. Still laying down, she stretched her arms out toward him, wanting him to join her.

"No, Mina. You want me, you're going to have to come over here. It's almost noon and you need to get up." Aiden said quietly, letting the calling do its work.

Mina really wanted to stay in bed, but her desire to be close to Aiden, as well as the gentle pull from the calling won out as she slowly pulled herself out of bed.

Slowly, and still half asleep, Mina made her way over to Aiden, crawling into his lap.

"Good girl." Aiden told her, as she melted against him.

"Ok, arms up." he instructed, picking up her shirt.

Mina obeyed as Aiden slid the shirt over her head. Now that she at least had a shirt on, Aiden could properly focus on getting some food in her.

On the table was a variety of different fruits that Sylvia brought in earlier today. Knowing Mina's tendency to sleep in, she always brought food that didn't have to be heated up or cooked.

Aiden picked up a strawberry, taking a small bite, before offering it to Mina.

Opening her mouth, Mina accepted the food Aiden was offering her. Giggling, Mina reached over for another strawberry, taking a small bite before offering it to Aiden as well.

This little game of theirs went back and forth until most of the food had been eaten.

"Better?" Aiden asked, looking into her eyes.

Mina nodded, climbing off Aiden as she put the rest of her clothes on.

"What are Master's plans today?" Mina asked as she got dressed.

"I still have some business to attend to this afternoon." Aiden answered.

Mina's ears drooped a bit, hearing that.

"But first, I have to keep the promise I made to my girl." Aiden said, causing her ears to perk back up.

"Master will spend time with Mina? Just Master and Mina?" she asked excitedly, her tail swishing behind her as Aiden got up and walked over to her.

Wrapping his arms around her, Aiden whispered softly into her ear.

"Just us. For the next two hours, you have me all to yourself." he whispered, making the catgirl shake with excitement.

Mina pulled out of Aiden's arms, grabbing his hand and pulling him towards the door and out into the sun.

"And where are we going?" Aiden asked as he followed the catgirl.

Mina turned, pulling Aiden down into a kiss. Mina could taste the lingering flavor of strawberries on his lips as she kissed him. Mina bit down on his lip slightly before pulling away.

"To have fun." she answered, then took off running.

Aiden stood there watching her running off for a few seconds.

"What are you waiting for.. that's clearly a woman who wants to be chased." Siri said, looking up from the book she was reading by the campfire.

Not having to be told twice, Aiden chased after Mina.

Aiden purposefully ran slow, knowing he could easily catch her if he wanted. But this was Mina's game, and he would play by her rules.

"Now where could my little Mina be hiding?" Aiden teased, looking around the trees for her.

Aiden heard a giggle come from behind a large rock. Quietly climbing over the rock, Aiden saw Mina peeking around the corner, looking for him.

"Found you." Aiden said reaching for her as she squealed, taking off running again.

Climbing down from the rock, Aiden followed in the direction she had run.

Aiden spent the next half hour searching for Mina, only for her to squeal and run off each time he found her, before hiding again.

"Oh Mina, where are you?" Aiden called playfully, making his way through the trees.

Mina jumped out of a tree as Aiden passed beneath her, tackling him to the ground as she began peppering his face with kisses while giggling.

"Mina wins." she said, snuggling into his chest.

"And what exactly does Mina get for winning?" Aiden asked, tickling her side.

"A ride." Mina answered, sitting up and looking down at Aiden.

"Mina wants a ride?" he asked.

Mina nodded.

"Mina wants to ride on the back of Master's wolf. Mina wants to feel the wind in her hair. Wants to know what it is like for Master." she replied quietly.

Several seconds passed as Aiden stared at her.

"Is it okay with Master?" Mina asked.

Reaching up, Aiden began to twirl her raven hair in his fingers.

"I'd do anything for my girl." Aiden whispered, getting lost in the ocean of her eyes.

~ ~ ~ ~ ~

"Ready?" Aiden asked.

"Ready Master." Mina nodded.

Handing his shirt and trousers to Mina, Aiden shifted into his werewolf form. Even though smaller than his hellhound, or his hybrid form, his shoulders still came to Mina's chest in height.

Aiden knelt down, allowing Mina to climb onto his back.

She marveled at the softness of Aiden's black fur, running her hands through it, enjoying the feeling. Mina sat just behind Aiden's shoulders, with a fistful of his fur in each hand to keep her balance. Aiden stood and began to walk, letting Mina get used to riding.

"Faster Master." Mina asked as he began to trot.

Mina held on tightly, leaning down into his neck.

"Run Master!"

Aiden took off.

Mina was having the time of her life. Feeling more confident, she leaned back up, closing her eyes as the wind blew through her hair.

Opening her eyes, seeing the trees rush by and the land stretch out before them, Mina felt free.

"This is amazing Master!" she said, leaning back down, hugging his neck tightly.

"How fast can Master run?"

Mina had to tighten her grip even more as Aiden sped up. Mina spent the next hour riding atop the back of Aiden's wolf, sprinting across the plains, without a care in the world.

# Chapter 48

"Let me explain how this is going to happen."

Aiden's voice was loud as he spoke to the group that had gathered, seeking acceptance into his pack.

"Those of you who only wish to leave Alpha Logan's pack to escape him, should leave now. Only those with good reason will be given the opportunity to join my pack. Beyond that, it is at my discretion whether to allow membership or not. Let us begin."

Three chairs had been set up on a makeshift platform. Aiden sat in the middle, Mina and Siri sat to his left and right. Sylvia stood off to the side, mind linked with Aiden.

Over the next few hours, Aiden sorted through those who had come. Listening to their story, and choosing whether to accept or reject membership to his pack. Several times throughout, Sylvia would mind link with Aiden informing him when someone was hiding something, or lying. By the end, over two thirds of the applicants had been rejected. Leaving only twenty men, thirty women, and around twenty children, ranging from newborn to eighteen. Only a few applicants remained for Aiden to judge.

Halfway through, Mina had become increasingly nervous, so Aiden let her and Siri step off to the side so Mina would feel more comfortable.

A man and his family stepped forward presenting themselves.

"Alpha, my name is Tiberius, and this is my wife Rene." the man introduced himself.

The woman beside him looked as though she had been crying, but was trying to hide it.

"This is our son, Timothy."

A young man approached from behind them, kneeling in front of Aiden, before returning behind his father.

"And may I present to you, our daughter." he said, stepping aside.

A young girl slowly stepped forward from behind him.

"Go on girl, introduce yourself to the alpha." Tiberius said, pushing her forward.

She had been dressed in revealing clothes, her legs shaking as she walked a few feet forward.

"M.. my name is Evelyn, sir." she said, shakily.

Aiden could smell her fear.

"Come here, girl." Aiden commanded, motioning her to step onto the platform with him.

"Yes, Alpha.' she replied, stepping up and stopping in front of Aiden.

Aiden noticed the corners of her father's mouth curl into a smile when he told the man's daughter to come to him.

She had long, dark hair with natural waves in it, eyes a warm amber color. Aiden stood, circling the girl, observing the way she ever so slightly leaned away from his gaze. Her hands shook as she kept them at her sides, trying to remain calm.

"Do you fear me?" Aiden asked.

"Of course not, Alpha." her father interjected.

"You will not speak again unless spoken to!" Aiden spat, turning to the man, allowing his aura to force the man to his knees.

"The girl will speak for herself." Aiden said, releasing his aura before turning back to the girl.

"Do you fear me?" Aiden asked again.

"Y.. yes." she whispered.

"Why?" he asked, continuing to circle her, watching her reactions.

Something wasn't right... even if she was afraid of him, she shouldn't have this much fear. The way she pulls away from his gaze tells him she doesn't like him looking at her body, yet the clothes she wore, were clothes meant for seduction.

"Y.. you're th.. the alpha." she stammered.

"Why does that make you afraid of me?"

With a slight motion of his fingers, Andarii, Raizel, Sylvia and Alice began clearing the remaining people from the area, leaving Aiden, the girl, and her family alone.

"Th.. the alpha takes what h.. he wants." she answered.

"And?"

"And i.. it scares me, Alpha."

Aiden stopped in front of the girl, her eyes were glued to the floor, a puddle had formed where her tears were falling.

"Look at me." Aiden commanded softly.

Slowly, she looked up into Aiden's softly glowing red eyes.

"Why does it scare you?"

The girl's lip began to tremble.

"When I ask a question, I expect an answer. Why does it scare you?" Aiden asked, keeping his voice calm and quiet.

"Father ex.. expects you to li.. like me, t.. to be.. become your p.. pet." she admitted, turning her eyes away, unable to hold his gaze any longer.

Walking behind the girl, Aiden looked back at her father, who was sweating profusely. Her mother had a confused, but hopeful look on her face, not knowing what was going to happen. The girl's brother was staring at his father in disgust. Aiden could tell he hadn't known.

Ignoring them for the moment, Aiden turned back to the girl.

"Lift your arms." he told her.

Slowly, the girl began to obey, raising her shaking arms as she began to cry louder, closing her eyes, afraid of what would happen next.

Evelyn felt a warm, soft cloth being pulled over her arms, slowly being drawn downward, covering her.

Opening her eyes, the girl looked down. She was now wearing the shirt that Aiden had been wearing, covering the girl down to mid-thigh.

"Do not be afraid of me." Aiden whispered into her ear, motioning for Mina and Siri.

Evelyn turned to see that Aiden had walked away from her and was now standing over her father.

Feeling two sets of soft hands on her shoulders, she turned. The alpha's lunas were there, asking her to follow them, saying that it would be ok.

Nodding her head, Evelyn looked back at Aiden one more time before following them.

"I do not appreciate being taken as a fool." Aiden said, glaring down at the girl's father.

"Alpha please, I can explain." Tiberius began saying.

"Do not speak another word." Aiden commanded.

"Boy." Aiden said, looking at the man's son.

"Alpha?" Timothy asked, looking up from a kneeled position.

"I take it you did not know of your fathers plan?"

"No, Alpha." he answered.

Turning to the girl's mother, Aiden had one question. "Do you support your children, or your husband?"

Tiberius gave her a mean glare.

She looked at him, then to her son, and then back at Aiden.

"My children, Alpha." she said.

"You two timing bi..."

Aiden grabbed the man by his throat before he could finish his statement. Motioning with his free hand, Andarii came forward.

"Take them to see the girl... and send Alice back when you go." he commanded.

The woman and her son followed Andarii as Aiden kept his eyes on the man in his grip.

"Alpha, you sent for me?" Alice asked, bowing slightly when she arrived.

"Please retrieve the former city guard and his three sons that have joined the pack. I have a task for them."

"Right away, Alpha." she replied, bowing before rushing off to follow Aiden's instructions.

Several minutes later, a large man and his equally well built sons knelt before Aiden.

"What would my Alpha ask of us?" he asked.

"Your name was Tyrien, correct?"

"Yes, Alpha."

"This man has attempted to deceive me, and attempted to use his own daughter's body to buy favor from me. I do not appreciate being thought of as a fool, or the blatant disrespect of my mates. He is banished from my pack. Give him three minutes head start to run, then... you and your boys may begin your hunt."

Aiden released Tiberius as he fell to the ground, begging.

"Please Alpha, I'm sorry, I was wrong to attempt to buy favor with you using my daughter. Please forgive me." he begged.

"You're wasting precious time." Aiden replied.

"Alpha please, three minutes is hardly fair."

"I guess you're right."

Tiberius let out a sigh of relief.

"Two minutes... and by my calculation, you've already wasted thirty seconds." Aiden finished.

Tiberius' eyes went wide as he took off into a sprint.

Tyrien and his sons had already begun to shift as they awaited their alpha's command.

Turning to head back into camp, Aiden looked over his shoulder.

"Leave him in pieces."

Tyrien and his sons bounded after their prey, eager for the hunt. Their howls... and the screams that followed, echoed across the camp.

~ ~ ~ ~ ~

As Aiden neared his tent, he could hear two people talking. Rounding the side of the tent, he saw Evelyn's mother and brother standing outside. Seeing Aiden approach, Timothy knelt on one knee.

"Alpha." he said.

Aiden walked past them, entering the tent before closing it behind him.

Sitting on the edge of the bed, still wearing his shirt, with a blanket over her shoulders, was Evelyn. Mina and Siri sat next to the girl, comforting her.

The moment Aiden entered the tent, Evelyn's eyes snapped to him. Aiden could still smell her fear, but it was substantially less that it was earlier. Evelyn's eyes never left Aiden as he crossed the room, grabbing a blanket from the end of the bed.

"She can stay here tonight." Aiden told them before leaving the tent.

Just outside the entrance to the tent, was a tree. Aiden spread the blanket on the ground before sitting down, leaning against the tree. After such a long day, Aiden quickly fell asleep.

# Chapter 49

Aiden woke just before dawn. Looking down, he saw Mina. At some point during the night, she left the tent and had curled up against him, her head resting in his lap as she slept. Aiden placed his hand on her head, gently rubbing her ears as she began to stir.

"Mina, what are you doing out here?"

"Master shouldn't have to sleep alone." she replied, turning her head to look up at him.

*"I really don't deserve you."* he thought to himself, seeing the love reflected in her sapphire eyes.

Mina shivered slightly in the chilly morning air.

Despite not wearing a shirt, Aiden wasn't cold. Since becoming the hybrid, his body produced an abundance of excess heat. Helping Mina sit up, he pulled her close, wrapping his arms around her as she straddled his lap, pressing herself closer to him.

"mmmm... Master's always so warm." she nuzzled into his neck, enjoying the heat.

Soon, she was once again asleep, her deep, even breaths against his neck soothing and drawing Aiden back to sleep himself.

Siri stepped outside, careful not to wake Evelyn, who had spent the night in Aiden's tent after her father attempted to use her body to gain favor with him. Halfway through the night Mina had disappeared from the tent. Siri knew she had gone to find Aiden, and was not surprised to find her missing this morning.

Closing the tent behind her, Siri went to help Sylvia prepare breakfast. She glanced over at Aiden leaning against a tree, with Mina sprawled on top of him, both still asleep.

After their talk a few days ago, Siri no longer felt jealous when Aiden showed more attention to Mina. She now understood Mina's need to be close to him, to touch, and be touched by Aiden wasn't a choice, but a fundamental drive of her species. It was engraved into her very DNA, a part of her very being, an instinct she had no control over, nor the ability to resist, even if she wanted to. Just as she had accepted Aiden, immortal and all, she also accepted Mina.

Siri smiled as she walked off to find Sylvia before starting breakfast.

~ ~ ~ ~ ~

Evelyn woke, finding the tent empty. Remembering where she was, she quickly shot up in bed. She must have cried herself to sleep last night.. as she didn't remember actually falling asleep.

The girl literally leapt out of the bed when she realized that she had just spent the night sleeping in her new alpha's bed, a deep crimson washing over her cheeks. The girl quickly inspected herself. Finding she was still wearing the shirt the alpha had given her, as well as the embarrassing clothes her father had forced her to wear still on underneath the shirt, she began to calm down a bit.

"Good morning, sleep well?"

Evelyn jumped as Siri entered the tent, greeting her.

"Sorry if I startled you. Are you feeling better this morning?" Siri walked over and sat down at the table, looking over at Evelyn.

"I'm not sure how to answer that question, Luna."

Evelyn was still looking at herself, unsure of how to handle the situation.

"I see."

Siri put her hands in her lap as she waited for the girls response.

"What happened last night, Luna?"

"Do you not remember?"

"The girl shook her head. "I remember what my father tried to do. The alpha putting his shirt on me before you and the other luna brought me here. Then... I woke up this morning in the alpha's bed."

Siri crossed the room, kneeling down next to the girl.

"Nothing happened... since you were scared, Aiden slept outside underneath a tree. You ended up crying yourself to sleep, so Mina and I tucked you into bed."

Siri took the girl's trembling hands in hers.

"Aiden's not that kind of alpha."

"Really?" the girl asked.

"See for yourself." Siri helped Evelyn off the floor, leading her to the entrance of the tent.

Opening the corner of the flap, Evelyn peeked outside to see Aiden and Mina still asleep beneath the tree.

"How about we get you some proper clothes to wear before we eat?"

Evelyn nodded, closing the tent, as relief flooded her.

~ ~ ~ ~ ~

"My lord."

Aiden opened his eyes.

Sylvia stood above him holding two plates of food.

Nodding, Aiden gently shook Mina.

"Wake up Mina, time to eat."

Mina sat up, rubbing her eyes as Aiden took the two plates of food from Sylvia.

"Thank you Master." Mina said, taking one of the plates from Aiden and began to eat.

*"I think it's time I should check in with our guest."* Aiden moved Mina off his lap, handing her his plate as he got up, heading over to the tent.

Entering the tent, Aiden found Siri and Evelyn sitting at the table eating breakfast. Evelyn was now wearing a set of clothes that Siri had given her to wear. Momentarily ignoring the girls, Aiden crossed the room, grabbing a shirt and pulling it on.

"Alpha Aiden?"
Evelyn was fidgeting in her seat.
Aiden turned to face her. "What is it?"
"Thank you for what you did for me last night."
"It was nothing."
"But it was." Evelyn lowered her head.
"At least... it was to me." she whispered.
"So you're not afraid of me anymore?" Aiden asked.
The girl shook her head.
"Good. I don't want you to fear me."

Stepping up to Siri, Aiden leaned down, giving her a quick kiss.
"Make sure she gets back to her mother before we leave."
Aiden turned to leave.
"Are you leaving us here because of my father?" Evelyn stared at her hands, tears welling up in her eyes.
"No. You, your mother, and your brother are all coming with us. The three of you are now a part of my pack, and I take care of my own."
Aiden was walking back to the entrance when Evelyn spoke up.
"Thank you, Alpha."

Aiden turned his head, nodding to the girl before exiting the tent.

Stepping outside, Aiden returned and sat next to Mina. Having finished her plate, Mina had now begun to eat Aiden's food as well.

"And just what am I supposed to eat?" Aiden teased as the catgirl stuck her tongue out at him.

"May I at least have a few bites of my food?"

She handed his plate back, half empty.

Aiden sat and ate the remainder of the food, watching as the pack gathered, preparing for departure. Several who had been rejected had attempted to sneak in, hoping to go unnoticed, only to be run off by those who were accepted.

"Alpha." Aiden turned his head to see Alice standing a few feet away.

"What is it?"

"The pack is assembled and ready for departure." Alice bowed slightly, then left.

Aiden got to his feet, looking off in the direction of the distant mountains. Turning, he held out his hands to Mina. After she placed her small hands into his, Aiden lifted her to her feet.

"Ready to go?"

Mina nodded.

# Chapter 50

After a long day's journey, Aiden had decided to set up camp next to a small river for the night. Weary from their travel, most of Aiden's new pack had turned in early for the night. Inside their tent, Siri sat at the table, several books, papers and scrolls scattered around her as she read. Aiden lay face down on the bed, Mina sat on the back of his legs, leaning over him.

"How does it feel Master? Is Mina doing it right?"

"Yes, thank you Mina. It feels Wonderful."

Mina had seen Siri give a massage to Aiden plenty of times, and wanted to try it herself. Though inexperienced, Aiden enjoyed the catgirl's attempt to ease his stress. Closing his eyes, he focused on the attention Mina was giving him. As she ran her hands along his back, occasionally her claws would inevitably leave small scratch marks on his skin, disappearing and healing almost as fast as they appeared. Aiden barely noticed, and Mina no longer felt guilty every time her claws accidentally scratched him.

"Hey Aiden, come take a look at this." Siri held a piece of parchment as she continued reading it.

"What are you reading?" Aiden sat up once Mina got off him.

Walking over to Siri, Aiden leaned his head down into her neck, kissing it before looking over her shoulder at the parchment she held.

"You remember the scrolls and documents we found at that abandoned cabin?"

"What about them?"

"Well, several of them keep referencing a "Tarnaak." I'm not familiar with the word, and I can't find anything related to it in any of my books. Does it mean anything to you?"

Aiden's eyes glazed over as a memory from Sebastien surfaced.

*A dark hallway stretched before him as he made his way through, opening up into a large audience chamber. Four figures seated atop four thrones overlooked the chamber.*

*"This council recognizes Lord Sebastien. Hybrid... first of his kind." one figure spoke, standing from his throne.*

"It's a place." Aiden replied, the memory fading.

"Where?"

Siri turned to look at him.

"I can't remember."

"That's too bad, I'll keep looking. Maybe one of these will have some answers." Siri picked up another book and began to go through it, searching for any clues about Tarnaak.

"Take a break. I'm going for a walk." Aiden turned, finding Mina directly behind him.

"Can Mina go with Master?"

"Of course.. care to join us?"

Siri waved the two of them off, placing her book down as she went and laid down on the bed.

Aiden held out his arm, which Mina happily took as they exited the tent.

Aiden and Mina strolled through the camp, arm in arm. It was a quiet night, the nearly full moon shining brightly overhead. Hearing a strange noise, Aiden looked up at the sky, but found nothing there. Continuing their way between the different tents of the pack, once again, Aiden heard the noise from earlier, as well as movement up in the sky. Aiden knew something was up there, yet disappeared each time he looked.

Aiden and Mina were startled by a crash, followed by people yelling and a few loud screeches coming from several tents away.

The two rushed over to an already gathering crowd, forming a circle around something. Whatever was making that noise came from the center of the crowd.

"What's happening here?"

"My Alpha, something was caught digging through our storage crates." someone from the crowd answered as the crowd parted to allow them through.

Huddled on the ground, struggling to escape a net that had been thrown over it, was a creature Aiden had never seen before. This creature had a human appearance, mostly. The creature had the body and face of a human, but that was the only thing human about it. Though her face was human, two long, pointed ears stuck out from the side. Small down feathers sprouted along her cheekbones and forehead, growing slightly larger before blending into her long, deep purple hair. Her eyes were the same amethyst color as her hair. Her arms had soft feathers extending from her wrists, to halfway up her upper arm. She wore animal skins to cover herself. Just below the knee, the creature's legs transitioned from those of a human, to those similar to an eagle, ending in four long toes tipped with talons. The feathers covering her large wings were the same color purple as her hair. One of her wings was broken, and had an arrow sticking out of it, bleeding and preventing her from being able to fly.

"Be careful Alpha, it's a harpy." one of his pack members warned. "They steal people's children, carrying them off before eating them."

One man stepped forward, drawing a knife. "They won't be taking my child."

The man began to approach the harpy still struggling in the net, her struggles intensifying as she watched the man approach.

Mina ran forward, stepping in front of the man, holding her arms out.

"Luna, move, we have to kill it."

He tried to step around her, but Mina kept blocking his way.

"Leave harpy alone. Harpies not steal children." Mina stood her ground defiantly.

"We can't let it live." Finally managing to push past Mina, he raised the knife to strike.

"Master please save harpy!" Mina screamed.

"Enough." Aiden commanded, causing the man to stop, the knife inches from the harpy's chest.

"Alpha, it's too dangerous to let live. We must kill it."

"You heard what your Luna said... do not make me repeat it." Aiden's voice dripped with authority as he stepped forward.

"Yes, of course. Apologies my Luna, as you wish." The man moved aside as Mina pushed past him, kneeling down next to the frightened harpy.

"It's okay now, no one will hurt you. Master will protect."

Looking around at the crowd that was watching, Aiden spoke up.

"Go back to your tents. Get some rest, we have a long journey ahead of us."

The crowd slowly began to disperse, returning to their own business while Aiden knelt down on one knee beside Mina.

"Care to explain?" Aiden's voice was soft, and without judgment as he looked at Mina.

"Harpies do not steal children, Master. Please set harpy free." Mina answered.

Aiden looked at the frightened harpy in the net, her eyes wide, staring at him.

"Can you understand me?"

The harpy nodded.

Extending his claws, Aiden sliced through the net holding the girl. The young harpy didn't try to flee as he thought she would, but instead shifted into a kneeling position, lowering her eyes while cradling her injured wing.

"What is your name?" Aiden asked, after several moments of silence.

"Nephylia, sir." the harpy answered quietly, not lifting her eyes to look at Aiden or Mina.

"What were you doing here? Why were you going through our supplies?"

"Mother is sick, unable to leave nest. Needs medicine or she will die."

"Why not just ask for some?"

"Your kind kills harpies. I was afraid to show myself."

Aiden knew she was right. Even if she had tried to ask for some medicine, the result would be the same as it was right now. Seeing her injured wing, he reached his hand out. Nephylia pulled away from his reach.

"Please... let me help. I'm not going to hurt you."

Slowly, the harpy offered her injured wing for Aiden to inspect.

Aiden gently inspected her injured wing. From the looks of the injury, she tried to fly off when she was caught going through the supplies and took an arrow while trying to flee. She must have broken her wing when she fell.

"I need to remove the arrow. It will hurt, but I will be as gentle as I can." Aiden looked into the harpy's eyes for a few moments, waiting for permission.

"Mina, hold her wing still."

Mina held onto Nephylia's wing, as Aiden broke the arrow off as close to the wound as possible.

"Ready?" he asked.

Mina and Nephylia both nodded.

"On three."

"One."

"Two."

Aiden pulled the arrow from the wound, Mina gripping the wing firmly as the harpy stifled a scream.

"Three."

Tossing the arrow aside, he placed his hands over the open wound and began to mutter a spell. Soon, his hands began to glow as the flesh beneath his palms began knitting itself back together. Aiden repeated this process on the broken portion of the girl's wing. Once done, Aiden stepped back.

"Try it now."

Nephylia carefully flexed her wing, testing it before wrapping her wings in front of her. The claws on the tips of the wings clasped them together in front of her, creating a makeshift cloak.

"Thank you, sir." The harpy bowed her head to Aiden in thanks.

"What kind of medicine were you needing for your mother?"

"I don't know. Mother has a very high fever, no strength to leave the nest and hunt. Other harpies in the area have all died. Hunting has been difficult the last few months. My Mother and I are all that remain. I fear if she dies, I will soon follow her to the grave, as I am not yet able to hunt on my own."

The girl was crying as she told her story to Aiden and Mina.

"I heard that humans had medicine for fever, and even though it was dangerous, I had no other choice but to try and get some. I either succeed, or mother and I both die."

"Mina, go back and tell Siri what has happened. I will accompany Nephylia to help her mother. I will return as soon as possible."

"Yes Master, be careful." Mina hugged Aiden tightly for a few seconds, then ran off to tell Siri what he had said.

"How far is it to your mother's nest, Nephylia?"

"If I fly, it will take just under an hour. But with you following on the ground, it will take much longer."

"Then let's fly." Aiden held out his hand, helping the girl to her feet.

Nephylia shook her head. "I'm sorry, my wings are not strong enough to carry both of us."

"No need."

Closing his eyes, Aiden began a partial shift. His fangs, and claws extending, while the muscles and bones in his body broke and rearranged themselves as his two large wings burst from beneath his skin. His skin darkened, and his body changed shape slightly, although not enough to rip out of his remaining clothes. Aside from the change in skin color, and a few slightly more animalistic qualities, his face remained relatively human. In this partially shifted state, Aiden was still capable of speech.

"I've got my own."

Aiden grinned at the shocked harpy in front of him.

Aiden walked over to a supply crate. Pulling several different potions out, he placed them into a small bag before returning to Nephylia.

"Lead the way."

Nodding, Nephylia took off into the air, followed by Aiden.

As they made their way across the sky, Nephylia cried tears of happiness, knowing that there was now a chance to save her mother. Picking up speed, the two of them sped off into the distance, heading towards her nest.

# Chapter 51

Aiden followed Nephylia for an hour, coming to a small cave entrance hidden halfway up a cliff face.

Crouching through the entrance, Aiden shifted before following Nephylia through the narrow opening into a large open portion of the cave.

In the center of the cave, dimly lit by a single torch, was a very large nest. It was composed of twigs, leaves, bits of animal hides, fur and feathers. Curled up into a ball in the center of the nest was Nephylia's mother.

"Mother, I have returned. I brought help... and medicine." Nephylia rushed to the nest, stepping over the rim and crawling next to her mother.

"Neph?" her mother asked weakly, opening her eyes to look at her daughter.

"Yes mother, it's me. I'm back, I found help." The young harpy motioned across the room towards Aiden.

"Who are you stranger, and why would you help us?" The older harpy struggled to sit up, with help from Nephylia.

"My name is Aiden. Your daughter stumbled across my camp earlier tonight, and unlike most people, I do not judge others by their looks or by their species. She told me of your situation, and I offered to help."

The woman looked at Aiden and then at her daughter.

"Is this true?"

Nephylia nodded her head.

"May I examine you?" Aiden asked, stepping closer to the nest, but not entering.

"I do not know you, but my daughter seems to trust you, and I will trust her. You may examine me if you must."

Carefully stepping into the nest, Aiden knelt down beside the two harpies and began to examine Nephylia's mother. She appeared much like her daughter, albeit older and more mature. Her feathers were a pure white, transitioning into a bright, vibrant crimson halfway through. The down feathers along her arms and cheekbone were a matching crimson.

"May I ask your name?"

"Fa`ena." the harpy responded weakly, before starting to cough.

As the coughing subsided, Aiden placed his hand on her forehead. She truly did have a very high fever, as her skin was very hot to the touch. Pulling a flask from the bag, Aiden handed it to Nephylia.

"Have her drink this, it should help bring the fever down."

Nephylia pulled the cap off and placed the flask to her mother's lips.

"Please mother, drink this. It will help."

After several attempts, Fa`ena finally managed to drink the potion, despite the difficulty of swallowing.

"If it is alright with you, may I take a few drops of your blood? I may be able to better know what the problem is." Fa`ena nodded weakly, closing her eyes and resting in her daughter's lap.

Taking her hand, Aiden pricked one of her fingers with his claw. With a drop of blood on his finger, Aiden placed his finger in his mouth, tasting the harpy's blood. The moment the drop of blood touched his tongue, Aiden knew what was wrong. It tasted wrong, had a slight bitterness to it. Though diluted, Aiden recognized the taste.

"Fa`ena, have you or your daughter eaten any dead animals recently?"

She nodded, trying to answer before erupting into a fit of coughing.

"Hunting has been difficult. We take what we can get." Nephylia answered for her.

"Based on her blood, your mother fed on an animal that had been killed by a feral vampuric, essentially poisoning her."

Both Fa`ena and Nephylia's eyes widened in terror, they knew what that meant.

"Is there nothing we can do?" Nephylia asked, crying as she held her mother.

"There is no cure, young one. You know this." Fa`ena held her daughter's hand.

Aiden felt sorry for the pair of harpies. Not knowing what else to do, he turned to leave when he remembered something Raizel had once told him concerning his own blood.

"There might be a chance." he said softly.

The two harpies looked at him in disbelief.

"How?" Fa`ena asked.

"My blood is unique. I can't tell you why, but my blood may be able to counter the poison in your system."

Both girls began to get excited.

"It is risky though. My blood could just as easily make it worse. There is vampuric blood inside you, poisoning you. I am also an immortal, but not like any other. My blood could possibly fight off the infection caused by the vampuric blood. My blood is stronger than other species of immortal, but there is still a chance that it won't work, or that my blood could even make it worse."

"I am going to die anyway. But if there is a chance to live and to see my daughter grow up, no matter how small of a chance, I will take it." Fa`ena struggled onto her knees facing Aiden.

"Please sir. If I die, Will you protect my daughter? She is not yet old enough to survive on her own."

"I would protect her as if she were my own." Aiden swore to her.

"What must I do?" she asked.

Aiden extended a claw and slashed his wrist, offering it to Fa`ena. "Drink."

Several drops of Aiden's blood dripped into her mouth before the wound could heal.

"How long before we know anythi.. ungh." Fa`ena doubled over, as pain shot through her entire body.

"Mother!" Nephylia cried.

Aiden's blood began to burn its way through the harpy's system at an alarming rate. The battle between Aiden's blood and that of the vampuric blood poisoning her caused immense pain.

"What's happening to her?" Nephylia asked, holding her mother as she cried in pain.

Aiden walked over and sat down on the floor of the cave.

"My blood is literally burning the poison out of her. All we can do now is wait."

Several minutes passed as Fa`ena continued to scream in Nephylia's arms.

Eventually, she passed out.

"Mother?... mother!" Nephylia shook her mother, but got no reaction out of her.

Stepping back into the nest, Aiden knelt beside her and placed his hand against her mother's forehead. It had only been a few minutes, but the fever was already gone, and the harpy's breathing was slow and even.

"She's alive, just let her rest."

Fa`ena remained unconscious for two hours as Aiden's blood finished burning the remainder of the poison from her system. Slowly, the harpy began to stir in the nest.

Opening her eyes, she was met by the face of her daughter looking down at her, tears in her eyes.

"Mother?" Nephylia whispered, gently stroking her mother's hair.

Reaching up, Fa`ena took her daughters face in her hand. "My sweet... beautiful Neph."

"Mother." the girl cried, collapsing into a hug with her mother.

"I'm alright dear. I'm ok."

"It worked mother, it really worked!"

The young harpy could barely contain her excitement as she hugged her mother tightly.

"How do you feel?"

Aiden's voice caught their attention as the pair looked over at him sitting against the cave wall.

"Better, I think." Fa`ena released her daughter.

Standing up, Fa`ena wrapped her wings around herself just as Nephylia had done. Stepping out of the nest, she walked over to Aiden as he stood up from the wall.

"Stranger, you have showed a great kindness to both myself and my daughter this day. You have proven yourself to be a friend to the harpy race, and we will not forget what you have done. Thank you."

Fa`ena knelt in front of Aiden, bowing twice before looking up at him while remaining kneeled.

"What do you plan to do now?" Aiden held out his hand, helping the woman to her feet.

"I don't know. We have lived here our entire lives... but we cannot survive if we stay." Fa`ena looked around at the cave, eyes full of sorrow. "We will search for a new nesting ground. Somewhere that my daughter can grow up in safety. The outside world is a dangerous place, especially for two lone harpies, but we must go... there is nothing left for us in this place."

Nephylia walked to her mother and hugged her tightly, tears beginning to fall from both of their eyes.

"What if I had an alternative solution?" A smile formed on Aiden's face as he looked at the mother and daughter.

"What kind of solution?" Fa`ena asked, giving Aiden a confused look.

"I wish to offer you, and your daughter refuge within my pack. No one will raise a hand against you, or Nephylia as long as you are under my protection."

"That is a generous offer, but we would not want to be a burden to you, or your pack.. and having harpies in your camp may upset your pack members." Fa`ena replied sadly.

"They only fear what they don't understand, but we can make them understand, show them that harpies are not the monsters they think they are. Besides, I can't turn away from someone in need, not when I have the power to help."

"You would do that for us?" Nephylia asked, a sparkle of admiration in her eyes as she looked at Aiden.

"I would. It would be my honor to have you stay with us."

"Mother can we?"

Nephylia looked at her mother, her eyes pleading with her. Nephylia and Fa`ena looked into each other's eyes for several moments in unspoken conversation.

"Are you sure this is what you want, Neph?"

Nephylia nodded. Her mother kissed her on the forehead before turning to Aiden.

"Very well, we will accept your invitation. We already owe you my life, now, our lives are in your hands." Fa`ena bowed slightly.

"Take some time, and get some rest. Tomorrow, you and your daughter can fly to the camp. Your daughter knows where my pack is camped. I will assemble the pack at dawn to inform them of your arrival. I look forward to seeing you in the morning."

"Of course, and... thank you again."

Aiden nodded before leaving the cave and beginning his journey back to camp.

# Chapter 52

Fa`ena and Nephylia arrived at the camp an hour after dawn. The entire pack had been assembled, with Aiden, Mina and Siri standing at the front as they awaited their arrival. The two landed twenty yards from Aiden, wrapping their wings around themselves before approaching.

"My lord." They both said in unison, kneeling to one knee before him.

"Stand, please." Aiden said, motioning them to stand up.

"Fa`ena, Nephylia... I would like to introduce you to my mates." As Aiden turned to his right, Siri stepped forward.

"This is my mate Siri."

"It's a pleasure to meet you." Siri said as she curtsied.

"Thank you, my lady." Fa`ena answered, bowing her head.

Turning to his left, Aiden took Mina's hand as she stepped forward.

"And this lady here is my other mate, Mina." Mina smiled at the two harpies, but did not speak.

"Momma, she's the one I told you about." Nephylia whispered to her mother while motioning at Mina.

Fa`ena stepped forward, kneeling once again.

"My lady, I wish to thank you for stepping in and saving my daughter's life last night. I am forever in your debt."

"I..It was nothing." Mina tried to hide behind Aiden as she became the center of attention.

Seeing Mina's discomfort, Aiden placed one of his arms around her waist, shifting the focus off her as he began to speak.

"Are the two of you ready for travel?"

"Yes my lord." Fa`ena stood and returned to her daughters side.

Turning around, Aiden addressed his pack.

"These two harpies will be joining us from now on. I expect each and every one of you to show the utmost respect and courtesy. Any acts of violence or unfairness towards them will result in immediate expulsion from the pack. They wish to live in peace with us, and as long as they do, they are under my protection. Is that understood?"

"Understood Alpha." the pack responded in unison.

Aiden turned back to Nephylia and Fa`ena, giving them a smile.

"Welcome to the pack."

The remainder of the morning was spent packing up camp. During that time, Siri sat down and spoke to Fa`ena and Nephylia, getting to know them. Once everything was packed, it was time to continue on their journey.

~ ~ ~ ~ ~

Despite Aiden telling her it was unnecessary, Fa`ena insisted on flying ahead and scouting from the skies.

Around mid-afternoon, Fa`ena came flying back to the pack as fast as her wings could carry her, landing a few meters from Aiden before taking a moment to catch her breath.

"What is it? Are you okay?" Aiden placed a hand on her shoulder as she caught her breath.

"Lord Aiden, a massive army is camped just beyond the next ridgeline." she told him between gasps of air.

"What?" Aiden was shocked.

"We have to hurry if we intend to go around them before nightfall." Fa`ena straightened, her beathing returning to normal.

Aiden motioned for Sylvia, Andarii, Raizel, and Alice to come over and hear what the harpy had to say.

"My lord?" Andarii placed his fist over his heart as he approached.

"Aiden." Raizel said, walking up.

"What do you need, Alpha?" Alice bowed slightly to Aiden when she arrived.

"An army has been spotted beyond the next ridgeline. Alice, I want you to take the pack and go around."

Pulling out a map, Aiden had Fa`ena mark the location of the army.

"The army is currently camped here." Aiden pointed to the spot. "Take the pack and go around the outskirts of the ridgeline, take care to not be seen. Raizel... you, Andarii, and myself need to go take a look at what we are dealing with. Sylvia, I want you to keep the mind link open so that we can communicate with the rest of you."

"Be careful." Siri said, taking Aiden's hand in hers.

"I will, I promise." Aiden gave her hand a gentle, reassuring squeeze.

Letting go of Siri's hand, Aiden turned to Mina.

"I'll be back as soon as I can."

Mina hugged him for a brief moment, burying her head in his chest as he rubbed her ears.

"Come back quickly Master."

Once Mina let go, Aiden stepped back, turning to Raizel and Andarii.

"Alright let's go."

~ ~ ~ ~ ~

Laying on his stomach, Aiden peered over the edge of the cliff looking down at the encampment.

"Vampyres." Raizel whispered from beside him.

"How many do you think there are?"

"From the looks of it, I'd say there are at least twelve hundred vampyres among them, and probably several hundred vampurics for them to use as front line fighters."

"This is bad my lord." Andarii spoke from his other side.

"Yeah, I know."

"It just got worse." Raizel pointed to a banner posted next to one of the tents, his eyes going wide.

"What is it?"

"Carden." Raizel said, gritting his teeth.

"Who's Carden?"

Aiden had never seen Raizel so shaken before.

"An elder vampyre, extremely powerful. One of the oldest and most sadistic and bloodthirsty vampyres I know. We need to leave... now."

The three of them quickly and quietly left the area to rejoin the pack.

~ ~ ~ ~ ~

Alice had pushed the pack to move as quickly as possible. In only a few hours, they had travelled more ground than they would in a day otherwise. Having made it to the location that Aiden had directed her to take the pack, Alice finally allowed the pack to stop and make camp.

"He'll be fine." Siri spoke up from behind her, getting her attention.

"I know, but I still worry. An alpha is strongest when he is with his pack." Alice looked out in the direction they had come.

Siri sat down beside her.

"I'm not sure the same rules apply to him though."

"I guess not."

"We're back." Aiden called as he and his companions got to the camp.

Siri stood up, walking over and giving Aiden a hug. "Welcome back."

Leaning down, Aiden gave her a kiss.

"Where's Mina?"

"She is resting in the tent. The journey was rough on her."

"I can imagine."

"So? What did you learn?"

"Nothing good. It's the vampyres, they are tracking us.. more than a thousand men."

"That many?"

"What's worse is they are being led by an elder vampyre named Carden."

"Why would they send an elder vampyre?" Concern filled Siri's voice as she looked up at Aiden.

"Apparently they "Really" want me dead. Come on, let's get some sleep. Tomorrow we head into the Whitetooth Mountains."

"Master you're back!" Mina yelled as she tackled Aiden, her small body colliding with his chest as he entered the tent.

"I missed you too."

Aiden kissed the top of her head as Mina nuzzled against him. Pulling himself from the catgirl's arms, Aiden removed his clothes and climbed into bed as Mina and Siri joined him. Soon the three were fast asleep in each other's arms.

Over the next few days, Aiden and his pack made their way into the Whitetooth Mountains. For several days now, Aiden had been dreaming of the mountains. In his dreams, a large grey wolf would beckon him to follow, leading him through the mountains. Each day, they followed where his dreams led them.

~ ~ ~ ~ ~

Snow covered the ground this morning as Aiden exited the tent. It was still a few hours before dawn, but Aiden couldn't sleep. He expected to have another dream telling him where to go, but none came.

Aiden held out his hand, watching the flakes of snow land on his palm before melting.

*"Where do we go from here?"*

Brushing the snow from a nearby rock, Aiden sat down.

"Can't sleep?"

Andarii's voice caught Aiden's attention as he approached.

"No, figured I'd step out for some fresh air."

As the two of them talked, the flap to Aiden's tent opened as a half asleep catgirl stepped out.

"Master?"

Mina looked around for Aiden, eyes heavy and half closed, wearing only a simple robe she had put on before going to look for Aiden.

"Over here Mina." Aiden called.

Walking over and wrapping her arms around Aiden, Mina let out a small sigh.

"What are you doing out here Mina? Shouldn't you be asleep?"

"Mina woke up and Master was gone. Mina couldn't go back to sleep without Master."

Looking down, Aiden saw that Mina was still barefoot. Pulling the cloak he was wearing off and wrapping it around her, he picked her up out of the snow, placing her in his lap as she wrapped her legs around him.

"Next time you go looking for me, please put on some warmer clothes. I don't want you getting hypothermia. Okay?"

"Yes Master." she whispered, her head laying against Aiden's shoulder as she fell back asleep in his arms.

Aiden chuckled to himself, knowing that she wouldn't listen.

Mina had a one track mind. Once she had a goal, everything else became secondary. Aiden let the calling slip out and wash over Mina, causing the catgirl to purr in response.

Half an hour later, Siri exited the tent.

Seeing Mina and Aiden sitting over on a rock, she smiled.

"Let me guess, she forgot to get dressed again?" Siri asked, sitting down beside them.

"Yep." Aiden answered, as Siri kissed him.

As Siri cuddled up to his side, Aiden took the edge of his cloak, pulling it around so that both Siri and Mina were covered.

Siri stared at the landscape around them.

"The snow is beautiful."

Hearing the crunch of snow, Aiden and Siri looked over in the direction of the sound.

Walking through the snow towards them was a large grey wolf. Aiden recognized it immediately.

"That's the same wolf from my dreams." Aiden whispered to Siri as he softly shook Mina to wake her up.

The wolf continued walking towards them, stopping twenty feet away before sitting down and looking at them.

"Why did Master wake Mina up?" Mina complained, rubbing her eyes.

"Look."

Turning her head, Mina saw the wolf and her eyes went wide.

"What does Master think it wants?"

As she spoke, the wolf stood, turning and walking back the way it came. The wolf stopped and turned its head, looking back at them.. waiting.

"I think it wants us to follow it." Siri said.

"I believe you're right."

"Can we go, Master?"

Looking at the wolf, Aiden felt no hostility from the creature.

"Sure, we can go."

Mina climbed off Aiden, wrapping his cloak around her to stay warm.

Not wanting to waste time, Aiden pulled his own boots off, handing them to Mina.

"What about you, Master?"

"You really think this snow will bother me?"

Mina giggled, stepping into his boots.

The three of them walked over to where the wolf was waiting. As they got closer, it turned and began to lead them through the snow.

"Where do you think it's taking us?" Siri asked.

"No idea."

After a while, the wolf led them to the side of a cliff. A waterfall cascaded down from the top of the cliff, forming into a freezing cold river.

"Why did it bring us here Master? Mina stared at the waterfall.

As if to answer her question, the wolf walked through the waterfall, disappearing behind it.

Siri looked at Aiden. "I guess it wants us to go in?"

"Mina, come over here." Aiden pulled Mina and Siri close together, wrapping the cloak Mina was wearing around the two of them.

"My cloak is waterproof, it should protect you from the majority of the water. Removing his shirt and trousers, Aiden handed them to Siri to keep dry beneath the cloak.

"I'll go check it out, you follow after.

Taking a breath, Aiden stepped into the waterfall, the freezing water chilling his warm skin as it flowed over him. Stepping out on the other side, Aiden found himself in a hollowed out portion of the cliff face.

A large, room sized hole had been carved out of the mountain behind the waterfall. The walls were smooth to the touch, the floor transitioning from natural rock into chiseled stone. From the outside, Aiden had no idea this space was even here. Looking around, he could find no trace of the wolf they had followed, not even a trail of water.

Turning back to the waterfall, Aiden called for Siri and Mina.

"Okay, come on through!"

Stepping through the waterfall together, the girls screamed as the cold water hit their heads.

"That water is freezing." Siri said, handing Aiden's clothes back to him.

"Mina didn't like that, Master." the catgirl pouted, trying to wring her hair out.

Aiden handed his shirt back to the girls to dry their hair with as best they could while he put his trousers back on.

"What is this place?" Siri gazed around the room as Mina dried her hair.

"What happened to the wolf Master?"

"I'm not sure, it was gone when I stepped through."

A popping sound could be heard as the far wall of the room opened up, revealing a tunnel. Over a dozen guards with swords, spears and bows poured out of the wall, completely surrounding them.

# Chapter 53

"Get behind me!" Aiden exclaimed, pushing Mina and Siri up against one of the walls, placing himself between them and their unknown assailants.

"Who are you people?"
Aiden wanted to fight, but with so many opponents in such an enclosed space, he couldn't guarantee the girls' safety, not when they were surrounded.

"Trespassers are not welcome here." one of the men to his left spoke, pointing a spear at Aiden.
Grabbing the tip of the spear, Aiden pulled the man towards him, taking the spear from him before kicking him back into a group of his companions. One of the archers let loose an arrow at the three of them.
Using himself as a human shield, Aiden took the arrow in his chest, but refused to fall to the ground.
Aiden's eyes changed and began to glow, his fangs and claws slipping out. A loud roar escaping his throat in defiance. Several of the guards were shaking as the rest pressed further in, closing the circle around Aiden and the girls.
"Hold!" a voice from the tunnel called, halting the advance of the guards.

A man stepped out of the tunnel, accompanied by two women who looked to be mother and daughter.

As he stepped towards Aiden, the guards moved aside for him.

"I apologize for my companions, we do not get many visitors.. even fewer who are not hostile towards us." The man opened his arms in a welcoming gesture.

"My lord, we can't risk it." the guard Aiden had disarmed spoke up.

"Fool, open your eyes, it's him." the man replied, turning back to face Aiden.

Aiden remained where he was, claws extended, and fangs bared, a deep growl reverberating through the room. Mina and Siri had both dropped to the floor behind him as he stood in front of them defensively.

The man and the two women knelt down at the edge of the circle of guards.

"What do you think you're doing my lord? This is beneath you."

The guard grabbed the man and one of the women's arms, trying to pull them to their feet.

"Enough! Can't you see who this man is? He is the Hybrid."

A look of shock and terror filled the soldier's face when he heard that. The man began to sweat, realization dawning on him as he slowly turned to look at Aiden once more, finally noticing the color and glow of his eyes.

"Please, forgive us. We have been awaiting your arrival for centuries." the man kneeling said.

Every soldier in the room immediately knelt to one knee.

Looking up from his kneeled position, the man in charge could see that Aiden was still positioned in a defensive stance, his eyes darting around the room, prepared for a sneak attack.

"Everyone, disarm yourselves immediately."

The sound of weapons falling to the ground echoed through the room.

Aiden felt Siri's hand on his arm. "Aiden, it's alright, we're both safe."

The tension in his arms slowly began to relax, his claws disappearing as his eyes returned to normal. Aiden looked at the soldiers around him one more time before turning to Mina and Siri.

"Master, you're hurt."

Mina gently touched his chest where the arrow was still protruding.

"It's nothing, Mina. Don't worry."

Handing the spear to Siri, Aiden reached up, grasping the shaft of the arrow. Taking a breath, Aiden clenched his teeth and ripped the arrow out of his chest, dropping it to the floor as the wound began to heal.

"See? Nothing to worry about." Aiden gave her a reassuring smile. "Are you both alright?"

Aiden began looking over both of them. Even though Siri had said they were both fine, he needed to be sure.

"I'm fine." Siri answered, letting him look her over.

"Mina is also unharmed, Master."

"I apologize for our misunderstanding earlier, we were..." the man in charge tried to speak, but was cut off by Aiden growling.

"Misunderstanding?" Aiden spat, standing and turning to face him.

"Your men attack me, put an arrow in my chest, and threaten my mates... choose your next words very carefully."

Aiden's aura pouring out of him in waves. Barely keeping himself from shifting, Aiden stared at the man, a low growl escaping his throat

"I... I..."

The man was paralyzed by Aiden's eyes. The intensity of his gaze, with the promise of violence just beneath the surface instilled a primal fear in him.

Seeing the situation, the woman beside him spoke up.

"Darling, allow me to handle this."

Standing, she folded her hands in front of her and addressed the guards in the room.

"All of you, return to your posts."

As she spoke, all but two guards stood and silently returned through the tunnel they had come from, leaving their weapons on the ground.

"My name is Elena. Your name is Aiden, correct?"

She remained where she was, allowing Aiden to make the first move, keeping her voice soft.

Aiden nodded, looking at the woman.

While the man beside her was nearly paralyzed by fear, this woman showed no sign of fear. But rather, she radiated compassion. The look on her face was one of concern. Not for herself, but for him, and his mates.

The anger inside him began to die down, as the muscles in his body slowly began to relax further.

"And may I know the names of your mates?"

Elena looked past Aiden at the two girls behind him.

Siri got up and stood next to Aiden. "I am Siri."

"You're an elf, aren't you?"

"Yes."

"It's nice to meet you Siri... and what is your name?" Elena leaned to the side, peeking around Aiden at Mina, giving her a warm smile.

Mina hissed, hiding behind Aiden's leg.

"Oh... did I say something wrong?" Elena brought her hand to her chest, surprised by the catgirl's reaction.

"Shot Master with arrow." Mina hissed.

"I see..." Elena lowered her hands to her side.

Aiden turned around, helping Mina to her feet. Wrapping her in his arms, he kissed her before whispering in her ear.

"But..." Mina looked up at Aiden.

"...Okay." Mina sighed.

Mina turned her head towards Elena, but kept staring at the ground.

"Mina is sorry. Mina knows it wasn't you who shot Master."

After apologizing, Mina hid her face in Aiden's chest.

"She does not forgive easily." Aiden said, looking at Elena.

"Understandable." Elena replied.

"Now, who are you people, and how do you know who I am?"

"That is a long story, but first, we would be honored if you would accompany us inside. It is not safe out here."

The woman held out her arm, gesturing to the tunnel they had come from.

"Most places we've been, have not been very hospitable." Aiden replied.

"That will change here. This place was founded by the hybrid. So you and your mates will be safe here, and treated as our own."

"My pack is camped not far from here."

"You have a pack?"

"I do, we are being pursued by an army of vampyres."

"Then the time has finally come." Elena turned to one of the two guards. "Send an envoy to guide his pack to the safety of our walls. There is much to do before the vampyres arrive."

"As you command." The guard ran back into the tunnel, following his orders.

Elena gestured back to the man and young woman behind her. "This is my husband, Marius."

The man nodded in Aiden's direction. "An honor to meet you."

"And our daughter, Alexis."

Standing up from the floor, the young woman smiled brightly at Aiden and the girls before curtsying.

"A pleasure to meet you my lord, my ladies."

"Please, allow me to show you around." Elena offered her hand out in Aiden's direction.

Aiden glanced around the room, finding his shirt on the floor near Mina, still wet from being used as a towel for her hair. Reaching down, Aiden picked up his shirt, wringing it out as best he could before putting it back on.

"Do you have a room we could stay in? I would prefer to get me and my mates dry before taking a tour."

"Of course." Elena turned, looking at her daughter.

"Alexis, please show our guests to their chambers. I'm sure it has been a difficult journey for them."

"Yes mother." the young woman replied.

Elena took her husband's arm in hers. Before speaking to the remaining guard.

"Collect the weapons and return them to their owners once they leave."

"It will be done." the guard answered, walking over to the opposite side of the room.

Elena and Marius left the room, leaving Alexis to escort Aiden, Mina and Siri.

"My lord, my ladies... if you like, please follow me. I will show you to your room."

# Chapter 54

Aiden, Mina and Siri followed Alexis through various tunnels and rooms, eventually coming to an entrance of a large, open area.

Stepping out of the tunnel, Aiden was amazed at what he was seeing. It was as if the entire mountain had been hollowed out, making room for large plots of farming land, with many different crops growing. Dozens of people could be seen tending the fields.

On the outskirts of the farms, along the walls, a great spiraling staircase encircled the entirety of the outer wall, ascending up at least forty levels. Each level had additional rooms and tunnels leading off them, creating more space for people to work and to live. Large wooden elevators were placed at different locations, providing easy access to all floors.

"How do you grow crops without sunlight?" Siri asked, looking around.

"We use sunlight... look up there." Alexis pointed to a spot above them.

A series of large crystals hung from the ceiling of the cavern at varying levels.

"There is an opening in the top of the cavern that we seal off at night or if attacked. It allows light to enter. The sunlight is reflected, and scattered across the farmland by the crystals you see, allowing us to grow our crops."

"It's impressive." Siri marveled, as they continued following her.

"The dwarves built and maintain this place. No one can match their stonework or craftsmanship when it comes to construction and building."

As she said this, several short men appeared from a nearby tunnel, covered in dirt, and carrying tools.

"Ah.. Miss Alexis, how are ya this morning?"

"I am well Valik, heading home?

The man had a long red beard streaked with dirt. Placing his pickaxe against the ground, the man leaned against it as he spoke to Alexis.

"Aye. Me and me boys just finished opening up a new passageway. Should be fit for use in about a week. Who's this ya got with ya?" Valik looked at Aiden and the girls.

"I'm Aiden."

"A pleasure to meet ya Aiden, my name's Valik. I'm in charge of construction.. and who are these two lovely lasses ya got with ya?" Mina giggled behind Aiden.

"My name's Siri." Siri held out her hand.

"A fine name, welcome."

"Short man talks funny." Mina said.

"Stone's breath... you're a Nekomata." Valik stared at Mina for a moment. "I haven't seen one of your kind in ages."

"There's not many of her kind left." Aiden replied.

"Aye, I heard. Hunted down for their blood. Crying shame that. But I'm glad to see at least one survived."

Mina gripped the back of Aiden's shirt. Seeing her distress, the dwarf quickly changed the subject, not wanting to upset her further.

"So, how did ya come to be acquainted with both an elf and Nekomata, young man?"

"I was a servant in Aiden's household for three years." Siri said.

"Master saved Mina's life." Mina added.

Looking between Aiden and the girls, Valik spoke.

"They are your slaves then?"

"They are not my slaves. They are my mates." Aiden's eyes glowed softly, a hint of anger in his voice.

"Ah, I see... I apologize for misreading the situation. You must be an immortal then."

"I am."

"If ya don't mind me asking son, what kind of immortal are ya?"

"Lord Aiden here, is the Hybrid." Alexis said.

"By the stone.. is what she says true?" Valik looked at Aiden.

"It is." Aiden answered.

"Well lord Aiden, allow me to be one of the first to welcome ya to Tyr`endalle, the sanctuary of stone."

Valik extended his arms, gesturing around them.

"The sanctuary of stone?" Aiden asked.

"Aye. We are all that remains of the allied races who stood up to the immortals. After losing the war, many fled here, to live free. Others scattered and went into hiding. Your predecessor commissioned the dwarves to build this place for those seeking to escape the war. Many generations have been able to grow up in relative peace without fear from the immortal empire."

"And now I've brought war back to your home." Aiden turned his head, unable to look the dwarf in his eyes.

"Son..." Valik placed a hand on Aiden's arm.

"We always knew that one day this place would be found. Today, or two hundred years from now, it makes no difference. This ain't your fault, lad."

"Thank you, Valik."

"Anytime my boy. Now, I'm sure you and your mates have had a long journey and would like to get some rest, so me and me boys will be taking our leave now." Valik turned to Alexis and bowed.

"My lady, do tell you father and mother I said hello."

"I will Valik, thank you." Alexis replied as Valik and his sons walked off.

"This way, lord Aiden."

Alexis continued walking as Aiden, Mina, and Siri followed.

~ ~ ~ ~ ~

"Here we are."

Alexis stepped off the elevator platform, followed closely by Aiden and the girls.

Looking around, Aiden could see they were standing on a small outcropping in the rock. At the back wall was a single door. Aiden looked at Alexis in confusion. The other floors they past had been made up of multiple hallways with connecting rooms.

Seeing Aiden's confusion, Alexis gave him a warm smile.

"This floor is different than all the others. This floor was made specifically for the Hybrid. A place that he could be alone without being bothered by others." Taking a few steps forward, Alexis opened the door, ushering Aiden and the girls through.

The room was huge, with a large living space big enough to comfortably seat fifty people. Nice furniture decorated the room. Animal skins had been sewn together, completely covering the stone floor beneath them. Multiple doors connected to the room, two on each side. The far wall was completely made up of thick, transparent glass, allowing the occupants to look outside at the snowy landscape around them.

"Wow." Mina and Siri said in unison.

"The far wall is protected by an illusion. From the outside, it looks and feels like stone. There are four rooms, a master bedroom, a bath, and two guest rooms. Please, feel free to make yourselves at home, I will send someone to inform you when your pack has arrived." Alexis bowed slightly before closing the door, leaving them alone in the room.

Taking his cloak from around Mina, Aiden hung it from a hook on the wall as she stepped out of his boots and began to explore.

"Master hurry!" the catgirl yelled, running up to the nearest door.

Opening it, she found a small room with a bed, small table, and a chair.

"Boring." she said to herself, closing the door and moving to the next one as Aiden stepped up behind her, followed by Siri.

Aiden opened the next room and his mouth fell open. They had found the master bedroom.

A large crystal chandelier hung from the ceiling, with several small tables, dressers and chests decorating the area. A large stone fireplace sat imbedded into one of the walls with several fancy chairs, and a sofa sitting next to it. across the room from the fireplace was the largest bed Aiden had ever seen. The bed was large enough to hold ten people comfortably.

Aiden just stared at the bed for a second before Mina squealed, running past him and launching herself onto the bed.

"Great, now she really won't want to get out of bed in the morning." Siri commented, stepping up beside Aiden.

"At least there's plenty of room. Maybe I'll finally get to wake up without being pinned beneath the two of you." Aiden grinned at Siri, causing her to laugh.

"Don't count on it." she replied, reaching her hand behind his head, pulling him down for a quick kiss.

Hearing a knock on the door, Aiden slipped out of Siri's grasp, leaving the bedroom to answer the door.

Opening the door, Aiden found a young girl and a middle aged man standing outside. Based on their posture, and the way they were dressed, Aiden could tell they worked as servants.

"My lord." the older gentleman spoke up.

"We've been told to see to anything you may have need of, and that your mate may be in need of some clothes."

As he said this, the young lady accompanying him held out a set of clothes to Aiden.

"Thank you, I appreciate it." Aiden said.

Taking the clothes from the girl, Aiden looked to the man.

"I'm grateful, but I don't need to be waited on or served by either of you. I prefer to do things myself, and my mates' handmaiden will be arriving shortly with the rest of my pack."

"Of course my lord, we will not bother you any further. I will see to it that your mates' handmaiden is sent up immediately upon her arrival."

"Thank you. If you would, have two of my subordinates, Andarii, and Raizel, sent up with her, I have things to discuss with them."

"It will be done."

The man bowed, before turning and leaving with the young girl.

Closing the door, Aiden brought the set of clothes given to him back into the bedroom.

"Mina, some clothes have been brought for you. Get dressed please."

Hopping off the bed, Mina walked up to Aiden, taking the clothes from his hands before standing up on her toes and giving him a kiss on the cheek.

"Thank you Master." she whispered, before turning and wandering off to get dressed while Aiden turned and went back out to the common room.

Two hours later, Aiden heard another knock on the door followed by Sylvia's voice.

"My lord?"

Aiden recognized the voice of Sylvia through the door.

"You may enter."

The door opened as Sylvia, Andarii, and Raizel entered the room.

"Sylvia, see to the girls, I must speak with Andarii and Raizel alone." Aiden motioned to the door leading to the master bedroom.

Sylvia bowed slightly before heading to the bedroom, shutting the door behind her.

Aiden spoke as the elf and vampyre found their seats.

"Raizel, tell me everything you can about Carden and the vampyres."

"Does this mean..."

"Yes. I'm done running. We stand, and fight."

# Chapter 55

Looking down over the fields of indoor farmland, Aiden let out a sigh.

Four days of preparation had turned the farmland into a field of traps.

The crops had all been cut down. Pits full of spikes had been dug, and explosive barrels have been half buried and covered to disguise them. Barricades have been made and the dwarves have sealed off most of the tunnels leading to the residential areas. Towers for archers had been built, and sentries were placed at all times to keep watch.

Turning from the balcony he was standing on, Aiden headed back into the room. Huddled around a large table with a diagram of the farmland on it, stood a group of ten people.

"We need to keep the fighting contained as best we can within the farmland. Otherwise we risk the lives of those unable to fight." one man said, pointing at a location on the diagram.

"This plan, it's going to wreak havoc on your farmland." Andarii stated.

"Better it than our people." Marius answered, his wife nodding in agreement.

"The most likely breach point will be here." Valik pointed to one of the tunnels connecting to the farmland.

"Once they enter the farmland, my archers will rain down arrows from overhead." the guard captain commented.

Walking up, Aiden joined the conversation. "Don't get reckless, try to keep yourselves safe at all costs. After all, it's me they're after. I don't want anyone else dying for me."

"This isn't just about you anymore lad, this is our home, our families. We will defend it." Valik looked across the table at Aiden as the others nodded in agreement.

"Very well. But still... be careful. They have superior numbers and strength."

"Once the majority of the army has entered the fields, we will light the trenches on fire, trapping them inside. Then, we let the traps we've set do the hard work for us." Raizel stated.

"Any stragglers left outside the field will be picked off by our pack members." Alice added.

"Should we get overrun, we fall back to this rendezvous point." Elena pointed to a tunnel on the far side of the farmland. "Within that tunnel, the vampyre's numbers will count for nothing. That allows us to fight them on an equal footing."

"What will you be doing during all this, lord Aiden?" Marius asked.

A smile crept across Aiden's face.

"I will be taking down the vampyre commander, and causing as much damage to the enemy ranks as possible while I do."

Aiden looked across the table to Andarii.

"Andarii, come to my room after this. I have something special for you to do."

"Yes, my lord." Andarii nodded.

~ ~ ~ ~ ~

Andarii knocked on Aiden's door, pausing a few moments before entering.

"Good, you're here." Aiden motioned him inside and over to the table he was sitting at.

"What is it my lord requires of me?"

Aiden motioned to eight jars on the table, filled with a dark red liquid.

"Over the last few days, I have been filling these jars with my blood. I want you to take them and have all of the archers dip their arrows in my blood. With this, they won't need to aim for a fatal wound, even a scratch will be enough to guarantee a kill. Any leftover blood is to be applied to the frontline fighters weapons."

"It will be done." Andarii said.

"Go."

Andarii placed his fist over his heart before gathering the jars into a sack and leaving to do as instructed.

Standing up, Aiden made his way to the other side of the room. Opening the door, he was met with the sounds of combat. Inside the room, Mina and Siri each had a weapon in their hands, fighting against Raizel.

"Master!"

Mina dropped the dagger she was holding and ran to Aiden.

Leaning down, Aiden kissed her forehead before looking up at Siri and Raizel.

"How much progress have they made?" Aiden asked, as Raizel sheathed his weapon.

"They are quick learners, but four days is hardly enough time to teach them to fight."

"If all goes according to plan, they won't have to."

Aiden released Mina as Siri stepped up, giving him a kiss as well. The four of them left the room, heading back into the common room.

Sitting down on one of the sofas, Mina climbed into Aiden's lap. Siri sat beside him, leaning against him with her head on his shoulder.

"I have something for you." Raizel said.

Raizel held out a sword wrapped in cloth, placing it on the short table in front of Aiden.

"What is it?"

"You have used this weapon once before."

Raizel slowly unwrapped the sword from the cloth, careful to not touch the silver hilt of the sword.

"Against the horde of vampurics. I remember." Aiden said, admiring the craftsmanship of the hilt.

Mina gazed at the large moonstone pommel. "It's pretty, Master."

"This sword is called Silthr'aca. It was created by Sebastien centuries ago using ancient magic, his own blood, and an extremely rare ore found only in one place. Brought together and forged under the light of a full moon. The blade has the ability to absorb and store moonlight, and is stronger than any other metal ever before seen."

To demonstrate his point, Raizel wrapped the cloth around the handle, partly unsheathing it. Pulling a dagger from his waist, he struck the blade with the dagger. The blade cut into the dagger as if it were made of wood, lodging itself halfway into the blade of the dagger.

"The edge does not dull, nor can it be bent or shattered." Raizel pried the dagger off and sheathed the sword before offering it to Aiden.

"No immortal can stand before it. It can also be wielded only by you."

"What do you mean? I've seen you wield it." Aiden asked, sliding Mina off him as he took the weapon.

"No, you haven't. I can carry it, but not wield it."

"Why not?" Siri asked leaning forward to inspect the blade.

"The magic Sebastien used when he forged it, combined with his own blood, bound the blade to him."

"What does that mean?"

"Basically... the blade is alive. If anyone other than the hybrid attempts to hold the sword with the intent to use it, the blade will kill the wielder, draining them of their life."

Aiden slowly drew the weapon from its sheath. "Fascinating."

"It also tends to have an adverse reaction if an immortal other than you touches it with their bare hands."

"That explains why you always keep it wrapped up."

"Indeed... now if you will excuse me, it's going to be a long day tomorrow, so I am going to get some rest."

Raizel stood and left the room as Aiden sheathed the blade, placing it back on the table.

Several minutes passed in silence as Aiden stared at the blade on the table.

"Aiden, you ok?" Siri placed her hand on his, locking their fingers together.

"What's wrong Master?" Mina looked at Aiden with worry.

"Am I strong enough?" Aiden finally answered.

"The last time I fought the vampyres head on, my family had to sacrifice themselves so I could get away."

"You didn't know how to use your power yet. It's not your fault Aiden." Siri lifted his hand, caressing it with her thumb before kissing it.

"I know. But even now, with training, I can only just barely keep up with Raizel. Do I really have a chance against an army of others just like him?"

Aiden turned to look at her.

"Yes, you do." Siri replied.

"How do you know?"

"Because..." Siri held his face in her hands. "You're not fighting alone."

Siri leaned forward capturing his mouth in a passionate kiss.

Breaking the kiss, Aiden turned to Mina, pulling her against him before she kissed him with equal passion.

Once Mina released Aiden's mouth from her own, he looked at both girls for a moment. A single word came to mind as he looked at the two of them.

"Seyh`aiya." he whispered.

The two girls looked at him in confusion.

*"It means My Beloved, my reason for being."*

Siri and Mina heard Aiden's voice in their head. A smile spreading across both girls' faces.

Both girls took him by the hand as they stood up.

"Don't worry about tomorrow." Siri said, helping him to his feet.

"Master should be more worried about surviving tonight." Mina whispered into his ear as they dragged him into the bedroom.

# Chapter 56

"Lord Aiden, open up, its urgent!"

Aiden could hear someone outside his quarters frantically banging on the door as they called his name. Looking down at Mina and Siri still fast asleep in his arms, he was glad the quarters they were given had multiple rooms, otherwise the banging would have woken them.

Carefully disentangling himself from the girls, Aiden pulled on a set of trousers before entering the common room and closing the door behind him. Whoever was outside the room still had not stopped banging on the door and calling his name.

Now rather irritated by the constant banging, Aiden yanked open the door and grabbed the man outside his room by his tunic.

"If you continue making noise and wake up my mates, I'm going to throw you off this ledge." Aiden angrily tossed the young man back a few feet, stepping outside and closing the door.

"Now what do you want?"

The young man quickly got to one knee, nervous and out of breath.

"Apologies lord Aiden, but something has happened, and you are needed."

"A few knocks is more than enough to wake me. Don't ever beat on my door like that again."

"Of course my lord, I'm sorry. Marius, Raizel, Andarii, and Valik have already been awakened and are awaiting your presence." the young man managed to say between gasps of breath.

"Fine, I'll be down shortly." Aiden turned and headed back into his room to get dressed.

"Don't bother waiting for me." Aiden growled as he shut the door.

~ ~ ~ ~ ~

"So, anyone want to tell me why I had a lunatic frantically banging on my door?" Aiden asked, stepping up to the group of people already gathered atop the makeshift battlements just above the battlefield.

"See for yourself."

Raizel lifted his hand, motioning down to the far edge of the battlefield. Down by the entrance to the battlefield stood a single person surrounded by four archers, with their bows drawn on him.

"Alright, I'll bite. Who is he?"

Marius ran a hand through his hair before answering. "We do not know, he claims to be sent to deliver a message."

"And what is the message?"

"He won't tell us. He claims that he is to deliver the message to you personally."

"Is that so?"

Aiden leaned against the battlements, observing the messenger for several seconds.

"Alright, let's go see what he wants."

~ ~ ~ ~ ~

"What is it you want?" Aiden asked as he neared the messenger.

The man bowed his head slightly as Aiden approached.

"You are Lord Aiden, I presume?"

Aiden stopped ten feet from the messenger. Raizel and Andarii stood just behind him.

"I am. Now say what it is you've come to say." Aiden's eyes glowed softly as he stared at the man before him.

"Very well, straight to business then."

The messenger held his arms out as he bowed. "My name is Dimitri Valkov. My master, Lord Carden, wishes to have a word with you. He asks that you come to this location at noon."

Dimitri pulled a piece of paper from his coat pocket and held it out. Andarii stepped forward, taking the paper and reading it before handing it over to Aiden.

"My master wishes to find a peaceful solution to the current predicament. You may bring three men of your choosing to this meeting. No harm will come to anyone at this meeting, as it will be considered neutral ground."

"And how do we know this isn't just a trap to draw us out?" Raizel asked.

"You don't.. but that is between you, and Master Carden. My message has been delivered. I bid you good day, and I shall take my leave." The man turned to leave, only for the archers to block his way.

"Let him go."

Aiden signaled the archers to stand down.

Once the man left back the way he had come, Marius walked up.

"You sure it was wise to let him go?" he asked.

"No... but if his message is authentic, killing him would cause more trouble than letting him go."

Aiden looked at the location written on the paper he was holding, then handed it back to Andarii.

"I want you to scout this location beforehand Andarii. If you feel anything is off, let me know. I have no intention of walking into a trap."

"Right away."

"And be discreet."

Andarii nodded, then turned, running off to follow Aiden's command.

~ ~ ~ ~ ~

Aiden, Raizel and Valik arrived at the location requested early. As they approached, Andarii revealed himself from the place he had hidden himself. Meeting up with the group, Andarii brushed the snow from his cloak.

"My lord, no one other than us have been here yet." the elf said, kneeling before Aiden momentarily, before rising to his feet.

As the group waited, off in the distance, a group of four people could be seen walking towards them. As they drew closer, Aiden studied the man in front. The man was tall, with a light tan. He wore what appeared to be expensive, custom made, formal clothes. His shoulder length, light brown hair was slicked back. He had a hard jawline, and cold, steely blue eyes that glowed. Aiden couldn't shake the feeling he had seen this man before, but couldn't remember where.

"Thank you for coming. I am Carden, and you must be Aiden."

The vampyre held out his hand to Aiden as he stepped up. After several seconds of silence, he withdrew his hand.

"What is it you want? Why did you request this meeting?" Aiden asked, as Raizel and Andarii held their hands on their weapons, just in case.

"Two reasons. One... I wanted to see for myself the man who has successfully evaded me so far, and two... I have a proposition for you."

"What could you possibly have to offer me that you think I would want?" Aiden glared at the man, still trying to figure out where he had seen this guy before.

"How about peace?" Carden replied, holding his arms out slightly from his sides, palms facing Aiden.

"Peace? Your people killed my family!"

Aiden clenched his fists, his claws threatening to cut into his palms.

"Technically... your family killed themselves. Took out several dozens of vampyres and vampurics while they were at it. It was quite the impressive blaze." Carden gave a small laugh.

Aiden's jaw tightened, but remained calm, not allowing the vampyre to get under his skin.

"And to think, we may never have figured out you were the hybrid if you hadn't shown a blatant display of power in the market of your hometown. All to save an elven servant girl... how is she, by the way? Your servant... or should I call her your mate?"

Aiden's body tensed up at the mention of Siri.

"Yes, I know all about your mate... both of them."

Aiden's eyes began to glow a searing red. He was about to attack when he felt Raizel's hand on his shoulder.

"Easy." he whispered, getting Aiden to calm down slightly.

"I must say... finding two mates is very impressive, but getting a Nekomata as a mate, talk about lucky. Tell me.. have you drank her blood yet?"

"You leave them out of this." Aiden hissed.

"That depends entirely on you. Apparently the Vampyre Lords would rather negotiate with you than to start another war. You see, even though I'm quite certain we would win, they have other interests they would rather be pursuing, than to chase a single man across the country. You see, your predecessor caused them a great deal of trouble, so they are willing to offer you peace."

"Peace? In exchange for what?"

Aiden's skin crawled as the conversation continued.

"Simple. The Vampyre Lords promise to cease hunting you... to let you.. and your mates, go. You are free to go wherever you want, and live your lives without having to constantly look over your shoulder. In return... you are to keep your existence as the hybrid a secret. No one may know that you are a hybrid. You, and your mates must also promise not to interfere with us or our plans. Now... or in the future."

"Why send an army if you are offering peace?" Aiden asked.

A wicked grin crossed Carden's face.

"That's quite simple. We knew the memories of your predecessor would eventually lead you to the remnants of the resistance. We are here for them, not you. You and your mates need only stand aside."

Valik tried to charge forward, but was stopped by Andarii, doing his best to restrain the dwarf.

"After all... you don't owe these people anything. You barely even know them. Their very existence threatens the society we have worked so hard to establish. Isn't the safety and future of your mates worth more than the lives of these few strangers?"

Carden snapped his fingers and the two men accompanying him parted, revealing a young girl.

"Come here, girl." Carden commanded.

Slowly the girl approached him, shaking with fear.

"This pretty thing here comes from your hometown. She was the daughter of a local shopkeeper that I had the pleasure of interrogating about your identity. Now... she is my pet." Carden lifted her arm, biting her wrist and drinking her blood as she cried and shook with fear.

Suddenly, Aiden remembered where he knew this man from. He was the one who gave the order to hunt down and kill him and his entire family.

Pulling his fangs from her wrist, Carden pulled the girl in front of him, with his hands resting on her shoulders.

"Apparently my little pet here was a friend of your mate. So as a gift, and a show of good faith... I'm giving her to you. I've had my fun and have grown bored with her."

Leaning down, Carden whispered into the girls ear.

"Go to him, pet."

Slowly and weakly, the girl walked towards Aiden, ignoring the blood dripping from her wrist. Tears filled her eyes and fell down her cheeks as she stumbled, falling into Aiden's arms, before passing out.

"You have until nightfall to contemplate our offer. At sundown, we will destroy this place, whether you are still in it or not." Carden swiftly turned and walked away, followed by his men.

Aiden picked up the unconscious girl in his arms. Looking down at her, she was covered in dozens of bite marks up and down her arms, as well as her neck.

"Bastard!" Aiden said, through gritted teeth.

Aiden held the girl's arm up, placing the fresh bite wound to his mouth, licking the wound to stop the bleeding.

This was the cost of saving himself and Siri, Aiden realized. And this innocent girl had paid the price.

"I'm so sorry. This is all my fault. Instead of trying to help you and your mother, I ran like a coward. You suffered all this time because of me." he whispered to the unconscious girl in his arms.

"This is what they do, Aiden."

Raizel's words cut sharper than any knife.

"Give her to me, lad. I'll carry the little one back for ya." Valik said, stepping forward, holding his arms out for the girl.

Aiden shook his head, pulling the girl closer.

"No, this is my fault, she's my responsibility. I have to make this right." Aiden said.

"Losing one's family ain't something you can make right, son. Let me take her."

Valik reached for the girl.

"I said no!" Aiden snapped at Valik, his eyes glowing.

"As you wish, lad."

Valik lowered his arms as the group turned and headed back to Tyr'endalle.

~ ~ ~ ~ ~

Siri sat on the couch holding the young girl's head in her lap as Aiden explained the events that transpired.

"I can't believe they did this to her. Marie didn't deserve this." Siri stroked the girl's head as she slept on her lap.

"This is my fault, Siri. I should have stayed and done something. I should have..."

"No." Siri interrupted him.

"This is not your fault Aiden. You didn't do this. If we had stayed, you would have been killed and he would have done this to Marie anyway. Don't you dare say this is your fault... this is on Carden. He alone is to blame, you understand?" Siri looked at Aiden, anger in her eyes.

"Sister mate is right, Master. You can't blame yourself." Mina stood up from the chair she was sitting in.

Walking over, Mina sat next to Aiden, pulling his head to her chest, wrapping her arms around him and holding him.

Several minutes passed in silence as they sat there.

"I want him dead, Aiden."

Siri looked up from Marie, over to Aiden.

"I want you to kill him. Promise me you will kill him." Tears fell from Siri's eyes as she pleaded with Aiden.

"I promise... I'll make him pay. I promise."

Aiden sat up, pulling out of Mina's arms as he stood.

"Go. You need to prepare for battle." Siri said.

Aiden leaned over, kissing Mina before moving over to Siri and kissing her as well.

"I love you, both of you."

"I love you too, Aiden."

"Mina loves you, Master."

Walking back over to Mina, Aiden placed his palm against her cheek, causing her to nuzzle into his hand.

"Mina, please say it, just once." he asked.

Mina nodded, looking up at him.

"Mina loves you.. Aiden."

Robert Stasny

# Chapter 57

Aiden could be seen pacing back and forth across the battlements, nervously waiting for the attack to come. Seeing Aiden like this set the soldiers around him on edge. He had been pacing like this for the last half an hour.

Raizel stood off to the side. He had silently been watching Aiden for several minutes, simply observing him.

Letting out a sigh, Raizel leaned off the wall he was against, walking over to Aiden and placing a hand on his shoulder.

"Come with me." Raizel said, pulling Aiden away from the others.

"But what about the battle? They could attack at any moment."

"This can't wait. Follow me."

Raizel led Aiden off the battlements and into a hallway.

Aiden didn't understand what Raizel was doing, but he trusted that there was a good reason for being pulled away from the battlements. Following him down the hall, they came to a stop at a wooden door.

Pulling a key out, Raizel unlocked the door, pulling it open and ushering Aiden inside.

The room was dimly lit, and completely empty other than two floor mats in the center of the room, placed facing each other. Between the mats was a bowl of sand and a small box.

"Sit." Raizel commanded.

"Raizel, what is this?" Aiden glanced at the floor mat before giving Raizel a questioning look.

"You're not ready for battle. Your mind is distracted, and your anxiety is placing your fellow soldiers on edge."

Raizel held his arm out, motioning for Aiden to sit on one of the floor mats.

"This is stupid, we need to get back to the battlefield."

Aiden turned to leave.

Before he could take another step, Aiden was shoved up against the wall by Raizel. His face pressed roughly against the stone with one of Raizel's hands against the back of his head, his other arm pressing into Aiden's spine as he held him against the wall.

"What the hell is wrong with you Raizel?" Aiden yelled, trying to free himself from the vampyre's grasp.

"Carden got in your head. That was the whole point of bringing that girl to the meeting... and now it's all you can think about."

Raizel slowly released his grip, allowing Aiden to push himself off the wall.

"Yeah... so?" Aiden turned to face Raizel, rubbing his face.

"So.. you've been shaken, and the men know it. They look to you for inspiration and courage."

Raizel sat down onto one of the floor mats.

"But right now, all they see is a man who is already defeated. Every soldier has to go into the battle believing he's coming home, otherwise, he's already lost." Holding out a hand, he motioned for Aiden to take a seat across from him.

As Aiden sat down, Raizel continued his lecture.

"Aiden, you are our greatest weapon in this battle. A finer warrior even than myself, and I do not say that lightly. But right now, you're stuck inside your own head, you are so focused on that little girl, that you can't see anything else. Your empathy is one of your better traits, but right now, it's going to get not just you, but every single person in Tyr'endalle killed. You need to calm your mind and see clearly for the battle to come."

"How do I do that?" Aiden asked.

"Start by closing your eyes, remember why you are here. It's easy to fight for someone else, but right now you need to fight for yourself. Why are "you" fighting? Why do you need to survive? What reason do you have to come home after the battle is over?"

Slowing his breathing, Aiden cleared his mind and began listening to everything Raizel had to say.

~ ~ ~ ~ ~

Ten minutes had passed in silence before Aiden opened his eyes, finding himself alone in the room. Raizel was nowhere to be seen. Instead, an armor stand sat before him with a set of armor on it.

Standing up, Aiden stepped up to the stand and inspected the armor. The armor was unlike anything he had ever seen before.

Thin black plates overlapped each other in a fish scale pattern creating an under armor of mail, providing maximum mobility when worn. Over the mail, larger plates of black metal were fitted onto the shins, thighs and chest, as well as both the upper and lower arms. Gauntlets, with their fingertips removed, designed for easy use of claws. Thin veins of silver coiled around the armor like vines. A matching black cloak draped down the back of the armor. Attached to the cloak was a hood. The inner rim of the hood had a set of magical symbols woven into it that glowed a soft silvery white. Where the cloak connected to the shoulders, where each collarbone would be, hung a short, braided silver cord several inches long. At the tips of these cords, woven into the fibers, were two different locks of hair. One a bright red, and the other as black as a raven's feather.

Aiden reached out, gently fingering the locks of hair, a smile forming on his face.

"Alright, let's do this." he said, pulling the first piece of armor from the stand.

~ ~ ~ ~ ~

Fastening the cloak and attaching his sword to his waist, Aiden stepped out of the room and returned to join the others waiting out on the battlefield, a clear and unmistakable confidence in his stride. As he stepped out from the hallway, all eyes turned to him.

"How does it fit?" Raizel asked, stepping up to Aiden.

"Like a second skin." Aiden replied, reaching out and gripping Raizel's forearm.

Raizel beat his fist lightly against the breastplate of Aiden's armor. "Good, because that armor is special. It's enchanted to either stretch, or even disappear completely when you shift.. then returning to its original shape, or reappear when you shift back."

"Thank you."

"You can thank me after the battle's over. Besides, I only made that for you because I'm tired of seeing your naked ass every time you shift."

"Oh, really? I hadn't noticed."

Both men started laughing as they turned to the rest of the men.

Having seen the change in Aiden's demeanor, the soldiers were eager to hear what he had to say.

"Your audience awaits." Raizel bowed, leaving Aiden standing alone.

Stepping up onto the wall of the battlements, Aiden held up his arms, getting the attention of all the soldiers.

"Many of you are afraid of the battle to come, and that's ok. Nobody wants to die.. but death comes for us all eventually, even for those of us who call ourselves immortal. You all look to me to win this battle, but I am only one man, and the enemies numbers are much greater than our own... but it doesn't matter, they will not claim victory over us this day. Not because of me.. but because of each and every one of you standing here." Aiden's voice rang out over the soldiers.

"That army out there is comprised of soldiers simply following orders... and that is exactly why we are going to win. They have nothing to fight for, no reason for this battle beyond orders. But you... you are fighting, not just for yourselves, but for your families, for your friends, and loved ones. If we are to die, then let it be for them... but make no mistake, I have no intention of dying today. My mates still need me, just like your families still need you. So no matter what happens today, I'm making it home to them. Who's with me?"

A chorus of yells filled the battlefield, threatening to shake the very mountain as every man raised their voice with the man next to them. Weapons were drawn and beaten against their shields. They had regained their will to fight.

Hopping down, Aiden made his way through the ranks as men parted for him, stopping briefly at the commander of the guard.

"Commander Val, have your archers been informed of the special properties of the arrows provided for them?"

"Yes my lord, thank you. You can count on us."

The commander placed his fist against his heart as Aiden continued on his way.

Stepping down from the battlements and onto the battlefield, Aiden was met by a group of twenty werewolves from his pack, led by Tyrien and his three sons.

"Alpha."

Tyrien knelt to one knee, followed by his sons and the other pack members.

"I want you to split your group into two teams." Aiden said. "One will be dedicated to fighting the vampyres in full force. The other, I want circling the perimeter. Should any vampyres get through our traps, or try to peel away from the main group, I want your wolves to either turn them back, or tear them to pieces. They can't be allowed to flank us, or breach the residential areas."

"As you command, Alpha."

Leaving Tyrien and his sons to prepare, Aiden headed up the spiraling staircase, disappearing into a tunnel.

~ ~ ~ ~ ~

Stepping out onto the ledge, Aiden looked out over the battlefield. The tunnel he had gone through led him to a small outcropping in the roof of the mountain directly above the battlefield. From this vantage point, he had a clear view of everything going on below.

Looking out over the edge, his vision began to blur, distorting, like ripples on a pond.

"Why have you come back?"

Aiden turned to see Sebastien standing behind him.

"Hello Sebastien." Aiden nodded his head in acknowledgment of his predecessor.

"Walk with me."

Sebastien turned, and began walking through the dreamscape, Aiden following close behind.

"I must congratulate you on finding your second mate, and a Nekomata at that... you are very fortunate, even amongst immortals."

"What do you mean?"

"Although it does occasionally happen, it is exceedingly rare for an immortal to be mated to another of a different race. On the rare occasions that it does happen, it is usually with a human or an elf, like your first mate Siri. The fact that Mina is also one of your mates is beyond exceedingly rare. In fact, Mina is the first Nekomata to ever form a mate bond with an immortal."

"Why?" Aiden asked.

"Why indeed... whatever the reason, it is to your great fortune." Sebastien waved his hand, a table and chairs appearing before them.

"Meaning?" Aiden asked as the two of them took a seat.

"Setting aside what you already know about the mate bond, there are a few more things you should know. The bond allows the two individuals to be connected, and with that connection, comes certain perks. First... because you are an immortal and they are not, normally they would eventually grow old and die, unlike yourself. But since they are both mated to you, through the mate bond, they share your immortality. Neither one of them will age a day from the moment the mate bond formed, just as you have not aged from the moment you became the hybrid. Second... the strength of one can be drawn on by the other. In the case of Mina, this is especially fortunate for you. Nekomata are born with an exceptionally powerful form of primordial magic that allows them to control magic without the need for spells, incantations, or even the use of ancient elvish. Most... never learn to take advantage of the gifts they are born with."

The image of Mina taking down the ogre from the elven village appeared beside them.

The blood of a Nekomata holds a small bit of that primordial magic inside of it. That is why an immortal can become stronger by drinking their blood, it gives them a temporary boost in power while the blood is in their system.

"So your saying Mina can use this kind of magic?" Aiden asked.

"Yes and no. Honestly, the only reason she was able to do what she did back then was because she drew on your own reserves of strength through your bond in order to cast that magic. Currently, she is not powerful enough... yet. But thankfully, she doesn't need to be. As her mate, you now have access to her magic through your bond with her. Have you noticed that there seems to be no effect on your body when you drink her blood?"

"Yeah." Aiden answered. "I don't understand the hype around Nekomata blood. It just seems like regular blood to me."

"That is because through your bond, you have a direct line to her power. It flows through you at all times, just like her. Your bond with her boosted your own power far beyond what simply drinking her blood could ever offer."

"Can I learn to use that power?"

"That depends." Sebastien rubbed his chin in thought.

"Depends on what?" Aiden leaned forward in his chair, waiting for Sebastien's answer.

A grin spread across Sebastien's face as he looked at Aiden. "That might just work."

# Chapter 58

A thunderous boom could be heard echoing across the battlefield, repeating every few seconds.

"Steady men! Prepare for battle!" Captain Val commanded, just as a portion of the cave wall exploded across the far end of the battlefield.

Out of the newly formed hole, poured dozens of vampurics. Each one violently pushing past one another trying to get inside, their claws scraping across the stone, gouging out pieces of rock as they sprinted into the farmland seeking their prey.

All sources of light other than a few torches here and there atop the lookout towers had been extinguished, plunging the cavern into darkness.

As more and more vampurics poured into the farmland, the first ones there began sniffing the air, trying to catch the scent of warm bodies to sink their claws into. After several minutes of sniffing the air, the vampurics began milling about, unable to pinpoint any prey. By this time, three hundred vampurics had poured into the farmland, along with around two hundred vampyres, with more pouring in by the second.

Above the battlefield two specks of light were noticed as they sped across the blackness. Before anyone could react, the two flaming arrows landed on the edge of the battlefield on opposite sides near the hole the vampyres had blown open. Flames erupted from the points of impact, the explosion catching many on fire as the flames raced across the ground.

Within moments, the farmland went from dead quiet, to filled with shrieks as the vampyres and vampurics were surrounded on either side by a wall of fire.

As the vampyre's tried to make sense of what was going on, torchlights began to appear across the battlefield, revealing the soldiers of Tyr'endalle on the other side of the farmland.

Seeing their prey, the vampurics gave a high pitched shriek as they charged across the farmland towards the enemy. Halfway across the farmland, a series of explosions began to blow apart the enemy ranks as the soldiers set off the explosive barrels they had buried beforehand. Others became victims of the pitfalls that had been dug, skewering them on sharpened staves in the ground. The calm from moments before had turned into pure chaos. The soldiers of Tyr'endalle cheered as the smell of burning flesh and blood filled the air.

Drawing their weapons, they charged forward to meet the immortals in combat as their archers rained death from above.

~ ~ ~ ~ ~

Aiden opened his eyes as the sounds of battle, and the smell of blood reached him. Standing up from his kneeled position, he looked out at the battle going on beneath him.

*"Better late than never."* he thought, seeing the battle had already been going on for some time.

Tightening his sword belt, Aiden pulled the hood of his cloak over his head before stepping off the ledge, free falling for several hundred feet. As he fell, the wind around him picked up, slowing his fall enough to not be injured as he collided with a vampyre who was too preoccupied with the battle to bother looking up.

Letting out a threatening roar across the battlefield, his call was echoed by the howls of his pack as they fought, along with the shouts of his soldiers, rising into a battle cry that renewed the spirits of those fighting.

Stepping aside as a vampuric lunged at him, Aiden disemboweled the creature as it soared past him with his claws. Looking out across the battle, Aiden could see that the soldiers behind him would soon be forced to retreat to the fallback position, as there were just too many enemies to deal with. The memory of his family barely holding back against the vampyres at his home came to Aiden's mind.

*"Not this time."*

Raising both hands, Aiden slammed his palms down into the earth as the ground in front of him began to shake.

Large fissures opened up in some areas, swallowing the immortals, and crushing them within the depths of the earth. On the surface, large spikes of stone erupted from the ground, impaling even more immortals as they struggled to take their last breaths.

From behind him, the cheers of victory rose from the men.

Thinking the battle had been won, the soldiers started hugging each other, happy to have survived. All seemed calm for a few moments as Aiden stood up, exhausted from the strain of the spell.

Suddenly, the sky seemed to catch fire. Dozens of fireballs rained down from overhead, tearing though their ranks and decimating Aiden's forces.

Directly across the battlefield, at the edge of the breach point, stood a circle of ten mages, conjuring fire magic. In the center of the circle stood Carden, with his arms folded across his chest. A look of annoyance was written across his face as he stared across the battlefield back at Aiden.

Aiden shifted into his hybrid form, digging his feet into the dirt as he darted between the pillars of stone he had summoned, running as fast as he could at the group of mages. From the corner of his eye, Aiden saw four of his wolves ahead of him, sprinting for the group as well.

*"No, don't be stupid!"* Aiden thought to himself, picking up even more speed.

The four wolves pounced on the nearest mages as they reached the circle, tearing the mages apart. Soon, all the mages were dead as the four wolves circled Carden.

Carden flashed a smile at Aiden as the first wolf lunged at him.

"No!"

Faster than the wolf could react, Carden drew a sword and cleanly severed his head from his body.

In the blink of an eye, Carden had killed all four wolves, blood dripping from his blade as he stood there waiting for Aiden.

Reaching Carden, Aiden swiped at him with his claws. Shifting his feet, Carden grabbed Aiden's arm, yanking on it before spinning and throwing Aiden into the stone wall.

Pain shot through Aiden's shoulder as he felt it dislocate, just before slamming into the wall, causing him to see stars momentarily.

Crumpling to a heap on the ground, Aiden shifted back as he tried to regain his footing.

"I'm sorry... were these friends of yours?" Carden taunted, kicking the dead body of one of his pack members over at Aiden's feet.

"I'm gonna kill you." Aiden said, drawing his sword.

"Oh, really? And just how do you intend to accomplish this?" Carden taunted, holding his sword out in front of him.

Aiden's eyes blazed a searing red in a sea of swirling black as he stared at Carden, raising his own sword.

"I'm gonna rip your throat out... with my teeth."

Aiden lunged towards Carden.

As their two swords clashed, Carden grinned wildly.

~ ~ ~ ~ ~

Raizel slowly lifted himself from the debris of a collapsed archer's tower, burns covered half of his body as he staggered towards the nearest soldiers.

"What the bloody hell happened?" he asked.

"Lord Raizel, you're injured." one of the soldiers said, grabbing his arm and offering support for him to stand.

"Never mind that, where's Aiden?"

"Lord Aiden is currently engaged in combat with the enemy commander."

Another soldier pointed across the battlefield at two individuals, trading blows with their swords.

"Quickly, we have to go help him."

Raizel tried to take a step towards Aiden's location only to collapse after a few feet.

"My lord, you're in no condition to help anyone. Besides, lord Aiden is holding his own right now. Take a moment to heal, then we can go."

"You don't understand... by then it may already be too late."

~ ~ ~ ~ ~

Aiden panted as he prepared for another attack. Each blow he made felt like he was striking an anvil. The impacts sending shockwaves of pain up his arm, threatening to knock his sword from his hand.

Lifting his sword, Carden blocked Aiden's blow before smashing the pommel of his sword into Aiden's jaw with a sickening crack.

"I really must commend you boy. This is the most fun I've had in centuries. You have no idea how boring it is to not find a worthy opponent to fight."

Carden took a step back, taking a few deep breaths before the two opponents clashed their swords together once more. As Carden swung his sword, Aiden waited for an opening to strike. Just as their swords met, he found his opportunity.

Reaching his offhand up, Aiden slammed his palm into the bottom of Carden's elbow, dislocating it with a pop and causing him to lose his grip on his sword.

Yelling in anger, Carden brought his own offhand up, the claws on his fingers finding a weak point in Aiden's armor.

Pain shot through Aiden as Carden buried his claws deep into his side, curling his fingers inside his flesh.

Aiden screamed, dropping his own sword, pulling away from the vampyre as Carden ripped open his side.

Holding his hand to his side, Aiden could feel his own blood seeping between his fingers. With it, Aiden could feel his strength leaving him. His body wasn't healing as fast as it should be, the magic he used to defeat the army took too much out of him... and this wound was fatal.

If he could get away, his body would be able to heal, but Aiden knew Carden wouldn't allow him that luxury. If he wanted to beat Carden, Aiden only had one option left. He just prayed it would work.

Popping his arm back into place, Carden stared at Aiden with hatred in his eyes, stepping toward him.

As Carden neared him, Aiden rolled forward, attempting to trip him while grabbing Carden's sword from the ground just as Carden dropped his elbow into his upper back, shattering his shoulder blade.

Fighting through the pain in his back and the wound in his side, Aiden held Carden's own blade up in front of him.

"*Come on... do it.*" he thought to himself as he watched Carden's reactions.

Carden looked at Aiden, wielding his own sword against him, then at the ground at his feet where Aiden's sword lay... then began to laugh.

"You really thought I was that big of a fool? I know all about the special properties of that blade of yours."

Stepping over Aiden's blade, Carden walked up to Aiden, sidestepping a swing from the sword before knocking the blade out of Aiden's hand.

Carden grabbed Aiden around the throat, lifting him up.

Aiden's strength had all but left him at this point, unable to fight back as the elder vampyre closed his fingers around his throat.

"Any last words, oh Great and Powerful Hybrid?" he mocked, holding Aiden a few inches off the ground.

Aiden spoke, his voice was barely a whisper.

"What was that boy?" Carden pulled him closer in order to hear what Aiden said.

"Y.. you've already lost." Aiden whispered.

Carden dropped Aiden as his own body became racked with pain. A searing pain was moving throughout his body as he fell to his knees in anguish.

"Wh.. what have you done to me?" he screamed, doubling over in pain.

Struggling to his feet, Aiden stood over Carden, hand still holding his side.

"In your eagerness to kill the hybrid, you forgot one very important thing about fighting the hybrid... look at your leg."

Carden looked at his leg. Just below the knee, on the outside of his left leg was a smear of blood, and a small nick.

"How? When?" the vampyre asked, his eyes wide.

Blood begun to fall from his eyes like tears.

"When you shattered my shoulder blade... you thought I was going for the sword. In reality, my hand was already covered in my own blood, all I had to do was cut you."

Despite the severe pain his body was in as Aiden's blood poisoned him from within, Carden managed a small laugh.

"Congratulations... well done. You've beaten me, but it's not over. The Vampyre Lords will never let you go as long as they live."

"Then I'll just have to kill them as well."

Aiden knelt down in front of Carden, grabbing a fistful of his hair, tilting his head back.

"But first..."

Aiden extended his fangs.

Leaning forward, Aiden closed his mouth around the elder vampyre's throat, ripping it out with his teeth.

As the blood spilled from Carden's throat, Aiden leaned back forward and began to feed from the rapidly dying vampyre, using the blood to heal his own injured body.

As the last drops of blood left Carden's body, Aiden dropped the lifeless body to the ground, collapsing beside it.

# Chapter 59

"Hurry!" Raizel yelled as they ran towards the place where Aiden and Carden had fought, a group of twenty men following him. As they approached, Raizel saw the bodies of both Carden, as well as Aiden slumped onto the ground. The body of Carden lay face down, with Aiden lying next to it, in a large pool of blood.

Rolling Carden's body over, Raizel could see the tears of blood, as well as his torn out throat, confirming the elder vampyre's demise. Looking over where Aiden lay, he could see that there was a large, bloody tear in the side of Aiden's armor. That, coupled with the pool of blood he was laying in gave Raizel a reason to be worried.

"Quickly, he needs blood if he is going to heal, and a lot of it." Raizel pulled a dagger from his belt, drawing it across his wrist.

Captain Val knelt on the other side of Aiden, reaching down and holding his mouth open as Raizel poured his blood into Aiden's mouth and down his throat. Eventually, Raizel had to stop, and was replaced by another man who offered to give some of his own blood to save the life of the man who saved them. All the men present took turns cutting their wrists and pouring their blood into Aiden's mouth.

After the last man bandaged his wrist, all they could do now was wait and see if Aiden would regain consciousness.

"Should we bring him back to the rest of the men?" Captain Val asked Raizel.

"No, it's too risky, we don't know what all injuries he sustained in the battle. Until he starts healing on his own, we can't risk moving him, otherwise we could make his injuries worse."

"Understood."

Raizel turned, waving another soldier over.

"What can I do to help?" the man asked.

"Go to his chambers and retrieve his mates... they should be here."

Raizel turned back to Aiden as the man ran off to fetch Mina and Siri. He stood there watching Aiden for several minutes, looking for signs of life.

"Please wake up Aiden. You can't leave your mates alone, not after you swore to them you would return." he whispered, turning back to the rest of the men.

"You know me better than that."

Every head turned as Aiden spoke.

"Mind helping me up?" Aiden winced as he tried to sit up.

Raizel knelt down, helping him to his feet.

"What were you thinking facing Carden alone? You could have been killed." Raizel threw Aiden's arm over his shoulder for support.

"Oh, well.. you know... seemed like a good idea at the time."

"You're lucky to be alive. Besides, if you had died, Mina would never forgive me."

Both men laughed as the rest of the men surrounded them.

After several minutes, Aiden now had the strength to stand on his own. Reaching up, Aiden undid the clasps that were holding his armor on, removing the chest and arms.

Looking down at his side, Aiden inspected the wound that was now mostly healed.

"Doesn't look like it's going to scar at least." Aiden chuckled.

"Why would it?" Raizel asked.

"Well for one, it was worse than the injuries that gave me these." Aiden gestured to the scars across his arms and chest.

"That's different. Those were caused by your mate."

"Speaking of..."

Aiden moved the man in front of him aside, seeing Mina and Siri off in the distance.

"If you will excuse me gentlemen, I've got more important things to do right now.

Stepping out from the group of men, Aiden began walking across what remained of the farmland toward Mina and Siri. Mina, having better eyesight than Siri, noticed Aiden first and broke out into a sprint toward him.

"Master!" the catgirl screamed at the top of her lungs, jumping into Aiden's arms, colliding with his chest.

Looking down, Aiden could see her eyes were puffy, and that she had been crying.

"Hey, what's wrong? Why are you crying?" Aiden held her close, stroking her ears as she cried, burying her face into his chest.

"Mina was so scared Master. Man told sister mate you were dying, and for us to come quick."

"Hey.. I'm alright, see? I'm not going anywhere. I promised I wouldn't leave you and Siri alone."

"Aiden!" Siri finally caught up to them, throwing her arms around Aiden's neck, as he leaned his forehead against hers.

"They said you were injured in the battle." she whispered, closing her eyes as Aiden held both her and Mina in his arms.

"I was.. but nothing a little blood couldn't fix. Don't worry, the two of you are still stuck with me.

"Shut up." Siri commanded, lifting herself up onto her toes and capturing his mouth with a kiss.

Breaking the kiss, Siri stepped back, allowing Aiden to pick Mina up as she wrapped her legs around Aiden's waist before kissing him.

"Never scare Mina like that again Master." she whispered, looking into his eyes after they broke the kiss.

Staring back into those ocean blue eyes of hers, Aiden could only nod before kissing her once more.

~ ~ ~ ~ ~

"Does it still hurt?"

Siri gently touched the wound in Aiden's side. She noticed it on the way back to their quarters, but decided to wait until they were alone to ask about it.

"Still a bit tender, but it's healing. By tomorrow, it'll be like it never happened." Aiden reassured her, pulling her against him as he wrapped his arms around her, pulling her down onto the sofa.

Siri leaned back against Aiden's chest, feeling the warmth of his skin and the strength in his arms as they held her against him. Wrapped in his arms, Siri felt completely at peace. She closed her eyes and let out a soft sigh as Aiden's lips began leaving a trail of kisses from her jaw, slowly making their way down her neck and across her shoulder.

"What about Mina?"

Siri gasped as Aiden found a particularly sensitive spot on her neck.

"Mina went to bed early, it's just us. Now relax." Aiden's hot breath blew across Siri's ear as he whispered.

Aiden continued his attack on the elf's neck and shoulder for several minutes.

Tired of his teasing, Siri pulled away slightly, giving her just enough room to turn around and kiss Aiden long and hard. Finally breaking contact to regain their breath, Siri stood up in front of Aiden, dropping the robe she wore at her feet, and placing his hands on her waist as he stared up at her.

Siri loved the way his eyes glowed ever so faintly with desire whenever Aiden looked at her, sending chills racing along her skin and a shiver down her spine. Every part of her came alive under his gentle touch. With his hands on her waist, Aiden guided her back to him, shifting his weight so that he could lay her down comfortably on the sofa beneath him. His hand traveled up her side before stopping and tracing the edge of her lower ribs, his thumb gently caressing her skin. A low growl escaped his throat as he gazed longingly at the woman beneath him. Reaching up, Siri pulled him down into a slow passionate kiss as her fingers ran through his hair, just before surrendering herself to him.

~ ~ ~ ~ ~

Opening the door to the guest room, Aiden peeked inside to check on Marie.

Aiden was surprised that the girl was as calm as she was when she learned he was an immortal. He figured she would be afraid of him after what she went through. But the first thing she did when she awoke and learned what had happened since Esenor, she gave him a big hug.

"Thank you for saving me." she had told him.

Seeing the girl sound asleep, Aiden quietly closed the door, and made his way across the common room.

Aiden stood, looking out the window.

Seeing it was still a few hours until dawn, Aiden turned back to the sofa where Siri lay sleeping. She had decided to sleep out here on the sofa in case Marie woke up.

Noticing the blanket had fallen down around her waist, Aiden walked over, picking it up and pulled it over her shoulders. Aiden kissed her on the forehead, then turned, walking back to the master bedroom.

Closing the bedroom door, Aiden turned to the bed to see Mina, her naked form sprawled across the middle of the bed, clutching his pillow.

Aiden watched as she lay there, her tail swishing back and forth gently.

A smile crossed his face as he took a step towards her.

He knew she was awake. Even though she was pretending to be asleep, her tail told another story, swishing back and forth in growing excitement as she listened to him draw closer to the bed.

Climbing onto the bed, Aiden crawled his way to her, running his hand from her ankle, up her leg and onto her thigh.

Mina's ears twitched, but she continued pretending to be asleep.

Aiden continued, moving his hands upward, slowly tracing his fingers across her backside, to dance his fingers lightly up and down her spine.

"mmmm... more Master." she purred, finally giving up the act.

Leaning over, Aiden whispered in her ear.

"Thank you for giving Siri and I some time alone... but I haven't forgotten about my little kitten."

Mina purred louder as he traced his lips across her shoulder, slowly working his way down her back, sending sparks through her skin where they touched, leaving a trail of fire behind them as her body came alive beneath him.

Rolling over, Mina sat up, pushing Aiden down onto the bed. Throwing her leg over his waist, she began placing a trail of kisses of her own across his chest, then up his neck, to his ear.

"Mina loves you Aiden... so much. Mina loves Master."

# Chapter 60

Four days had passed since the battle with the vampyres, and the people of Tyr'endalle were still recovering.

"Aye, the damage can be repaired, but I hardly see the point. Even if we repair the wall, the Vampyre Lords know where we are. Staying here is not an option."

Valik gave the city's damage report to Marius and the other leaders. His left arm was in a sling, and he now sported a cut across the side of his face that would eventually heal into a scar.

"I see your point, but we have hundreds of families who live here, just where are we supposed to go?" Marius countered, rubbing his temples in frustration.

"Actually..." Raizel's voice came from across the room where he stood next to Aiden.

Everyone in the room turned to look at him.

"I might have a solution to our problem."

"What do you suggest?" Elena asked, standing next to her husband.

"It's a long shot... but it might be just what we need. Until I know for certain, that is all I can tell you."

"Very well, when will you be able to know for certain?" Marius asked.

"A few days at most. Valik, I could use your expertise in the field if you would join me."

"If it can help to give our people a chance, then I am at your disposal." The dwarf gave an exaggerated bow.

"Thank you, please meet us in Aiden's room in half an hour."

Valik nodded to Raizel before discussions resumed amongst the leaders.

~ ~ ~ ~ ~

Valik sat in a chair in the common room of Aiden's quarters. Aiden sat opposite him, reclining on the sofa. Mina had crawled into his lap as Siri sat beside them. At a nearby table, sat Andarii and Sylvia. Standing by the window looking out at the snow, stood Raizel.

"So what exactly is your plan Raizel?" Aiden asked, running his fingers over Mina's back, causing the catgirl to purr into his shoulder.

"There is a place we might be able to go. Though it will have been abandoned now for nearly eight hundred years."

"That's why you asked me to come along, to make sure the place is still structurally sound?" Valik ran his fingers through his beard as he looked at Raizel.

"Yes. But technically, the place would belong to Lord Aiden, as it was once the property of Sebastien. So the final decision will be up to him on whether to let anyone stay."

"Just what is this place you're speaking of?" Aiden slid Mina off his lap, despite her small protests.

"See for yourself."

Raizel walked across the room as Aiden and the others stood and followed.

Entering into Aiden's master bedroom, Raizel walked over to the fireplace. Reaching up, he placed his hand on one of the stones and pushed. A pop, followed by the sound of rushing air could be heard as the fireplace retreated further into the wall.

Inset into the frame of the wall were a series of magical runes.

"This is a magical doorway that will lead to the location I am speaking of."

"How do we activate it?" Siri asked.

"Aiden.. if you would be so kind, we need some of your blood." Raizel handed a knife to Aiden.

Running the blade across his palm, Aiden drew blood, then handed the knife back to Raizel.

"Now what do I do?" Aiden asked, looking down at his hand.

"Hold out your hand and speak the words "Take me home" in ancient elvish."

Doing as he was told; Aiden spoke the words as he held out his hand.

As he spoke the words, several drops of his blood floated from the wound on his hand through the air, landing on the magical runes, causing them to start glowing. The air between the frames began to shimmer and distort as the doorway activated.

Raizel stepped through the doorway and disappeared right before everyone's eyes.

Several seconds went by before Raizel reappeared back in the doorway.

"Are you coming or what?" he asked before disappearing again.

"I guess that means it's safe then." Aiden said, pulling Mina and Siri near him as the three of them stepped through.

Aiden and the girls found themselves in what appeared to be a courtyard of some sort, right next to a large wall too high to see over. Looking about, Aiden saw Raizel standing a few feet away waiting for them.

Miles of open land and grassy hills dotted the landscape around them. Several feet away, Aiden saw a tunnel, overgrown with vines, leading through the wall.

"Welcome to the home of Sebastien Arlet."

Raizel pulled the vines aside as Aiden stepped into the tunnel with Mina and Siri beside him.

Stepping out from the other side of the tunnel, Aiden and the girls' eyes went wide.

Aiden, Mina and Siri were at a loss for words as they looked at one of the most beautiful castles they had ever seen.

"Master, it's so big." Mina whispered.

"It's absolutely beautiful, Aiden." Siri said, admiring the dark colored stone used to build the castle.

"By the Stone, that's a big castle." Valik said, walking up beside them, followed by Andarii, Sylvia and Raizel.

"Where are we? Andarii asked, looking around.

Aiden placed an arm around Mina's and Siri's waists, looking down at each of them and smiled.

"We're home."

Together, the three of them ascended the steps of the castle.

# <u>Acknowledgements</u>

I wish to give a special thanks to all those who have supported me in this nearly three year journey writing this book.

Patricia Newman, your support has meant the world to me, your willingness to sit down and re-read my book over and over throughout the writing and editing process has been instrumental in this project. Thank you.

Ilene McCune, your constant enthusiasm, excitement, and eagerness to read each chapter as they were written, helped me to push through, even when I didn't feel like writing. For talking with me for hours about the details of the book and its characters. Without you, this book would have never been completed. Thank you.

Thank you to all those who worked on the artwork and illustrations for the book, you brought my characters to life.

Finally, I want to thank my readers for choosing to pick up my book and go on this journey with me throughout the world I created, laughing, and sometimes crying along with the characters in the story. Thank you so much.

# About the Author
## Robert Stasny

'Creativity', that one word describes Robert's whole life. As a young child, he would put together plays or skits for his brother and sister to help him perform with his stuffed animals. His love for reading led him into his favorite genre of Sci-fi, Fantasy, Superheroes, and the Supernatural.

In high school, he created a complete story about an alternate planet and lifeforms for his language arts class.

Now, his creativity has led him to produce something that others can enjoy as much as he has enjoyed the creativity of others.

Name Pronunciation and Translation Guide

| **Ancient Elvish** | **Translation** |
|---|---|
| Nar Talas: (Nar  tall_oss) | Don't move |
| Meir't: (Me_air_t) | Come |
| Nohkra: (Nah_kra) | Wind |
| Nihckt: (Knee_k_t) | Twist |
| Sal Theur: (Sal Th_ur) | Shatter |
| Seyh'aiya: (Say_hi_uh) | My Beloved |

**Names**

Raizel: (Rye_z_el)
Andarii: (And_are_e)
Linorra: (Lin_or_uh)
Sylvia: (Sill_vee_uh)
Nephylia: (Nef_eel_e_uh)
Fa`ena: (Fay_en_uh)

**Places**

Esenor (Ess_eh_nor)
Nurki'l (Nur_kill)
Plains of Aerindor (Air_in_door)
Tyr'endalle: (Tear_in_doll)

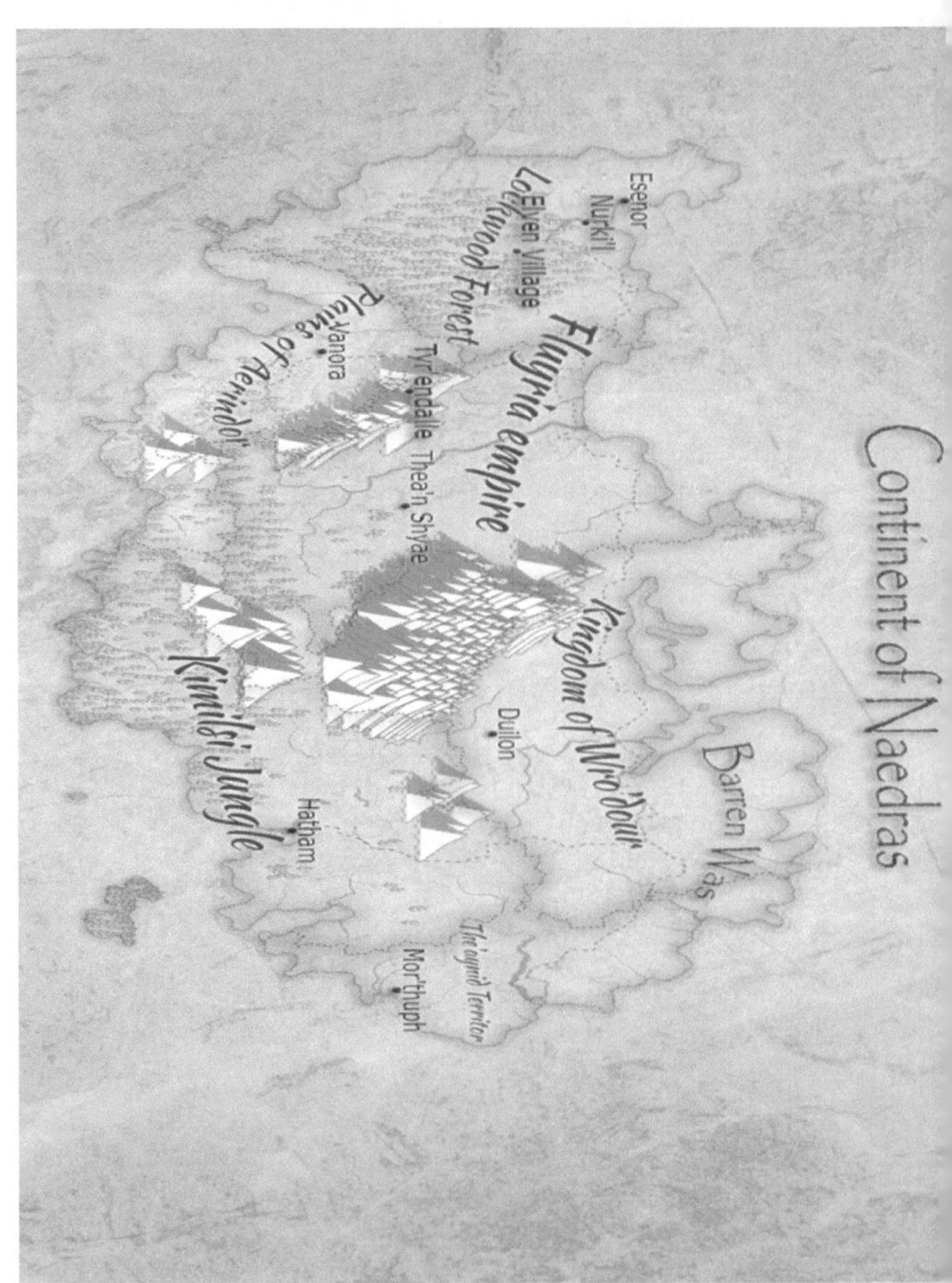

www.ingramcontent.com/pod-product-compliance
Lightning Source LLC
Chambersburg PA
CBHW030757260626
47169CB00001B/97